# SEATTLE QUAKE 9.2

By
Marti Talbott

D1490335

They knew it could happen - scientists had been warning them for years. Yet, nearly two million people living in the greater Seattle area went about their daily lives as usual. A Detective Agency thought they had found a missing woman, an upstart radio station was on the air, and an eccentric banker had just started a round of golf. Thousands were driving on freeways, shopping in malls, awaiting flights, working in downtown high-rises, and on buses in the bus tunnel.

They knew—they just didn't believe it could happen to them.

(Seattle Quake 9.2 is dedicated to Ham Radio Operators all over the world who open the lines of communication after a disaster. Although it was written over 20 years ago and the technology may be a little out of date, this book still honors their hard, behind the scenes work.)

(**Author's note:** This book was written in the early 1980s and many places and things in Seattle have changed since then.)

# CHAPTER 1

A LITTLE MORE THAN 33 kilometers below the earth's surface, two massive sheets of solid rock strained to move in opposite directions. Beginning deep in the Olympic Mountains, the jagged and deadly fault line stretched beneath the town of Bremerton, under the waters of Elliott Bay and directly below the City of Seattle. For centuries the mammoth walls remained quiet and in place, with thousands of tons of pressure prevented from shifting by the slanted ledge of the southern wall locked tight against the slanted ledge of the Northern. Week after week, month after month, year after year, and decade after decade, the tension increased - until at last, a tiny crack appeared in the northern ledge.

Sunday Afternoon, July 7

From a small landing pad in the foothills of the Olympic Mountains a Sikorsky CH-54A Sky crane slowly lifted into the air. At first glance, its royal blue bubble face resembled a mutant dragonfly, with two dark tinted windows set in silver frames for eyes and a wide, threatening silver slit for a mouth. Long rear legs with hydraulic joints extended from the round, thin body and the tail sloped upward. Dual, free turbine Pratt and Whitney engines powered the matching blue blades, whipping the air with the sound of a hundred stampeding horses and generating enough shaft horsepower to lift twenty-five tons. Originally designed to hoist cargo off ships, the air crane belonged to an unlikely trio, had a modified body and housed a sophisticated, satellite linked tracking system.

At the age of twenty-four Jackie Tate married Private Detective Dane Harlan. He taught her everything he knew, worked exotic exciting cases and showed her the world. But when the baby came they bought a house in Jefferson, Iowa, accepted less provocative assignments and settled down. A short two years later, someone simply walked away with their son Brian. For months, they feverishly followed every lead, ran background checks on hundreds of people and imagined all possibilities. But in the end, the best private detective team in the world couldn't find their own son. Jackie withdrew and Dane drank himself to death.

It was Carl Kingsley, a nearly forgotten high school friend and chopper pilot, who brought Jackie back from the abyss. He owned a floundering air crane business, a shabby mobile home and part interest in a small drug company he hoped was on the brink of discovering a new wonder drug. He also had an ex-wife determined to take it all.

In less than two days, and with the help of Michael Sorenson, Jackie tempted the ex-wife to settle for the sure thing—the riches soon to be derived from the drug company. Or so the wife was led to believe. Carl retained his beloved air crane and his mobile home, Jackie awoke from her nightmare and the three of them began the Harlan Detective Agency. Not surprisingly, the drug company went out of business.

The new Harlan Detective Agency specialized in finding lost people, even those who didn't want to be found, and the company flourished. A few well-paying jobs later, they bought two new mobile homes complete with backup generators and roof mounted satellite dishes. Carl gave the air crane a paint job, Jackie designed a new modified body, and Michael installed every conceivable electronic device on the market. Relocating between jobs was easy. The huge air crane simply lifted the mobile homes and flew away. For each assignment, Jackie found remote locations for their home base so Carl and Michael could hike, hunt, fish, and occasionally get lost in all parts of the world. And so it was, that their latest home setting was tucked away in the dense foliage at the base of the Olympic Mountains.

Their thirteen-year record of finding people was excellent, so when one of the wealthiest men in the world contacted them, Jackie wasn't surprised. She was surprised however, to learn Evan Cole wanted them to find his first wife Christina—a woman lost at sea nearly thirty years before. Lost at sea, he thought, until her diamond-and-ruby wedding ring turned up in a New York pawnshop. It took Harlan Detective Agency six months to track the ring back to a robbery recovery in Los Angeles. But the LAPD had no record of the ring's original owner and no one filed a claim with any known insurance company. The trail went cold.

In the off hours with nothing but cold trails to contemplate, Jackie often ran her son's fingerprints through a Department of Motor vehicles. Soon, Brian would be old enough for a learner's permit. The question was, which DMV, which county, which state and which country? For fun, she ran the name Christina Cole—nothing. She expanded the search, eliminated the name, added 5' 6" in height, 125 pounds, give or take 25, dark hair, age 54, and blue eyes. The numbers were astronomical.

It was Michael's genius with computers that led them to Seattle. Christina was born with two birthmarks, one the size of a quarter hidden beneath her dark hair, and a dime-sized one midway up her right forearm. Birthmarks sometimes turn to melanoma, a deadly form of cancer. It was a long shot, but Michael found thirty-six cases of birthmark melanomas in the US. Three were dead and the rest were the wrong age, sex or height. But suppose Christina Cole lied about her age? Yes, there was one—a woman living in Seattle. Upon hearing the news, Evan Cole was ecstatic.

SEATTLE'S BEAUTY WAS breathtaking and for a long moment the air crane held its position just above the Olympic Peninsula, allowing the snow-capped, spiny ridges behind it to showcase the chopper's long, sleek lines. Just across the Strait of Juan De Fuca, Canada's Vancouver Island lay less than twenty miles north of the American coastline. To the east, a multitude of large and small islands dotted the intricate, sparkling waterways of Puget Sound. And beyond that, an imaginary line separated Puget Sound from Elliott Bay, a four-mile wide inlet lapping against Seattle's waterfront.

Computer whiz Michael Anthony Sorenson kept his thick, brown hair cropped short and wore gold-rimmed glasses. As soon as the air crane was away, he darted inside the first mobile home, sat down at a counter, and turned to face six monitors. Three were blank, while the others used the computer-aged image of Christina as a screen saver.

Along the far wall of the modified air crane body, Jackie Harlan sat in a plush chair securely bolted to the floor. A pretty, brown eyed woman in her late thirties, she was surrounded by still more computer equipment and watched an identical set of six wall-mounted monitors. In the tail section, four empty chairs faced front, with a narrow hallway between them and full-length windows on each side. On the outside, just below the passenger windows, one-by-four foot panels contained hundreds of tiny light bulbs flashing the chopper's 'HDA1' identification.

Jackie was smartly dressed in blue high heels, nylons, a white blouse, and a royal blue suit, with strands of long auburn hair resting on the shoulders of her jacket. She entered her password and watched her exclusively designed software program light up three of the monitors with different images—an aerial map of Seattle, a recent picture of Evan Cole and the computer-aged likeness of Christina. Along the bottom of Christina's picture ran a grid that normally displayed her heart beat, but just now it was flat-lined.

She spoke to Carl through her headset microphone, typed commands on her keyboard and waited for the air crane to begin its flight over the wide Olympic Peninsula. Mounted on the under-carriage, three oddly shaped video cameras with high tech antennas and telescope lenses, clicked into action. Instantly, her remaining monitors lit up. Just then, a small red light flashed in the lower, right-hand corner of the first monitor. She quickly hit a hot key at the top of her keyboard, opening the line so both Carl in the pilot's seat and Michael on the ground could listen. She took the call, "Good afternoon, sir."

Thousands of miles away, the mature man's English was sprinkled with an Irish accent, "I cannot bear the suspense. Is this the one? Have you found her?"

Jackie directed her answer toward Evan Cole's photograph on her far left screen, "I wish I could say yes and be sure of it. Our subject has dark hair, is the right height, has the right blood type, and closely resembles the computer-aged picture. "She's old enough and her medical records mention a scar matching a childhood appendectomy. But she wears long sleeves even in summer, and we have yet to get a picture of anything resembling a birthmark on her arm. Without that, I can't be positive."

"I see. It is a small birthmark, less than..."

"I know, sir."

"Of course you do." Evan Cole stood near a large office window with an exceptional view of the Statue of Liberty. A touch of gray along the sides of his neatly trimmed dark hair made him look distinguished and his Irish eyes glistened. He wore an expensive, charcoal suit with a pristine white shirt open at the collar, and highly polished black shoes. "Forgive me, I do not think straight where she is concerned. What's happening now?"

"Well, right now we're off to see if we can get a closer look. She lives in an apartment with large picture windows facing the Bay and we're hoping to catch a glimpse of her without long sleeves. We've hidden a camera in the fire alarm across the hall from her front door and we've tapped her phone. I've also become good friends with her over the Internet. She thinks it is a chance meeting in an art chat room."

"An art chat room?"

"She's taken up painting and she's really quite good at it. Mister Cole, the woman has a daughter."

"...a daughter?"

"Yes, sir. Her daughter is married with two daughters of her own. She was born five months and four days after the day your wife was reported missing at sea."

Evan did not speak. Instead, he aimlessly stared at the rose-colored carpet on the floor of his expensively decorated office, "A daughter? Christina hid a daughter from me? Is she mine?" He paused to think for a moment, "Five months ... she must be mine. Does she look like me?"

"Sir, I don't think you should get excited just yet. Thousands of women fit Christina's profile and without your wife's dental records, only the birthmark can give us a positive identification."

"You're right, of course. I've been disappointed too many times to get out of hand now. Anything else?"

Jackie hesitated, lightly biting her lip, "Well, we have stumbled across something unusual. Our subject has two bank accounts. She works in an office, deposits her paycheck and pays all her bills with one account. The other has a balance of exactly $10,000.00 in checking with nothing in savings."

"You mean it does not draw interest?"

"Not a cent. She hasn't touched the account for a long time. It appears she drew out large sums to pay for her daughter's college education, and then left it alone. The odd thing is, no matter how much she spent, the balance remained at exactly $10,000.00."

Evan Cole turned away from the window and stared at the five-foot painting of his young wife hanging on a far wall. Christina wore a satin blue, strapless gown the exact color of her eyes with a delicate diamond-and-ruby necklace and tiny white diamonds in her long, dark hair. Her eyes were filled with love and her smile was adoring. "But Christina had no money of her own and nothing was missing. How old is this account?"

"We're checking into that now. I'll call when we have something more definite."

In the mobile home, Michael studied his upper, middle screen. The mock figure of a woman was lying on a bed in a three-dimensional composite of an apartment, and in this screen as well, the still flat-lined graph at the bottom was supposed to be monitoring her heartbeat. In a second screen, he replaced Evan's picture with an image generated by the hallway camera. As soon as Evan Cole hung up, he spoke into his headset, "You didn't tell him about her heart condition."

"I see no reason to just yet. Michael, she hasn't moved in more than an hour. Are you sure the equipment is working?"

Michael frowned and folded his arms, "I'm sure, she's just sleeping on her side again. The system only works when the necklace is flat on her chest, you know, and we wouldn't have this problem if you'd let me put a microphone in her bedroom."

"And how would I explain that to Mister Cole? We promised not to invade anyone's privacy and we've already put in a lot more equipment than he authorized. Besides, what if she finds it, panics and runs?"

"Okay, I get the point." He unfolded his arms and typed a new command on his keyboard. Instantly, the aerial map changed to a close-up of a necklace, "By the way, the necklace matches the ring perfectly, except for the slightly altered mounting we had our guy put in when she wanted it cleaned. Mister Cole had the necklace and the ring made by a jeweler in London."

"That's wonderful, Michael."

"So tell me this. Why does a woman fake her death to get away from a husband, and then faithfully wear the necklace he gave her? She only takes it off to shower. And I found something else, she's got scars around both wrists—like maybe she's been tied up."

"Tied up?"

"Yes. I wish I could think of some other explanation."

Jackie turned in her swivel chair and thoughtfully looked out the window. "You think she's been abused and that's why she faked her death?"

"Maybe. Our background check on Evan Cole didn't indicate anything violent, but I think I'll have a little chat with his second wife's sister. If anyone knows his history, she does."

"Good idea, the last thing we want to do is find a wife for an abusive husband."

IN THE SUMMER AFTERNOONS, when it wasn't raining, sixty-six-year old Sam Taylor liked sitting on the end of a West Seattle pier with his legs dangling over the edge. His milk-white hair complimented his blue eyes, and more often than not, he wore headphones connected to a transistor radio in his shirt pocket. His favorite was KMPR, a new talk radio station owned by his son, Max.

Behind him, homes and apartments dotted the hillside where thousands of people enjoyed an impressive view of the water and Greater Seattle. On both sides of the pier, rows and rows of moored pleasure boats sloshed with the rhythm of the sea. To his right, in the wide southern curve of Elliott Bay, Harbor Island's multiple docks displayed huge land cranes capable of lifting full railroad cars off enormous cargo ships. Overhead, airplanes of varying sizes passed every three minutes, completing their final fifteen-mile descent into Boeing Field or SeaTac Airport.

Further around the curve tugboats, cruise ships, dinner ships, and the Victoria Clipper dotted piers jutting out from shops and restaurants. And behind the waterfront lay the colorful and magnificent city of Seattle. Eight blocks deep and twenty-six blocks long, downtown Seattle loomed high on a hill, with graduating levels of glistening sky scrapers. Among them, the impressive Winningham Blue Building stood forty-seven floors high, covered an entire city block, and was a mere three blocks from the waterfront.

On the northern end of the twenty-six blocks, an enormous water fountain and the Space Needle marked the middle of The Seattle Center. And just northeast of the Seattle Center, the ground sloped upward toward the top of Queen Anne Hill. Named for a time when the weight of one trolley going downhill pulled another trolley up, the steep grade of the nine block "counterbalance" ascended four blocks, leveled off, and then continued up the next four blocks.

From where Sam Taylor sat, the view was magnificent. The air was fresh and free of pollution, the "Emerald City" was its usual green, and never did he have to wait more than an hour to see something new or unexpected. Sam opened his box of order-out fried chicken, set it on the pier beside him, and popped the pull-tab on a can of soda. He took a sip, put it down, and reached for a chicken leg. Wearing an old brown fishing hat, he laughed at something said on the radio and started to watch two tugs maneuver a freighter toward Harbor Island.

Something unique caught his attention. A loud clapping noise signaled the slow descent of the largest chopper he had ever seen. And there was more—there was some kind of a disturbance in the water.

QUEEN ANNE HILL WAS only ten minutes from downtown by Metro bus and sported three and a half vital communication towers on her top. Vital that is, until 60 and 70 story skyscrapers were built downtown. After that, radio and television had a higher place from which to transmit, and after that came satellites and satellite dishes. Still, the towers on top of Queen Anne Hill were useful for other things such as cell phones, weather and traffic cameras, and one Amateur Radio repeater. Between two of the towers, in the attic of an old two-story house, Sam Taylor's son, Max, built his talk-radio station, KMPR.

A tall man with shoulder length blond hair, Max spent weeks putting in a plaster ceiling, adding three coats of lusterless paint and setting up the soundproof booth with an adjoining studio. The control room was small and housed the "board" with inputs for each mike. Cartridge players ran commercial spots, promos, show intros, and news sound bites. In addition, the board held a four-track tape deck, a CD player, and a computer complete with monitor. On the opposite side of the control room sat a 5 kW transmitter the size of a phone booth with more equipment on both sides. Overhead, a long florescent light hung from chains and offered a pale white glow. The console, dotted with tuning dials and switches held a ten-line telephone and faced a large, soundproof window overlooking the studio. In the studio, another console sat lengthwise with its own hanging light, a ceiling fan, a ten-line phone, various switches, dials, and a second computer monitor.

As soon as Max put the finishing touches on his station, he began scouring the countryside for an energetic, fun loving host willing to work long hours. Finally, he lured Collin Slater away from a small station in Denver, Colorado. For two weeks, handsome, African American, Collin Slater's picture was splashed across TV screens, appeared on billboards, in newspapers and filled every inch of advertising space on the sides of fifty percent of the city's metro buses. In the background, on separate pieces of a jigsaw puzzle, was an artist's rendition of the rest of Seattle's radio and television commentators looking bored and listless. The caption read – KMPR, expect the unexpected."

Max Taylor was a family man. He lived on the first floor of the two-story house with his wife Candy and their three small sons, Jason, Cory, and Adam. Collin Slater brought his bride of three months with him from Denver and happily moved into the second floor apartment. Just before dawn on the first day of May and just at the beginning of Monday morning rush hour traffic, the station went on the air.

Collin's first few months at KMPR in Seattle passed quickly. His stool in the studio was beginning to soften, his coffee cup was honorably dirty, and the Denver fan's favorite three-inch Dallas Cowboy replica hung from the ceiling—with a noose around its neck. His thick black microphone was connected to a wide, silver stand and just beneath the console, a drawer held Tums, cigarettes, candy bars, matches, picks for his hair, and every flavor of hard candy known to man. At the far end of the narrow room, a well-stocked refrigerator stood next to the only outside window.

Wearing his usual jeans, T-shirt and sneakers, Collin casually adjusted his large, black earphones, "You're listening to KMPR, Seattle's newest talk Radio. "I'm your host Collin...as in call-in...Slater. You can find us at 760 AM on your radio dial and the number to call is 789-1001. Expect the unexpected. With me is Max Taylor, the guy who owns this little station and works the controls in the sound proof booth. Today's news, in case you missed it, is just as boring as yesterday's." Collin paused while Max tapped a sound effects switch. Soon, his headphone filled with the funeral march.

"Wait, here's something. Jan Farnsworth, the same Jan Farnsworth who claims to be in constant touch with the long deceased Winston Churchill, says..."

AT 2:10 P.M., ON JULY 7th, the tiny crack in the northern wall of the fault suddenly splintered. Instantly, a small portion of the vertical shelf disintegrated. In the University of Washington's Seismology Lab, a needle abruptly began to etch sharp horizontal lines on paper. Outside, dogs barked, birds took flight, cats dashed under beds, and the water in Elliott Bay began to jiggle.

STILL TALKING INTO his microphone, Collin suddenly stopped. The walls made a popping noise and he looked to his right just in time to see the windowpane wave. Confused, he glanced down. The coffee in his cup was rippling. His eyes darted up, and then he looked left and right again. But it was over, nothing else was moving. Finally, he turned to Max. His boss looked puzzled, but not upset. His headset was still in place and both hands were working the controls.

Collin shrugged, adjusted his microphone, and began again, "Jan Farnsworth, who claims to be in touch..."

AT FIFTY-FOUR, SEELY Ross enjoyed the safety of a security building. She lived in a spacious, sixth-floor apartment just a few blocks down Queen Anne Hill from KMPR. Three picture windows faced southwest offering a spectacular view of Elliott Bay, the islands, the Peninsula, and the Olympic Mountains. With long black hair and warm blue eyes, she doted on her grown daughter Michelle, lovable son-in-law Theo and her two glorious granddaughters, Ausha and Brianna. She loved painting landscapes and her job, on the forty-third floor of the Winningham Blue Building paid well and kept her busy.

Up from her doctor prescribed nap, Seely turned her radio to KMPR, sat down at her computer and logged on to the Web. By 2:10 p.m., she was engrossed in an Email from Jackie, a woman she met in an art chat room. Suddenly, her huge picture windows all creaked at the same time. The opposite wall popped and Collin Slater stopped in mid-sentence. Seely held her breath and waited.

IN THE EARTH, THE SAME immeasurable pressure that caused the snag to crack shoved the newly disintegrated rock onward. The vertical shelves freely moved less than a centimeter before they caught again. But now there was a new snag, a weaker one, and one closer to the surface of the earth. It held for a little more than fifteen seconds before it too yielded to the mighty strength of a moving earth. The motion generated a 4.3 magnitude earthquake.

AT 2:10:46, SAM TAYLOR's brow wrinkled. Sitting on his West Seattle pier, he mentally estimated the distance between the mysterious chopper and the surface of the water. But the chopper was too high to make the bay ripple. Besides it wasn't rippling – it was jiggling. In an apartment building behind him, a door flew open and a man ran out into the street.

WITH THE SECOND JOLT, Seely abruptly scooted her chair away from the computer. She ran to the door of her apartment, yanked it open and quickly braced herself. The hallway was empty. Plaster, wood, and concrete groaned as the eight floor, twenty-five-year old building shook. The easel holding her latest acrylic painting bounced. Both elevators banged against their shafts, dishes rattled, pictures swung and the floor rolled. And lying flat on her chest, a chip on the back of her necklace recorded the sudden increase in her heart rate.

On a monitor in the body of the sky crane, Jackie watched the mock woman abruptly race across the simulated living room. She noted the woman's palpitating heart and quickly turned to study the picture fed from the camera in the Building's hallway. But no strangers stood knocking and the fire alarm was not flashing its red light. Even so, the front door flew open and Seely Ross grabbed hold of her door jamb. Bewildered, Jackie wrinkled her brow, "What's happening?"

# CHAPTER 2

COLLIN SLATER CAUGHT his breath. In KMPR's studio, the whole console was bouncing. Instinctively, he spread his arms wide and grabbed hold. Glass clinked, walls popped and the window waved. Coffee sloshed on his shirt, papers slid, the Dallas Cowboy replica swung back and forth, and his hanging ceiling fan started an odd circular motion.

In the soundproof booth Max flew out of his seat, threw his two hundred-twenty pounds against the transmitter, and held it flush to the wall. He watched helplessly as disks stacked too high, slid off his console. Coke sloshed and splattered on his papers and a hairline crack appeared in the ceiling plaster. Then it stopped.

Still seated on the pier, Sam's eyes steadily grew larger. The jiggling water suddenly turned to an odd ripple – a wave crossing the Bay at lightning speed. "Uh oh!" he said, swinging his legs up half a second too late. The small wave smashed against his feet, hit the pier, rocked the boats, and then dissipated.

Seely's building was still in motion. She whispered a short prayer and waited. At last the building quieted, the dishes stopped tinkling and the elevators quit banging. Still she stood motionless – watching, listening, and waiting. The last object to stop swaying was a heavy, full-length mirror on her living room wall.

When the quake ended at KMPR, Max quickly checked the equipment and retook his seat. He turned dials, flipped switches and glanced at Collin. He grinned. Less than three feet away, on the other side of the sound proof window, Collin was staring at him, wide eyed and shaken. With mischievous blue eyes, Max pulled his hanging mike closer, "Not from around here, are ya?"

Tiny beads of sweat glistened on Collin's brow. He shoved his headset back, closed his eyes, and took a deep, forgotten breath. His hands were trembling. Slowly, he replaced his headset and leaned closer to his mike. "Earth..." he started, pausing to clear his throat, "Earthquake, right?"

"Right." Max brushed a lock of curly blond hair off his forehead and expertly adjusted the sound. "We get a little shaker now and then; you'll get used to it."

But Collin Slater rolled his eyes, "I doubt that." He took another deep breath and tried to stead his nerves. "We still on the air?"

"Yep."

"Okay folks, the number is 789-1001. Give us a call. I thought I heard rumbling, anybody else hear it?" He paused, watched four lights on the ten-line phone begin to blink, grinned and punched the first button. "KMPR."

"Wow man, did you feel that? I was just getting out of my car, and..."

SEELY ROSS DID NOT quickly let go of the door jamb. Instead, she waited until she was certain the earth wasn't still moving. She crossed her hands on her chest, took three deep breaths and tried to quiet her racing heart.

Two apartments down and across the hall, a man stood in his doorway watching. "You alright?"

"Yes, just scared."

"Me too." He was a stout, middle-aged man with light brown hair and a kind face, "Looks like you and I are the only ones taking this seriously."

Seely stepped out, leaned against the hallway wall, and then folded her arms. "They don't know any better." Her long dark hair hung loose, her light pink shirt had short sleeves and one knee peeked out of well-worn blue jeans.

The man chuckled. "I guess not. I was in the Northridge quake in LA. On any given day, I can still feel a truck going down a street four blocks away."

"I know what you mean, I was in the San Fernando Quake in 1971. Any kind of sudden movement and I'm rattled. I think that's good though, at least we know when to run."

Just then, a young couple came out of their apartment and headed for the elevator. Seely intentionally raised her voice, "The last thing I'd do right now is get in an elevator." But the couple only stared at her, waited for the door to open, and then stepped inside. Seely closed her eyes and listened as the elevator made its way down six floors. Endless seconds later it stopped and the door opened.

The man across the hall shook his head. "You can't tell them. People just don't understand until they've been in a bad one."

"I know, I've got a daughter and son-in-law who think I'm a whacked out alarmist for making them keep their earthquake kit up to date."

"Good for you. Speaking of family, I better see if my wife's okay." He pulled a cell phone out of his pocket and stepped back inside his apartment.

Cautiously, Seely slipped through her foyer and grabbed the phone off an end table next to her pastel peach sofa. Untangling the long cord, she quickly walked back to the open door, dialed the number, and listened.

In the suburb of Crown Hill, ninety-seven blocks north of Queen Ann Hill, the familiar voice of her son-in-law answered, "Yes?" Theo Wesley held the phone in one hand and a TV remote in the other with his tall, thin frame sprawled out on the living room sofa.

Seely tried desperately to control the quiver in her voice, "You guys alright?"

Theo quickly sat up, "Why, what's happening?"

"We just had an earthquake."

He frowned and abruptly turned the volume down on the television, "Ah Ma, are you sure? I didn't feel anything."

"Lucky you."

"Hang on, Ma, there's the other line."

Seely listened to the familiar nothingness of hold, took another deep breath and cautiously made her way across the living room. Careful not to get too close, she peeked out her picture window. The older, brick apartment buildings below looked undamaged, the water of the Bay seemed calm, and the chopper hovering above it didn't seem alarmed. Even so, she quickly went back to the hallway.

"That was Michelle...Ma, are you there?"

"Yes, I'm here."

Theo turned the television off, set the remote down and absent-mindedly toyed with the phone cord. "She's downtown shopping and scared out of her wits. She says they're evacuating so she's coming home."

"Good. Have her call me when she gets there."

"Dang, I never feel anything. How big this time?"

Seely thought for a moment, "A Four."

"Four it is then, you haven't been wrong yet. Dang, I'd like to feel it just once."

"Careful what you wish, son."

"Are you okay?" Theo paused for a long moment before he continued, "Ma, I gotta tell you, we worry more about your heart than we do about earthquakes. You get so scared."

"One bad quake and you'll be just like me...scared the rest of your life. Have Michelle call me, okay?"

"Okay. You sure you're all right?"

"I'm sure." Seely hung up the phone, and then cautiously went back inside. She sat down on the edge of her easy chair and concentrated on calming her nerves. On the opposite wall, a landscape painting hung askew. Above and below it, jagged new cracks stretched through the plaster. With her eyes, she followed the upper one to the ceiling where it turned toward the windows and stopped. Behind her, both sides of the door to her bedroom displayed angled, hairline cracks four to six inches long. Still unnerved, she lifted her hands and rubbed her forehead – exposing a half-inch, pear shaped birthmark midway down her right forearm. Finally, Seely relaxed and turned to gaze out the window. Only then did she realize the radio was still on. Collin Slater's deep rich voice was comforting, but the female caller was near hysterics.

"No kidding?" Collin asked.

"I'm telling you, a man fell off the Aurora Bridge. I was watching him when the earthquake hit and now he's gone...oh wait, there he is. I guess he just fell down. Maybe he sat down to keep from falling. I..."

For nearly five hours, all ten lines on Collin's console lit up repeatedly. Firsthand accounts reported only slight damage. Cans fell off shelves, a few windows break and one back porch slumped, but no one died or was seriously injured. At ten p.m. he helped Max shut down the station.

THE EARTHQUAKE WAS over. Or was it? Directly below the city of Seattle, the enormous shelves tested the strength of the newest snag.

BY THE NEXT DAY, COLLIN had questions, serious questions. "Folks, I'm looking for the name of a good book on Earthquakes. If you know of one, call in. Meanwhile, our friend Louise has been kind enough to stay on the line while we took our little station break. Louise, are you still with us?"

"Like I said, I'm real tired of you young folks trying to run me down when I try to cross the street. Slow down! My feet don't go as fast as they once did."

"How old are you, Louise?"

"Ninety-four. I've lived through four wars and 'twas'nt a one as dangerous as crossing Third Avenue during rush hour. Tell them to slow down, afore they splat me clear across the road."

"I'll tell them, Louise. Do you still live on your own?"

"Sure do, Hazel died, you know."

"No, I didn't know. I'm sorry."

"Well I'm not, meanest nurse you ever did see. My granddaughter lives with me now. She's forty-three and don't cook so good, but we manage. Well, that's all I got to say." With that, Louise hung up.

Collin chuckled and looked at Max, "That's what I like about the older generation, they get right to the point. And before I forget, here's tomorrow's excuse for not going to work—someone pulled the wiring out of my car. Okay, let's get back to the earthquake question. If you know of a well written, informative book on the subject, let me know. What I don't get is, some people felt the earthquake and some didn't. Why is that?"

With his feet on his console, his hanging microphone lowered to his mouth and his blond hair pulled back, Max grinned, "We're on a hill. People who felt it were on hills. People who didn't, either live farther away or are in the low-lands."

"In that case, I say we move the station."

"Can't. Can't afford the rent anywhere else."

"Figures." Collin sipped his coffee and went on, "And now for other news. Remember Jan Farnsworth, the woman who claims Winston Churchill tells her the future? Well, it seems the ghostly Mister Churchill wasn't as forthcoming as he might have been. The body of Jan Farnsworth was found in a hotel room in Portland early this morning. The cause of death has not been determined."

Collin intentionally paused before he went on, "Now this is interesting. The Aircraft Carrier USS Carl Vincent is due to arrive next month for maintenance and repairs. Man those babies are beautiful and a real pleasure to watch. We don't see a lot of Aircraft Carriers in Colorado and in my opinion, they are the essence of well spent, hard earned American tax dollars.

And guess what else folks, the Medical Profession has issued yet another public awareness announcement. You know, those fillers the mega-media uses on their nightly news ... when they're out of real news to report. Well, now they claim smoking causes cancer in cats. I ask you, who can afford to let their cat smoke? And why aren't all the cats dead by now? I smoke and..." He hesitated and watched Max through the window. Right on cue, Max played Chubby Checker's, "I feel fine," interrupted by the sound of uncontrollable coughing.

Days Later

The oldest of the three, Carl Kingsley was a tall, slender man with blond hair and mischievous brown eyes. His beloved air crane was the same one he'd flown in the Viet Nam War, later convinced the army to sell and floated an enormous loan to buy. His air crane was his one true love and when she stood idle on her landing pad, he delighted in checking the engine or climbing a ladder to polish her bubble face. Even now, he still chuckled at the thought of his ex-wife's failed drug company.

To outsiders, the three made an odd trio – Jackie usually dressed as though she stepped out of a magazine, Michael was the epitome of a computer nerd and Carl thought of flying as a pleasure, not a job. Each of them was happy. The money was excellent, vacations were frequent, and Jackie always consulted them before taking on new cases. Neither man ever turned her down

Dressed in her usual royal blue suit, Jackie stood in the doorway of her private mobile home and grinned at Carl, who was standing on a ladder with a can of polish in one hand and a rag in the other. When Michael appeared, she stood aside, let him in, and offered a seat in her recliner. Cramped but immaculately kept, Jackie's private quarters held a much smaller version of their computer system, a television, a radio, and the best in audio equipment. Just now, soft music played and the smell of pine trees filtered in through an open window. She made herself comfortable on a bar stool, crossed her long slender legs and began to fiddled with a diamond wedding ring on her left hand.

At the age of twenty-nine, Michael Sorenson gladly gave up the conventional business world as soon as Jackie offered him a job. Short men, in his opinion, were never taken as seriously as tall men. Nor did Corporate American allow him the freedom to expand, embellish, and investigate new ideas. With Harlan Detective Agency, all that changed. Jackie gave him a free hand, spoiled him with more equipment than he knew what to do with and greatly valued his opinion.

But today Michael looked confused and bewildered. He pushed his glasses up and stared into her eyes, "I think we might be in over our heads."

"In what way?"

"I talked to the second Mrs. Cole's sister. She knows Evan is looking for Christina and at first she was friendly, asking me more questions than I asked her. But after a while, her voice got sort of cold. I don't think she's going to be real pleased if we find Christina."

"What did she say?"

Michael got up, walked to a kitchen cupboard, and opened the door. He withdrew two glasses and a bottle of scotch, and then walked to the refrigerator for ice.

"Not much really. She said Evan never hurt his second wife, Jennifer. In fact, her sister had a good life and the best doctors money could buy before she died. I asked her a few more questions, and then all of a sudden she blurted out, 'Oh hell, he's going to find out anyway. You want to know what happened? Go to Evergreen Cemetery,' abruptly, she hung up."

"Evergreen Cemetery...where?"

"As it turns out, right here in Seattle."

"And?"

"And I found a very interesting grave."

"Let me guess, Christina is buried there."

He handed her a drink, and then retook his seat in the recliner, "No, Evan is."

"What?"

"The head stone reads: Evan Cole, beloved husband of Christina. Born June 13, 1945...died April 10th, 1970."

"The same day Christina supposedly drowned off the coast of Maine?"

Michael raised an eyebrow and took a quick sip, "The very same day."

"What is going on here?"

Ten days later

At KMPR, Collin plopped a piece of hard candy in his mouth and quickly tucked it between his teeth and cheek, "Enough of boring national news, here's a little local news. Guess what Charlotte Bancroft dug up in her back yard? Charlotte lost her husband of twenty-three years to heart disease, and having finally recovered from her grief, decided to dig up Harold's garden. But what she dug up was a metal box containing the records of Harold's—other identifies. Yep, old Harold was also John Peters, Clay Wilson, and Steve Watts."

In the booth, Max slammed a stuffed toy in the palm of his hand and quickly raised it to the mike. With an English accent, the toy echoed, "Oh no!"

Collin smiled and went on, "Our Power Company says they're still powerless to explain last night's brown-out. Some little something went wrong somewhere. And, at about two this morning, Seattle's fire and rescue trucked, and I do mean trucked, to the corner of 28th Avenue and Northwest Market in Ballard. Get this folks, a garage collapsed crushing a car. The owner of the twenty-year old garage had it inspected right after last month's earthquake and was told...it's as solid as a rock.' Don't they get it? Rocks break. That's why we have earthquakes!"

Max narrowed his eyes and glowered, "Been reading that book again, huh Collin? That stuff will fry your brain man, make you too scared to get out a bed in the morning."

"Forewarned is forearmed." Collin stuck his tongue out, and then quickly pretended to brush something off his blue jeans. "Gonna have a big one, you know."

"Sure we are, right after the sky falls. It's propaganda man, that's all."

"And there you have it folks, the Titanic syndrome. This ship is unsinkable! Seriously my friends, if you're not as sure footed as Max here, you can get a free pamphlet on surviving earthquakes from the office of Disaster Management. They're located at..."

Max tipped his water bottle, drank, and then glanced at the phone. A single light was blinking. He tapped on the window, got Collin's attention, and then pointed at the phone in Collin's console.

Collin nodded and quickly punched the button, "KMPR, what's on your mind friend?"

"I'm not a friend, I'm your mother."

Taken aback by the unfamiliar voice with just a hint of a southern accent, Collin turned to Max, put a hand out palm up and shrugged, "Oh hi, Mom. What's up?"

"Well, I got a letter today from your Aunt Jo in Cincinnati, you know, the one determined never to cut her hair. I swear it's longer than a month of Sundays. Her boy Carl just got a promotion. Carl, your Aunt Jo's boy, never did a lick of work in his life till three years ago last December, and then he happened upon an old man claiming to be homeless. Homeless, my Boston behind, the man owns half of Ohio. He's just miserly, that's all. Anyway Carl, that's your Aunt Jo's boy, took a liking to the old man right off and three years ago last December started the all-important job of tending the old man's canaries. Oh, it's a full time job, you know, what with the birds allowed to fly freely though the mansion. And son..."

"What Mom?"

"The way I got it figured, your job is far more high-flute'n than his. You ask that Max for a raise, you hear?" With that, Mom hung up.

Surprised, Collin's eyes widened. He timidly looked at Max and shook his head.

But Max was unconvinced. He glared, flipped a switch, and brought up the sound of screeching tires followed by a fatal crash. Then slowly, the tips of his mouth curled upward into a wide grin.

Relieved, Collin chuckled and punched line two.

Abruptly, a man's deep voice loudly boomed across Puget Sound's airwaves, "The Lord hath sent his Prophet Daniel to warn Thee."

Instantly, Collin pulled both sides of his headset away from his ears, "What?"

"Thou art an evil and rebellious people, whom the Lord God shall chasten with a mighty shaking of the earth." Unexpectedly, the line went dead.

Speechless, Collin hung on a full ten seconds more. He disconnected the call and stared at Max, "What'd he say? Can you play that back?"

Max nodded, quickly rewound the tape and played it again.

# CHAPTER 3

MONDAY, JULY 21

SPECIFICALLY BUILT to withstand an 8.0 earthquake, the forty-seven-floor Winningham Blue Building faced Third Avenue directly across the street from the Mainland Tower. Spread over an entire city block, it had two sub-floors, five parking garage levels, giant criss-crossed pillars, and a glass observation deck on the top floor. Inside, three sets of six elevators were centrally located with a stairwell on the end of each set. Both the interior and exterior of the building were decorated in shades of blue with gold trim. Built into down-town Seattle's hillside, it served as a miniature shopping mall complete with restaurants, coffee shops, a bookstore, a cobbler shop and a flower shop. The sub-floors opened on to terraces facing Second Avenue and the Federal Building. Two blocks down the hill lay the Alaskan Freeway, the waterfront and the Bay. And every day at noon, a pianist played a grand piano in the first floor lobby, offering classical music to customers of a prominent bank branch.

The consecutive floors of the plush building held ample bathrooms, thick carpets, potted plants, and decorative art. Custom designed executive offices on the outskirts of each floor exhibited full length, blue glass windows. Across wide hallways lay a second row of internal offices, more hallways and a third row of still smaller offices. In addition to a reception area and a break room with a sofa and comfortable chairs, each contained a centrally located kitchenette complete with sink, refrigerator, coffee maker, and microwave.

As was their policy, the building management encouraged individual companies to modify their offices, an offer eagerly accepted by the accounting firm of Paul McGill on the forty-third floor. The northern half of the floor remained unchanged with the reception area, the conference room, executive and internal offices intact. But ten years before, Paul McGill ordered the other side – just beyond the kitchenette, virtually gutted, leaving only one office and a large room filled with crowded desks, equipment and busy employees.

Twenty-year-old Jenna Swenson casually poked her head into the only remaining office on the southern half of the floor, "Hey boss, did you hear that Prophet guy on KMPR last night?"

Seely Ross waved her in. Two blue lounge chairs faced her desk and all three walls were lined with matching oak bookshelves and cabinets. Seated behind a large oak desk, she kept her eyes on her computer spreadsheet, "Uh huh. Pity he didn't say when to expect the earthquake, we could all take the day off."

"No kidding." Jenna leisurely walked to the huge, blue tinted windows. Forty-three floors up and facing east, the panoramic view included the University of Washington Campus to the north with Lake Washington, Mercer Island and the city of Bellevue straight ahead. To the south, she could see the I-5 freeway "S" curves, Boeing Field and the Cascade Mountains. Suddenly, Jenna's eyes lit up, "Oh look, the mountain is out."

Seely scooted her chair away from her desk and walked to the window. With a dusting of soft white clouds at its base, Mount Rainier's glacier capped peak towered high in the distance. "It's about time. We've had so much rain this year; I thought we'd never see it again."

"Hard to imagine it's nearly a hundred miles away." With short blond hair and light brown eyes, Jenna stood a full head taller than her boss. "Seely, you're the religious freak around here. Does God send earthquakes to punish people?"

"He has, on occasion. He sent one to wipe out a golden calf and another to destroy Sodom and Gomorra."

"Really? And does he send Prophets?"

"I've never met one, but that doesn't mean they don't exist. The test of a true prophet is in the prophecy. If it doesn't happen, the guy's a fraud."

"Yes, but God could sent a Prophet to warn us, couldn't he?"

Seely smiled and walked back to her desk. "Far be it for me to tell God what he can or cannot do. But Sugar, try not to take this too seriously. It's probably just a publicity stunt. Let's go home, this 'religious freak' is tired. And in the elevator you can tell me all about Kevin. He's coming home soon, isn't he?"

"Yep, Sunday. That's five days, seven hours and..." Jenna paused to look at her watch, "six minutes."

"My, how time flies. Seems like only yesterday you were shrouded in gloom over his leaving."

Jenna lifted her chin and headed for the door. "It's been six whole months, I'll have you know. And the next time the Army sends him overseas, I'm going with him."

"Good for you. While we're on the subject, how about working Saturday and taking Monday off?"

"Really?"

"Really. I could use the help and if you promise not to tell, I might be persuaded to throw in Tuesday."

"Oh Seely, you're just like a Mom...the greatest mom in the world."

"Uh huh, this week anyway." Seely closed all her programs, turned off her computer, grabbed her purse, and walked out the door. In the large room across the hall, thirty-six people kept her department of McGill Accounting Services running smoothly. Copiers lined the far wall, separated by industrial size scanners, fax machines and a walk-in vault. Seven rows of desks faced east, each with a bookcase, a chair, a computer, an adding machine, and mountains of reports.

Tuesday, July 22

Seated at his console, Collin finished rolling up his shirt sleeves and leaned closer to the mike, "...and by Saturday, 86 degrees. However, the clouds are coming back, folks. I'm afraid this kind of weather is just too good to last." He set a weight on his papers and then flipped a switch on his console. Slowly, the overhead ceiling fan began to pick up speed. "It's five o'clock, the traffic is backed up for miles and I've got something to say. As you may have heard, John Simony got arrested today for molesting a child. Thing is, he's been convicted before. Folks, I'm fed up with these dirt bags. A mistake over and over is a lifestyle. Twenty years ago we would have hung him. Now we give these slime balls free room and board, cable TV and a physical fitness center. And who pays for all that? We do! Then, a few years later, they let guys like him out to rape again. If a law needs to be changed, it's this one. As soon as they're convicted, we should put them on public display and then we should hang them...publicly! Call me, tell me what you think."

Max stared at the un-lit phone, looked at Collin and shrugged.

"Speaking of taxes," Collin went on, "They've done another traffic study. Seattle now has more traffic jams than LA or New York. What I want to know is, why do we need another tax funded, outrageously expensive study? Can't they just watch the traffic reports on the Internet?"

Max chuckled and flipped on his mic, "Maybe that's how they do their study." Finally, line one flashed. Max quickly tapped the window and watched Collin answer.

"KMPR, what's on your mind, friend?" Collin asked.

Again, the deep, mysterious voice blared in his ear, "Behold, the Lord sends his doves as a sign unto thee."

"Who is this? Hello...hello?" Collin listened to the click, and then the abrupt dial tone.

Further north of downtown, on the roof of the Ballard Independence Bank, Sam Taylor put his cell phone back in his pocket. Next, he pushed the stop button on a small tape recorder and slipped it into a second pocket. He unhooked the clasp, lifted the wire mesh and watched six snow-white doves fly out of the cage.

"That should do it," he muttered. He shoved the empty cage behind a roof vent, and then covered it with an old blanket. "For what they cost, that better do it." When he turned, one of the doves sat perched on the edge of a vent. Sam glared and pointed toward town, "That way. See those tall buildings? Right in there is Interstate Five and that traffic jam. All you gotta do is swoop down now and then, okay?" The dove cocked its head to one side and then took flight, soaring in the wrong direction.

His white hair newly trimmed, Sam straightened his expensive suit jacket, opened the door and descended the narrow flight of stairs. He walked down the hallway, strolled past his Administrative Assistant, admired his name in gold above the words 'Bank President,' and then went into his office. Quickly, he closed the door, took a seat behind his desk and turned the radio up. His son, Max, was playing the song "Nearer My God to Thee."

In the station, Max flipped his microphone off and gingerly tapped a button until the music faded. "Come on people," he mumbled. He worked the controls, repeatedly glanced at the un-lit phone and listened to more of Collin's chatter. "Call in people, call in. How's a guy supposed to stay in business if you don't call in?" Finally, the first line lit up and before he could signal, Collin answered it.

On the other end of the phone, a woman immediately started talking, "There's a dove in my back yard."

Collin spilled his coffee. He looked around, grabbed a paper towel, and quickly wiped it up, "You're kidding, right?"

"I'm not kidding. It's white and sitting in my pine tree."

"Are you sure it's a dove? I mean, have you ever seen one?"

"No, but I've got an encyclopedia with a picture. It's a dove all right, I'm positive. I'm scared. Are we going to have an earthquake?"

Collin quickly softened his voice, "Don't be scared. On the other hand, we did get a report from the University of Washington Seismology lab this morning. They say seismic activity is increasing."

Max puffed his cheeks and flipped his mike on, "Collin, we live in volcano land. It wouldn't be right if seismic activity didn't increase occasionally. The time to worry is when the seismographs stop moving." Suddenly all the lights on the phone began to blink.

Collin grinned and quickly punched the next button. "KMPR, seen any doves lately?"

"No," a man answered, "but you do know there really was a Prophet named Daniel in the Old Testament, don't you? I mean, it's not impossible to think..."

Collin took six calls in the first ten minutes, and then reached for the seventh, "KMPR, what's your name?"

"Skip."

"Hi Skip, you believe in Prophets?"

"Sure do. I think this guy might be for real. Thing is though, the voice sounds vaguely familiar. I can't quite put a name to it."

"I know what you mean. It sounds a little like Tennessee Ernie Ford without the accent. You figure it out, you let me know, okay Skip?"

"You got it."

"Thanks for calling." Collin sipped his coffee, and then took the next call, "KMPR, you're on the air."

The eighth caller was another man. "Listen, I run a pet shop in Federal Way and some guy came in here yesterday looking for doves."

"Really? What'd he look like?"

"Old, gray hair, shabby hat, you know. Looked like one of the street people except he was wearing after shave."

Collin sat up just a little straighter, "You sell him any doves?"

"Two."

"He didn't happen to pay by check or credit card, did he?"

"Nope, had a big wad of cash. Thing is, there was something about his eyes. They were blue, a real bright blue like...like he had some sort of, you know, fire in his eyes."

In the booth, Max switched off his mike. "Fire in his eyes, this is great stuff." Lightly tapping two soft switches at the same time, his lips parted in a wide smile. Quickly, he shoved a pile of papers aside, typed six words on his keyboard and hit enter.

Collin set his coffee down, punched the next button on the phone, and then glanced at the huge words on his monitor.

**Let's see the competition top this!**

He smiled and gave Max a thumbs up, "KMPR, seen any doves lately?"

At closing time, Max opened the door, waited for Collin to walk through, and then pulled the attic door closed. "Good show. That Prophet stuff might just put us on the map. I signed up two new advertisers today, and you took twenty-six calls in forty-five minutes. I like your style man, I truly do."

Collin grinned and started down the steel reinforced concrete stairs, "Thanks. Beth's getting pretty good at disguising her voice, but she's already tired of calling."

"So is Candy. With any luck, they won't have to do that anymore. By the way, Dad's been thinking about earthquakes, thanks to you. He's put up the money for better backup generators, plenty of fuel and some heavy-duty batteries. They should be delivered tomorrow."

Collin paused on the second floor landing and turned to face him, "Like that'll do us any good. This place is wood. Anything over a 5.5 and we're doomed."

"Not so. My grandparents lived here during the Cuban Missile crisis. They thought the Russians were coming, so they had the whole thing reinforced with steel and concrete. After they died, Dad divided it into apartments. It's a bomb shelter, complete with a place in the basement for generators. All we gotta do with the new stuff is hook up exhaust pipes and run more wiring."

Collin leaned against the wall and rested his hand on his apartment doorknob. "Amazing."

"What?"

"You're not as tough as you sound, are you? This earthquake thing has you just as rattled as me."

Max looked him in the eye for a moment, and then turned away. "The truth is, I'm probably more scared. Some seismologist found evidence of an old, cataclysmic earthquake out on Neah Bay. He thinks we're due for another one. There's not a day goes by I wished he hadn't said that. He says our 'Big One' will be between 8.0 and 9.5. If it is, Seattle will tumble like a house of cards. We're not ready, Collin, we're not even close to ready. We've got a double-decker highway just like the one that collapsed in Oakland, only in worse shape. We've got sky scrapers built on hills and floating bridges that swing every time the wind blows over 40 miles an hour."

Max stopped to take a long, deep breath. "A couple of years ago, one of the bridge sections popped up and a friend of mine hit it head on. It killed her instantly. If those bridges start twisting..." He closed his eyes and shook his head. "We've got brick buildings with shoddy mortar everywhere, not to mention wooden ones that should have been condemned years ago."

"And four million people?"

"Yes, half of which work downtown. The truth is, Seattle's business district is just a tiny stretch of land with Elliott Bay to the west, Lake Washington to the east and Lake Union's bridge canal to the north. We've got water, tons of it on three sides and if the bridges go, all those people will be stuck downtown. Been through the bus tunnel yet?"

"Not yet."

Max pulled a rubber band out of the back of his blond hair and let it hang loose, "Good, stay out of it. Rumor has it, the sides are starting to bulge."

"You're kidding."

"I wish I was. It runs right under Third Avenue with skyscrapers on each side. You should see the taxes we paid...are still paying to build it. And guess where they put the new stadium?"

Collin raised his eyebrows, "Downtown."

"You got it. Most of our hospitals are on hills. A freeway, complete with overpasses, runs right between downtown and the hospitals. And should we have fires, which we will, the main fire station is downtown too. And we've got rain, man. Every winter more and more houses slide down the hills. Now they're using recycled glass in the foundations of new buildings. You know what recycled glass, mixed with all this soppy land does in an Earthquake?"

"Not a clue."

"Neither do I."

Collin narrowed his eyes and glared at Max, "And you got me to leave Denver for this? I want hazard pay."

"Get in line, pal, get in line." Max playfully socked Collin's shoulder, and then hurried on down the stairs. When he reached the first landing, he opened the door. "Honey, I'm home!"

Collin listened to Max greet his three rambunctious little boys and waited until he heard the door shut. He closed his eyes and rubbed his forehead. Finally, he opened the door to his own apartment, crossed the living room, walked into the kitchen, and wrapped his strong arms around his wife of only a few months.

She was by far the prettiest girl to grace the campus of Colorado State University and from the moment he saw her, Collin was taken. But Beth Carpenter was notorious for turning down dates, hated immaturity, and intended to get the best education available. So Collin used a novel approach. He made sure they shared at least one class per semester and kept his distance. Yet each time he saw her, he whistled his favorite song.

She recognized the 60's tune and finally, in the hallway outside of class, she turned around and looked at him. Now she was his wife and her beauty still took his breath away, "Have you any idea how much I've missed you?"

Nearly as tall as he with her hair in small, long braids, Beth's smile was warm and genuine. "Indeed? Did you miss me enough to buy me a new car?" Her brown eyes twinkled as he lowered his lips to hers. But when his kiss seemed somehow urgent, Beth pulled away to look at him. "What is it?"

Collin ignored the question and drew her close again.

"Something's wrong. What? We promised to be honest, remember? I can take it, just spit it out."

He kissed her forehead, took her hand, and led her to the sofa. When she sat down beside him, he wrapped his arms around her again. "It's just that I love you so. You're beautiful, you're funny, you're so alive, and I can't imagine what I did before I met you. Beth, if I ever lost you, I'd..."

"Baby, I'm pregnant, not terminally ill. Women live through this kind of thing every day."

He chuckled and laid his head on top of hers, "It's not that. I didn't check it out before I brought you here. I didn't think to. Seattle has earthquakes like LA, and the more I learn, the more frightened I am. It could happen, Beth, it really could."

"Yes, but maybe not for another hundred years. Honey, there are no safe places. Our other choice was Dallas where they have hurricanes, floods, and tornadoes. Even Colorado has killer blizzards. We're as safe here, with a maybe earthquake, as we are anywhere else. Besides, it's so beautiful here."

The two-story house faced south, yet the living room had an extension with side windows offering views both east and west. Collin gazed through the picture window at the multitude of downtown city lights glistening against the crystal clear, night sky. "It is beautiful, isn't it?"

"Yes, it is. And you like working for Max."

"I like Max very much. I got a good look in the booth today. Remember he said it was rustic? Well, he forgot to mention the bobby pins."

"Bobby pins?"

"Uh huh, and tape and who knows what else. The guy's either a genius or the biggest miser I've ever met. And he's so inventive with the sound effects."

Beth moved just enough to tuck her feet up under her body and nuzzle deeper into his neck, "So I've noticed. I love it when you're talking about the Prophet and he plays Titanic music."

"Titanic music?"

"Don't you remember? They played 'Nearer my God to Thee' on the Titanic right before it sank."

"Oh great, that's just great. Max is warped, you know that. Am I the only one who gets frazzled when that Prophet calls in?"

"You mean you don't know who it is?"

"Not a clue, neither does Max. Tell me, don't you get a little freaked?"

"Well sometimes, when I let myself think about it. But the guy's not for real, he can't be."

"I sure hope you're right."

Beth pulled away and smirked, "And this from a man who isn't sure there is a God. If there is no God, he can't have Prophets, right?"

Collin wrinkled his brow and lightly bit his lower lip, "Right."

"So, can we stay?"

He took a deep breath, stared at the city lights a moment longer and then smiled, "On one condition."

"What?"

"Tomorrow we make some serious survival plans, complete with dried food, water and enough diapers to last for months. Deal?"

"Deal." Finally, she lifted her lips to his

# CHAPTER 4

KMPR, THURSDAY, JULY 23

"...LAST NIGHT, AN EARTHQUAKE measuring 2.9 on the Richter scale rattled windows and woke several residents. They say, seismologists that is, it was an aftershock from July's 4.3 quake. They say that, because it was centered in the same area. Most folks don't feel small quakes. Actually, I was reading my earthquake book last night and..."

Max slapped both hands against the side of his face and quickly interrupted, "Oh boy, here we go again."

"No wait, this is interesting. Did you know that in China and Japan, they sometimes see red and white flashing lights in the sky right before an earthquake?"

"Red?"

"That's what the book says. The flashes are sort of like the northern lights and they're so bright, they wake people out of a sound sleep."

Max scratched the top of his head, and then the side of his face, "So okay, if I see a red light I should run, right?"

"Unless you're at an intersection."

"Very funny."

Collin reached in his drawer, grabbed a candy bar and began unwrapping it. "Did you hear about part of that new shoe store collapsing? Bet last month's shaker weakened it."

"Collin is eating again folks. That's what all that noise is."

KMPR's host ignored Max and went on, "Bet our Governor thinks so too. He's trying to get new funds to fix the Alaskan Freeway, you know the double-decker that runs along the waterfront. I say, tear it down and put in a park, Mister Governor."

While Max brought up the music, Collin took a quick bite, chewed and swallowed, "And now for the latest Prophet news. This morning, a local Minster found a man matching the Prophet's description asleep in his sanctuary. Pastor Jack couldn't explain how the Prophet got in since he always locks the church up tight. And no, the Pastor didn't see any fire in the Prophet's eyes."

Once more, all ten-phone lines lit up.

"KMPR, go," Collin said, winking at Max.

The man's voice sounded angry and demanding, "Look Collin, you're gonna cause a panic if you keep this up. Everybody knows it's a publicity stunt and all you're doing is scaring people."

"Tell me, how do I prove KMPR has nothing to do with this? I swear we're not behind it."

"Then stop letting him on the air. Don't you know panic is just as deadly as earthquakes?"

"My friend, when we first went on the air we made our listeners a promise. We don't screen the calls. We believe people are intelligent enough to know when they have something important to say. Besides, people don't panic over something like this, not after 'War of the Worlds.' They're smarter than that. On the other hand, no one denies we live in an earthquake zone. Maybe it takes a Prophet to make people pay attention. Call him a wacko, call him an extremist, call him anything you like. But the truth is, right after work tonight I'm getting prepared just in case...and so should you."

In the booth, Max pulled out his cell phone and placed a call to his father. "Dad, Collin wants a raise."

IN THE FAULT BELOW Elliott Bay, small sections of earth repeatedly crumbled. The shifting rock caused only minimal shaking in the 1.0 to 1.5 range, but at the University of Washington, seismographs recorded every tremor. A man spread yesterday's graphs out on a table and carefully examined them. His eyes still glued to the jagged marks, he reached for his phone, punched an auto dial number, and listened.

As always, he found comfort in the sound of his wife's voice. "Hi babe...No, nothing's wrong. I was just wondering if our stored water is out of date...I swear nothing's wrong. At least nothing I can put a finger on. You know me, the least hint of a major occurrence and I start running down the list. Have we used anything out of the medical kit? Mark's in a new school this year, and..."

Harlan Detective Agency had all the pictures of Christina, AKA Seely Ross they needed. So instead of flying, Carl took up his fishing pole and headed into the woods. Once more Jackie sat across from Michael in her mobile home, nestled beneath the shade of several pine trees. This time, both were dressed in casual clothing and the music was livelier. "How did this get so complicated?" she asked.

"I have no idea. The sister-in-law still won't take my calls. I did reach the cemetery caretaker, however. Once a year someone, a woman, comes to lay flowers on Evan Cole's grave. The caretaker doesn't know who she is and says it's not his place to ask. I faxed him a picture of Seely Ross and he says she is definitely not the one. The woman who comes is short, frail and probably in her seventies."

Jackie stood up, walked two steps into the kitchen, and grabbed a plate of freshly baked cookies. Retracing her steps, she set them on a small table beside Michael's easy chair and retook her seat. "What are we going to do? We can't keep Evan at bay much longer and we can't expose Seely Ross until we know what's going on. She's got the classic symptoms. She goes to work, buys groceries, and goes home. She has no friends, goes out only to see her grandchildren and does all her other shopping over the Internet. She's frightened Michael, she must be."

"I agree, but of whom? Evan Cole is not an abuser. In fact, he raised two good sons who are successful in their own right; he made his money honestly and is quite generous." Michael helped himself to a cookie and paused to savor the taste. "Are you sure you don't want to marry me?"

Jackie laughed and reached for a cookie, "It's against company policy. I never marry the men I work with."

"In that case, I quit."

"Michael, be serious. We have nothing new on the sister-in-law or the bank account, right?"

"Nothing. Banks are not so easy to break into, you know, and so far, sister-in-law Loraine Whitcomb is squeaky clean. Don't worry, I'm still on it. I do have one little jewel to offer. I talked to Evan Cole's best friend and business partner. He agrees with everyone else, Evan wouldn't hurt a fly. Besides, Mister Cole deeply loved Christina. He nearly went nuts after she died. He spent a fortune trying to recover the body, built a shrine in his house and refused to part with a thing she ever owned or touched. Unfortunately, the house burned down about six months later, which is why there are no dental records."

"I see. What about her dentist?"

"Evan doesn't remember which Dentist she went to and all his cancelled checks burned. The portrait he hung in his office was all he had left. According to his friend, the painting was a great source of irritation to his second wife, but Jennifer eventually learned to live with it." Michael helped himself to another cookie and watched Jackie's thoughtful expression.

"Okay, so Evan Cole loved his wife and probably isn't the one who hurt her. That leaves us with a dead second wife, a sister-in-law who won't talk, an old woman, and a burial site for a man who's very much alive. Got any suggestions?"

"Yes. Let's go ask her."

"The sister-in-law?"

"No, Seely Ross. You're her Internet friend, ask her to dinner. Maybe you can get her to talk."

Saturday, July 26

For Sam Taylor, Saturdays meant only one thing – golf. As bank president, Country Clubs eagerly sought his membership. But Sam preferred the old golf course of his youth, in the community of Mount Lake Terrace several miles north of Seattle. It had a small clubhouse and down to earth members. As he always did when he arrived, he put on his highly polished, white golf shoes, opened the trunk of his car and tossed his old fishing hat in. Next, he withdrew a new, red golf cap. He put it on, lifted his chin, and lowered the trunk enough to examine his reflection in the back window. He smiled. Wearing all white with a red-checkered vest, he carefully examined the rest of his appearance. Satisfied, he grabbed his red golf bag, closed the trunk, and headed for the clubhouse. The time was 8:45 a.m.

WITH FRESH AIR, A CLEAR sky, and the bright morning sun in their faces, Jackie poured coffee for Carl and Michael, and then sat down in a lawn chair beneath the second Mobile home's awning. At ten minutes past nine a.m., Jackie took a deep breath, picked up the satellite phone and placed a call to her client's private line in New York City. "It's me, Jackie."

"And..."

"Good news, the birthmark is a perfect match."

"I'm on my way."

"Wait! Mister Cole? ...Mister Cole?" But the line was dead. "I knew he'd do that." She hung up the phone, turned and stared at the grin on Michael's face. "Give him half an hour, and then start checking the airlines. I want to know what flight he's on and exactly where his layovers are."

"Doesn't he own a plane?"

"Yes, but yesterday the pilot detected a malfunction in the engine."

Carl chuckled and set his coffee cup down on the round metal table, "A malfunction? How convenient."

"I want him on a commercial airline. In a private jet, he could land anywhere."

Michael helped himself to sugar and cream, reached for a spoon and began to stir his coffee, "Are you sure we're doing the right thing?"

"No. But I can't think of any other way. It took a lot of convincing to get Seely Ross to see me and I don't think we'll get another chance. You got all the papers?"

Michael scooted his small frame back in his chair, crossed his feet and laid his spoon down, "Yep. Airline tickets, hotel rooms and a man in Chicago ready to make new ID's. You give the word, we pick up the two of you first...then her daughter and family. We fly them to the compound, take them by ferry to Canada and put them on a flight to Chicago...where they disappear off the face of the earth."

"Good. We're all set then. All we have to do is get Evan Cole in a hotel room. He pays our fee and we give him Seely's address."

"And," Carl put in, "if it turns out he's not the one she's afraid of and she wants to see him, he's right here in Seattle waiting."

"Right. What have we forgotten?"

Carl's mischievous grin slowly widened. "Nothing. A royal blue chopper will land in the play field across the street from the daughter's house and it'll be the talk of the neighborhood for weeks."

Jackie buried her face in her hands and shook her head, "Good point. Set up a new paint job in LA."

"Red?" Carl asked.

"We used red last time."

"I know, but baby likes it when she's red."

Jackie glanced at the blue chopper sitting quietly on its landing pad, and then smiled. "Okay, red." Suddenly, she turned her attention to Michael, "You took care of the flowers, right?"

"Don't worry. I picked them out myself yesterday and the mike is in place. All the guy has to do is deliver them. And before you ask, I know she's working today. The flowers will be delivered to her office at exactly 4:30. And if she leaves early, he'll take them to her house. Relax, will ya?"

Finally, Jackie returned his smile, "Flowers always make a woman feel good."

"I'll keep that in mind."

WHEN KATIE MOORE GLANCED at the clock it was 11:15 a.m. She lived eight miles south of the Kingdome, just west of SeaTac airport and as usual, her dog Spook lay sleeping on the floor. Katie had a migraine headache and the noise of planes taking off wasn't helping. She rested her elbows on the kitchen table and massaged her temples with her fingertips. Suddenly, her black Labrador shot up and raced to the door.

"What is it, boy?"

Spook pawed and whined, wagged his tail, and then deserted his position and lay back down.

Katie watched him a moment more, and then went back to her massage, "Guess that's why we call you spook." Overhead, the roar of a 747 grew louder.

IN CHICAGO, THE FLIGHT from New York landed at O'Hare International Airport without incident. Evan Cole looked haggard and tired as he dug his commercial ticket out of his jacket pocket and walked to the flight monitors. Flight 414 to Seattle, originally scheduled to leave in less than half an hour, was delayed. Furious, he turned toward the ticket counter. But before he could head that direction, his cell phone rang.

Clumsily, he stuffed his ticket back in his pocket, pulled out the phone and extended the antenna, "Hello."

"Evan, this is Loraine."

His eyes lit up and his smile was warm, "Loraine, I found her. She's in..."

"I know. Evan, we've been friends for a long time...long before you married my sister and I love you like a brother. You know that, don't you?"

"I love you too, Loraine. But just now..."

"Evan, Christina didn't fake her own death."

Hundreds of people wandered the corridor or hurried off to catch flights. Children cried, teenagers laughed and couples argued, but Evan Cole noticed none of it, "What?"

It was early afternoon in New York. Even so, Loraine Whitcomb walked to the bar in her well-furnished, dark mahogany library, poured herself a brandy, and took a drink. "It's a long story and I haven't got time to tell it to you now." She was his same age, kept her gray hair bleached blonde, and lived a life of luxury at Evan Cole's expense. Loraine never married, handled Evan's many contributions, and loved to grow flowers.

Stunned, Evan found a row of seats and sat down. "You've known Christina was alive...all these years? Why didn't you tell me?"

"At first, Jennifer needed a wealthy husband. And later, there were your sons to consider." It was stormy in New York with black billowing clouds yielding thunder, lightning, and a downpour of hard rain—a lot like the day Christina vanished. Brandy in hand, Loraine walked to the window, pulled the sheers aside and looked out.

"Loraine?"

"I'm here."

"Are you going to tell me what happened or not?"

Lightening streaked across the sky and thunder quickly followed, booming loudly and ominously, "It's all so very complicated."

"What's complicated? Loraine? ...Loraine talk to me."

But Loraine didn't answer. Instead, she slowly set the phone and her drink down on a table. She turned, walked out of the library, and closed the door behind her. Her four-million-dollar house with its five acres of gardens was well known and admired. One last time, she walked down the gold-capered staircase with its dome windows and crystal chandeliers. She crossed the white marble foyer, picked up her clutch bag and pulled out her keys. Quickly, she removed the house key and laid it on a table next to the door.

The expression on Loraine Whitcomb's face was subdued when she climbed into her luxury car and turned on the ignition. In the midst of the dark storm, she calmly drove away.

WITH LITTLE LEFT TO do but wait, Carl Rhodes took the air crane up for a "spin around the block." His spins usually involved photographing wildlife from high in the air or flying a bit too low over houses to get people to come out. In thirteen years, Jackie paid nearly that many fines and the cost of replacing five cracked windows. But it was a harmless prank, at least so far.

Michael was on to something. He'd been completely engrossed in his work for hours and declined to share anything with her until he was sure, so Jackie decided on a long shower—at least until the small hot water tank ran cold. Just before she stepped in, she glanced at her watch. It was time for Evan Cole's delayed flight to leave Chicago.

WITHOUT AIR CONDITIONING, KMPR's attic was hot and sticky in the summer sun. Collin wiped his brow with a paper towel, and then pulled off his T-shirt. For nearly an hour, music played while Max connected wires from the booth to the new generators in the basement. In a few more minutes, they would shut the power down completely. No big loss. Saturday morning brought few calls anyway. Collin shoved one side of his window open, stuck his head out, and lit a cigarette.

"The minute my back is turned," Max teased, shaking his head as he set his toolbox down on the floor. He pulled the new wiring through a hole that was drilled in the outside studio wall, and then threaded it through another hole into the control room. Next, he checked the length, and then applied caulking to seal both holes. "And where's your shirt? There are laws in Seattle, you know. You gotta wear a shirt, shoes and you can't smoke in a public business."

"So fire me. It's too hot to work up here anyway."

Max put the cap back on the caulking tube and tossed it in his toolbox. "Man, we only get three days of summer a year and you can't take it? What a wimp. Hey, see that spool? Hand it to me, will ya?"

Collin took a drag, laid the cigarette in an ashtray, grabbed the spool of wire, and followed Max into the booth. When he glanced at the console, three lines were lit up. "What the...? Max look!"

Max quickly wiped his hands on his pants and closed the booth door. He waited until Collin was in place, flipped the switch, and mumbled, "They're probably calling to complain about the music."

"KMPR, what's on your mind?" Collin asked.

"I've been trying to get you guys to answer for fifteen minutes," a woman blurted out. "Something weird is going on. There's a blue chopper..."

"Hang on a second. Tell me who you are, where you're calling from and slow down. You talk faster than most people can listen."

"Okay. My name is Cynthia. I'm in Bremerton. Anyway, there's a huge blue chopper flying too low. The noise was so loud, it broke out one of my windows. Course, the window was already cracked, you know, from that earthquake."

"Did the chopper crash?"

"No. It lifted off again. By the time I ran outside, it was high in the air and headed for the Olympic Mountains. But my neighbor got a good look at it. It's got guns mounted on the bottom."

"Guns? Is she sure?"

"She's certain. The barrels are long and about six inches in diameter."

Collin rubbed his forehead thoughtfully, "Maybe it's ATF or FBI."

"She said it wasn't marked. It doesn't even have numbers. Aren't government choppers supposed to be marked?"

"I always thought so."

"Me too. Anyway, you find out who they are. I want them to pay for my window!"

"I'll do my best, Cynthia." Collin glanced at Max, shrugged, and then pushed the next button."

This time the caller was a man, "This is Brian, and I'm over here on Bainbridge Island. I saw it too. It's a sky crane, you know, like they use to haul logs out of the forest. And it dropped something in the water. Maybe something fell off, I don't know. There was another chopper with red markings. It looked like Channel Eight news, or maybe it was channel six. I never can remember which color is which. Anyway, the news chopper started to come closer and when it did, the sky crane turned and took off."

"Did you see any guns on it?"

"I couldn't tell what they were. They don't look long enough to be guns, but these days, who knows? I'm ex-army and it's a Sikorsky 54A all right, but it's been modified. The blades are longer, it has a full body, and the aft windows are bigger."

"Aft windows?"

"Yes. In a sky crane, there are windows in the back of the cab so the crane operator can see what he's doing. Like I said, normally these choppers are used to haul logs or fight fires. But this one's got a full body with windows along the sides where the water tank should be."

"I see."

"I called every TV station from Seattle to Tacoma, and none of them admit to having a news chopper anywhere near Bainbridge. I saw the sky crane another time too. It was hovering over Elliott Bay on the day of the earthquake. Hey, I just thought of something. Didn't a cabin cruiser sink in the Bay a couple of months ago?"

"I remember that. It belonged to some rich guy in Florida."

"Maybe he hired the crane to lift it out of the water."

"Maybe so. Thanks Brian. Give us a call if you see it again."

"Will do. I'm curious now."

In the booth, Max flipped his mike on, "Know what I think? I think it's another right wing, Christian Coalition conspiracy."

Collin sneered and put his finger on the next button, "KMPR, you see a blue chopper?"

"No. But I've been in an earthquake."

"Really. Where?"

"In San Francisco in 1906. My name is Amanda and when I went to San Francisco, it was so cool because I'd never been there before, but I remembered the streets."

"Wait, you'd never been there...but you were in the 1906 earthquake?"

"I must have been...in another life."

Collin shook his head and glanced at his burned out cigarette. "Thanks Amanda. Call again sometime." With the phone lines once more quiet, he took his headset off and lit another.

In the booth, Max was busy jotting down places to call—Ft. Lewis, McNeil Air Force Base, Bremerton Naval Station, Whidby Island, Seattle Police, Boeing and Paine Field. He laid the pencil down and studied his list. "One of them has to know who owns that blue chopper. But first, the generator." He flipped on the music and went back to work.

Collin returned to the window and leaned one shoulder against the wall. Across the street and just beyond a small park, two identical, six floor apartment buildings stood side by side. Below, kids played on the park swings and climbed on bars, while their mother's basked in the rare summer sun.

Max changed the intercom music from Jazz to Soft, making Collin smile and think of Beth. He started to go down stairs to see her, and then he thought better of it. The time was 4:08, Saturday afternoon.

THE MORNING HOURS PASSED quickly for Seely and Jenna on the forty-third floor of the Winningham Blue. Seely bought lunch and promised an excited Jenna they'd finish before five. The love of Jenna's life was finally on his way home and only a few hours remained until Kevin's plane was due to touch down at SeaTac Airport. But by 4:10, Seely was thirsty and needed a breath of fresh air.

She took the express elevator down to the lobby, and then entered a small shop on the upper sub-floor, where she smiled at the clerk and paid for her orange juice. She walked to a long, narrow bar against the wall and grabbed a napkin. Wearing blue jeans and a white shirt with her long hair in a bun, she leisurely strolled out on the terrace. The fresh warm air was just what she needed.

When she reached the four-foot high brick wall, she set her juice down and took a deep breath. On the street level below, Magnolia trees offered large white blossoms and shoppers sat on benches in the flower garden.

On weekdays, Second Avenue was bumper to bumper with traffic, including a multitude of city buses opening their doors, letting people off, and then allowing others to board. But on Saturday, buses ran less frequently and today, there were only two in sight. The first came and went without incident. But in the second, a blind man seemed unable to get his guide dog to budge. Finally, he spoke stern words and the dog relented. The canine led his master down the steps and away from the bus, but as soon as the master urged him south, the dog abruptly sat down. Perplexed, the blind man issued more commands. Still the dog disobeyed, whining and barking instead. At a loss, the man leaned down, spoke softly, and rubbed the dog's ears. Even so, the dog refused to move.

In front of the Federal Building across the street, seagulls watched an elderly lady toss pieces of bread from a bag. The gulls circled and landed. But instead of retrieving their easily obtained meal, they quickly took flight again.

Slowly, Seely searched the cloudless sky. She could feel no wind and other birds were doing the same—landing, but not staying. "I don't like the looks of this. I don't like it at all."

Forgetting her drink, she hurried back inside. She raced across the Bank foyer, rushed around a delivery man with a huge bouquet of flowers, jetted into the hallway, and jammed her finger on the express elevator button. Urgently, she pushed the button again, and again, "Come on."

At last, a door opened. She stepped in and quickly pushed the button marked 43. Endless seconds passed before the door closed and the elevator began to climb. Alone, with her heart racing, she nervously toyed with her necklace and backed into the corner of the small room. Finally, the express elevator increased its speed, whirling past the first thirty-six floors. Even so, Seely remained on edge. Her eyes were glued to numbered lights above the door and her thoughts poured out of her mouth, "Thirty-six floors of solid wall. What were they thinking of?"

# CHAPTER 5

AT 4:14 P.M., MAX THREW the power switches in the basement of KMPR. Just as he hoped, the backup generators kicked on. He hurried up two flights of stairs, raced across the studio and dashed into the sound proof booth. All the appropriate lights were lit on his console, the equipment along each wall buzzed and Max was pleased, "Perfect."

Collin snuffed out his third cigarette and grabbed his T-shirt. "Guess that means I have to go back to work." He sighed, put his shirt on and waited while Max flipped what seemed like dozens of switches on the control panel. Two minutes later, the new backup generators were off and KMPR was back on public power.

JUST SOUTH OF THE SAN Juan Islands, a pod of Orca whales abruptly turned and headed into the Strait of Juan de Fuca toward the open sea. At the same time, the Victoria Clipper sailed past a Port Townsend Lighthouse and started for Vancouver Island. In Everett, two police officers parked their cars outside a restaurant and went inside for coffee.

Just north of the Snohomish County line in Mountlake Terrace, an eight-year old boy in a little league baseball uniform wound up to throw a pitch. On the 405 freeway heading south, a drunken motorist in a station wagon quickly changed lanes without signaling for the third time. Just out of sight, a family of six lounged on the deck of their cabin cruiser on the waters of Lake Washington.

South of Seattle, soldiers marched across an open field at Fort Lewis while at McCord Air Force Base, pilots climbed out of cockpits on the runway. Nearby, the California Zephyr whizzed through Fife on its way north.

In Federal Way, thousands of kids with half as many parents played in swimming pools, rode amusement rides or slid down tall water slides. At Boeing field, a new 777 made a perfect landing, successfully completing its maiden flight. On Seattle's waterfront, a half filled ferry blasted its horn, and then pulled away from the dock.

At the Seattle Center, children frolicked in the water fountain or paused to count the state flags in the Flag Pavilion. On the second level of the Center House, whole families boarded the Monorail and prepared for the three-minute ride to the heart of downtown. Others paid the price, and then climbed into glass-encased elevators for the lift to the top of the Space Needle.

In the southbound lane of the short I-5 tunnel under the Convention Center, none of the Saturday drivers noticed when three small yellow tiles popped off the western wall.

Seventy-six-year-old Morgan Toliver stood in his living room window and waved good-bye to his five-year old great-grandson. For no apparent reason, the lower left hand corner of his window suddenly cracked.

On a wide window ledge of a third story apartment house built in 1932, a faded red brick set in old gray mortar slipped a full inch out of place.

And Spook was spooked again. This time, the dog whimpered and pawed on Katie Moore's kitchen door until she let him out. Befuddled, Katie stepped outside to watch. Spook raced to the back fence, abruptly stopped, lifted a paw, and whimpered – this time louder. Just as abruptly, he turned and darted back to her. At her feet, he quickly jumped into the air, and then he was off again, speeding toward the back fence.

"What on earth has gotten into you?" Katie muttered.

In the bathroom of her expensive home facing Lake Washington, Silvia Graham applied lipstick to her top and bottom lips, and then rubbed them together. She put the cap back on and tossed the lipstick tube in her bag. But just as she was about to leave, she noticed movement. When she glanced down, the water in the toilet bowl was rippling.

ANY OTHER TIME, SEELY would have marveled at the speed of the express elevator. But now, it seemed painfully slow. "Come on!" she nearly shouted. At the thirty-seventh floor, the elevator slowed to normal, passing each level at a snail's pace. The necklace still in her right hand, she deliberately took a long, slow breath. "Calm down old girl, this could be a false alarm." But as soon as the door opened, she dropped the necklace back in place and flew out. She ran down the center corridor, dashed through the kitchenette, burst into the main room, and shouted, "Everybody, go home now!"

Three desks back, Pat Timberly peeked over a mountain of printed reports. "Just gotta run these off, then I'm done."

Seely quickly made her way across the room, "No, you have to go now!" She darted across the hall and into her office, and then raced around her desk, yanked open a bottom drawer, and grabbed her purse. Soon, she was back in the large, center room. But when she looked, Pat was still standing there – staring at her. "I'm dead serious. Put those down and go home."

"Okay," Pat said. She set the papers back on her desk, grabbed a backpack, and disappeared down the outer corridor.

Seely looked at Jenna's empty desk, and then quickly glanced around. Just as she turned, the door to the walk-in-vault opened and Tim Garton came out. "What are you doing here?"

Tim smiled and sarcastically curled the corners of his mouth, "If you must know, I came to steal all the money." Young and muscular, Tim mockingly bowed, and then twirled the corner of his imaginary mustache. He had a full head of red hair, brown eyes and a silly grin.

"Timmy, go home...please."

"Oh I get it, you don't trust me."

"This is not a joke, I'm worried. Outside, the animals are acting strange and I think we're going to have an earthquake."

"Earthquake?"

"Just humor me and go home. Please."

"Well, since you put it like that." Tim closed the vault door, locked it and headed for his desk. He sat down and quickly began flipping off all his printers and computer equipment.

Finally, Seely spotted Jenna in the kitchenette pulling pop cans out of a carton, and then shoving them in the refrigerator. She hurried back across the large room.

Jenna grinned and brushed blond hair off her forehead, "I hate hot pop on a Monday morning." She was a pretty girl, with a teenage figure and a matching giggle, wearing a soft green short set.

Seely leaned down, took the pop out of her hand, set it on the counter, and closed the refrigerator door. "You won't even be here Monday."

"Yes, but you will."

"I appreciate the thought, but I'd rather have you gone. Go get your things. And do it quickly."

Jenna stared into Seely's serious eyes for a moment, and then got up. "What's wrong?" But Seely muttered something she didn't understand, walked through the kitchenette and disappeared into the center hall. As soon as she was out of sight, Jenna shrugged and went back to filling the refrigerator with pop.

On her left, Seely walked past the heavy steel door leading to the stairs and then three upright file cabinets. She paused outside the woman's bathroom, stared at the door nervously, and then sighed, "Settle down. It's a false alarm...it must be." With that, she opened the door to the ladies' room, stepped inside, tossed her purse on the counter, and headed into a stall. "Some things can't wait."

The time was 4:18.

Crossing three zones, Evan Cole wasn't sure what time it was and didn't care. He was in the first class window seat of a Boeing 757 somewhere over Washington State. Outside, the view of thick wooded mountains and deep valleys went unnoticed. Instead he stared aimlessly, reliving the last night he spent with Christina. She was wearing a long flowing dress when he took her gloved hand and led her onto the dance floor. He'd looked long into her loving eyes, touched her glistening black hair, and then took her in his arms. Even now, he could still hear the music and smell her perfume.

IN THE SOUND PROOF booth, Max logged onto the Internet, and then located a national news service. In disbelief, he narrowed his eyes and read the lead story. "Prophet predicts earthquake in Seattle." Suddenly, his eyes lit up. He pushed the print icon and waited. Ten seconds later, the story printed out. He scanned the page, located the letters KMPR, and then tossed the paper on his desk. Using his mouse, he copied the page, pasted it into an email and sent it to Collin in the next room.

Collin was on the air and engrossed in a phone conversation with an elderly man recounting a war story. Instinctively, he opened his e-mail and allowed his eyes to dart down the page. Not only did the story mention Max, the Prophet and the predictions, but his name was in bold print. Grinning, he turned to look at Max through the sound proof window. Max had on a paper party hat and his eyes were crossed.

The time was 4:23.

IN THE LOBBY OF THE Winningham Blue Building, the flower deliveryman waited for an elevator to take him up to the forty-third floor.

LESS THAN TWO WEEKS earlier, the vertical shelf of the northern wall yielded to the hairline crack, and then shattered causing the 4.3 quake. On this day, it was again the massive northern wall that began to give under the unfathomable pressure of a continuously whirling world. A new, more profound – longer and deeper hairline fracture appeared in the snag. Seconds later, the solid rock ledge fragmented, sending a multitude of fractures in all conceivable directions, until it abruptly disintegrated. The instant collapse of thousands of tons of rock created a massive explosion and sent the noise and the first earthquake jolt on its way through 33 kilometers of earth – toward the water in the bay and the foundations of the city of Seattle.

SEELY ROSS WAS WORRIED. Her nerves were on edge, the short hairs on her neck felt as though they were standing straight out and never had she washed and dried her hands so quickly. She grabbed her purse and headed toward the door.

A short three blocks away, the water in Elliott Bay began to swirl and churn. All over Seattle, birds took flight, dogs panicked and cats ran for cover.

Seely opened the door and stepped out of the bathroom. But her right foot took a fraction of a second too long to reach the floor. Instantly, she drew in a sharp, urgent breath and her eyes widened with terror. She filled her lungs and with all her might she screamed, "Jenna!"

Alarmed by the elder woman's scream, Jenna shoved the refrigerator door closed and ran out of the kitchenette into the hallway. Seely's face was filled with an unfamiliar, frightening expression and for a moment, Jenna hesitated. But as soon as she neared, the older woman grabbed both her arms, turned her and shoved her into the small bathroom foyer. "What...what is it?"

Seely's face grew ghastly white. Even so, she managed to close the bathroom door, brace her back against it, and then pull Jenna to the floor. Just as she began to answer, the sudden, colossal, heart-stopping explosion erupted from the bowels of the earth.

Suddenly, the city came alive with motion. The southern wall of the fault hurled its gigantic bulk upward ten feet. At the same time, it shifted twenty-seven feet away from the water – carrying with it the Kingdome, Safeco Field, Pioneer Square, the Coast Guard Museum, large and small businesses, the railroad station, the fire station, China Town, the southern end of the bus tunnel, the southern end of I-5, railroad tracks, four skyscrapers, and the Smith Tower. Like a row of falling dominos, the tops of the tall buildings leaned toward the water, and then snapped back with unthinkable cruelty, hurling everything within them against eastern walls.

The earth's horrendous discharge reached the 43 floor of the Winningham Blue Building at exactly thirty-seven seconds past 4:26 p.m. Instantly, the lights flickered and went off plunging Seely and Jenna into total darkness. A tenth of a second after the southern wall lifted and moved away from the water, the northern wall dropped, causing the other two thirds of the city to abruptly sink. At the same time, it fell, the northern wall shifted thirty feet into the Bay – and the foundation of the Winningham Blue Building moved with it.

The rapid motion caused the building to free-fall at an angle, and then come to a crashing halt. Impacted steel and concrete screamed in agony. Hundreds of windows simultaneously shattered, flinging lethal shards of glass outward, and then down forty-seven floors to the ground below. The bathroom door burst off its hinges and fell in-to the hallway taking Seely with it. Plastic covers over ceiling lights ruptured, the wall mirror exploded and water bounced free of toi-lets. Displaced dust threatened to choke their breathing and with the door now missing, tiny splinters of glass glistened in the afternoon sunlight. The overburdened seventh and eighth floors collapsed in swift succession, causing Seely and Jenna to fall straight down once more. Endless, dreamlike fractions of time passed before the parking garages, the sub-levels and the first six floors grudgingly absorbed the building's grisly weight.

Just as the southern portion of the city leaned west, the northern part leaned east. And the sudden displacement of the foundation caused the top of the Winningham Blue Building to dangerously tip away from the water. Only four floors from the top and with Jen-na's arms around her, Seely began to slide across the fallen door into the hallway. Then the top floors snapped back, lifting the door and throwing both women back into the bathroom.

Seely's eyes bulged and her arms flailed for something to grasp. But the foyer offered nothing.

ON THE WATERFRONT, artificial fill turned to Jell-O and a vast chunk of land instantly sank taking restaurants, terminals, parking lots, a trolley, and the Alaskan Freeway with it. Suddenly displaced, the water in Elliott Bay began drawing away from the shore, pulling small and large ships from their moorings.

Soon after, the steep incline of the second block began to crumble and slide toward the Bay. High-rise apartment buildings teetered, and then broke into splintered sections. Small parks and adjacent streets quickly succumbed to the eroding earth, snapping buried water pipes, sewer pipes, telephone cables, and power lines. In unison, a stretch of land one block wide and five city blocks long started a painful slide into the sunken waterfront. Saturday shoppers lost their balance, fell to the ground, and then became buried in moving earth and debris. Others tumbled off high walkways while driver-less cars rolled down hills. Atop the rising waters of the bay, a ferry urgently blasted its' horn.

Five blocks east of the water, hundreds of small yellow tiles snapped off the ceiling of the Convention Center tunnel all at once. The freeway began to twist and turn, cement behind the tiles cracked, and then crumbled – sending unthinkable, horrifying chunks down on helpless motorists. Coming fast from behind, the drunk in the station wagon plowed into the back of a hatchback and started a chain reaction, multiple car pileup.

The first gigantic jolt raced through the city at 14,000 miles per hour. In the Seattle Center, flag poles shuddered and swayed, the Center House buckled, the Space Needle leaned and children screamed. South of Seattle, Boeing's runway violently rolled, sending the still moving 777 off the end and into a field. Parents helplessly watched their children fall off water slides and amusement rides, and old wood and brick buildings collapsed in rapid succession.

AT KMPR, ONLY FORTY-six blocks from the epicenter, everything popped at once—the walls, the floor, the windows, and the ceiling. The old soldier was still talking, but Collin wasn't listening.

Instead, his eyes darted around the room. He too heard the explosion in the ground. Collin threw his earphones down and started out of his chair.

ONE HUNDRED AND TWENTY-one blocks north of KMPR, Sam Taylor stood near the eighteenth hole, wet his finger and tested the air. There was no wind. He set his golf ball on the small plastic tee, carefully placed his feet, wiggled his butt, and took a swing. He missed. But the ball flipped into the air anyway. It dropped back to earth, rolled in the opposite direction and oddly picked up speed. Greatly disturbed, Sam watched it cross the green toward two other men with equally perplexed expressions. But before the ball reached them, it mysteriously dropped out of sight.

Suddenly, the ground split apart. In an instant, the fracture widened causing both men to lose their balance and plunge into the deep, foreboding fissure headfirst. Sam started to take a step toward them, but just as suddenly, the ground under him shot up, buckling him at the knees. Next came the horrifying rumble in the earth.

DOWNTOWN, HORRENDOUS shock waves quickly replaced the initial jolt. The deadly rolls forced one side of the city to rise one fifth of a second before the other. The top floors of the tall buildings swayed forward and back, while the middle floors bulged one way, and then the other – straining to keep up with the rapid movement of the foundations.

In the Bay, the churning water was still drawing away from the sunken waterfront. In the marinas, more boats snapped off moorings and joined sailboats, ferries, fishing vessels and cargo ships in the deadly upsurge of a massive wave. Directly across from the water-front, mothers, fathers, sisters, brothers, and grandparents on the beaches of West Seattle stared, unable to take their disbelieving eyes off the murderous rising water. Others struggled against the viciously thrashing ground to run inland. And still, the water climbed.

THE SWAY OF THE TOP floors of the Winningham Blue Building caused Seely to slide into the inside wall of the bathroom foyer, only to slide back out the door again. Jenna's head banged against a wall one moment and her knees knocked against another the next. She screamed, "Momma!" But the unyielding, relentless rumbling in the earth coupled with the heinous discord of the tortured building muted her cry. Ceiling tiles broke free and pitched downward, exposing steel rafters and gray insulation. Blood gushed from the top of Seely's forehead and began to run down the side of her face. Another tile hit her left jaw, causing an immediate red mark that would soon bruise.

In the rooms beyond, the extreme sway of the top floors caused pictures to swing away from walls only to slam back again. Desks repeatedly shifted from side to side, inching ever closer to windowless outside walls. Computer equipment toppled, plaster crumbled, file cabinets fell, and papers whipped into a sea of white. And still the earth heaved, the building screeched and the thunder roared.

THE GIANT SHOCK WAVES expanded in a perfect circle causing Seattle's hills, suburbs, and waterways to violently and repeatedly pitch. Not long after, precariously placed cans and jars fell off shelves in Portland, Oregon. Windows cracked, loose bricks toppled and people ran out of buildings in Vancouver, British Columbia, Canada. Just off the coast of Washington, a ship lost at sea in 1856 rolled on its side. In Yakima and Spokane, wood split and foundations cracked. In Boise, Idaho dogs yelped and cats scurried out of rooms. Swimming pools jiggled in Northern California, and before the earth fully absorbed the initial quake, a church bell rang in Mexico City.

UNDER SEATTLE, ONLY a fraction of a second passed before the next mammoth wave hit, and then the next and the next—each churning, twisting, rolling, heaving—and violently moving everything on the face of the earth with it.

In KMPR's attic, the glass in both the booth and the outer windows shattered the instant the first wave hit. Only half out of his seat, Collin struggled to keep his balance. His mike tipped over and his console bounced a foot high with his arm and elbow banging against it. The hanging Dallas Cowboy replicate swung wildly and the ceiling fan increased an exaggerated circular motion. He took a step toward the stairs. But the convolutions made his foot take too long to hit the floor, and then his knee was higher than it should have been. He took another step and another, each time at war to keep his balance, but movement was slow and excruciatingly difficult.

His facial muscles tightened and his whole body shook with fright, but when his foot sank again, he lunged for the doorknob. The upward movement of the room caused him to miss and nearly fall on his face. He regained his balance, braced his feet, reached for the knob again, got hold of it, and yanked. But the twisting, buckling walls made the door rapidly tilt this way and that; throwing it out of alignment and making it impossible to open. Collin froze. Wall and ceiling plaster cracked, and then crumbled to the floor and the dangerous swinging ceiling fan hung just over his head. Suddenly, the electrical rubber casing around the fan's cord split down one side exposing blue, black, and red wires.

Objects fell off shelves and repeatedly bounced on the floor. A book slid forward, and then back, and the horrendous roar in the earth seemed to be increasing. At last, he noticed a hand gripping his leg.

Crouched just inside the sound proof booth, even Max's shouts were lost in the thunder. One arm protectively over his head, Max ignored the control room door relentlessly banging against his body, let go of Collin's leg and motioned him down.

Reluctantly, Collin obeyed and sunk to his knees.

"She's not down there!" Max shouted. But Collin returned with a blank stare. Max drew closer and tried again, "She's not down there, man!"

Finally, Collin understood. On all fours, he fought the ferocious arching of the building, inched his way into the control room and crept under Max's console. He was too tall, and the bouncing movement caused his head to bang against the underside of the table. He lowered his head, only to find his shoulders taking the blows. Collin leaned forward, wrapped his arms around a bolted metal leg, and glanced back. Max was lying on his side in the fetal position with his hands folded over his head.

More plaster plunged to the floor, its white powder sending clouds of choking dust into the air. The continuous rumble in the earth sounded like a high-speed freight train, no farther than an arm's length away. Finally, the phone booth-sized, teetering transmitter shifted and fell, hitting the console, and then crashing to the floor. Collin panicked and spun his body around. He shoved the equipment away with his feet and started out.

But Max lunged for Collin's shoulders. He pulled him back under the console just seconds before the hanging light fixture dropped to the floor, sending exploding bits of plastic in all directions. "No, man, you'll die out there!"

"We'll die in here!" Collin struggled, but Max held on. The heavy amplifier bounced, thrashed and slid closer. Something wet began pouring over the edge of the console, its liquid flowing at odd angles.

More chunks of ceiling plaster fell from above, shattering on the transmitter before bouncing to the floor.

And still the earth moved

# CHAPTER 6

RIGHT BEFORE HIS EYES the huge fissure on Sam's golf course closed, trapping the two men between tons of earth. Four feet from it, another quickly opened spitting mud, sand, and water fifteen feet into the air. And on the top of the waterspout was Sam's rapidly spinning golf ball.

His sudden island measured ten feet by sixty feet and repeatedly rolled with the convulsions of the ground. On both sides, a patchwork of broken green slabs twisted and turned, sank and rose. On the edge of the course, trees danced, tipping one way and then the other while water in the pond surged north, only to surge south again. In the distance, a man attempted to run. He fell, struggled to his feet, and fell again. Stunned and still on his knees, Sam slowly lifted a hand and held on to his bright red golf cap.

DURING THE INITIAL earthquake, only forty seconds passed before the walls of the fault caught on another snag, once more binding the earth's unfathomable strength. Yet the quake sent out its violent waves for more than four minutes. Finally, it's overpowering roar decreased, but then it was replaced by another, more frightening sound – the sound of a billion rusty nails being pulled from age-old wood, as rock against rock ground to a screeching halt.

IN THE CONTROL ROOM of KMPR, the rumbling finally began to subside and the retching heaves of the earth tapered into kinder, gentler rolls. Wood, steel and concrete yielded its tortured anguish to less frightening rattles and clatter. Finally – it stopped.

His whole body trembling, Max cautiously loosened his grip around Collin's neck and let his body relax. He reminded himself to breathe, closed his eyes, and laid his head on the floor. Then he waited. He waited for the white dust to stop drifting downward, the earth's screech to become softer and for distant car alarms to grow louder. Somewhere outside, a window lost its final battle and shattered on a sidewalk.

The top of the Winningham Blue Building was still in motion. Slowly, it too tapered off until finally, the forty-third floor came to a full standstill. Somewhere in the midst of the chaos, Jenna stopped screaming. Now her cheeks were stained with dried tears and she was seated on the buckled floor with one of her bruised and battered legs straight, and the other bent outward and back. For a long moment she did not move, listening instead to the hellish screech in the earth. When it began to fade, she rested her head against the wall and watched Seely's chest rise and fall.

The older woman had somehow managed to move out of the doorway into the foyer and now she lay on her back with her head jammed against one wall and her feet against the other. Seely's face was gaunt and her eyes were closed. Still Jenna did not move. Little by little, the squeal in the earth grew softer and yielded to a sound not unlike that of a faraway train, moving slowly and patiently on its tracks.

A FULL MINUTE AFTER the shaking stopped, Collin's eyes still darted. His body remained tense and his breathing shallow. The room smelled of dirt and white plaster dust still filled the air. Somewhere, a book fell off a shelf causing him to jump. He too waited and watched until at last, he drew in a long, deep breath. His voice was unnaturally calm and quiet when he turned to look at Max, "Where did she go?"

Max still had his eyes closed. A bruise from the banging door was already beginning to darken under his short-sleeved shirt. His tan pants were speckled with blood and his head ached, "Candy took her shopping. Tomorrow's your birthday and Beth wanted to surprise you."

Collin hesitated, half afraid to ask the next question, "Where?"

"South Center."

"Where the hell is South Center?"

Max struggled to sit up in his half of the cramped space. "I'll show you, if I can find the map. First we gotta get out of here." He turned and twisted his body until he could put his feet against the fallen transmitter. "Help me move this thing, will you?"

But Collin didn't budge. Instead, he glared at Max. "How far, just tell me how far?"

"I don't know, man. Ten, maybe fifteen miles."

"Fifteen miles? It might as well be a hundred. Did Candy take the boys?"

"Yes, but maybe it's not so bad down there."

Collin rubbed his face with both hands, and then began to shift his weight until he too could put his feet against the transmitter. "Maybe. What about your Dad, where is he?"

"Golf, probably."

"Golf? That's good. Not much can fall on you on a golf course."

In the back of the air crane high above West Seattle, Jackie was aghast. Her eyes shifted from monitor to monitor and her heart felt like it was stuck in her throat. Four minutes before, a voice recorder hidden in the bouquet of flowers sent terrifying screams into her earphones just before the earth exploded. The chopper's first camera captured the sudden rise of the Southern half of the city and the abrupt drop of the Northern half, sending pictures to her screen of thousands of tons of earth sliding into the Bay. Commands from her keyboard instructed the second camera to zoom in on the tormented Winningham Blue Building just in time to watch the sixth and seventh floors collapse.

And now, the third video recorder was aimed at a passenger ferry, a cargo ship, and a multitude of smaller boats rising with the waters of Elliott Bay.

Several miles north, the USS Carl Vincent slowly sailed down Puget Sound. Caught standing on the deck in dress whites when the quake hit, the confused and befuddled crew dashed below and were just now slowly reappearing.

When the small red box flashed at the bottom of the screen indicating a call from Evan Cole, she ignored it. Instead, Jackie studied the graph on the upper monitor. Seely was alive but her heart rate was way too high. She took a deep breath, and then opened a line to Michael on the ground, "Michael, Seattle just had..."

"You think I don't know? I saw it start on the monitor and ran outside. It's big Jackie, the whole place went nuts."

"Even that far away? Are you alright?"

Michael tried to calm himself. Standing in the middle of the landing pad, the only cleared land for miles, he held a satellite phone to his ear and watched the tops of the swaying pines finally come to a standstill. "Yes, I'm okay. You've got a couple of trees on your trailer though, and I don't know if we can get to the standby fuel tanks. Is she alive?"

"Barely, but the building could go at any moment. Michael, we have to find a way to get her out. Let me call you right back." She disconnected him, and then connected the waiting call. "Mister Cole, we have a problem."

"What kind of problem?"

"Seattle just had a major earthquake."

Seated in first class, Evan Cole instantly snapped out of his tired, listless state and sat up straight in his chair, "How major?"

Jackie didn't quickly answer, her eyes held instead on her view of the rising tsunami, "It's very bad, sir. You wife is alive, but ..."

THE GIGANTIC WAVE IN Elliott Bay crested and began to curl, sending frothy, white foam over its top edge toward West Seattle's beaches. On the backside, the fully loaded cargo ship's bow lifted completely out of the water. Terrified men jumped overboard, railroad cars on the deck began to slide, and the passenger ferry rammed into its port side. Instantly the ferry's hull splintered into chunks of wood and metal. The rushing water hurled the damaged ferry and its precious human cargo over the top of the wave, forcing it toward West Seattle. The quick thinking captain of the transport ship turned hard to starboard and steered down the backside of the wave.

At an unimaginable speed, the five-hundred-foot high crashing wave thrust the ferry, several small boats, and tons of water onto the West Seattle beaches and up the side of the sloping hill. Instantly, the ferry broke apart hurling her human cargo into the violent water. The edge of the Tsunami gushed upward, and then it paused for several agonizing moments before it began a deadly withdrawal – sucking belongings out of houses, cars off of streets and barely alive people off of beaches. And now, the wave was headed back toward Seattle's waterfront.

HIS CAP IN HAND, SAM cautiously stood up in the middle of his sudden island. Slowly, he turned full circle. The golf course was a total disaster. Whole clumps of trees were tipped in opposite directions and the pond was empty. Car alarms blared in the far off parking lot and somewhere, a woman screamed.

Timidly, Sam lifted his eyes to heaven. "Okay, so I lied about being a Prophet." Just then, he heard faint yelling in the distance. Normally hidden behind a large knoll, the clubhouse was oddly visible from the eighteenth hole, and a man stood near it waving his arms. Not far from the fifteenth hole, another man and a woman got to their feet. Sam watched as they disappeared into a ravine, and then reappeared on the other side.

Suddenly, he heard more rumbling. Frightened, he quickly got back down on one knee and waited. But the earth didn't shake. Instead, a 757 passed overhead, lowered its landing gear and continued its gradual descent toward SeaTac Airport. Sam held his breath and watched until the plane flew out of sight. Painfully, the seconds ticked by until at last, he heard the urgent thrust of the plane's engines, and then caught a far off glimpse of it, a tiny speck climbing and turning east.

Inside the 757, a stunned Evan Cole helplessly watched out the window as the jet flew over block after block of a devastated and shattered city.

JENNA STILL HAD NOT moved. Broken plaster, pieces of mirror, strips of insulation, shards of blue glass, splinters of wood, and ceiling tiles littered her lap and the floor around her. At length, she lifted her trembling hands and covered her face. The blare of a cargo ship horn seemed to be growing louder and now she could hear the odd sound of rushing water. Thoughtfully, she pondered the peculiar vibration and the disquieting noise.

Four minutes earlier, the Winningham Blue Building sat high on a hill, three full city blocks away from the Bay. Now only the Federal Building stood between it and the tsunami. High above and unable to comprehend, Jenna listened to the rebounding wave crash against the land, its lapping foam spilling into broken windows on the Winningham Blue's demolished sub floors.

Again the tsunami sucked the carnage away, taking a dropped bouquet of flowers with it and retracing its path back across the bay to West Seattle. Twice more it slammed against opposite shores before losing its strength and dissipating. At last, the bay settled into its new boundaries and the surface of the water became calm and smooth.

Except for the strange "shhhh" of an elusive train, Jenna's world grew silent. Slowly, she pushed the rubble off her lap, and then gently untwisted her leg. It wasn't broken. Blond hair lay matted against her forehead. She reached up, touched it, and then examined her fingertips. Whatever the liquid was, it wasn't blood. Finally, she turned her attention to the older woman. "Don't you die on me, I need you. ...Seely?"

Seely struggled to open her eyes and force breathless words from her lips, "I think...my heart...is going to explode."

"I know what you mean, mine too. Did you break any bones?"

Seely closed her eyes again, "I...don't know."

Out of sight in the hallway, a chunk of plaster broke free and fell, sending more particles of brown dust into the air. Jenna let out a startled squeal. She waited, the terror welling up inside her, but nothing else moved. "We've got to get out of here, we're forty-three floors in the air." Abruptly, she started to rise.

But before she could, Seely tightly grabbed her arm, "No...stay here."

"Why?"

"Aftershocks."

Jenna's eyes steadily grew larger, and then her expression abruptly changed to fury, "You mean it's going to start again?"

Seely nodded.

"Oh, no!" In a panic, Jenna broke free of Seely's grasp, got to her feet and darted across the fallen door into the hallway.

Too late, Seely grabbed for her again. But the sound of Jenna's movements were already fading down the debris filled hall. Seely allowed her arm to relax and concentrated instead on regulating her breathing. A little while later, she lifted her hand, wiped some of the blood away from her eye and then wiped her hand on her clothes. She thought she was going to make it through, but when she started to get up, she felt a sharp pain in her chest. She clutched it and quickly slumped back down.

Seely's eyes darted in search of her purse, but it was gone – lost beneath mountains of rubble. Defeated, she slumped, closed her eyes, and listened to her hurting, pounding heart. Then the building groaned and shifted and Seely's eyes shot wide open. Something in another room fell and crashed to the floor, but soon the world quieted again until nothing was left but the eerie, muffled sound of the phantom train. At length, Seely closed her eyes and tried to rest.

Another two minutes passed – long, empty, quiet minutes with nothing rattling, breaking or moving. Seely took a cautious, deeper breath and opened her eyes. Dust still lingered in the air, tears began clouding her vision and her voice quivered, "Please God,... let my little family...be alive." She settled down again and was quietly lost in thought, but then she began breathlessly muttering to herself as if to fend off some unthinkable loneliness. "I never should have...let them send us to...Seattle." Again she was quiet, her mind spinning, her heart aching and her tears freely flowing. At last, she pulled her thoughts together enough to whisper, "Jenna, don't...get in the elevator."

Jenna was long gone.

IN THE CHOPPER, JACKIE suddenly lost her temper, "Damn it Seely, you can't die now!" She intertwined her fingers and cupped her hands over her eyes. "Think, Jackie, think." For several long moments, she peeked through her fingers at the heart monitor, comparing the latest readings to the previous ones. Finally, she dropped her hands and took a forgotten breath. "Good girl, you've slowed your heart rate. Hang on, Seely. Just hang on."

A good thirty miles from the epicenter, Michael couldn't believe the destruction around him. The chopper pad had huge cracks, trees were slanted at odd angles, and the leveling jacks on the back of the command center lay in the dirt, allowing the trailer to tilt.

Even so, he gathered his courage, yanked open the door and got back to work. A few minutes later, he placed a call to Jackie, "I've got the equipment back up."

"Good, what can you tell me about Seely's daughter?"

"Michelle's house is totaled, but they're alive and out in the front yard. She's got a nasty cut on her arm, probably from flying glass and her husband is limping. The girls look scared, but uninjured. Both cars got buried in the garage." Michael paused to catch his breath, "Good thing we put that hidden camera in the sprinkler head last week. You coming to get me?"

"No. If the equipment is working, you'll be more help to us there. ...Uh oh."

"What?"

"The Bay is churning again. Get out, Michael! Run!"

THE NEW SNAG HELD ONLY six minutes and twenty-three seconds before the intense pressure crushed its outer perimeters and sent hairline fractures coursing through its mass. When it disintegrated, it created another resounding explosion. The opposing walls of the fault once more moved in their predetermined directions, sending forth a new round of appalling, ring-shaped shock waves across the surface of Washington State.

From the bowels of the earth, the boom of breaking rocks again surged upward. Instantly, the windowless steel and concrete Winningham Blue skyscraper dropped another two feet while slipping three more feet toward the water. And again, already loosened land dropped into the bay. Just as before, the top floors of all the buildings snapped back, and then pitched, twisted, swayed, bulged, and loudly protested. Yet their anguished cries remained obscured by the gigantic rumble of the moving earth.

The terror caused Seely to lose her breath. Instinctively, she clutched her chest and gasped for air, again finding herself powerless to prevent her body from sliding back and forth with the cruel sway of the top floors. The building's possessions took on new life, sliding, bouncing, falling, and crashing.

THE COLOSSAL AFTERSHOCK hit a short two minutes after Max and Collin finally shoved the heavy transmitter aside and crawled out from under the control room console. Collin made it across the studio and yanked on the doorknob just half a second before the earth jolted again. Nearly the strength of the first quake, the new impact quickly caused him to lose his balance.

Behind him, Max grabbed Collin's shoulders, and then he shoved until Collin was in the doorway. A second later, Collin had a hold of Max's shirt. Both men paused just long enough for the building to thrust upward again, and then Collin yanked Max into the doorway beside him. The thin door jamb offered little protection. More glass shattered, equipment bounced, nails popped out of walls, objects crashed and Collin's futile groans were drowned out by the clamor in the earth. Above them, more chunks of plaster peeled away and dropped to the floor, and then insulation fell, leaving bare rafters. In the walls, added steel I-beams suddenly became exposed.

Intermittently, Max shifted his gaze from the studio ceiling to the smaller one over the stair landing. The smaller one had yet to lose all its plaster and seemed to be holding better. Still, Max kept an eye on both. High above the studio rafters, a crack appeared at the top seam of the "V" shaped roof. With each new wave, the crack widened—inch-by-inch – until rays of hot July sunshine streamed down from above. Still, the earth continued to move. The gap in the roof steadily grew wider, causing shingles and boards on the northern side to slip further and further down. One whole half of the roof slid completely away, exposing KMPR's attic to sunshine and clear blue sky. Max listened, but the noise of the quake completely obliterated the crash.

Next, he turned his eyes toward the southern half of the roof.

THIS TIME, SAM HEARD the explosion and hurled himself to the ground. His narrow strip of land surged still farther upward, and then once more followed the rapid roll of the earth. Face down with his arms spread wide, the constant movement offered different abstract views of the golf course. He watched in disbelief as the clubhouse collapsed, forcing a cloud of dirt high into the air. Large chunks of green grass began splitting into smaller ones and trees renewed their unnatural tilt forward and back. A woman several feet away fell and didn't get up again.

A three-foot strip of earth crumbled and slid away from Sam's island. Suddenly, his right hand was dangling in midair. Sam's heart skipped a beat and his mouth dropped open, "I repent, Lord!"

It was headed straight for Sam's dangling hand. Already belching dirt and water, the threatening fissure quickly shot through the empty pond and started across the sunken, gyrating patchwork of grass.

IN THE WINNINGHAM BLUE Building, only ten seconds had passed since the earthquake roared back to life. Sucking in great gulps of air and tumbling with each sway of the top floors, Seely too cried out, her words mute in the horrendous noise of exploding earth, screaming metal and breaking concrete. "Please, make it stop."

On Third Avenue forty-three floors below, the reinforced cement ceiling of the buckled and ruptured bus tunnel quickly gave way. Whole sections plunged downward, taking with it electric and telephone cables, water and gas pipes, dirt, pavement, cars – and people. As well, the ground hastily eroded beneath buildings on both sides of the sudden ravine.

Across from the Winningham Blue, the thirty-five-story Mainland Tower shifted off its imbedded foundation and tilted toward the sunken street. Caught in its own gigantic swaying motion, the twenty-forth and twenty-fifth floors bulged, straining to hold the structure upright. Suddenly, steel girders snapped at the seams where the twenty-fifth floor joined the twenty-forth. The strained and agitated top ten floors of the Mainland Tower plunged toward the Winningham Blue.

WEDGED IN THE DOORWAY beside Max, Collin held fast to the top ledge and bent his knees in an effort to absorb the repeated bouncing. In the studio, plaster, glass, fallen pictures, dirt, and equipment rapidly hopped across the floor. The overhead fan dangled by a single wire and again swung violently.

Then he saw it. Through the open space where the window once was, he watched the six-story apartment building across the street begin to crumble. Bricks broke free of mortar and hurled to the ground, and then the entire face of the building slid away, briefly exposing inside carnage and terrified people huddled in corners. Suddenly, the rest of the building dissipated and crashed to the ground, its noise absorbed by the rumbling earth and all the other ongoing carnage. Behind it, a smaller apartment building buckled and shook, but then the dust storm from the first building rose to obstruct his view.

Horrified, Collin's heart sank and his mouth dropped open. He watched until the folding, dust filled cloud lifted higher, and then at length, he dropped his eyes. The floor beneath his feet rolled, the walls twisted and the taste of dirt filled his mouth. Even so, he let out a wounded, disturbing whimper, "...Beth."

SEELY WAS DISORIENTED. The earth still convulsed, the thunderous noise still roared, the building still shook, and steel girders still squealed, but the top floors of the Winningham Blue oddly stopped swaying and now her body bounced instead of sliding. Perplexed, she put aside her pain and deeply wrinkled her brow. She lowered her eyes and concentrated until she was convinced that the violence was decidedly less. Yet, lying on the bathroom floor, high above the fallen Mainland Tower building that was now embedded against the Winningham Blue, the cause for the change escaped her.

JUST IN TIME, SAM TAYLOR jumped off his golf course island and slid down the side of the newly formed embankment. Less than a foot away, the fissure ripped through the earth, widening as it went. Instinctively, he rolled in the opposite direction, righted himself, and then scrambled toward the trees. His attempt to run on land that moved beneath his feet made his legs look and feel disjointed. Odd patches of green turned in different directions. Beside him, another island jutted five feet higher than his sunken valley. He clawed at the dirt, shoved one foot into the hole, grabbed a hold of the grass, and hoisted himself up.

Sam wasn't watching when the belching fissure ripped through his deserted island and swallowed his red golf bag. Instead, he sprinted as best he could toward the trees, his heels often sinking into newly displaced earth. As soon as he reached the forest, he lunged for the lower branch of a pine, and then scurried up. When he was high enough, he wrapped his arms around the swaying trunk and held on for dear life.

Finally, the earth slowed, the ground movement stopped and the bending tree came to a rest. A small white dot sailed past his face, hit a branch, and dropped to the ground. Sam narrowed his eyes and leaned forward. There, four feet below him, a golf ball rolled to a stop.

AT LAST, THE VIBRATIONS in the Winningham Blue building diminished. Somewhere, glass still tinkled, dust still rose and plaster still fell, but Seely only heard the thud of her own heart beating against her ribs. Crumpled on her side, she was afraid to move. Blood stained her dark hair, her face was the color of ash and her body quivered with fright. For nearly two minutes, she lay in the same cramped position, struggling to quiet her breathing and steady her violated nerves. It was then that she noticed the near total silence – no traffic, no buzz of electrical equipment, no clatter of computer key boards, no whining elevators, no planes, no traffic, no generators, and no wind. Only the 'shhhh' of that illusive train and the tedious, bit by bit settling of the now fragile and frail structure, which was the only thing that was keeping her from falling nearly 600 feet to the ground. At length, a new involuntary tear rolled from the corner of her eye and dropped to the floor.

JACKIE MADE SURE MICHAEL was still okay, and then ordered the air crane moved. Carl quickly banked and soared to a new position just south of downtown – and the three dimensional diagram of the Winningham Blue changed with it. But the heart monitor was flat-lined and the mock image of the woman was gone. Deep in thought, Jackie checked and rechecked the equipment, typing in new commands and over-riding old ones. Still, the mock woman did not appear.

Slowly, she turned in her swivel chair and looked out the window. The ghostly, windowless building seemed to stare back at her. Pieces of gold trim hung from the windowsills and large chunks of fake blue marble were missing. Beyond it, a new wall of water was pulling away from the shore, leaving live fish flopping on the exposed seabed.

Just then, Michael's voice came through her earpiece, "Hang on, I'm going to reboot." She watched as all the screens went blank, and then held her breath as one by one, color, images and graphs came back up. The heart monitor remained flat-lined, but at last the mock woman was there – deep within the walls of the building.

SEELY TRIED TO CONCENTRATE on saving her own life, but her thoughts were of her family, "My babies...please help my babies." Her eyes filled with more tears and she just let them flow. The vibration caused by the tsunami increased again and she thought she could hear roaring water crash against the lower floors of the building. Alone and afraid, she waited until all was once more quiet, and then cautiously tried to turn her upper torso.

Her bruised and cut body cried out in pain, yet nothing hurt as much as the cramp in her chest. She stopped moving and waited for it to let up. A minute passed, and then another. When it subsided some, she tried again, turning on her back, and then putting her hands on the floor. Straining, she inched herself up until her back was against the foyer wall and her necklace fell back in place. Seely clutched her left bicep and held on tight. Above, a small piece of paper seesawed through the air and landed in her lap, but she didn't notice. Seely slowly lifted her shocked and hurting eyes toward heaven, "I am old, let me die." Then faintly, she heard movement in the hallway.

As abruptly as she had left, Jenna tromped across the fallen door and poked her head back into the foyer. A new set of tears stained her cheeks, a ghastly bruise covered the left half of her forehead and she was furious. "The elevators are broken!"

Seely opened her arms and allowed her dear friend into her embrace. But as she began stroking Jenna's hair, the crushing pain intensified. Gasping for air, the sound of her own voice seemed weak and somehow foreign, "Jenna...help me. Heart...attack."

The younger woman quickly let go and sat up," What? What can I do?"

"Find...my purse."

In a whirl of urgent movement, Jenna shoved rubbish aside and tossed tiles away. Finally, she spotted the thin purse strap. She grabbed it and pulled until the purse came free. She knelt down, unzipped it, and dumped the contents on the floor. Finding the small bottle at last, she unscrewed the lid and poured six small tablets into her hand. "How many?"

"One."

Jenna poured five back in the bottle, and then held out her hand. She watched Seely get hold of the pill and slip it under her tongue. Then she screwed the lid back on, put the bottle back in the purse and waited. In a little while, the older woman's color started to return and her breathing eased. Still Jenna quietly waited until Seely opened her eyes. "The elevator doors won't open."

Seely forced a comforting smile, and then struggled to spit out her words, "Jenna, you must not...get in the elevators. It's better to take the stairs."

"Okay. We'll go down the stairs then."

"...too soon. Let's rest, okay?"

"But Seely, we're going to fall. Besides, my Mom and sisters are down there. I have to get home."

Seely paused to breathe several more times before she spoke, "I know, my family...is down there too." To her relief, the pain in her chest was beginning to ease.

Jenna stared into Seely's haunting eyes for a long moment, and then she slumped against the opposite wall, "Don't die Seely? If you die, I'll be all alone."

"I don't think I'm gonna die. Not yet."

AT KMPR, COLLIN WAS still braced in the doorway. He watched Max get up, scoot rubbish off the top landing, and test the railing. It held. Next, Max eased his weight down on the first stair step. It too held. Meticulously, he tested another, and then another until he stood on the landing outside Collin's apartment.

He glanced up at Collin, and then turned the knob and pushed the door open. Cautiously, he eased inside. All the windows were gone. Cast iron I-beams stood in each corner of the living room, minus most of their concrete reinforcement. Beth's china hutch lay face down with chips of broken dishes scattered across the floor. Globs of broken cement and plaster, mixed with glass lampshades, pieces of knickknacks and broken light bulbs littered the carpet. Most of the furniture was completely overturned. The ceiling light dangled by one wire and rafters showed.

Easing his right foot inside, Max felt the sturdiness of the floor. It was safe. "Where is it?" he shouted.

"What?"

"The medical kit you bought the other day?"

"In the closet. Why?"

Max stuck his head back out the door and looked up. "You're bleeding man."

Only then did Collin notice the three inch cut on his right arm and the blood dripping off his fingertips. He covered half his face with his other hand and shook his head. "I've never been so scared in my life. Now I see why guys wet their pants." Suddenly, he uncovered his eye and looked down. His blue jeans were dry. Collin puffed his cheeks, let out a long breath and started to chuckle.

"What's so funny?" Max shouted. But by the time he grabbed the medical kit and started up the steps, Collin had disappeared. When he reached the attic, he paused to look around the demolished studio. Months of hard work lay in ruins and Collin stood in the carnage, less than two feet from the pane-less window.

Collin inched a little closer and strained to look down. The small park was deserted. Across the street, the four-story apartment building looked less than ten feet high with its black tar roof broken in odd chunks on top. Already, three men and a woman were furiously digging in the rubble. Another man ran down the street screaming the names of his wife and child. Still more people poured out of the identical apartment building next door and Collin could bear no more. He sharply turned and started for the stairs.

Max quickly grabbed his uninjured arm, "Wait!" Collin's furious eyes bore into his, but Max ignored it, "Let me fix your arm first."

"To hell with my arm, there are people dying down there."

"There are people dying all over the city. They need you here, Collin. They need both of us to stay right here."

"Why? What good does it do to stay here?"

Max set the medical kit on the rubble, glanced around until he spotted a newspaper, and then quickly swooped down and picked it up. Shaking the dust off, he rolled it up leaving a hollow center, and then he stepped through the carnage to the window. Pointing the newspaper toward the men below, he raised it to his mouth and yelled, "Turn off the gas!"

The confused men stopped to look his direction. "Turn off the gas," Max repeated. Finally, one of the men waved and started down the street, yelling at others as he went.

Collin listened to the man's fading voice, and then headed for the medical kit. He knelt on the floor, unhooked the latch, and flipped the lid up. "We've gotta get on the air!" Reaching inside the kit, he grabbed a roll of gauze and began wrapping his injured arm.

IN THE EARTH, NEWLY crushed rock settled, and allowed the shelves to slip half a centimeter more, sending forth another aftershock. This time, the ground rumbled instead of exploding and the sound of the rumble carried less than a mile.

Spreading from the fault line, the first roll took only a second to reach what was left of Sam's golf course. Holding fast to the trunk of the pine, his body tilted back and forth with the movement of the tree, until the waves tapered into gentle rolls and stopped.

IN THE STUDIO, BOTH Collin and Max were back in the doorway. In the rapid shaking, more plaster fell and the room again filled with dust. But the shock wave lasted a brief ten seconds and both men soon breathed easier.

THIS TIME, THE WINNINGHAM Blue didn't sway at all. Just the same, Seely's heart raced and her body trembled long after it stopped. With Jenna right beside her, she listened to the last groans of strained metal, tinkling glass and falling plaster and she waited, but the sound of crashing waves never came. At length, the tiny pill relieved more of her pain and her breathing grew less strained, "Good," she whispered.

Abruptly furious again, Jenna's eyes turned wild and the muscles in her jaw tightened, "Good? How can you say that?"

"Calm down, Sugar. I was talking about the pain. It's better."

"Oh."

"And, I think the worst is over," Seely said.

"But the ground keeps moving. What if we fall?"

"I don't think we'll fall. I think this building is going to hold."

"You do?"

Seely didn't answer. Instead she closed her eyes and prayed for the rest of her pain to stop. Her face was smudged with dirt and blood, and the hair on top of her head held a thick layer of plaster dust. It seemed like an eternity but the pain finally let up a little more and her breathing returned to near normal. "I think we're going to survive this, like it or not. Best we get to work."

But Jenna didn't move, "What sort of work?"

This time Seely's eyes held a hint of mischief when she answered, "First, we have to see if anyone else is still up here. Then we need to go get the earthquake kit."

Her whole demeanor rapidly changed and Jenna began to giggle, "You mean the one you and Paul had that awful fight over?"

"Uh huh."

"You bought it anyway?"

"I did. It's not the big one, but it will do." Cautiously, Seely began moving her legs to check for broken bones. They hurt, but they moved and her chest pain didn't come back. "I ended up buying most of it myself." Playfully, she put one hand on her hip, "I hope that old tight wad is alive somewhere and hasn't got a drop of water to drink. And when this is over, I'm going to kick him in the shins."

"Me too," Jenna giggled.

Seely brushed the debris off her lap and straightened her blood stained, white blouse. "We have to get to the earthquake kit before dark. We've got flashlights, food, medical supplies, and water." She waited for Jenna to get up, and then tried to get to her knees. Every bone in her body signaled its bruised and battered state and her chest hurt again. Instinctively, she sat back down.

Jenna's face filled with concern, "I can do it by myself. You rest."

"Maybe you're right." Seely eased into a more comfortable sitting position and rested her head against the wall.

"I know, you could lay down on the door." Jenna grabbed the side of the fallen door, groaned as she lifted it, and then leaned it against the wall. Next, she began scooting rubbish out of the way with her feet so she could lay it down flat.

Just then, the muffled sound of a man's voice filled the hallway, "Help! Is anybody there? Help me!"

Seely's mouth dropped, "Timmy? I thought he went home."

In the hallway, loose cables dangled through holes left by missing tiles in the ceiling, broken tiles cluttered the floor, and three metal filing cabinets with spilled drawers completely blocked the pathway back to the kitchenette and the large room.

# CHAPTER 7

AS THE CROW FLIES, sixteen-year-old James McClurg lived 140 miles southwest of Seattle, in the small town of Yakima, Washington. Between the farmlands of Yakima and the bustling city, lay the Cascade Mountain range and the dormant volcano, Mt. Rainier. He lived with his parents and fourteen-year old sister in a modest, three-bedroom home surrounded by four acres of land. An array of large trees and well-kept gardens gracefully surrounded the house and lined the two-lane driveway.

Seated in a well-worn easy chair and engrossed in a magazine, James was startled by both the first and the second Seattle earthquake. It was little more than a hard jolt each time, but the foundation of the house creaked and his cat dashed under his bed. With light brown hair and blue eyes, James cautiously got up, walked to his bedroom window, and looked toward Mt. Rainier. He saw no rising smoke and no ash filling the hot summer sky. Whatever happened, Mt. Rainier had not erupted—not yet anyway. He sat back down and returned to his reading.

His was a typically-cluttered teenage boy's room with a life-sized poster of Michael Jordan on the wall, dirty dishes on shelves, scattered clothing, an unmade bed, a baseball on the floor, a basketball next to his chair, an exercise bike, and a CD player. Suddenly, his bedroom door flew open and his sister, Heather, burst in, "Seattle had an earthquake. It's on the news."

James grabbed the remote off his bed, turned the television on and flipped to a national news service. The announcer looked solemn and the words "breaking news" flashed across the screen. "I repeat, the USGS in Golden, Colorado is reporting a major earthquake in Seattle. The quake hit just a few minutes ago and tentatively measured 9.1 on the Richter scale. The Seattle Quake is the biggest quake to hit the United States since the 1964 Alaska quake. We have no reports of damage or injuries yet, but we'll keep you posted. Meanwhile..."

James turned the television off and tossed the remote back on his bed. Thoughtfully, he ran his hands through his short, brown hair, and then turned to stare at the High Frequency, Amateur Radio on his desk. It was off. He walked to the desk, pulled a chair out and sat down. With Heather watching his every move, he flipped the switch and began turning the large dial. Briefly, he listened to a conversation between two women discussing a recent trip to Hawaii. He dismissed them, turned the dial to the left, and increased the volume. His lips parted and a single word escaped, "Max."

The same brown hair and eyes as her brother, Heather plopped down on the bed and crossed her long, skinny legs. "Who's Max?"

"A guy I know. He's got a radio station in Seattle. He'll know what's happening." James turned the dial, found the desired frequency, and leaned closer to his mike. "W7LGF, this is KB7HDX." He waited, but Max didn't answer. "W7LGF, this is KB7HDX. Max, can you hear me? Over." Still nothing. "Maybe the repeaters are down."

Wearing blue summer shorts and a matching shirt, Heather uncrossed her legs, put her elbows on her knees and rested her head in her hands. "What's a repeater?"

"Heather, I've explained all this a hundred times. Haven't you been listening?"

"Yes, but I never really cared before. What's a repeater again?"

"It's an electronic device with antennas on high mountains or tall buildings. Repeaters receive weak transmissions, amplify them, and then re-transmit." Once more, he began inching the dial toward emergency frequency 145.33. Suddenly, his room filled with the voice of a man.

"K7LQ emergency."

No one answered.

"K7LQ emergency. We've had an earthquake. Anybody there? ...Net Control?"

Again, no one answered.

Heather wrinkled her nose and blinked her eyes. "So what's Net Control?"

James huffed and turned a glaring eye on his little sister, "Heather, I'm trying to listen."

"I wanna listen too. Just tell me what Net Control is."

"Okay." James thought for a moment. "Groups of guys get together and form a network of Hams. There's maybe thirty or forty in a net, all living in the same area and most owning a hand-held. That's a hand-held Amateur Radio. Usually Hams go to fires or help find people who are lost, but once a year we practice in case there's a major disaster. After a disaster, each guy or lady, checks out his assigned area and reports damage or injuries to Net Control. See, Net Control is the one who decides who gets to talk when. Okay? Now leave me alone." With that, he ignored Heather's indignant stare and turned his attention back to the radio. Two men were talking.

"K7LQ, this is AB7JSJ. Where are you Ed? Are you okay? Over."

"K7LQ, I'm at home...what's left of it. I've never seen anything like this. My house is totaled, Carl, totaled. But we're okay. Listen, can you take Net Control? I can't raise Gary and I'm at least a mile from his house. Over."

"LQ, will do if I can steady my nerves. Okay, this is Net Control, let me have reports of injuries first, over." A single bleep sounded as

Net Control released the push-to-talk button on his Ham Radio. But after that, the airwaves remained quiet. "LQ you still there?"

"K7LQ roger, I'm still here. You got any damage? Over."

"I don't have anything left that isn't damaged. The china hutch fell on me before I got out the door. I think my arm is broken, but I'll live. The floors are buckled and power is out. My earthquake gas valve must have worked, I don't smell anything. I've got water in the basement though. Don't know where it's coming from. This is AB7JSJ, over."

Suddenly, a woman screamed into her hand-held, "Help us, oh God, help us!"

"This is Net Control, give us your call sign please. Is that you Mattie? Over."

"WJ7V. The Cleveland Department store fell. Help us! Over."

"Mattie, how many inside? Over." He waited, but she didn't answer. "Mattie, how many inside? Over."

"Hundreds! Today's Opening Day. It's a four-story building that's only about half that high now. People are starting to crawl out of the top floors and some are hurt bad. We need help now! Over."

"Okay WJ7V. This is Net Control, has anybody got phone service? Over?" When no one answered, Carl tried again, "Do we have any Hams at a police or fire station? Over." Again, no reply.

"K7LQ."

"LQ, go ahead."

"K7LQ, it's too soon Carl. It's just too soon."

Before Carl could answer, another man's voice interrupted, "NJ7RBG emergency."

"RBG, go ahead."

The man sounded nearly out of breath and his voice was quivering, "NJ7RBG, we've got two heaves in the I-5 freeway with a section missing. Several cars and a truck went off the end. Three seriously injured and one fatality. What hit us? Was it a bomb? It looks like..."

A mechanical voice curtly superseded him, "Time out. Wait." After that, there was complete silence.

Heather scooted forward on the bed with her huge eyes glued to the radio, "What's that? And where are they?"

"It's an automatic timer used to limit how long people can talk at one interval. And how should I know where they are?"

Finally, the mechanical voice came back on, "Repeater time out."

Net control instantly began to talk again, "Okay, RBG, give us a cross street, over."

"NJ7RBG, I'm at 228th street SW in Mount Lake Terrace, over."

Still seated at his desk, James turned to his sister. "There's a map of Seattle in the glove compartment of the truck. Go get it will you?"

Instantly, Heather flew out of the room. A short second later, a screen door slammed.

IN BOISE, IDAHO, GLEN Brown listened to the same frantic exchange over the emergency frequency. He reached in his desk drawer, pulled out an unused notebook, and opened it to the first page. Next, he withdrew a sharpened pencil; poured himself a fresh cup of coffee, changed frequencies on his Amateur Radio, and began alerting the Hams on his net.

In San Francisco, Ham Operator and earthquake survivor John Meting bowed his head for a moment, and then pulled a checkbook out of his pocket. He entered a $1,000.00 amount, reached for an envelope, and sealed the check inside. On the front he wrote the words – Salvation Army.

The only thing Ham Operator Belinda Case ever survived was two sets of twins, the youngest of which was finally and happily out of diapers. Without a second thought, Belinda went to a closet, opened the door, and removed two full bags of disposables. Next, she located several spare blankets, and then began rummaging through her kitchen cupboards for extra canned food. Less than half an hour later, she made the first of many trips carrying generous donations from friends and family to Spokane's Red Cross collection center.

SOON REPORTS OVER THE Ham Radio began to come in more frequently and James listened intently to each new transmission.

"AC7UP."

"UP, go ahead."

"AC7UP. We just had a gas station blow up on the corner of Greenwood Avenue North and 92nd. We have heavy...make that severe damage to several homes on 92nd. Roads are impassable. We have broken water mains and injured people lying in the streets. I count seven dead so far, over."

KMPR'S BACK-UP GENERATORS should have kicked on automatically, but nothing on either console had power. Confused and still in shock, Max stood in the middle of the broadcast studio and scratched the back of his head. Half the room remained shaded by the still intact southern half of the roof, but a hot sun beat down on the other half. At length, he turned to Collin, "Well, the best place to start is the control room...I guess. In the closet by the front door, there's a snow shovel. Get it will you? We need to clear this mess out. And be careful on the stairs, go slow."

Collin was already halfway out the door when he answered, "Will do."

Cautiously, Max made his way through the rubble and started into the control room. "I can't believe this." He paused for a moment and scratched the back of his head again, "I can't believe we *lived* through this." He pushed on the broken door until it came free, and then leaned it against the wall. Next, he bent down, grabbed hold of the broken light fixture and dumped the plaster out. He leaned it against the wall as well, and soon, he disappeared inside.

Just as Max had done, Collin carefully tested each step, scooting plaster aside as he went. Remarkably, the reinforced steps felt solid. When he reached the closet, he easily found the shovel and hurried back upstairs. First, he picked up the larger chunks in the studio, carried them to the window, and dropped them into the lush Seattle vines below. But each time he went to the window, he intentionally avoided looking across the street. Next, he used the shovel to start clearing a path. His injured arm had begun to ache, but he ignored it. Bruises on his head grew darker but none were serious. When Max was ready, Collin went into the control room, helped lift the fallen transmitter, and then listened as loose parts fell to the bottom.

"Don't worry, it'll work," Max said. He scooted more debris out of his way, and then got down on his knees. The summer sun beat hot on his skin, but Max didn't seem to notice.

Collin watched him get a wrench out of his toolbox and start removing screws from the front panel of the transmitter. "I know we need to get on the air, but I'm worried. Maybe we should try to go get them. Beth is pregnant, she can't walk fifteen miles."

Max kept working, beads of sweat beginning to glisten on his brow, "Let's hope they don't try. Go look out your front window, man. What's left of Seattle is, or soon will be, on fire."

Instantly Collin spun around and rushed out the door. He hurried down the stairs, charged into his living room and abruptly stopped. The sofa lay face down and twisted, the coffee table was on its side and his chair sat beneath the china hutch. But all these things he ignored. Cautiously, he made his way around the furniture until he stood only four feet from the open-air windows. In the distance, the bay looked calm, but oddly void of ships and summer sailboats.

On the Olympic Peninsula, multiple columns of smoke rose from Bremerton and outlying areas.

He picked up a toppled wooden chair in his way, set it upright, and then moved farther forward. The fire was nearer than he imagined. The Space Needle was still there, although it slanted westward and one of its outside elevators, with people still inside, precariously hung by cables. Key Arena's newly built dome sat closer to the ground than it had before. The Opera house was gone as was the aging Center House and now he could see the Ferris wheel. Just behind it, billowing black smoke drifted straight up. The fire had completely engulfed at least two city blocks – the same blocks where three of Seattle's major television and radio stations were. On the roof of a building, orange and yellow flames grew in intensity, licking at a parked News chopper. Abruptly, the chopper exploded, adding fifty-foot flames to the smoke. Transfixed, Collin stared at the spreading fire for a long time before he looked away. Behind the smoke, what he could see of the city loomed dark and broken against the bright sky.

More columns of smoke drifted from structures on Capitol Hill. Beyond that, still more fires burned out of control, spreading their brown, white and black clouds of smoke into the windless air. Farther south, an even larger blaze was beginning – a great wall of fire would soon burst forth from broken gas mains in the ground.

Again, he eased another step forward, and then another until he could see down the steep, southern slope of Queen Anne Hill. Eighteen square blocks of homes and apartment buildings lay in shambles. Stronger, newer structures rested askew on broken and damaged foundations. Older buildings lay heaped in odd shapes of mangled brick, metal and wood. Others were missing roofs and walls. Still more threatened to fall, precariously leaning or collapsed on one end. Yet none were on fire. Relieved, Collin sighed, and then went back upstairs.

THE ROYAL BLUE CHOPPER drew closer to the Winningham Blue, and then paused. At a snail's pace, it circled the building, turning and tilting until its video cameras captured every inch of the damage. In the modified body, Jackie paid particular attention to the collapsed 6th and 7th floors, and then asked Carl to move them higher.

Rising two hundred feet higher, the chopper hovered for several long minutes over the demolished observation deck. The glass dome was gone and broken steel window frames jutted up from the outside rims. Tables and chairs were missing, as were flowerpots, vending machines and seven decorative water fountains. In the center, only the hull of a devastated luncheon counter remained with its back to the back of the elevator shafts. The other side of the shafts still held six closed doors.

Jackie zoomed camera two in on the damaged elevators, and then slowly guided it to a dark hole on the northern end where the entry to a stairwell once was. The door was gone and only one wall of rafters remained intact. She typed in a new command, changed to night vision and zoomed closer – peering into the black hole, but the images were too small and unclear. She continued to increase the size of the zoom until finally, her monitor displayed a pile of crumpled and broken concrete steps in a heap two floors down.

Solemnly, Jackie spoke into her headset, "You guys got any ideas?" Neither Carl nor Michael answered.

In the mobile home, Michael pushed his glasses back up his nose and tried to think. He stared at the monitor, and then caught a glimpse of something. "Look at that!"

"What?"

"Screen six. Look behind the building. There's a man hanging off the top of the Columbia Tower."

Ninety stories tall, the windowless, forbidding, black Columbia Tower still stood on its damaged and broken, multi-level foundation. Jackie adjusted the angle of camera one and zoomed in, "A window washer?"

"Yes, and still alive. Looks like the cables on one end of the scaffolding snapped. Move the camera up. Let's see what's holding him." Almost instantly camera one moved, sending pictures of the dangling man with his safety harness hooked to wires leading to the roof. Behind him, loose wires hung from the bottom of the flat metal scaffold and above, more cables led to the end of a steel I-beam that stuck out almost two feet over the edge. On the other end of the I-beam, another steel cable stretched to an oversized hook mounted in the center and except for the I-beam, nothing remained on the roof of the tallest building in Seattle. Missing were transmitters, satellite dishes, television cameras and a mountain of communication equipment.

"Don't window washers usually work in pairs?"

In the pilot's seat, Carl slumped, "I wouldn't think about that, Jackie. The question is, how do we get him down?"

"Down? Why not up? We could land on the roof and..."

Carl shook his head, "No way, not with aftershocks like the last one. You ever see a chopper fall off a ninety-story building? It ain't pretty. Besides, all the equipment is down there with Michael. We don't even have the hook up here."

"We can't just leave him."

This time it was Michael who spoke, "We won't, we just need to think of a better way. Meanwhile, tell him you're coming back, okay?"

"Okay." While Carl moved the chopper closer and turned it broad side, Jackie hit a different hot key at the top of her keyboard. This time, monitor five went blank. At the same time, all the little bulbs on the outside identification board just below the windows lit up. In black font, Jackie typed the words, "Hang on, we'll be back." She zoomed camera one again, closer and closer until she could read the expression on the terrified, man's face. He looked in pain, yet his clothing was free of blood. Finally, the man lifted his right arm and halfheartedly waved.

# CHAPTER 8

WHEN COLLIN RETURNED, Max had his head halfway inside the base of the transmitter. "How can you concentrate? All I can think of is Beth."

Max paused in his work just long enough to choose a smaller wrench, "My wife is smart, and she'll take care of Beth and the boys. Besides, Dad packed an earthquake kit in the trunk of the car. They've got water, food, and medical supplies. If they can get to the car, they can make it another three or four days."

"If they can get to the car."

"Yes." Max sighed and turned his attention back to the transmitter. "And if we can get on the air, maybe we can tell them we're alive. They're probably just as worried about us as we are about them. Go to the window and see if the towers are still up. Okay?"

Collin nodded and obeyed. Outside, more men and women were gathered at the collapsed apartment building feverishly digging for survivors. The bodies of two men lay side-by-side in the street and three injured people huddled on a neighboring yard. Cautiously, he leaned out the window and looked left. He saw no towers. In fact, on a street once lined with a multitude of houses, he saw only the remains of three severely damaged buildings and the roof of a forth. Straining, he leaned out just a little farther to get a better look across Queen Anne Avenue North. Suddenly he gasped, "The hill slid!"

Instantly, Collin jerked his head back inside, covered his face and sucked in an urgent breath. For a long moment, he held it. He let it out, lowered his trembling hands and leaned back out the window to look right. This time the houses and businesses looked in pretty good shape and a block away, he spotted the only remaining tower. It no longer stood tall. Instead, it leaned south, as though bowing in homage to the fallen city. But south was where Beth and Candy were. With renewed optimism, he hurried back to Max. "The one to the south is leaning, but it's there."

"Good. Check the phones, will ya? Maybe they're ringing and we can't hear them. Don't forget my cell phone...though I doubt there are any cell towers still up. It takes one every three miles, you know. And see what you can do with the equipment in the studio."

At last, Collin grinned, "Aye, aye, Captain. Hey, want a soda?"

"Sure," Max answered. As he worked, he listened to Collin scoot rubbish aside, and then open the refrigerator. Suddenly he noticed something on the floor. Half hidden beneath a chunk of plaster was a picture of Candy and the boys. Thoughtfully, he picked it up and dumped the broken glass out of the frame. He stared at them for a long moment, and then closed his eyes and bowed his head. When he opened his eyes again, Collin stood in the doorway with two cans of soda.

Any other day, Collin would have snickered at the sight of someone praying and turned away. But today he simply handed Max the soda, and then went back to the window to get his shovel. Tears lined the rims of his eyes.

EIGHTEEN MINUTES AND forty-six seconds after the first jolt, the fault was still settling into its new position. Small rocks and crushed earth tumbled into voids, and then larger rocks gave way, causing a 6.3 aftershock.

IN YAKIMA, JAMES SPREAD the map of Seattle across his desk and hunted for Mountlake Terrace. "There!" he said, pointing to a northern suburb just across the Snohomish County line. He yanked his dartboard down, grabbed his tape dispenser, held the map against the wall, and taped all four corners. Next, he searched in his desk for a small box of adhesive dots, found them, and placed a tiny red dot on the map near I-5 and 228th Street S, eight miles north of downtown. He held the box out and grinned at his sister. "You're in charge of the dots, okay?"

Heather's eyes instantly lit up. She took the box, rushed to a steel fold up chair, and carried it to the wall.

Just then, someone on the radio screamed, "Aftershock!"

"Copy that, NJ, after..." Background noises burst over the radio waves. A child screamed, and the sounds of crashing mixed with the rumbling of the earth.

AT THE SAME TIME, THE thunder and movement in the ground made the shaking of the Winningham Blue Building begin anew. "Come here!" Seely shouted. She waited endless seconds while Jenna struggled to walk in the jostling building. Finally, she grabbed Jenna's arm and pulled her back into the bathroom foyer. The rumble was not as loud. Still, the twisting metal and concrete shrieked as the building rode the waves. Toilet water mixed with glass and plaster bounced across the tile floor and more chunks of ceiling fell. In the hallway, hundreds of feet of dangling wiring dropped from exposed beams and danced with the jousted building. But the top floors did not sway, the sides did not bulge and no more floors collapsed.

ON TOP OF QUEEN ANN Hill, Collin nearly fell out the window. At the last second, he let go of the shovel, threw his soda in the air, and hurled his body toward the center of the room. He crumbled to the floor, and then covered his head with his hands. Above him, the loose ceiling fan renewed a circular motion with its long, wide blades dangerously tipped downward.

ON THE GOLF COURSE, Sam scurried back up a tree. This time the golf ball was in his pocket. He watched for new fissures, but he saw none. He watched with fascination as the golf course rolled like the waves of the sea. His tree bent rhythmically, but he was not in danger and found it oddly thrilling.

Heather McClurg held her breath and waited. Peaceful Yakima, where the ground had not moved since the initial quake, lay in stark, inconceivable contrast to the horror unfolding in her mind. In silence she watched as the battery operated wall clock ticked off thirty-two seconds. Finally, a woman's stone cold voice came on the air, "K7LIZ."

"LIZ, this is net control, go ahead."

"K7LIZ reporting a death in Snohomish County. Name, Bill Wright, age 41, reason, heart attack...My husband, over."

"K7LIZ copy" For a moment, there was a different, more heartfelt silence. "AP... AP7RB, can you get to her? Over."

"AP7RB, on my way. I'm about four blocks from her house."

"Thanks AP7RB. Any more reports of damage? Reports of injury or damage only please, over."

"W7HEU emergency. We've got a fissure that did not close. I repeat, a huge fissure that did not close. The hill split apart. It's just north of the University of Washington Campus running diagonally across Revena Boulevard. It looks like a giant tear in the earth. It's about half a mile long, fifty or sixty feet across and real deep. I can see part of a house and several people down there, over."

"Copy. Jeff, can you see the hospital from there? Over."

"W7HEU, I'm on the wrong side and too far away."

"Roger HEU. Do you have any help? Over."

"A couple of guys went to see if they could find some ropes. We've got heavy damage to houses all around me. Cars are buried under buildings, people are trying to crawl out...I don't know who to help first. W7HEU, over."

"Copy that, Jeff. Keep us advised. This is Net Control, who's next?"

"NY7E."

"NY, go ahead."

"NY7E, heavy damage at Central Elementary School. It's got walls missing, the playground is buckled and the roof collapsed. One injury, not serious. Thank God it's summer."

Nearly in tears, Heather puckered her lips in a childish pout, "Isn't Net Control going to do anything?"

James glanced at his sister's sad expression, and then reached over and laid a tender hand on her shoulder, "Net Control isn't supposed to do anything. See, other people are listening too, like police and firemen. When you think about it, it saves everybody a lot of steps. This way, Net Control doesn't have to make any 911 calls. See?"

Heather nodded. Her eyes brightened, but only a little.

SAM WAITED A LONG TIME after the earth stopped moving to breathe a sigh of relief and climb down out of the tree, "You know Lord, Max is all I've got. Max, Candy and the kids. Annie, she's up there with you. Course, you already know that." He removed his golf cap, smoothed his white hair, and pulled his cap back on. He adjusted it slightly and looked around for the safest route to the clubhouse, and then headed off on the long walk from the 18th hole. "If you let them live, I promise to confess, openly, to the whole world. I'll tell them I'm a fake, a fraud and a liar."

Abruptly, he stopped walking and winced. "Well now, maybe not a fraud. That wouldn't set well with my customers. Liar's okay though, people expect that from a banker." He puffed his cheeks, blew his breath out, and renewed his clumsy walk across the broken ground near the slanted trees. "And if you let me live, I promise..."

STILL CRUMPLED ON THE floor with his hands over his head, Collin waited for the last tinkle of glass to stop. Slowly, he removed his hands, lifted his head, and cautiously looked up. Max was standing above him, holding the ceiling fan with both hands. Relieved, he rolled over on his back and allowed his body to relax. "You got earthquake insurance?"

"No," Max answered. He yanked hard and the ceiling fan came lose. He studied the wiring a second, and then leaned the fan against the wall. "Earthquake insurance is expensive and I didn't really think it would happen."

"Me either." Grudgingly, Collin sat up, and then got to his feet. "The book says the aftershocks last a week or more. I vote we pull the rest of the ceiling down before it kills us."

"Good idea. Hop to it man, I'm going down to check the generators." With that, Max headed out the door. His shoulder length, blond hair was filled with sweat and dirt. And out of Collin's sight his blue eyes revealed growing pain.

Collin watched Max leave, looked up and surveyed what little was left of the cracked and broken plaster, "Might I remind you, I'm a radio announcer not a carpenter." He shrugged, found an overturned stool, and climbed up. Thoughtfully, he grabbed hold of a one-foot section and yanked. It fell to the floor with ease, barely missing his console and giving rise to thousands of dust particles. Collin quickly closed his eyes. He waited a moment, and then brushed the dirt out of his hair and reached for the next section. This time he shoved until if fell away from what was left of his damaged console. As soon as the dust cleared, he turned to look at the smashed phone. None of the ten lines were lit up. Nevertheless, he climbed down, picked up the receiver, and listened. The phone was dead.

JUST MOMENTS AFTER the rapid, unmerciful bouncing of the last aftershock ended, Jenna and Seely heard a huge, frightening crash somewhere beyond the Winningham Blue Building. The boom reverberated inside the grossly damaged building, echoing again and again before their world quieted. Even so, both women continued to hold their breaths – listening, wondering, fearing and trying to remember to breathe.

Finally Jenna scooted away from Seely and coaxed her sore body back into a more comfortable sitting position. "What was that?"

"I have no idea. It sounded like..." Seely paused to contemplate her words.

"A building fell?"

"Yes."

The silence lasted but a few seconds more before the building groaned, and then see-sawed north to south in an effort to settle back on its foundation. Terrified, Seely stiffened her legs against the weakened foyer wall and braced herself. Almost instantly, the pain in her chest returned. Jenna screamed, and then curled into a ball and began to sob inconsolably. But the seesaw did not last and the building held.

Tim's faint and muffled voice again drifted down the hallway, "Help! Anybody up here?"

Seely tried to shout. But her scratchy, unrecognizable voice came out weak and useless. She turned instead to the frightened, weeping girl, "Jenna...stop crying. Answer...him."

"We're going to die. We're all going to die." With that, Jenna burst into a new round of sobs.

"Fine. We'll just die."

Slowly, Jenna lifted her head and looked into Seely's determined eyes. "We can't just leave him there." She brushed at her tears and sniffed her nose, "Timmy? We hear you Timmy."

"Louder, Jenna."

She drew in a deeper breath and started to get up off the floor. "Timmy?"

"Jenna?"

"Yes. We're coming Timmy."

"Thank God. I'm stuck."

Jenna sniffed her nose again and made her way into the narrow hallway. The heavy metal filing cabinets still lay half tipped with their drawers spilled. She stooped down, grabbed an armload of loose files, and flung them down the hall. "Timmy, the hall is blocked. You'll have to wait a minute."

Tim's muted voice came back almost cheerful, "Am I glad to hear your voice. I'd love to help, but I'm a little indisposed."

Jenna got down on her knees, shoved more files aside and then stood up and tried to lift the first cabinet. Still too heavy. She reached in the top drawer, grabbed another armload of files and set them on the floor. When the drawer was half empty, she shoved it back into place, turned the lock, and started on the second drawer.

"Hey Jenna, what's taking so long?"

"Be patient Timmy, I'm doing the best I can."

"Well speed it up, will ya? A guy could die out here."

Jenna stopped, put her hands on her hips and turned to look at Seely, "Still think we should help him?" But when she turned, Seely looked ghostly white and was tightly holding her left arm again. "Is it your heart?"

She tried, but the words wouldn't leave her lips so she simply nodded.

Jenna quickly found Seely's purse, unscrewed the cap, poured another small pill into Seely's palm, and watched her put it under her tongue. She waited until it appeared the pill was taking effect, and then screwed the cap back on the bottle. Next, she examined the cut on Seely's head. The bleeding had almost stopped. Jenna made her way into the bathroom, came back with a wad of toilet paper and started cleaning Seely's face.

"Go help Timmy."

"But what about you? I can't leave you."

"Go."

Jenna hesitated, turned and went back down the hall. This time, she attempted to climb over the cabinets. At first, she slid and fell back on the slippery metal, reaching too late for a cable dangling from the ceiling. Her already bruised body cried out in pain and she moaned in misery. She closed her eyes, relaxed her body, and waited for the aching to subside. Finally, she grabbed hold of the cable and pulled herself up. Using it for support, she carefully walked across the tilted cabinets and hopped down. "Tim? Timmy, where are you?"

"Over here!"

She pushed more rubble aside with her feet and more wiring out of the way with her hands, quickly passing the heavy steel stairway door. Horrified by what she saw, Jenna took a careful step into the Kitchenette. All the blue tinted windows were gone and the feel of fresh air so high off the ground made her skin crawl. Near the south wall, a section of the floor sagged, offering a horrifying view of the mangled and twisted I-5 freeway "S" curves. In the distance, columns of smoke drifted upward from large and small fires. Stunned, her words just barely came out, "Where Timmy?"

His voice was still muffled, but louder, "Over here." The rubble in the room was piled high on one side. Desks, filing cabinets, and equipment were shrouded in miles of paper, wiring and fallen plaster. A huge steel I-beam stood in the middle of the large room, its bare metal exposed. Clumps of broken cement lay in clusters around it. Splintered boards hung precariously and all but one landscape painting lay on the floor in ruins. The kitchenette bar was tilted outward, the refrigerator door was open, and ruptured pop cans added their sticky liquid to the carnage. But the microwave was still in its built-in cabinet and looked completely unharmed.

Mesmerized, Jenna took another step toward the microwave. Not one scrape or scratch marred the tinted black door.

"Hey, you gonna help me or not?" Tim shouted.

"I can't see you."

"Well I can see you...your feet anyway. I'm under a desk. There's another desk in front of me."

Jenna stared at the horde of desks crunched together on the east side of the room. "Are you hurt?" Timidly, she started over the rubble.

"I'm bleeding. I didn't duck fast enough. Reflexes must be slowing down. Course we were falling at the time and that might have caused the delay. The window exploded and the glass got me in the face. Is Seely okay, I heard her scream?"

"I think she's having a heart attack. Keep talking so I can find you. Are you cut bad?"

"Well, let's put it this way. My wife used to call me pretty boy Floyd. Now I'll be scar face. Don't worry. She'll love me just the same...if she's still alive."

JAMES MCCLURG SLOWLY moved the radio's tuning dial until he reached the desired, non-emergency frequency. "W7LGF, this is

KB7HD, over." He paused, but heard only weak voices, transmitted on a frequency close to his. He adjusted the dial and tried again. "W7LGF, this is KB7HD. Max, can you hear me?"

Heather sat on the metal chair with four red dots stuck on the tip of each finger on her left hand, "Is he the one who taught you how to hook up free Cable TV."

"Uh huh. And if you tell Mom and Dad, I'll string you up. "W7LGF, this is KB7HD, Max?" Nothing. James eyed his cluttered bookcase and then grabbed his ARRL Manual. He quickly turned the pages until he found a list of emergency frequencies. With the snap of his wrist, he ripped the page out and laid it on the desk. He turned the dial, found the designated Yakima frequency, and spoke into the mike, "W7CC, this is KB7HDX, over. W7CC, this is KB7HDX."

"Who's W7CC?" Heather asked.

"Boyd Smith, the section manager."

Finally, an answer came over the radio. "W7CC. Hey kid, what's up?"

"KB7HDX. Haven't you heard? Seattle had the big one. 9.1 on the Richter Scale."

"You're kidding. I've been up on the roof fixing the repeater. Come to think of it, I did feel something. Thought it was the wind. It's Saturday, there's nobody here at the courthouse except me. Are you available? Over."

"KB7HDX, you bet, over."

"Standby KB, let's see how fast we can staff this place."

"Copy Net control, KB7HDX out." James moved his mouth away from the mike and stared at his desk. Even without homework, the desktop was covered. It held electronic manuals, magazine articles and hand written notes. "They'll use the more experienced guys to staff the courthouse."

"What'll we do, then?"

"Pass messages along to other stations. In the disaster area, guys will have their hands full with injury and damage reports, but out here away from Seattle, hundreds, maybe thousands of people are gonna wanna know if their families are alright."

Heather sighed. "I'd rather listen to what's happening. Can't you find that one channel again?"

"Frequency, you mean? Sure."

# CHAPTER 9

IN THE MIDDLE OF THE largest room on the forty-third floor, Jenna suddenly froze. The world was moving again and she was at least ten feet from the kitchenette. The building rose, humped, dipped down and then shuddered. She turned and started back, but as abruptly as it began, the earth stopped moving. "Timmy?"

"What? You think I'm going somewhere? Get me out of here Jenna before I lose my lunch!"

Jenna rolled her eyes and headed back toward the desks. "You do and I'll tell everyone I know what a coward you are. Just hold on, I'm doing the best I can." A large, overturned bookcase blocked one corner of the first desk and its contents blocked the other. First, she tried moving the bookcase. When it didn't budge, she began tossing the thick accounting records out of the way, scattering the unbound papers. Finished, she scooted rubbish off the desk and knocked on the top. "You hear that?"

"Yes. I must be farther back than I thought...maybe two desks."

Jenna cleared a space on the floor, got down on her knees and peeked under the desk. Instantly, she reeled back in horror. His face was covered with blood and she could only see one eye. Feverishly, she began scooting more debris out of the way. She tried to stay calm, but her cracking voice betrayed her approaching tears, "The good news is, you're only one desk back after all. The bad news is..."

"Yes? Go on."

"You're probably gonna bleed to death before I get you out."

"No, no, won't bleed to death. It doesn't run in the family. Besides, I think most of the cuts are only skin deep. Maybe one or two worth fretting over, but I've still got my neck. Juggler veins are working perfectly and..."

Jenna listened to him talk while she struggled to maneuver her body around the desk. Pulling on one side, she managed to move the corner nearly six inches away from the other desk.

"Hey, watch it will ya? Dust is falling everywhere. Warn me next time so I can cover my good eye."

"Okay, Mister Cranky. You don't need to take it out on me. Cover your eye." She wedged her body between the desks and shoved hard until the heavy desk moved another five inches. "How am I doing?"

Tim lowered his hands and looked, "Good; real good for a kid. Another shove should do it."

"Okay. Cover your eyes now." Jenna groaned and applied all her strength. The desk moved another four inches.

"My hero," Tim said. He waited just long enough for her to move out of the way, and then crawled on all fours until he could stand up.

When he turned to face her, she gasped. Splinters of blue tinted glass dotted his face and a jagged, one-and-a-half-inch piece jutted out of his forehead. Blood still oozed from the wound, dripping into his right eye.

"I couldn't get that one out. Too slippery. You got any tweezers?"

Jenna grabbed his arm and pulled. "Come on, it's not safe in here."

"You're telling me?"

AS HARD AS JAMES TRIED, he still couldn't find any other frequency on his Ham Radio with the same clarity as the one reporting from Seattle's North end. So he returned to the original frequency, got a pen, opened a spiral notebook, and began jotting down call signs, damage and injuries.

"KE7SRT emergency."

"SRT, go ahead."

"Carl, we've got three city blocks with heavy damage at 103rd NE between 36th and 37th Avenue in Inverness. They're brand new apartment buildings, four or five floors high, but they slid down the hillside. We have three dead and six injured so far. And we've got a lot of water coming from somewhere. Could be from that tower on the hill, over."

"Copy SRT. Phones are down here. Have you got service out there? Over."

"KE7SRT, we get a dial tone but nothing goes through, over."

"SRT, you got a phone number for your water company?"

"KE7SRT, roger. The number is 428-206-2838."

"SRT, copy. I can try from here, but we don't even have a dial tone. SRT, you have any contact with police or fire yet? Over."

"Negative control. I'm heading that way next."

"Copy, SRT."

HIGH IN THE CASCADE Mountains, a man from Spokane made a final adjustment to one of several tall antennas. He climbed down off the concrete and metal housing, and then walked back down the dirt road to his Ford Bronco. Reaching through the open window, he withdrew a hand-held Amateur Radio, brought it to his mouth, and pressed the Push-To-Talk button.

"AS7E to K7ZLP."

"This is K7ZLP, go ahead."

"The repeater looks pretty good. I replaced one of the antenna so it should work okay now, over."

"K7ZLP, copy. I've already picked up three more frequencies out of Seattle. Thanks my friend. You headed that way? Over."

"Yep, if I can get there. With five kids and no husband, my sister will need help. I'll stay in touch. AS7E, out."

With each new step down the two flights of stairs, Max slowed. When he finally reached the first floor landing, he sat down and gently pulled off his tennis shoe and sock. Just as he suspected, the corner of the falling transmitter left a bright red mark surrounded by a hideous purple bruise. Next, he eased his T-shirt sleeve up and examined his shoulder. It was bruised as well, but not as bad as he expected. Carefully, he put his sock back on and retied his shoe to allow more room for the swelling. Then he limped down the stairs to the basement.

Cans, once stacked on sturdy shelves, lay strewn across the room, with the shelves lying haphazardly on top of them. Broken glass containers added their gooey liquid. Candy's gardening tools and dirt for potted plants mixed in the wet mess. A crack large enough for a finger stretched up the side of both walls. But the generators were intact, each humming their call to duty.

Max stepped through the mess and quickly switched both generators off. Just hours before, he'd connected the wire to the generator, threaded it through a hole in the basement window, and then ran it up the outside of the building to the roof. Now, the window was gone. He carefully examined the connection to the generator, and then every inch of the cable. It looked okay.

He eased back up the stairs and opened the door to his apartment. The living room was in shambles. Mixed with overturned furniture, broken plaster and glass, high chairs were toppled amid scattered crayons, color books, toy cars and baby rattles. Max swooped down, picked up a small teddy bear, and gently laid it on the overturned sofa. Testing the floor, he cautiously inched closer to the window. When he was near enough, he grabbed a coloring book, scraped the broken glass out of the frame, and then tested the strength of the wall. It felt sturdy. Grabbing hold, he leaned out the window and scanned the cable. It was still tacked to the outside wall and ran unbroken from the basement window to the attic.

"Good!" Max breathed. He limped back to the door and out of habit, pulled it closed behind him.

On the floor, in what was left of the usually neat and orderly dining room, an upside down Ham Radio crackled to life, "W7LGF, this is KB7HDX. W7LGF, this is KB7HDX. Max...can you hear me? Max?"

YAKIMA'S DESIGNATED frequency was suddenly alive with call signs reporting availability. The section manager quickly became Net Control and gave each an assigned duty. Not once did Boyd call for assistance from James. He listened a while longer, and then glanced at his little sister. "I feel so helpless."

"Me too." Perched on his bed again, Heather toyed with the red dots. "We could go there, and help, maybe."

"Get real. Seattle's a long ways away and who knows if the roads are still in one piece. Besides, it'll get dark soon and Mom would skin me alive if anything happened to you."

"Yes, but I've got first aid. I took it last year, remember. And I could work that stupid radio if you'd let me. We could take shifts and report what we see."

James thought about it for a moment. "I don't think we should, it's not safe, Heather. For all we know there are dead bodies everywhere."

"I've seen a dead body."

"When?"

"When Grandpa died."

"It's not the same. Grandpa died in his sleep and wasn't bloody or anything." James folded his arms and thoughtfully blinked his eyes. "I'd like to go. I'd like to see what happened. But if I do, I'm not taking you."

"You have to. Mom and Dad are in Portland and I'm your responsibility. Where you go, I go!"

BY THE TIME TIM AND Jenna climbed back over the file cabinets and reached Seely, her color had greatly improved. Her head wasn't bleeding and she was on her feet. At first, she winced at the sight of Tim's face. She narrowed her eyes and looked closer. "I've got tweezers in the earthquake kit. You stay here. And sit down before you fall down."

Tim blinked his usable eye, "I just love it when a woman gets bossy." He put his back against the only portion of solid wall and slid down, bending his knees and then stretching out his legs. "Man that feels good. I couldn't stretch my legs under that desk. I thought I was going to die out there. First we fell, then..."

Seely just let him talk. Holding aside the dangling wires, she carefully stepped through the rubble and led Jenna down the hall toward the elevators. When she reached the end, she stopped. To her left, a wider hallway offered six closed elevator doors on one side and a badly damaged wall on the other. Beyond that, the inside conference room wall, once holding large windows in narrow frames was gone, leaving a wide open area surrounding the reception desk. Chairs and a hutch sat precariously close to the outer wall. And the oak table, large enough to seat twenty people, had disappeared. Gone also were the identical narrow frames that once separated four, floor to ceiling blue tinted, outer windows. Beyond that, sunshine, crystal clear air and a forty-three floor drop.

Seely stared at the unmoving, sheer curtains pulled to the right hand side of the windowless room. "Still no wind."

"What?" Jenna asked.

"No wind. We're so high up, there should be wind." She dismissed the thought and continued straight ahead. The door to the supply room at the end of the hallway was closed. Seely turned the knob and shoved, but the door only opened an inch. She put her head closer and peered into the darkness. "No windows, I can't see a thing."

Suddenly, Tim was standing right behind her, "Here, let me." When both women turned to stare, he shrugged his shoulders. "I don't want to die alone. So sue me." He waited until Seely moved out of the way, put a shoulder against the door, and pushed hard. The door abruptly opened another foot."

Seely grinned. "Perfect. The earthquake Kit is right inside the door, on the bottom shelf. Do you see it? It's a black, nylon duffel bag?"

"Okay." Tim knelt down, reached his hand in and felt for the bottom shelf. Suddenly, he jerked back, stood up, grabbed the doorknob, and slammed the door shut.

"What? What is it?" Jenna asked.

Tim's good eye blinked repeatedly and his breathing became labored, "A hand. I felt a dead hand."

Seely slumped against the wall and closed her eyes, "I thought Bob went home early. I didn't know he was still here. Are you sure he's dead?"

"I'm positive; his hand is ice cold and clammy."

Jenna started to cry again. "We've gotta get out of here!"

"We can't." Tim slowly turned the knob and eased the door open again. "We fell, remember?"

Jenna tightly folded her arms and huffed, "Yes, but that doesn't mean we can't get out. Don't say that Timmy!"

"Okay, so maybe I'm wrong. Try not to stress Jenna; I've been wrong before—once." Tim carefully reached in, avoided touching Bob's hand, and grabbed hold of the duffel bag. "I got it." He tugged, let the bag fall to the floor, and then dragged it through the doorway. Instantly, he pulled the door shut. "May he rest in peace."

Seely took the bag, but didn't move out of his way, "Tim, on the next shelf up, there is a gallon of water. Let me do it."

"No. I'm the guy, I'll do it." Tim quickly opened the door, grabbed the plastic bottle of water and brought it out. He handed it to Jenna and once more pulled the door closed. "I say we let poor Bob rest in peace." With that, he waved Seely aside, and then headed back down the hallway.

Before they reached the bathrooms, the earth shifted, sending another shiver up the walls of the Winningham Blue Building. Each of them stopped and waited to see if it would increase or pass. It quickly passed.

Her arms still tightly folded, Jenna lowered her voice and growled, "Doesn't it ever stop?"

Seely tenderly placed a hand on the young girl's shoulder and urged her forward, "No, baby, it doesn't. We left LA two weeks after the San Fernando Quake and it still hadn't stopped moving. But the aftershocks diminish in strength and frequency. We'll be all right, Jenna. We can survive here for days if we have to and eventually, someone will come for us. You'll see."

"Days? But Seely, Kevin's coming home tomorrow."

Tim sneered and continued on down the hall. "Don't count on it. If the airports can function at all, and there's a landing strip within fifty miles still in one piece, they'll use it for emergency flights only."

Seely agreed, "True. And worrying about Kevin is the least of our problems. We need to get Timmy bandaged, and then we'll see about finding food. I've always wanted to break into a candy machine, now's my chance." When they reached the ladies room, Seely waited for Tim to sit down, and then knelt down in front of him. She opened the bag and searched through the supplies until she found scissors, bandages, and the tweezers. She glanced at Jenna's worried expression, and said, "Sugar, right where we are, is the safest place to be."

Jenna rolled her eyes and reluctantly sat down. "Safe?"

"Think Jenna. Directly below the bathrooms are elevator shafts...the ones that only go two-thirds of the way up. With all those walls so close together, it's the strongest part of the building. And even if we fall, people on the top floors survive more often than those on the bottom."

"That makes sense," Tim said. He watched Seely bring the tweezers up, closed his good eye, and gritted his teeth. "Just yank. I can take it."

Seely took a deep breath, steadied her hand and grabbed hold. With a jerk, the jagged, blue tinted glass pulled free. She quickly covered the wound with gauze and applied pressure.

Jenna watched, and then folded her arms and studied the floor. "Well, if it's safer on the top floors, we should go up."

"We probably can't go up either," Tim said. "Fire locks, remember? All the doors are steel and lock automatically from the inside. On the other hand, maybe they fell off or one of you has a key."

Disgusted, Seely clicked her tongue on the roof of her mouth, "Don't look at me. If they had keys to the bathrooms they wouldn't give me one. I'm just a lowly supervisor, a religious freak, a nut, and an earthquake alarmist. And now that we've had one, I'm furious. How dare they build buildings we can't get out of? They knew the chances of an earthquake were high. We should have keys to the stairway doors, we should have two way radios, and we should have a big enough earthquake kit for the four thousand people who work in this building every day!"

This time it was Jenna who tried to comfort Seely, "Hey, calm down. It's okay. It's Saturday, remember, and there are only three of us that we know of." She suddenly frowned, and then cautiously went on, "Seely, do you think Pat made it down?"

"I don't know. I've been worried sick about her. I think she might have been in the elevator when it hit."

# CHAPTER 10

HIGH ABOVE SEATTLE, in the body of the chopper, Jackie eased her feet out of her high heels and leaned her head back against the headrest. Moments before, the mock woman moved thirty-seven feet west, stayed still for six minutes, and then moved back. Hopeful, Jackie placed a call to her employer, "Sir, I think she's going to make it, if we can get her out of the building."

Evan Cole's weary eyes drooped and circles were beginning to darken under them. His aborted Seattle landing took him to Spokane International Airport where the decor and hard seats were just like any other airport, only on a smaller scale, "Can you see her?"

"Well no, not exactly. We tapped into the building's security cameras but nothing down there works anymore."

"Then how do you know she's alive?"

"Well, you may not like this, but we put a computer chip in her necklace. It's a tiny sensor that allows us to know where she is and monitor her heart beat."

He was quiet for a time, rubbing his chin, and thinking, "Are you telling me there's more to worry about than injuries from the earthquake?"

"Christina had a heart attack a couple of months ago and the truth is, she's had another one today. But she's alive. We think she has medication with her. When does your next flight leave?"

"Twenty minutes. I'm flying to Vancouver, British Columbia, which is about 140 miles from Seattle. I'll take a car from there, or walk if I have to."

Jackie considered not asking, and then went ahead anyway, "Mister Cole, why did Christina go into hiding?"

"I don't know, not yet anyway. I think my sister-in-law has something to do with it, but I can't find her. Jackie, I hope you know money is no object. Please do whatever you can to get my wife to safety."

"We'll do our best."

The voice over an Amateur Radio on Mercer Island was clear enough, yet the words were slow and labored, "WA7Y emergency."

"WA, this is Net control, go ahead."

"WA7Y. The Mercer Island floating bridge over Lake Washington is out. Looks like it fell. A witness saw cars go in the water. I can see two, maybe three survivors, and a speedboat headed that way. Miles Landing is under water and firehouse sixteen reports heavy damage. We've got no power, no phones and thank God, no fires...yet. Crestwood Retirement home collapsed. We have seven elderly dead and I don't know how many injured – a lot. Over."

"WA, copy. See if you can locate Doc. Parker. He lives on Greenwood Avenue, in the three hundred block, I think. He's got an office over there with supplies and some equipment. Then let me know where they're setting up emergency services. Over."

"Will do. WA7Y, out."

OLD, TIRED AND CONSTANTLY muttering to God, Sam steadily drew closer to the clubhouse. Keeping the oddly slanted forest within reach, he strained to climb up ruptured chunks of green, and then cautiously slipped down into cracked and unstable valleys. Just as he was about to climb another, a shock wave zipped beneath his feet. Wide eyed, he took a clumsy step toward the trees and nearly fell. But the waves did not continue. "Oh good, a little one...maybe it was just my imagination." He righted himself, tucked his shirt in his pants, adjusted his cap, and started off again.

AT KMPR, THE CRACKED and slanted studio console was still without electricity. Collin cleared off the rubbish and used a paper towel to remove plaster dust. Once more he tried both the phone and the cell phone. Neither one worked. When the earth rolled again, he waited to see if it would worsen. When it didn't, he went back to cleaning up. The mike looked unharmed and the cord was uncut. Nevertheless, he checked it all the way to the control booth. It looked okay. He dusted off his stool, set it next to the console, and reached for a cigarette. Suddenly, he stopped and stared into the control room, "Hey Max, you turn off the gas?"

"Didn't need to. Everything's electric."

Collin lit his cigarette, deeply inhaled and blew out the smoke. He rubbed the back of his neck with his free hand, thought for a moment, and then grabbed his cigarette pack. It was half empty. "Uh oh."

"Collin, go down in the basement and turn on the generators. Let's give it a shot."

Quickly, Collin obeyed. He passed Max and Candy's apartment twice, once going down to the basement and once coming back up stairs. Neither time did he hear the voice of young James McClurg trying to raise Max on the Ham radio.

"I GIVE UP," JAMES SIGHED. He moved the dial and listened, but the chatter was not about the earthquake. He moved the dial again. This time he located a frequency occupied by Hams in the south end of Seattle.

A man's voice came in loud and clear, "Any Hams in the Fife area? I repeat, do we have any Hams in the Fife Area?"

Heather sprang off the bed and started scanning the map. Fife...Fife...there? It's down by Tacoma."

"KP7J."

"KP, go ahead."

"KP7J, we have heavy damage in Fife. There is a strong smell of gas in the area of 21st street and 356th. We have fire in the shopping center on Military Road and a report of a multiple injury accident on Highway 99. Fire station..."

Once more the mechanical voice came on the air. "Time out. Wait." And again, there was a silent void. At last the mechanical voice came back on, "Repeater time out."

"N7XRG, can you turn the timer off? Over."

"N7XRG, will do."

Heather cocked her head to one side and studied her brother's face. "You said the repeaters were on mountains or tall buildings. How can they turn it off?"

"Easy, they punch buttons on their hand-held and send a message to the repeater."

"Oh."

"KP, what about fire station six? Over."

"KP7J, fire station six suffered moderate damage, but part of the roof caved in on engine number one. Engine two is headed for the fire."

"B7XRG, timer's off."

"Thanks XRG. KP, have you been to city hall? Over."

"Negative. My assigned duty is to check the schools. But I can head to city hall if you want. KP7J. Over."

"Net control to all operators. There shouldn't be anyone at the schools. Let's delay the schools. KP7J, it'll be a while before the command center is staffed at City Hall. You're the only one checking in from Fife. Head for the fire, over."

"AZ7BLB emergency."

"BLB, go ahead."

"AZ7BLB we've got an orange cloud forming just east of I-5 and 277th in Auburn. Looks like it's coming from the industrial park. Might be Nitric Acid. Advise evacuation of the area immediately. The cloud is low to the ground and moving northeast. It's headed for the freeway, over."

"Okay, BLB. All stations, anyone got phone service? Can anyone call Auburn fire or police? Over." The lady net controller waited for an answer. None came. "Looks like all phones are out. BLB, can you get to the fire station? Over."

"KR7V."

"KR, go ahead."

"I'm about half a mile from fire station 12 in Edgewood. If I can get to them, maybe they can reach Auburn Fire and Rescue, KR7V, over."

"Copy that KR, go. BLB, what's traffic like on I-5? Over."

"NZ7BLB, bumper to bumper and stopped. Must be a buckle somewhere."

James hadn't noticed the sadness in his sister's eyes until she stood up, walked to him, and tapped his shoulder. "What Heather?"

"Is Tacoma close to Portland?"

"No, Portland's a long way south of there." He used his pencil and pointed to the bottom of the map. "Portland's way down here, see? Mom and Dad probably didn't even feel the earthquake." With that, he turned his attention back to the radio.

"...anybody got a CB? Over."

"WD7PRM."

"PRM, go ahead."

"WD7PRM, I've got a CB, over."

"WD7PRM this is AZ7BLB. I can see three tanker trucks in the danger zone. Tell them to blast their horns, over."

"Copy that AZ7BLB."

"This is Net Control; all operators stand by."

In the small rural community of Auburn, Washington, the frightening silence left by the quake was interrupted by one short and two long blasts from an eighteen-wheeler. Another added his horn, and another until the people, involuntarily parked on the I-5 freeway, turned to look. Standing on the hood of a tanker truck, a man held both his arms out, pointing toward the orange cloud.

"WD7PRM. It worked! The people are evacuating, over."

"Glad to hear it. AZ7BLB, out."

"W7GF."

"GF, go ahead."

"W7GF, Portland radio station reports two quakes centered under downtown Seattle. The first was a 9.2 and the other an 8.6. I repeat two quakes, over."

Net Control was silent for a long moment. "We could have told 'em that."

In Yakima, James abruptly turned the volume down and listened. Outside, the air was filling with sound. Quickly, he went to the open window and leaned out. He searched the sky with his eyes, and then watched as seven emergency rescue choppers lifted off from Yakima's Military Training Center. "There they go. I'm gonna do that someday."

"Yes, if you can pass the eleventh grade."

He glared at his sister and went back to his desk. "I'll get there, you just watch." He turned the volume back up and defiantly straightened his shoulders.

"NJ7E, emergency."

"NJ, go ahead."

"NJ7E, the earthquake set off an explosion and we've got black smoke rising fast. The fire is spreading south...we've just had another explosion...there goes another one straight down Parkland Avenue. Must be a gas line. Dear God in Heaven, it's headed for South Center..."

James lowered his eyes and bowed his head. "Mom's favorite shopping center. I bet there's ten thousand people there on Saturdays, maybe twenty." For a long moment, he remained shrouded in gloom. Suddenly, his eyes lit up. "The radio station. Maybe Max is on the air. Maybe that's why I can't reach him. Heather, go get the radio out of Mom's room."

AT THE SAME TIME HEATHER brought her mother's radio to James and Max got power back on to both his and Collin's consoles, Tim found the transistor Radio in Seely's earthquake kit on the forty-third floor of the Winningham Blue. "Oh cool. I get the radio."

Seely narrowed her eyes, tightened her lips, and took it out of his hand. "Let me tell you something, young man. The radio is mine. I bought it, I made sure it had batteries and it stays with me."

"Okay. But can I hold it a little while? Where are the batteries? I wonder if the stations are back up? Does the whole world know what's happened here yet? Where..."

Seely rolled her eyes, handed him the radio and fished out the first package of 9-volt batteries. She watched him quickly load one, close the plastic cover, and begin turning the dial.

AT KMPR, COLLIN CLEARED his throat and leaned closer to his mike. "This is KMPR, 760 AM, located on top of Queen Anne Hill. Seattle has suffered a catastrophic earthquake. We can see a huge fire downtown and several smaller ones in the suburbs. We also have fires in West Seattle and on the Peninsula across Elliott Bay. On the south side of Queen Ann Hill, buildings are in ruins. Others are leaning and with the aftershocks coming so often, who knows how long they'll hold up. People are stunned. They try to help dig for survivors, but most of us don't even own shovels. North of the station, it looks like the hill just slid away. Across the street, a six-story apartment building collapsed. The last time I looked, there were three bodies."

Collin stopped. He took a long breath, slowly let it out and closed his eyes. "Beth, if you can hear me, Max and I are alright. Stay where you are, Babe. Don't try to come through downtown."

Busy making corrections in what was left of the control room, Max only took a mental note when Collin stopped talking. He glanced into the studio, adjusted another dial, and then turned to stare. Collin was biting his lower lip hard. Max grabbed for his hanging mike, but along with the rest of the ceiling it was gone and he found himself waving his hand in thin air. Chagrined, he rubbed his forehead a moment, and then leaned through the broken window, "Tell them to honk."

"What?"

"We don't know if we're on the air, man. Say...if you're on Queen Anne Hill and you can hear us, honk your car horn."

"Oh, okay folks. If you are on Queen Ann Hill and you can hear us, honk your car horn." Collin waited. Outside, men were yelling, women cried and dogs barked, but no horns sounded. It was faint, but at last he heard someone honk. "This is KMPR, 760 AM. Do it again. If you're on Queen Anne and you can hear the sound of my voice, honk your horn three times." Again he waited. This time the faint horn sounded immediately. Honk...honk...honk. "Right on!" Collin shouted.

Downstairs, the Ham Radio once more came to life. "W7LGF this is KB7HDX. Max, you're up, you're on the air. Can you hear me

Max?" James narrowed his eyes and glared at the radio. "Heather, go pack some food."

"Why?"

"Because we're going to Seattle."

SAM'S CLUB HOUSE WAS completely unrecognizable. Built in 1932 of brick and mortar, it easily succumbed to the earthquake and following aftershocks, progressively crumbling where it stood. He climbed the last green knoll on the edge of the golf course, crossed the broken sidewalk, and started into the deserted parking lot. Just then, he saw a man raise the butt of a twenty-two rifle and break the window out of a Mercedes Benz. Yanking the door open, the man leaned in and bent down. A second later, the blasting car alarm stopped. The intruder helped himself to a CD player and fled into the forest.

"At least he got rid of that annoying alarm." Sam turned his attention to the oddly deserted, collapsed building. Amid the ruins, a lone woman tossed crumbled brick and rotting lumber aside. Cautiously, he drew nearer. "How many?"

"How many what?" the woman snapped.

Sam instantly reeled back, "How many still in the building?"

The tall, painfully thin woman paused in her work just long enough to glare at him, her brown eyes flashing with fury. "None! They all got out between the quakes."

"Well then, why do you dig?"

"My keys are in there. How am I to drive home without my keys?"

Sam watched her toss two more broken bricks away, and then grab hold of a two by four and try to wedge it free. Carefully, he stepped into the rubble and drew close enough to take the woman's arm. "My dear, it is best to walk. If the streets are serviceable at all, they'll be jammed with traffic."

At first, the woman tried to pull her arm free, her angry eyes boring into his. But at length, the words he spoke rang true. Suddenly, she threw her arms around his neck and began to weep uncontrollably. "My kids. I left them with a sitter. I..."

"There, there now, don't cry. I'm sure they're just fine." He held her a while longer and then tenderly pulled her away. "We've only a few hours of daylight left. How far away are your children?"

"A couple of miles, I guess."

"Good. You've plenty of time to walk it before dark." He took her hand and helped her climb out of the rubble. She hugged him once more, and then was off—hurrying past the parked cars and up the lane to the road. Then, something peculiar caught Sam's attention. He felt a gentle breeze against his face. "Wind? I hadn't noticed it missing. Feels good, Lord."

Sam walked to his car, opened the door and sat down. He glanced around looking for the guy with the twenty-two, and was relieved that he was nowhere in sight. He reached in his glove box and removed an old canteen. Unscrewing the lid, he gently pulled on a string until one-by-one, small rolls of cash came free of the rim. Stuffing them in his pocket, he looped the long canteen string around his neck and closed the glove box. Next, he grabbed his transistor radio off the seat, removed his cap, and mounted the small earphone set on his head. Collin was on the air, giving earthquake survival instructions.

Sam smiled. "Max must be all right, then. Thank you, Lord." He put his transistor in his pocket and pulled his red cap back on. Then he locked his car and headed in the same direction as the woman – down the tree-lined lane toward the grid of streets and avenues leading to Seattle.

# CHAPTER 11

ON THE FORTY-THIRD floor, Tim finally looked human again. Seely too noticed the wind, a soft gentle breeze at first barely ruffling the loose paper. Then it grew stronger. She sat down on the door with her back against exposed rafters and insulation, closed her eyes, and basked in the feeling of it hitting her face. Her heart no longer hurt and her drug-induced headache was beginning to let up, "I think I'm feeling better."

"Good." Jenna said. "You look better."

Tim turned the radio off and handed it to Seely "I say we go have a look around. We can see more from up here than they can tell us on the radio."

"Be careful, okay."

Jenna glanced from Seely to Tim and back to Seely again. "Is it okay if I go too?"

Seely giggled, "Sugar, you don't need my permission."

"I know, but will you be alright?"

"Sure I will. Go."

Suddenly, Jenna looked disturbed. She leaned her head to one side and listened. "What is that?"

"What?"

"That noise? That thudding noise?"

Tim focused on the sound, holding his breath until he recognized it. His eyes then lit up, "Chopper!" In a flash, he was stumbling through the rubbish in the hall. By the time he turned down the corridor and passed the six elevators, the noise of the chopper was overwhelming. Cautiously, he made his way into the conference room until he finally spotted it. The huge blue chopper with bulging eyes, a bubble face, and a slit for a mouth slowly descended until it hovered directly opposite the conference room. With Jenna right behind him, Tim inched closer to the middle of the room and waved his arms, but if the pilot saw him from behind the tinted windows, he gave no indication. Instead, the chopper tipped slightly upward and held its position. Just as it appeared, it slowly lifted above the top floor, sharply banked right, and was gone.

As soon as the noise dissipated, Tim took one more cautious step toward the outside edge of the building, "Jenna look!"

"What?"

"We can see the water."

"So?"

"So where's the Federal Building?"

Jenna felt sick. She wrapped her arms around her stomach and backed away.

JACKIE ASKED CARL TO move the chopper back to its original position over West Seattle where all three cameras were at a better advantage. She adjusted the focus on each, and then went back to her conversation with Michael, "Well, at least she's not alone."

Michael took off his glasses and rubbed his eyes. Comparatively, the small, compact mobile home suffered only minor damage – not counting broken windows, spilled cupboards and an upset coffee pot. He put his glasses back on and turned his attention to the middle monitor, "I ran a quick picture comparison through the company's personnel records. Both of them are co-workers and neither have any medical training."

"Oh Michael, what are we going to do?"

"We're out of our league here. I suggest we call someone."

"Good idea. See if you can find...let's see. I know, call fire and rescue in LA. They're experts in earthquakes."

"Okay."

"No wait, they might notify the press." Jackie sighed and tried to rack her brain. "Hey, let's call Colonel Shafer at the Pentagon. He's an engineer and he owes us a favor."

"Got it. By the way, I've picked up a local radio station. And a report just came in with a little history on Loraine Whitcomb. Ready?"

"Shoot."

"Loraine Whitcomb, AKA Eileen Black was arrested for murder in 1968. The case was weak and all charges were dropped. The victim was a twenty-three-year old college student and Eileen Black was one of two roommates. Guess who the other roommate was?"

"Christina?"

"Bingo. Loraine and Jennifer's mother is still alive. She lives in Seattle and is in her seventies."

"The old woman who visits the grave?"

"Could be."

"Michael, how do you get your mother to visit a grave with nobody in it?"

"Maybe somebody is in it."

"Great. That's one I hadn't thought of. Have you found anything on the $10,000.00?"

"Not yet, but who'd be surprised if it leads back to Loraine?"

"I sure wouldn't. So now what have we got? Christina marries well, Jennifer wants Evan and the money so Loraine sets up a revolving fund and convinces Christina to walk away because..."

"Because it was Christina who murdered the roommate?"

Jackie kept her eyes on the heart monitor strip at the bottom of the monitor. Seely's heart rate was near normal. "Blackmail?"

"Yes, but why the scars on Christina's wrists?"

"Maybe she needed some heavy duty convincing."

"Michael, we don't have time for this. You call the Colonel and I'll call Evan. It's time I had a little talk with him." Jackie quickly disconnected Michael and dialed Evan Cole's private number.

It seemed like forever before the seat belt sign in the 737 went off and Evan was allowed to turn his cell phone back on. When he did, it was already ringing. "Loraine?"

"No, it's Jackie. Mister Cole, have you ever heard of an Eileen Black?"

His jaw instantly dropped in dismay, "Eileen Black? She was Christina's roommate in college. She murdered Julie Wilcox."

"Did Christina tell you what happened?"

"She couldn't, she wasn't there. That was the weekend I flew her back to meet my parents. Jackie, what's..."

"Loraine Whitcomb and Eileen Black are the same person."

If Jackie was still talking, he didn't hear her. Nor did he hear the roar of the engines, the in-flight television, other passengers talking or a baby crying somewhere in the back of the plane. Instead, he let the phone slide from his ear. He remembered how Loraine stared at Christina's portrait the first time she saw it. He considered the peculiar way the house he shared with Christina burned to the ground, and how Loraine and Jennifer always seemed to be there when he needed comfort most. Finally, he remembered being told what happened in that horrible storm - two cabin cruisers traveling at high speed, one crashing into the other, and then a distress call from Christina's captain – sinking fast! Mayday! Mayday! Finally, there was nothing but a debris field. Both boats and all aboard lost...or so he thought.

Slowly, Evan Cole turned his furious eyes toward the window.

LONG AFTER THE THUDDING chopper engines dissipated, Tim finally turned and made his way back to Seely. Disappointed, he sat down on the floor and slouched his shoulders, "He saw me, I know he did. But he didn't do anything. I mean the chopper just sat there, and then it flew away." He lightly touched his bandaged forehead, and then ran his hand through his short, red hair.

Jenna moved files aside and sat down beside him, "At least they know we're here. Maybe they'll come back for us."

Tim dropped his eyes and fiddled with the button on his blood stained shirt. "Jenna, I don't know. We're not the only ones stuck in these buildings and that's the first chopper we heard. Where are the news choppers? And why didn't this one take a closer look at the other buildings. I don't know, Jenna. Something's not right."

"Was it blue?" Seely asked.

"Uh huh. Why?"

Seely lifted the radio off her lap. "Collin was talking about that chopper this morning. You're right, there's something odd about this one. Did it look like it had guns underneath?"

"Guns? No, not guns, more like cameras. Hey, maybe I'll make the five o'clock news. Who knows, maybe it's a Canadian television station. Then again, maybe not." Tim paused, and then quickly glanced at each woman before he continued. "You know, there is a bank on the first floor of this building. You don't suppose..."

Once more, the earth shifted. Jenna screamed and nearly fell over Seely getting back into the bathroom foyer.

At KMPR, Collin instantly scooted his stool away from the console and headed for the door. Max was already there.

On the tree lined lane leading away from the clubhouse, Sam found a new tree, quickly grabbed hold and watched for fissures.

Once more the world seemed to be coming apart. This, the second largest aftershock measured 7.1 and sent its rolling thunder at lightning speed in all conceivable directions. The land renewed its rumbling, its giant heaves, and its waves of horror.

NORTH OF DOWNTOWN SEATTLE, longtime friends, and a closely knit network of Ham Radio Operators darted outside or ran for the nearest cover, and then waited for the earth to stop shaking. Each suffered their own constant terror, waiting and watching until it was safe to go back to their duties. Yet, voices quivered and hands trembled.

"W7HEU, this is net control, how do you read?"

"Loud and clear, over."

"HEU, did the fissure close?"

"Negative. We count twenty-six adults, seven children and we've got a motorcycle cop down there in bad shape. W7HEU, over."

"Has help arrived?"

"Affirmative. Half the Husky Football Team is here. We've got a few ropes and one harness. Two of the guys are mountain climbers and were thinking about going down. Thing is, that aftershock scared us. The fissure did move some. One more like that and I think it might close. W7HEU, over."

"A7AQ, emergency."

"AQ, go ahead."

"Net control, this is A7AQ. The I-5 interchange at 244th SW in Mountlake Terrace just collapsed. There must have been a hundred cars stuck on the off ramps. Are the phones still down? Has anyone been able to reach emergency services? Can anybody help? People are dying here, over."

AT KMPR, THERE WAS little left to fall except the southern half of the roof. During the aftershock, Max kept a watchful eye on it, but it didn't fall. Nearly all the plasterboard was gone off the walls leaving exposed two by four's and torn pink insulation. Hanging off a nail in the wall just above Collin's console, a calendar swayed. When it stopped, Max rubbed his face with his hands, took several deep breaths, and eased back into the studio.

Once more, he carefully tested the sturdiness of the floor, and then he took a long hard look at the outer walls. At length, he walked across the room, turned and looked up. Only a small portion of the northern roof remained and above that, he could see the round, shiny rim of a satellite dish. "I don't believe it."

"What?" Collin asked.

"The dish is still there."

"You've got a satellite dish? Why'd you have me see about the towers then?"

Max walked into the control room, sat down and started checking switches. "There's an Amateur Radio repeater on that tower. By the way, I think we're still on the air."

Collin hurried in, picked up his toppled stool, sat down, and set his mike upright. "Okay folks, we've had another big aftershock and we need another check. If you are on Queen Anne and you can hear us, honk." Less than a block away, two car horns sounded. Collin smiled.

While Collin repeated instructions for turning off the gas, saving water, avoiding power lines and finding a safe place outside to spend the night, Max slipped down the stairs to his apartment. This time the door was stuck. He stepped back and examined the placement. In the last aftershock, the doorframe twisted. He pulled out his wallet, withdrew a credit card, turned the knob, and slipped the card between the lock and frame. Careful not to re-injure his foot, he stepped back and kicked with his good foot. The door opened.

In the dining room, he took a moment to pick up broken pieces of Candy's cherished antique teapot, an heirloom from her mother.

He cleared a place and carefully set them on the table. Max un-plugged his Amateur Radio and pulled a bottom drawer out in the adjoining kitchen. He grabbed six batteries and then paused to stare up at the cracked and broken ceiling. "I bought her everything I could think of. Why didn't I buy her a hand-held?"

A few minutes later, while Max was setting up his Amateur Ra-dio on Collin's console, James and Heather were still in Yakima, seat-ed in the pickup truck with two bags of groceries, extra clothing, and four gallons of water in the back. On the passenger side, Heather scooted down, and then propped her feet up on the dashboard. "Mom and Dad are gonna kill us for this."

James backed out of the driveway, shifted to first gear, and head-ed north on Interstate 82, which would take them to Interstate 90 and west to Seattle. "We can only die once. Besides, we left a message at their hotel and Dad knows how to reach us on the radio."

"And when he does, he's gonna lose his Ham license for the lan-guage he'll use." Heather switched on the truck radio and turned the dial to KMPR.

"THIS IS COLLIN SLATER in Seattle. We've had a major earth-quake and we need all the help we can get. What we don't have right now is incoming information. We're just two guys in a radio station with no phones, two backup generators, a lot of damage and only four cigarettes left. We need help world. We need help bad."

Back upstairs, Max finished loading batteries in the Ham Radio, and then he buried his face in his hands and shook his head. "Get a grip Collin. You need to give up smoking anyway, man."

"You want me to give up smoking now, in the middle of a dis-aster? I may be addicted, but you're crazy. I get mean when I don't smoke. Trust me, Max, you don't want me to give it up."

Max snickered and flipped the switch on the Amateur radio. He tuned the dial until he located his net's Magnolia/Queen Anne frequency, and then spoke into the mike, "W7LGF."

It was a woman who answered his call, "W7LGF, this is net control, stand by. BB, go ahead."

"A7BB, the Magnolia Bridge is down. I repeat, the west end of the Magnolia Bridge is twisted sideways and there's a sixty-foot drop. Traffic is backed up in both directions. We have heavy damage to the houses on both the east and south hillside area, but no report of injuries yet. Anybody know if we had a tidal wave? Over."

The Net Controller for Magnolia and Queen Anne was the only woman on this particular network of Hams. More experienced than most men and well known for keeping her cool, Sarah had a rich, flowing voice, a southern accent, and a calm manner. Her microphone system was voice activated, which sometimes was a nuisance since it often interpreted a noise for a voice. Yet, it gave Sarah free hands to take notes and in this case, it was invaluable, "Copy A7BB. Magnolia Bridge out and heavy damage to houses. No word of a tidal wave, but only three Hams have checked in on this net...four now, counting Max. W7LGF, go ahead."

"W7LGF, we've got the station back up. Mind if we listen in?"

"LGF, not at all. Good to have you aboard Max, over."

"W7LGF, thanks Sarah. Are you okay? Over."

Sarah glanced around her tiny duplex apartment. A wide crack ran down the middle of the hardwood floor in her living room. Half the ceiling sagged at one end; a large aquarium broke, spilling gallons of water across the room, and who knew where the fish were. Prized possessions littered the floor, but Sarah's backup generator worked, she was unharmed and her wheelchair wasn't broken. Her green eyes sparkled amid tousled dark hair and when she smiled, deep dimples appeared in her cheeks, "Lost my ramp, but this old house held better than I expected. Over."

"You'll let us know if you need help, right?"

"Roger handsome. LGF, national news says we've been hit by an earthquake measuring 9.1 and centered under downtown Seattle. That first aftershock was 8.6. The last one measured 7.1 LGF, stand by. Net Control to A7BB."

"A7BB, go ahead."

"BB, can you see downtown Seattle?"

"This is A7BB. Let me walk across the park and take a look." A normally good-natured young man, Jim Sarasosa had dark hair and brown eyes. He was twenty-eight, unmarried and a native of Seattle. A College graduate and full time teacher, he currently attended a summer course at the University of Washington. Now, next week's finals would be canceled.

Cautiously, A7BB walked closer to the edge of the park. Magnolia's land mass jutted out high above the Bay offering a panoramic view of the City, Harbor Island, several islands, the Olympic Peninsula and West Seattle—opposite where Sam Taylor often sat on the pier.

While they waited for A7BB to report, Collin took two heavy breaths and stared at his trembling hands. "Nine point two. Wow, that's almost as big as the Alaska Quake and we've got a lot more people in a lot more buildings."

Finally, A7BB's voice came back on the Ham Radio.

"BB, this is net control, go ahead."

"A7BB, the fire downtown is pretty big now. Probably five or six city blocks. I've only heard one siren since the quake. It stopped after that first aftershock. I'm almost to the edge of the park now. Holy Cow."

"BB, What?"

Stunned, Jim Sarasosa forgot to say his call signs. "Sarah, the city is ... there's some sort of split in the city. Some of the buildings are tilted and some are clearly gone."

"BB, are there any more fires? Over."

"A7BB, small ones but not right downtown. I can see a fairly large one in West Seattle and more smoke in the South, behind the.... Good grief, I think the Kingdome fell, and I can't see the Alaskan Freeway. We must have had a tidal wave, the waterfront is gone."

AT THE NEWS OVER HER transistor radio, Seely's heart sank. "This can't be happening."

"I wish it weren't," Jenna said.

Tim slumped his shoulders even more and slowly shook his head. "Who would have guessed it? An earthquake, sure...a little one, but this big? I mean, the whole waterfront gone?" Abruptly, he got to his feet and started down the hall. "I'm gonna go see. The waterfront can't be gone."

Seely immediately protested, "Timmy, the water front is straight down. You can't go that close to the windows, you'll fall out."

The farther away he got the more muffled his voice sounded. "Won't fall out. Falling doesn't run in the family."

Jenna raised her eyebrows, got up and hurried after him. "I wanna see too. I think I smell the smoke."

Seely watched until Jenna was out of sight, and then leaned her head back against the insulation. "Even if the fire is headed our way, we're stuck up here." When she tried to shift her position, she winced. "I'll bet the bruise on my rear end is the biggest one in Seattle." She eased her weight more on her left side, closed her eyes, and went back to listening to the radio.

SAM TAYLOR WAS LISTENING too. City block after city block still lay between him and Max. But this block was deserted. Tired, he paused to sit down on a large rock. The house behind him hardly looked damaged except for broken windows. The one next door was missing the front wall and would probably never be repaired. He removed his shoe, dumped dirt out and put it back on. Hair trapped under his earphone made his ear itch, so he removed his cap, set it on the rock, shoved his head set back, and gave his ear a good rubbing.

Only then did he hear the church bells. Connected to the church organ, the bells played, "In the sweet bye and bye." Sam grinned, got up and followed the sound. Behind him on the rock sat his red golf cap.

He'd gone half a block before he remembered it. Sam stopped, turned and looked back. Behind him, a little eight-year old, African American girl followed with the cap cock-eyed on her head. Sam waited until she caught up. "Mighty fine cap you got there, little girl."

"I know. Found it on a rock. And I ain't no little girl. I'm in the third grade."

"I see. Where are your parents?"

"At the church. Darn near everybody's at the church, Mister. You go'n to the church?"

"I thought I might. My name's Sam, what's yours?"

"Ashley."

"Well, Ashley, do you think you can show me where the church is?"

The little girl grinned, slipped her hand into Sam's and pulled him on down the street. "Come on Sam. We gots everything at the church. Pastor Kirby, he said 'get ready' and ready we gots. We gots water, food, blankets and..."

"Get ready for what?"

"The earthquake, course." Her big brown eyes filled with wonder, Ashley suddenly stopped and looked up at Sam. "Haven't you heard? God's Prophet Daniel called up on the phone. He called to warn Mister Collin Slater at KMPR."

Just above Sam's nose, two straight up and down wrinkles appeared in his forehead, and his eyebrows pulled closer together. "I see. And you believed this Prophet?"

Ashley tugged on Sam's hand again and started off down the cracked and broken pavement. "Pastor Kirby did. Last Sunday, Pastor Kirby said 'get ready' and ready we gots. We brung everything to the church; blankets, food, diapers for the babies, dried milk, water and candy just in case. And sure enough, we had an earthquake. When God calls on the phone, we best be listening!"

Sam looked up and searched the sky with his eyes. He shrugged and followed the little girl to the church.

IN THE PICKUP TRUCK, the Amateur Radio sat unused on the seat between Heather and her brother. Instead, they listened to KM-PR on the truck radio. But with only four Hams checking in on Sarah's net, Heather soon got bored. Mischievously, she glanced at James, and then slipped her hand close enough to turn the dial on the Amateur Radio. As soon as she found what she thought was the right frequency, she quickly flipped the truck radio off and the Amateur Radio on. The dial was set perfectly and the transmission from the north end of Seattle came in loud and clear. Heather ignored her brother's look of disdain.

"UES, this is Mountlake Terrace net control. Your transmission is weak, try again, over."

"N7UES, we've got severe damage at Roosevelt Hospital. The west wing collapsed. We have twenty-three dead so far, at least a hundred injured and more walking in. Roads are buckled. We desperately need blood donors. Elevators are stuck and only one backup generator is functional. Requesting all medical personnel come immediately. It's bad here, Dave, really bad. Over."

"N7UES, copy. Anybody been able to reach the Red Cross?"

"KB7C"

"KB, go ahead."

"KB7C, Tulalip Indian Reservation here. We have moderate damage, no deaths and only minor injuries so far. We can spare 26 units of blood if you can find a way to get it there. Over."

"WV7GRM."

"GRM, go ahead."

"WV7GRM, this is Whidbey Island. We've got another 30 units and should have a chopper airborne in five to ten minutes. Red Cross reports staffing problems. We have requests from six other hospitals. Happy to pick up, Tulalip. Can you spare any medical personnel?"

"WV7GRM, this is KB7C, I'll check and get back to you. Out."

IN THE CONFERENCE ROOM, Tim picked up a five-foot cork bulletin board and dumped the rubbish off. With a careful eye, he surveyed the damage to the room, and then placed the corkboard on top of the broken glass on the floor. Next, he got on his knees, crawled onto the board and lay down. With his hands and the tips of his feet, he scooted the board closer to the edge of the vacant window.

Standing behind him, Jenna was afraid to breathe, "Maybe we should wait until after the next aftershock."

"Could be another hour or so, who knows? Grab my leg will you? And don't let go." Careful to avoid jagged glass still in the frame, he eased his head over the thin windowsill. For several breathtaking moments, he scanned the damage far below. He scooted back, got to his knees and hurried to the safety of the inner room.

"What?"

"The waterfront's gone all right. It sunk. Come on, I wanna see the other side." Tim lifted the corkboard and hauled it through the door. When he reached the elevator hallway, he turned left. Another corridor led to the plush executive offices on the northern side of the forty-third floor, some with worse damage than others. Cautiously, he chose a middle office and just as before moved rubbish out of the way, put the board down and climbed on.

And again, Jenna held on to his leg, "Tell me what you see."

"Well, I can see the fire. It's a lot bigger than I thought. Looks like it's the television stations. No wonder we haven't heard any news choppers. The smoke is drifting out over the water, so maybe the fire won't spread this way. I can see people in the street and...wait, where's the Grand Rainier Hotel?" Boldly, he moved a little farther forward. "Jenna, the bus tunnel collapsed. Some of the buildings are leaning." Hurriedly, he pulled himself back inside, grabbed the board, and stumbled over the rubbish toward the corridor.

"Where are you going?"

Tim didn't answer. Instead, he turned down yet another walk-way. This one was filled with multiple filing cabinets, each toppled and spilled, making the hallway impassable. "Take a memo Jenna. From now on, no filing cabinets or furniture of any kind allowed in the hallways. Sheesh!"

Jenna giggled and quickly followed him in another direction. Soon, he'd led the way to an outer office facing west. Again, he moved debris, climbed atop the corkboard, and inched his way forward until his head stuck out over the edge of the building. And once more, Jenna grabbed hold of his leg.

# CHAPTER 12

BY THE TIME SAM AND Ashley arrived, the damaged church was filled to overflowing. Inside, a man stood near the altar and sang the last few lines of, "In the sweet bye and bye, we shall meet on that glorious shore..." Not one eye was void of tears. Then Pastor Kerby offered a prayer for the dead and dismissed his congregation. Sam slipped a hundred-dollar bill into the preacher's hand, glanced one last time at the golf cap still on Ashley's head and slipped away. More than a hundred blocks and a waterway yet separated him from his son. He adjusted his earphones and continued on.

"THIS IS KMPR IN SEATTLE. I'm Collin Slater with the worst news this announcer has ever had to report. At approximately 4:30 this afternoon Seattle suffered a catastrophic earthquake followed by several strong aftershocks. America, if you can hear me, we have severe damage and are in desperate need of help. The number of dead and dying increase by the moment, and personally, I could use another pack of cigarettes."

Seated in the control room, Max let his head flop forward, "Collin, it's against the law to smoke in a public building in Seattle, remember?"

"Let 'em come arrest me Max! Half of Queen Anne Hill is gone, people are dying across the street, we don't know where our wives are, and you're worried about some stupid ordinance? I can't take it Max, I really can't. Aftershock!"

TIM'S EYES BULGED. The building had begun to heave and his head was sticking out of a forty-third floor window, "Jenna pull!" The south side of the Winningham Blue sharply rose, the middle humped and the north side dipped in such rapid succession the top floors wildly bounced. The ground once more rumbled, metal and concrete screeched and the rubbish on the floor shifted.

Caught in her own terror, Jenna struggled just to hold on to Tim's leg. But the sharp jolts were inching her closer to the outside edge of the building as well. Two ceiling tiles sailed past her head and a heavy black cable abruptly snapped free of its lodging, and then hurled downward. Just in time, she jerked out of the way.

Tim's body scooted farther over the edge. He shoved his hands behind him in search of something solid to grab. There was nothing, but then he felt a sudden weight on his leg. Behind him, Jenna was sitting on it. Her hands free, she pulled the cable taut, and then repeatedly looped it around his other leg. Quickly, she tied a knot, grabbed hold of the cable and waited.

A LITTLE MORE THAN two blocks from the church, Sam heard the rumble and watched the wave beneath the pavement shoot toward him. He quickly glanced around, but the trees were too far away. So he simply sat down in the middle of the street. Parked cars tipped up and back, threatening to roll toward him. Wood-framed houses creaked and popped in agony. Telephone poles with dangling lines, leaned closer together, and then stretched farther apart. And frightened people flew out of doors.

Finally, the land eased and stopped moving. His tired muscles aching, Sam slowly got up off the pavement. He watched neighbors run to a collapsed house, listened to a woman scream something about her cat, and then turned to go.

AT KMPR, THE PAIN IN Max's eyes had increased. Still, he walked to the center of the studio again to make sure the satellite dish was still there. It was. He scooted the Amateur Radio back toward the middle of Collin's console, set the mike in front of it and went back to the control room.

Collin, on the other hand, hurried down the stairs and disappeared inside his apartment.

JUST OUTSIDE OF YAKIMA, James made the turn onto Interstate 90, increased his speed, and then turned the volume up on his Ham Radio. The dial was still tuned to reports coming out of Northern Seattle's Mountlake Terrace where Carl, a worried man with an increasingly alarmed voice was in charge of Net Control. Carl asked all his Hams to stand by, and the airwaves went quiet. James waited a moment more, and then flipped the Ham Radio off in favor of KMPR.

Surprisingly, the voice he heard was Carl's, "WB7JSS to NE7JT, over."

"JSS, Carl this is Sarah, go ahead."

"WB7JSS, I've got heavy traffic here with all kinds of calls backing up. I just can't handle it. We never trained for anything of this magnitude. Can you help? Over."

"Roger WB7SS. Don't know what's happened to our people ... nothing bad, I hope. What have you got?" Sarah flipped to a clean page in her spiral notebook and got ready to take notes.

"It's bad Sarah, real bad in the North. I'm sending you W7MX and W7HEU. Mattie has a collapsed department store with hundreds buried inside and Tom is at an open fissure just north of the UW."

"Copy WB7SS, send them to this frequency and take a break. You're no good to anyone if you're falling apart. Let somebody else take Net Control for a while. Over."

"I suppose you're right. Thanks Sarah. WB7SS, out."

Patiently, Sarah waited, staring at her radio and absentmindedly tapping the end of her pencil on her paper. The tapping filled the airwaves. Finally, W7MX called in.

"Mattie, this is Sarah. Can you give us a report? Over."

She tried to hide it, but even over the radio it was obvious Mattie was crying, "W7MX. Well, we're doing the best we can to get them out. We can hear people crying for help, but we can't get to them. We have fourteen dead and I don't know how many missing. People are bleeding and we only have one doctor. We need medical supplies and better equipment to dig with. Every time we have an aftershock, the building crushes that much more. Over."

"W7MX, copy. Mattie you're doing a great job, just hang in there. I need your location, over."

"This is W7MX. I'm in Northgate just west of North Seattle Community College on 97th and Wallingford Avenue, over."

"Okay, we need heavy equipment in Northgate. Anyone else? Damage or injuries only, please."

"AG7VHR."

"VHR, is that you Ronnie? I've been worried about you, over."

"Sarah, the roof on the bingo hall caved in. I don't know how many inside. It runs twenty-four hours, but this time of day, they've usually only got people playing the machines. We need equipment too. Guess there's not much hope of that anytime soon. Sarah, my kid's trapped inside, over."

Sarah hung her head. AG7VHR was the man who'd helped her settle in Seattle, came to check on her often and she adored his teenage son. He was a widower, ran a sports shop and never turned down an opportunity to help others. His son was an only child. "Roger VHR. Help will come – it has to. Over."

IN THE PICKUP, HEATHER changed positions, fiddled with her fingers, and then intentionally turned to stare at the side of her brother's face.

James pretended not to notice. He kept his eyes straight ahead, but he could always tell when she was watching him. Finally, he narrowed his eyes and glared back, "What?"

"I'm thirsty."

"Drink water, we brought four gallons."

"I don't like water. I want a soda."

"Where? Here? We're in the middle of the mountains, Heather."

"Yes, but we could stop somewhere. Take the next turn off, okay?"

James frowned, turned his head away, and softly muttered, "Women."

"NP7QRT."

Usually cheerful and relaxed, Sarah was oddly annoyed. Aside from all the other problems, something was causing her great discomfort and she'd been too busy to figure out just what. Finally, she turned her attention away from her Ham Operator duties and slammed her pencil down. "What is going on here?" She glanced around, and then turned her head as far as she could to look behind her. Already a good two inches lower than her walls, the split and cracked hardwood floor appeared to be sagging. Above, the ceiling sagged as well.

Sarah reached for her elongated, special made gripper, placed a doorstop between the pinchers and expertly wedged it behind her right rear wheel. "There!" Relieved, she easily returned to her normal, cheerful tone, "QRT, go ahead."

"NP7QRT, I'm over here in Mathias Park. The deer spooked and ran into an electric fence. Several have broken legs. What should I do? They sound like they're crying. Should I kill them or what? Over."

AT KMPR, Max waited for the answer. But Sarah was silent. Finally, he hobbled to the Ham Radio and leaned into the mike.

"W7LGF to NP7QRT."

"LGF, go ahead."

"W7LGF, listen the most humane thing is to put them out of their misery. Who knows how long it will be before we can find a vet in this mess, over."

Sarah sighed, "LGF, I sadly agree. Okay, who's next? Injury or damage only please. We can worry about traffic later."

"WT7RA."

"RA, Magnolia net control, go ahead."

"WT7RA. Wallingford Red Cross is requesting help moving their backup generator."

"RA copy. Where are they setting up? Over."

"WT7RA, Abraham Cook High School on 41st and Stoneway. Arrangements were made in advance with the Fairmount Church, but it fell in. The school's in pretty good shape and has cooking facilities. All we need to do is move the generator from the church to the school. A pickup truck would do. Shoot, we'd settle for a wheelbarrow. Looks like we're gonna have a lot of hungry people to feed, over."

"Copy that WT7RA, good to hear your voice. I was worried about you too. Okay, Wallingford Red Cross needs help moving a generator at 41st and Stoneway. Anymore?"

"A7BB."

"BB you still in Magnolia Park? Over."

"A7BB, affirmative. Got myself in a little trouble. Nothing Serious. Sarah, the Navy is coming. I can see an Aircraft Carrier sailing down the sound from Everett. Must be that one they were bringing in for repairs. Man am I glad to see those guys. And they've got three rescue choppers lifting off, over."

"Thank God. BB, what kind of trouble are you in?"

"A7BB. Well, when that last aftershock hit, I hugged a tree. The edge of the park crumbled and the tree took me with it. I'm about half way down the cliff. Don't think I'm hurt, but the tree's got me pinned and it's about a ninety foot drop from here, over."

"Copy BB. We got anybody available in the Magnolia Area? Over."

"NE7J, emergency."

"NE, go ahead."

"NE7J, we've got a gas leak in Freemont. I've been smelling it for three blocks. It's real strong, over."

"NE, you anywhere near the gas company's business office? Over."

"Yes, but it's across Lake Union. A section of the Aurora Bridge fell and the Freemont drawbridge is stuck in the up position. They've got a crew trying to lower it. I could steal a sailboat, I guess. Where is everybody? We've got thirty people on this net. Sarah, you don't suppose they're...dead? NE7J. Over."

AT THE RADIO STATION, Collin was back upstairs. He sat down and quietly listened to the exchange over the Amateur Radio, and then he shook his head and turned to Max. "All these years, I never even knew these guys were out there. I figured Hams just talked to people in other countries. It never occurred to me they were this organized. And they're so calm. You'd think this kind of thing happens every day."

Max slowly looked up from his controls, "We're on the air, you know."

"I know." Collin stopped talking and listened a while longer. He gently pulled the third from the last cigarette out of his pack and lit it. He took two long drags, and then quickly put it out. "I can't stand not knowing. Doesn't anybody know what's happening at South Center? At this rate, it could be days before we find out if our wives are alive."

Max closed his eyes, brought both hands up and rubbed his temples. "It's not that simple Collin. Hams need repeaters, most of which are on the top of buildings. If the repeaters are down, their transmissions are limited to a short distance and have to be passed along by other Hams. Besides, there are thousands of separated families. We train for emergencies so we can get help to the injured and prevent more tragedy by warning of potential danger. We're not doctors, we're not cops, and we're not fire and rescue. We're just Hams, scared out of our wits. We pass messages – that's all most of us know how to do. We'll hear from South Center, it just takes time."

At the unusually long outburst, Collin turned in his seat. His friend had his brow tightly wrinkled and was still rubbing his temples. "Hey Max, you got a headache or are you cracking up on me?"

"Think I might have broken my ankle."

"No kidding? You've been walking on it."

"Yes, but it's black and blue, it's swollen and there is no way to get to a doctor. You got any pain killers downstairs?"

"Could be, I'll go see." Collin swung around on his stool and headed for the stairs.

The Amateur Radio was still on and the man trapped by a tree over the edge of Magnolia Park lifted his hand-held to his mouth and pushed the PTT button, "A7BB."

"BB, go ahead."

"A7BB, possible broken ankle at KMPR. Age 32, name Max Taylor, over."

"Copy, BB."

SAM TAYLOR TURNED DOWN Greenwood Avenue, a four-lane street running straight through the suburb of Bitter Lake. After only ten blocks, his legs ached, his feet hurt and he was in need of something to drink. So when he reached the small shopping center near the Library, he paused to watch a crowd standing outside a corner store. People were angry, shouting and pushing each other.

Suddenly, in the midst of the crowd, he saw a hand raise a pistol and shoot into the air. Women screamed, men instantly began backing up and then a man in the center of the crowd yelled, "One at a time! No one gets in; my son will get what you need. Anybody with change goes first. We need ones and coins. Get back! Get back!"

"Who made you God?" someone else shouted.

"I'm not God, but I own this store and if you don't get back, I'll board it up and go home. You need me a hell of a lot more than I need your money. Now, who's got change?" Several in the crowd raised their hands.

Sam watched the people finally obey, forming a line into the buckled and torn parking lot. Some cars sat twisted and turned while others sitting on broken slabs were slanted slightly up or down. Thoughtfully, he gazed through the gap where a large window once stood. Sam's eyes lit up. Trying not to draw attention, he softly whistled, "Ally Cat," skirted the parking lot and headed down the alley. Just as he thought, the back wall of the store had collapsed. Just inside, an elderly woman sat in a rocking chair facing the alley. When he drew near, she raised her loaded rifle.

"I'll give you ten bucks for a bottle of pop and pack of cigarettes."

The woman thought for a moment and then glanced toward her son. "Fifteen."

"Fifteen for one pack of cigarettes, a bottle of pop and a bottle of water."

"Done!"

The feeble old woman eased out of her chair, slowly got up and started in, but then she thought better of it and turned back to Sam. "You mind the store?"

"Sure." A side tooth missing, the old woman smiled and handed Sam the rifle. Several minutes passed, but finally she returned. Sam exchanged the gun and the money for the bag, nodded his appreciation, and then headed for a nearby park and a place to sit down. He located a bench tilted only slightly on one end and sat down. When he opened the bag, the old woman had included a fresh sandwich.

Sam smiled and pulled it out, "I tell you, the Lord works in mysterious ways." Hungrier than he realized, he unwrapped the egg salad sandwich, opened his mouth and took a hearty bite.

# CHAPTER 13

TIM'S HANDS WERE STILL shaking when he sat down in the hallway next to Seely. "My exploring days are over. I might be wrong. Maybe falling does run in my family."

Seely turned the radio down and watched the tightness in Tim's jaw. "I've got a feeling I don't wanna hear this."

"You're right." Jenna eased down on her knees, and then leaned against the wall. Suddenly, she sat up straight again, "Listen."

"Chopper," Tim said. "I'll go have a look." With that, he was up on his feet again, hurrying down the hallway. He walked into the conference room just in time to watch a Navy Chopper slowly fly over. Unlike the sky crane, this helicopter seemed to be examining damage all over the city, crossing over, turning, and then....crossing over again in a zigzag pattern. A few minutes later, the thud of its engines diminished. When Tim returned, Jenna handed him the jug of water. He took a long drink and wiped his mouth on the back of his scraped up arm.

Seely watched him with growing concern. His hands were still trembling and his normally pale skin looked even lighter. "Was it the same chopper?"

"Nope, that one was Navy, but it didn't turn this direction. It doesn't know we're here."

"Maybe we could make a sign."

Tim screwed the lid back on the jug and set it down, "And hang it where? The truth is, I don't have the courage to go back out there. I'm the guy, I'm supposed to have all kinds of courage. But man, we're a long way up. A long, long way up."

"I wasn't thinking of hanging it out the window, I was thinking about going to the roof. The top floor is...or was all glass, remember. If the dome is gone, all we'll need to do is spread it out. We can stay one floor down, the 46th floor. And when a chopper comes, we'll go up."

Tim thought for a moment. "It might just work, if we can get on top. We got anything to make a sign on?"

Dropping her eyes, Seely hesitated before she answered, "I'll take care of it."

Jenna quickly puffed her cheeks. "You're going back into the storage room, aren't you?"

"There are a lot of things we still need in that room. If we plan carefully enough, we can get it all in one trip."

"But Seely, Bob is in there. And the big roll of paper is against the far wall. We'd have to..."

"You let me worry about that. Now Timmy, tell me what you saw out there."

Tim took deep breath and slowly let it out. "It's a mess. That guy was right, the waterfront is gone. The Federal Building, the one that used to be as tall as this one, is about six stories of rubble. The one next to it fell sideways. The whole harbor collapsed along with most of the first and second block. There's a freighter with its nose stuck up Madison Street and a long section of the Alaskan Freeway is out in the Bay, with cars still on top."

Seely's mouth dropped. "You're kidding."

"I wish I was. And it gets worse. We lost a floor, maybe two. I can see steel girders and rubble sticking out of the side of the building. I can't tell which floor, but if I had to guess, I'd say it's the tenth. Even if we take the stairs down, I doubt we can get past that floor, and the tenth floor is still too high to jump or climb down a fire ladder—if a fire truck could get to us, that is."

He took another deep breath and once more ran his shaking hands through his red hair, "The fire is about fifteen blocks north. At least we don't have to worry about that just yet. The twin towers of the Westin Hotel are still there, though they are badly damaged and one is leaning two or three feet to one side. The Monorail flew off its rails and is sticking out of the roof of Times Square. And the jail collapsed, the new one we just built. Hopefully, the prisoners who survived will have left town by the time we get out of here."

Jenna's short temper abruptly flared up again, "The new jail collapsed, how is that possible? Wasn't it strong enough? Didn't they build it right?"

It was Seely who answered, "Sugar, new buildings are built to withstand an 8.0, not a 9.1. An earthquake measuring 9.1 is huge and no one knows how to build a building that strong."

"Why didn't everything fall then?"

"I don't know. Go on Timmy, what else?"

Tim glanced at his trembling hands, and then tucked them between his wobbling knees. He managed to steady both. "Well, the building directly across Third Avenue hit us. It's the darnedest thing I've ever seen. The top is imbedded in this building, about ten or twelve floors down."

"So that's why we stopped swaying. Go on," Seely said.

"There's a tanker truck on fire on the freeway, about six blocks south of us and the freeway is a tangled, twisted, buckled mess. And, the top of the bus tunnel collapsed, street and all. There's a deep gash all the way down Third Avenue and I can see people still alive down there with water around them. They must have built the tunnel below the water level. It looks like some buildings fell into it and more are leaning that direction."

Seely put a hand up to stop him. "Wait, wait. I can't absorb this much at once. Is anyone helping the people in the bus tunnel?"

"A few, but real help won't arrive any time soon."

"Why not?"

"There are tons of glass and garbage in the streets. I could barely see the tops of cars."

Seely lowered her eyes and hung her head, "How could we let this happen? We knew about the fault under the city."

"Yes, but by then it was too late. What were we supposed to do, move Seattle to Boise?"

The wind was picking up, lifting the corners of loose papers and threatening to send them airborne. The haunting 'shhhh' of the illusive train yet seeped up from the ground below, and once more the building began a slow, sorrowful groan as more weight settled on the devastated foundation. All three held their breaths until the building quieted.

Finally, Tim broke the eerie silence, "Without a chopper, we're never gonna get out of here."

Seely nodded, "I think you're right. What else did you see?"

Tim suddenly chuckled, "You know the Smith Tower? Well it's still standing."

Seely's mouth dropped, "I don't believe it. It's the oldest high-rise in the city."

"Go figure. They must have known how to build back then. Not only that, it got taller. Looking south to the next block down Third Avenue, I can see ground."

"What do you mean, ground?"

"Raw dirt, maybe twenty or thirty feet high. And the rest of Third Avenue, the part on top of the cliff, shifted away from the Bay. The Grant Building is in the middle of the street. The train station is demolished and the train tracks moved over. The fire station is flat on the ground. Seely, I think the whole city shifted, only in different directions. We moved toward the water and the south side moved away from it. Are you getting what I mean?"

Seely looked deep into Tim's eyes for a long moment and then looked away. "We're sitting on the fault?"

"Right smack dab on the line. I can't imagine why we're still alive. And if we do find a way to get down, we can't go south because of the cliff. We've got fire to the north, water to the west and the sunken bus tunnel out our front door to the east. The only way to get out of here is by chopper and..."

Seely closed her eyes and slowly shook her head, "And there are thousands of Saturday shoppers down there needing more help than we...if any of them are still alive."

Jenna glanced at Tim, and then looked back at Seely, "Aren't any of the other buildings still standing. I thought some were on rollers. Isn't the Parkland Hotel on rollers?"

"I don't know," Tim answered. "Next time, I'll look for it. I'm feeling a little braver now, and yes Jenna, some of the other buildings are still standing. The US Bank building is still there, although it's not so pretty with all its glass blown out. One Union Square is up and so is the Columbia Tower. There's a guy hanging off the top from cables, poor guy."

"Are there any people in the streets?" Jenna asked.

"Alive you mean?" Instantly Tim regretted his abruptness. He watched the sorrow in Jenna's eyes a moment, and then took hold of her hand. "Yes, I saw a few trying to dig out. But Jenna, even if we could get out of this building, it would take weeks to walk out of downtown."

"I don't care if it takes weeks. I've got to get home. My mom..."

Tim wrapped an arm around her shoulders and drew Jenna closer. "We'll get out. Just you wait and see. We'll go up to the top floor, some nice man in a helicopter will let us in and we'll all go home, okay?"

"Okay."

WITH COLD SODAS, A full tank of gas and the ease of interstate driving, James took the onramp back to Interstate 90 westbound and continued up the winding, gradual incline to the crest of the Cascade Mountains. The higher they climbed, the cooler the air, a welcome relief from Yakima's 96 degrees. Again, he switched off the truck radio in favor of the Ham and before she could protest, flashed Heather a warning glance. Soon, he located the emergency frequency being used by Hams south of Seattle.

Heather folded her arms and frowned, "I'd rather listen to Max."

"I know. But we need to know how bad it is in the South end. That's where we're going, you know."

Heather fumed a while longer, and then started talking again just to keep her brother from listening, "So, what are the bleeps?"

"The repeater does that. It beeps three times to alert other Hams of an emergency. That way, they stay off this frequency."

"Oh. Then why does..."

"Heather, I'm trying to listen!" James watched his sister use her thumb and forefinger to pretend to zip her lips, and then turned his attention back to the Ham radio.

"WG7LRS"

"LRS, this is net control, go ahead."

"WG7LRS, I've got a report of two pit bulls out of their cage in South Tacoma. Last seen headed west on 66th. The dogs have been trained to kill and the owner says they are extremely dangerous, over."

"WG, copy. Okay, we're stacked up here. Stand by...okay, K7EQ, go ahead."

"K7EQ, Tacoma Police are asking our assistance. We got anyone available? Over."

"EQ, stand by. All Operators able to assist Tacoma Police check in, over."

Heather let the cool wind blow her short, brown hair. Quickly over her latest irritation, she watched the passing scenery, listened to the call signs reporting in on the radio, and then turned to her brother. "What'll they do with all the dead bodies?"

James shifted positions in his seat and glanced at her, "I don't know. They'll put them in body bags, I guess, until they can bury them."

"I've only seen one dead body."

"Heather, we're going to help the living. Try to remember that."

She stared out the window a while longer, and then asked another question, "When we get there, will you know where to go?"

"Sure. Mom's worked for the Red Cross for years and took me there lots of times. The Red Cross warehouse is easy to find, once you know where to look, and if we can't get to that one, we'll go to another one. There are dozens in Seattle."

"Yes, but will they have enough food and water stored up for this?"

"I hope so. If not, they'll fly more in. What they need most right now are people like us willing to help distribute the food and keep records of who's alive."

Heather got quiet again, gazing at the mountains and wondering aloud, more to herself than to her brother. "We still haven't heard much about downtown. How come they don't have any Hams downtown? James, do you think we should try to reach Max and tell him South Center is on fire? His wife is there, you know."

"I've been thinking about that. I don't want to be the one to tell him. He'll hear soon enough."

"You ever meet him?"

"Nope. Just talked to him over the radio. Don't even know what he looks like. Turn the radio on, will you?"

"Which one?" Heather asked.

"The truck radio."

"Cool."

JUST AS THE FCC REQUIRED, Collin regularly turned the volume down on the Amateur Radio to give the station's call sign and frequency. Next, he launched a new round of instructions for the sake of people who recently managed to find a radio. Yet, each station break reminded him of the amount of time passing without word of Beth. Faithfully, he reported the number of bodies laid out near the collapsed building across the street. When he was finished, he put the mike close enough to pick up the Ham transmissions and turned the volume up.

He tried the phones again. Still dead, not even a dial tone. He got up, walked to the window, and looked out. Less than a dozen people struggled to toss the rubble away, brick by brick and board by board – feverishly working without the benefit of equipment, engineers or even one police officer. Nor were there any Ham operators available to report the severity of the injuries. At length, he turned away.

"A7BB."

"BB, go ahead."

"Sarah, the Coast Guard got one of its fire ships running. Looks like they're going to try to put the fire out from the Bay. I don't know if they can, though. Don't think they can shoot their spray that far. On the other hand, maybe they've got some sort of extensions for the fire hoses. Oh well, not my problem. The Aircraft Carrier is dropping anchor and I saw a couple of divers jump into the water. Wait...Sarah, something big just blew up way down south. Man, I can see the flames from here, over."

"BB, anybody come to help you off that cliff yet? Over."

"A7BB, not yet. Hope it rains soon, I'm starting to get a little thirsty."

Sarah nervously giggled, deepening the dimples in her cheeks. She was getting tired and her southern drawl was becoming more pronounced, "BB, Rain in Seattle? Be serious. Can you tell what blew up?"

"I'm too far away. It's about as far south as that other big fire only farther toward the west. A7BB, over."

"BB, copy."

"AY7MMO."

Sarah winced when she heard the call sign. She paused, rolled her eyes, and then answered, "MMO, go ahead Mister Mayor."

"This is AY7MMO. Sarah, you tell your people I'm sending plows down Highway 99 to clear it for emergency vehicles. I catch anybody else on it, I'll have them arrested. You hear me?"

"Nice to know you're unharmed, Mister Mayor. I hear you. By the way, did you know we're on the air...the commercial airwaves? Tell me, you ever take the time to review Seattle's disaster plan, or are you still too new on the job? Over." Sarah waited, but AY7MMO did not answer. "Okay, KG7SD, you're next."

"KG7SD, this is University Hospital. We're in fairly good shape. Damage is only moderately heavy, generators are working so far, and we have two operating rooms functional. We need more personnel, supplies and as much morphine as we can get. We have fifty-six dead, 123 critical, and more than 200 serious so far. The Red Cross is understaffed, but setting up in the Hester Carson Building as soon as our engineer says it's safe. Meanwhile they're using a park across the street. People are walking in, some carrying injured and some injured themselves. Roads are impassable until we can get some of these uprooted trees and downed power poles out of the way, over."

"Copy that SD. Can you see the fissure from there?"

"Negative net control. But I took a walk that direction a little while ago. It's still wide open. Scariest thing I've ever seen. KG7SD, out."

"NP7WS."

"WS, net control, go ahead."

"NP7WS, Sarah, the Navy wishes to pass along a message, how do you read?"

"Loud and clear WS, go ahead."

"NP7WS, Navy has your man on the cliff in sight. They will attempt a rescue when they can, over."

"Thanks Navy. A7BB says he saw Navy launch choppers. Can they give us a report? Over."

"NP7WS, stand by, I'll ask." For several seconds, a soft static filled the Ham frequency air waves while NP7WS talked to someone on the USS Carl Vincent Aircraft Carrier. Then NP7WS came back on, "Net control, we have one ferry missing on Elliott Bay. Navy has divers in the water now. A tsunami hit shortly after the first quake and another after the second. All hospitals and government services have gone to disaster mode. Stand by." Again Sarah waited until finally, he returned, "Navy says the death toll reached seven hundred about ten minutes ago. They're getting ready to take injured aboard ship. Red Cross is mobilizing all across the country and the Canadian's are sending all the help they can, over."

Sarah heaved a big sigh of relief, "God bless Canada, over."

"One more thing, Sarah. Tell Max his little station just went nationwide. The whole country is listening in. NP7WS, over."

Sarah's lip began to quiver and her eyes suddenly filled with unexpected tears, "God bless America." She paused, breathed deeply and cleared her throat, "This is Net Control, thanks. Navy, can you tell us about the fire down south?"

"WP7WS, stand by. ...Navy doesn't know what just blew up, but they report several fires South of Seattle. They are Sherwood Library,

SeaTac Community Center, Air Traffic control, one city block in Thorndyke, South Center has been burning since the quake, a warehouse in Tukwila, gas explosion in West Seattle, half a block..."

COLLIN GRABBED A CIGARETTE, a lighter and walked to the window. His hands were shaking when he struck the flint and he couldn't hold the flame. Again he struck the flint, again the flame went out. When it finally lit, he struggled to bring the flame closer to the end of his cigarette. Suddenly, Max was beside him, steadying his hand. He took a long drag, blew the smoke out, and allowed the tears to stream down his cheeks. "I can't go on without her, there is no point. Beth is all I have."

"We don't know they're dead. They were gone a long time. Maybe they headed back before the quake."

"You think so?"

"Yes. I've thought about it a lot. The boys are a handful in a shopping center and Candy shops quickly. For all we know, they're sitting at the bottom of the hill trying to figure out how to get up the counterbalance. It's pretty steep, you know."

"I need to talk to Beth. I've gotta tell her something."

"Okay, go for it. We're on the air, talk to her."

Collin stared at Max for a moment, and then wiped the tears off his cheeks. He walked back to his stool, sat down, grabbed his mike, and then watched Max turn down the volume on the Ham Radio. "This is Collin Slater at KMPR in Seattle. As you know, we've had an earthquake. Max and I said good-bye to our wives this morning, just like we do every morning. We climbed the stairs to this attic studio and went on the air. How could we have known we might never see them again? Beth and Candy took Max Taylor's three little boys to South Center and as you just heard, South Center has been on fire since the Quake.

And if I had known I might not ever see Beth again, I would have told her this. My love...there are no words eloquent enough to tell you how much I adore you. I love your laughter. I love candlelight flickering in your eyes. And when you are asleep in my arms, I know I'm home...really home. Come back to me Beth. Please be alive."

Max bit his lip hard and turned the volume back up on the Amateur Radio. The Amateur airwaves were quiet.

IN THE FRONT YARD OF a house belonging to people he didn't know, Sam Taylor slumped to his knees. Traffic had not moved on Greenwood Avenue North since the quake and the cars were deserted. The air was crisp and fresh. Birds flew into the tops of trees and landed, the wind managed to cool the temperature and people were helping each other. But Sam noticed none of it.

He eased his headphones off his ears, placed his hands together and bowed his head. "For Thou art my candle in the darkness, my strength when my heart is heavy, the forgiver of my grievous sins, and the Savior of my soul. If it be Thy will, Lord, please let Beth, Candy and my grandsons be alive." Sam lifted his head and started to get up. Then he quickly retook his position, "Oh yes, and these cigarettes are not for me, they're for Collin. Amen."

# CHAPTER 14

IN THE PARKING LOT of the Cleveland Department Store, twenty-seven-year-old Mattie Campbell was fresh out of tears when she pushed the speak button on her hand-held and brought it to her mouth, "WJ7V."

"WJ, go ahead."

"Sarah, we've found a little girl. She's four years old and buried just inside the wall. She says her leg hurts, but she's alive. We need better equipment. There's a cement slab just above her and the building keeps settling, over."

"WJ, do you have any help there yet?"

"Not much, but people are doing what they can. Even injured people are digging. We need equipment, but there's not much chance of that. The parking lot is a mess and the streets are jammed with cars. Trees are slanted every which way and some are uprooted. We had a live power line to worry about, but one of the guys got it shut down. WJ7V, over."

"N7ORM."

"ORM, go ahead."

"Sarah, John Snider is with me. He owns a construction company and wants to help. Can you give us Mattie's location again? N7ORM, over."

"ORM, she's at the Cleveland Department Store on North 97th, just off Wallingford Avenue, over."

"Roger Sarah. Traffic is jammed, but we'll try our best to get there. N7ORM, out."

Collin thought for a moment, and then lifted the mike, "This is Collin Slater at KMPR, 760 AM in Seattle. Folks, I know a lot of you are trying to find loved ones, but please, if you've deserted your cars, go back. Pull them to the side as far as you can. Park on sidewalks or in yards if you have to, but clear the streets. It's the only way we're going to get help to that little girl and the hundreds of others trapped in buildings." Gently, he laid the mike back down near the Ham Radio speaker.

A few minutes later, he was standing at the window watching the pitiful scene across the street again. Unlike the department store, none of the floors remained high enough off the ground to allow people to crawl out. A new body had been added to the dead and a woman sat nearby, holding her bleeding head in both hands. Collin turned and walked into the control room. Keeping his voice down, he leaned toward Max, "I'm going down there."

"And do what?"

"I don't know, take a closer look, count the dead and see about the injured. Maybe Sarah can get them some help."

Max turned to look at the sincerity in his friend's eyes, and then lowered his gaze. "Collin, there's something you need to understand. Help is a long way off. You've been listening, we've got reports of damage, deaths, and injuries, but the only good news is about an Aircraft Carrier and four choppers. We don't even know if they're medical units. Real help takes 24 to 48 hours after a disaster. All we've got is ourselves."

"I'm going anyway. The least I can do is let them know somebody cares. Besides, I'll go nuts if I don't do something."

Max mulled it over, and then reluctantly nodded. "Don't take too long, I can't handle this place by myself."

"Great."

As soon as he was gone, Max got up, hobbled into the studio, and made sure the mike was close enough to the Ham Radio. Next, he turned the volume up a little, and then went back to the control room.

"A7BB."

"BB, go ahead."

"A7BB, good news! We've got more choppers coming in. I count six, maybe seven all coming from the east. And the Navy choppers are starting to come back. Guys in yellow jackets with sticks are telling them where to land and they've brought tons of equipment topside. Would you look at that, some guy is waving a white flag at me! Hello Navy, over."

Sarah smiled. Next to Max, A7BB was her favorite and she was relieved to hear him in a good mood. "BB, maybe they want to surrender."

"Ah Sarah, we ain't got no place to keep prisoners. I say we let 'em go. A7BB, over."

"BB, hasn't anybody come to help you?"

"Well, one guy peeked over the side of the cliff and looked down. But the truth is, the edge isn't safe. He nearly fell just getting close enough to lean over. Sure wish he'd come back with a jug of water though. A7BB, over."

"Copy, BB."

"N7JDX emergency."

Sarah immediately turned her attention to the new caller, "JDX, go ahead."

"We've got looters in downtown Ballard. The earthquake broke all the windows so people are just taking whatever they want out of stores. What should I do? Over."

"JDX, stay clear. You'll only get hurt if you try to interfere."

"Okay. I'm just sick about this. Looters? I never thought this would happen in Ballard. Haven't we got enough trouble? N7JDX, over."

"JDX, it's just stuff. We need to concentrate on getting help to the injured. Walk away JDX, let it go for now. You been to St. Luke's Church yet? They're a designated Red Cross center, aren't they? Over."

"This is N7JDX, I'll head that way now. Thanks Sarah. Out."

ON THE FORTY-THIRD floor of the Winningham Blue building, Seely cautiously opened the door to the supply room. Flashlight in hand, she allowed the beam of light to shine first on Bob's hand, and then she slowly moved the light toward his torso. Obscured behind an industrial copier, his body lay crushed between it and the mail machine. His face obscured, Seely let out a relieved breath and knelt down. She brought out two more gallons of water, a smaller duffel bag and then stood back up and started in.

"Wait," Tim said. "Suppose we can't get up the stairs. You'll have gone in there for nothing. I say we try to get to the roof first. Besides, maybe we can find paper in one of the offices."

Seely quickly pulled the door closed and sighed, "Sounds good to me."

"Okay." Tim picked up both jugs, made his way through the debris in the hallway, and set them on the floor near the ladies' room. "Jenna, help me move these filing cabinets. No use having to climb over them several times."

"Coming." With Tim's help the cabinets were easy to lift, even with the drawers falling out. One by one, they shoved the lower drawers back inside the cabinet, set them upright and moved on. Finally, the path was clear all the way to the steel door leading to the stairs.

Tim turned the knob and pulled, but the door didn't budge. He stood back, viewed the frame, and then tried again. This time he pulled harder. Finally, it screeched open. He held it while Jenna pulled a full drawer out of a filing cabinet and shoved it against the door to keep it from closing. Then he let go. "Well, best I go see."

Jenna hesitated. The stairwell was pitch-black and clammy cold. "I'll get a flashlight."

"Good idea." Cautiously, he stepped out onto the cluttered, concrete landing. "Hello? Anybody there?" He waited for the echo to subside, but no one answered. "Looks like we're the only ones dumb enough to work on Saturday." When Jenna and Seely came with two flashlights, he turned an inquisitive eye on Seely, "You're not going, are you?"

"What, and miss the best radio show I've heard in months? Not a chance."

"Good. You need to rest, you know, your heart?"

Seely grinned, "Yes, I do know."

Tim took one of the flashlights, flipped it on, and shined it against the cracked and broken concrete walls. The north and south walls showed the most damage with cracks wide enough for his entire hand. All the walls were missing large areas of concrete exposing steel mesh reinforcements and the missing chunks lay in heaps on the stairs.

Attempting to boost his own morale, he winked at Jenna, "And there you have it, an elevator shaft with stairs...hopefully." Timmy took another careful step, and then another until he reached the handrail. "I saw a movie once where even the stairs were gone. Think they used a fire hose and a chair to get down. Yep, that's what they used. Might be a handy thing to know...should we have an earthquake."

Jenna eased out onto the landing and watched him try the first step, "It is cold in here."

"Take a memo, Jenna. From now on, all death traps are to have heat in the stairwells. And another thing, put in for my vacation. I'm feeling a little burned out." He lifted his eyes upward and again shined his light on cracked and broken walls. "I'm going up now, Jenna. Stay here, okay? No use both of us getting killed." Ever so gingerly, Tim put one foot at a time on the concrete steps and eased upward.

"A7BB"

"BB, go ahead," Sarah answered.

"A7BB. Things are really look'n up now. I can see a second Coast Guard fire ship sailing around Alki Point. Must be coming from Tacoma. And I think...yes, I see two fire choppers. Yee haw!!! And guess what? There's a kitty cat perched on a piece of wood out on the water. Poor thing just sits there looking up at me, like I should be doing something to help. Poor dumb cat, over."

"Copy that, BB. You okay?"

"Yep. The tree slipped another few inches, but I'm still okay. A7BB, over."

"A7FLC emergency."

"FLC, go ahead."

"A7FLC, we've got houses and a ton of earth that slid down First Hill onto the I-5 freeway. And the East St. Johns overpass collapsed trapping cars under it, over."

"FLC, where are you? Over."

"A7FLC, I'm about four blocks from the Convention Center tunnel. It fell too. I'm up on St. John's Street looking down. There's a forty-foot drop to the freeway and I can't get down there to help. People are hurt bad. Sarah, there's a metro bus crushed by the overpass and a major pile up on the other side of the landslide. If we could get a fire truck up here with a long ladder, we maybe could get people out, over."

"NJ7Q."

"NJ, go ahead."

"NJ7Q, Fire station three reports heavy damage in that area. Many injuries and no way to get a fire truck through this mess. Suggest you try getting a cherry picker down on the freeway, over."

The man standing above the freeway instantly flared, "You idiot, we've got no phones. If we can't get a fire truck up here, how do you expect us to find a cherry..."

Sarah instantly interrupted, "This is net Control, all stations stand by. We are all overwhelmed here, try to calm down guys." She intentionally paused, allowing only dead air, and then moved her mouth closer to the mike. "Okay, A7FLC needs ladders at St. John's Street. Who's next?

GETTING FROM THE TWO-story radio station to the collapsed building across the street wasn't as easy as Collin expected. The narrow yard filled with daisies and pansy plants, now held the remnants of KMPR's northern roof. Glass littered the sidewalk along with bits of shingles, wood, brick and plaster. An antique weathervane from the roof next door lay in the middle. Power lines sagged, trees slanted and the declining sun made elongated shadows, pointing out the lateness of the hour.

UNDAUNTED, COLLIN SLIPPED around the side of the house, made his way across the street and walked through the small park to the collapsed building. He was greeted by stunned, cut and bruised faces, exchanged a few words and paused to take an accurate count of the dead. He looked over the wounds of the injured, placed a comforting hand on several shoulders, and then headed back.

When he came back upstairs, he walked straight to his can of soda and downed all that was left. Visibly upset, he opened the refrigerator, pulled out another and popped the pull-tab before he noticed Max was watching him.

Max slowly mouthed the words, "You okay?"

Collin nodded and then quickly turned away.

WHEN TWO HAMS TRIED to call in at the same time, Sarah started tapping her pencil, "That was a complete double. Let me have the one that starts with WC, over."

"This is WC7NJT, I have a message to pass on from the Mayor, over."

Sarah's green eyes instantly sparkled, "WC, is that the same Mayor who said most Ham Radio Operators were 'looky loos' just trying to get a cheap thrill by loitering around fire stations?"

"WC7NJT. No, this is his overworked and underappreciated executive assistant. You know, the one with the actual Ham license? May I continue? Over."

"Oh okay, might as well let him get it out of his system or he'll pester us till we do. WC, go ahead."

"WC7NJT. My fellow citizens of Seattle, the Mayor wishes to assure you he is doing everything in his power to help. He wants the voters to know..."

AT THE STATION, COLLIN narrowed his eyes and hurried back to his stool. In a flash, he turned the volume down on the Amateur Radio and grabbed his Mike, "This is KMPR in Seattle, 760 AM Radio. Here's what we know so far. We have an open fissure north of the University of Washington with several people still trapped at the bottom. Hillsides slid in several areas and overpasses collapsed.

We have a child trapped in a department store and fires burning out of control. Homes and apartment buildings have fallen and reports from downtown, where the quake was centered, are still nonexistent. And the ugly truth is, there isn't going to be enough help to go around for quite some time.

Folks, we're on our own. Darkness is only a few hours away and we need to think ahead. Try to find flashlights, batteries, blankets, and water. We can all live for a few days without food and like the book says, most of us have water stored in our water heaters, if we can get to them. What we don't need is more fires. Make sure the gas is turned off in your neighborhood. Watch for live power lines and find a safe place to sleep where nothing can fall on you. And most of all, expect more aftershocks. This is far from over."

Collin paused and quickly glanced at Max, "And if you happen to find a pack or two of cigarettes..."

Max quickly downed two more ibuprofen, swallowed, and then rolled his eyes, "Collin, you're twisted, man."

Collin smirked, laid the mike down, and then turned the volume back up on the Ham Radio. The Mayor's speech was over.

"NR7G"

"NR7G, go ahead."

The man caller spoke in a dull, monotone voice, slowly stretching out his painful words, "Mercy Hospital fell...collapsed. Don't bring your injured...there is no one left to help."

Sarah hung her head and softly mumbled, "It's too much. It's just too much." She put both hands on the arms of her wheelchair and lifted her body. Paralyzed from the waist down, her upper back was starting to hurt and changing positions was the only way to relieve it. She lowered her body back down, and then went back to her duties, "This is net control, copy. Mercy Hospital is incapacitated."

"WC7NJT."

"NJT, go ahead."

"I've got another message from the Mayor. The Army is closing all routes into the city and will turn everyone back except emergency staff and vehicles. Also, the Mayor is ordering an 8:00 p.m. curfew. All citizens are to be off the streets by..."

In a huff, Collin switched off the radio. "Great. That's just great! We've got people dying here and his answer to all our problems is to lock us down tight. It'll be dark soon. What are we supposed to do, stop helping people just because the Mayor is afraid of looters? I say..."

Bad foot and all, Max left the control room and walked to Collin, "Man, don't say stuff like that, you'll start a riot."

"I don't care! Are people like him born without common sense or do they just misplace it once they run for office? We've got work to do. We need every available man and woman to dig people out of the rubble. What about the fires, huh? Are we supposed to just let them burn all night? Where are the police? Where are the firemen? We haven't seen one since the quake and we've got a collapsed building right across the street. I'll tell you where they are, there are too few to handle this mess, and those we have are trying to dig their own families out. What about kids with missing parents and parents looking for kids? Think they're a big threat to pawn shops and jewelry stores. And what about..."

Suddenly, the loud, sorrowful groan of wood and metal interrupted Collin in mid-sentence. He held his breath, waiting to see if the earth would move again. But it wasn't the earth. Instead, the noise was coming from outside. Unnerved, he spun around on his stool, hopped down and raced to the window. Across the street, the second apartment building had begun to lean to one side – the side where the first one lay in ruins. Wide eyed, he listened as the unearthly moan of wood scraping against wood intensified and the building teetered.

People began to fly out the front door. A man jumped from a second floor window, quickly got up and held out his arms to a child above. In the doorway, a woman fell and mindless others trampled her. And still, the building lamented, leaning closer and closer to a torturous death.

The man on the ground screamed, "Jump, Jeremy, jump!" But the four-year old in the window above was frozen in terror, his arms out stretched and his face streaked with tears. Briefly, the father considered going back up, and then he thought better of it. Forcing himself to look angry, he glared at the child, "If you don't jump, I'll beat your butt!"

The child winced. Still in tears, he begrudgingly lifted one, and then the other leg over the windowsill. Again the building groaned and leaned yet another foot to the side. In the doorway, two men mercifully grabbed hold of the fallen woman and quickly pulled her to safety while still more people fled from inside.

At last, the child jumped into his father's arms. But before the man could turn to run, the building gave up its struggle. Old mortar suddenly disintegrated, allowing bricks to rain down on father and son. With a percussion as loud as a bomb, the building crumbled into a heap of rubble, burying both under tons and tons of rubbish.

Collin dared not move. In shock, he heard no sounds and felt no emotions. Nor did he allow his mind to accept what his eyes had just seen. The dust storm from the fallen building began to mushroom upward like some thoughtless, evil cloud of death and he still could not move.

It was Max, not Collin who quickly sat down at the console and grabbed hold of the mike. His expression was filled with anger, his hands shook and his jaw muscles flexed, "Listen people!" he nearly shouted. "The sound you just heard was another building falling. More people have just died. Please, please don't go back inside any building. There can't be anything in there important enough to risk your lives for. Take your children to a parking lot or a park. As soon as we can, we'll give you a list of places to go for food and water. Until then, get out of the buildings!" Still angry, Max shoved the microphone aside, got up and hobbled back into the control room. He would have slammed the door, but...

THOUSANDS OF PEOPLE all up and down the Puget Sound area were painfully aware of the approaching night. Some had transistor radios but most did not, relying instead on car radios. Some had water, medical supplies, stored food and extra clothing. But most did not, oblivious or uncaring when it came to preparing for that elusive earthquake they assumed would never happen. Now, survival gear meant everything. And fear consumed their very souls.

Ninety-five blocks north of downtown, Theo Westly sat his overwrought wife Michelle down in the front passenger seat of their 1963 Oldsmobile. Thousands of hours went into restoring the engine and just before the quake, he moved it from the garage to the street, planning to take it for a test drive. Now, it was the only undamaged car they owned. He closed the door, and then glanced around. No telephone poles or power lines were near enough to fall on them.

Next, he put his two daughters in the back seat, got in the driver's side, rolled down the window, and closed the door. "Honey, there is absolutely nothing we can do about your Mom. Absolutely nothing."

Her hair as dark and as long as Seely's, Michelle folded her arms and sniffed her nose. Tears streamed down her cheeks, her head already ached and her voice quivered, "There must be something we can do. We can't just leave her there. Oh Theo, if only she hadn't gone to work today."

"If she hadn't gone to work she would have been at home, in that twenty-five year old building with cracks already in the walls from the last earthquake. She probably has a better chance of surviving downtown." He watched her face, but his wife didn't find much comfort in his words. "Come here," he said, opening his arms, and then wrapping them around her. "Honey, we can't go downtown and we can't leave the kids even if we could. What can we do?"

"I don't know, something, anything."

"Well, there is one thing we can do."

Michelle sniffed her nose again and wiped her eyes with a handkerchief, "What?"

"We can stay alive. Your Mom made sure we had enough stuff to last two weeks, maybe more. But if people find out, we could be in danger. We need a plan, a safe place to keep ourselves and our supplies."

"Where? The house is ruined."

"I know. Let's just think a moment."

In the front yard, just below the third sprinkler head from the street, a tiny camera captured their worried expressions and tender moments.

"A7BB."

"BB, you okay? You haven't slid any farther down that hill, have you?"

"No, I'm okay. Just thought you might like an update on that dumb cat. He fell asleep, Sarah. Curled right up and fell asleep like he hasn't got a care in the world. But Sarah, it's the strangest thing ... the water is muddy. I didn't realize that before. I've never seen the Bay all muddy. And Sarah, I can see bodies. A7BB, over."

IN THE HALLWAY OF THE Winningham Blue, Seely sat on the floor with her legs outstretched. The bruise on her face seemed darker and her jaw was swollen. She laid the radio in her lap and watched Jenna's nervous eyes dart from side to side. "What's wrong baby?"

"How can you be so calm? We could still fall, Seely. We really could."

"I know, but there's not a thing we can do about it. Tell me about Kevin. What do you suppose he's doing right about now?"

Jenna suddenly giggled. "He's on the plane from Germany, I hope. He's probably heard about the quake and is trying to figure out a way to sneak through the barricades."

"Good for him. Think he'll make it?"

"Of course he will. He's smart, he's big, and he's got a uniform. But Seely, what if he can't land. I mean, Timmy said the airport..."

"Tim is guessing. We don't know for sure all the runways are out and SeaTac is not the only airport. There are military airports all up and down the coast, not to mention Spokane and Yakima. And we have small airports too, practically everywhere. He'll make it. And by that time, we'll be out of this building. Now, how about passing me the water jug?"

# CHAPTER 15

THE SIKORSKY AIR CRANE seemed to appear from nowhere, moving southwest, and gliding just above Lake Washington. But W7HEU didn't notice.

His mouth tight and his hand-held radio clutched in his hand, he stood a little more than six feet from the edge of the giant fissure. All around, houses lay in ruins. Telephone poles and uprooted trees were strewn across heaved and broken yards, some crushing homes or cars parked in the streets. From the top of the hill, the devastation yielded a clear, unexpected view of Lake Washington and occasionally he glanced that direction, only to find the destruction too cruel to contemplate.

Onlookers watched the activity around the fissure from a safe distance. Shirley Goodman, her face cut and one arm bruised, brought a pot of fresh coffee heated over a camp stove. But the Amateur Radio Operator and the young football players with blistered hands refused to pause. Once more, they lowered the only available harness over the edge. One hundred and sixty feet below, another of their team quickly slipped it around a teenage girl, buckled the belts and yanked on the rope. Slowly and carefully, the girl was pulled out of the chasm. Yet fear of the fissure closing grew with each passing moment and the rewards only numbered two women and seven children saved. People still waited amid the ruins of crashed cars and toppled houses—at the bottom of the frightening "V" shaped crevice.

Faintly, he heard the clap of the Pratt and Whitney engines coupled with the whine of the air crane's blades. W7HEU turned and looked – beyond the onlookers, beyond the crumbled houses and beyond the felled trees. Its bubble face was pointed directly at him and coming fast, but it was not the curious face that held his attention. Instead, he kept his eyes glued to something extraordinary. It was a brown, circular object hanging just beneath the undercarriage of the modified body.

Closer and closer it came, rising off the water with its repetitive whipping noise growing louder, and its size increasing. Finally, he threw up his arms and began to shout for joy. "A basket...they're bringing a hot air balloon basket!"

Instantly, he pushed the speak button on his radio, "W7HEU."

"HEU, go ahead."

"We got ourselves an Angel...a big, blue Angel!"

ON AN ORDINARY DAY, Heather and James would have found crossing over the Cascade Mountains amid such manageable traffic a pleasure. But as they drew nearer to Seattle, traffic markedly increased. Now, James was forced to keep his speed down to forty miles an hour and be prepared to stop at a moment's notice. Even more troubling was the unusual, bumper-to-bumper onset of traffic leaving the greater Seattle area. Heather watched the dull, lifeless expressions on worried, frightened faces. Some looked agonizing. The last car going east passed by, leaving a clear and free highway. Heather sat up straight and looked ahead for the reason. Inbound traffic slowed to twenty miles an hour and crept around a long, wide curve in the Interstate.

James tightened his grip on the steering wheel and frequently glanced to his left, "Must be an accident." Suddenly, he spotted a tangled web of cars with dazed people standing beside them. He pulled the truck over to the side of the road, applied the brakes, and stopped. With quick, precise movements, he turned his Amateur Radio toward him, found the Yakima emergency frequency and brought the portable microphone to his mouth. "KB7HDX emergency."

"HDX, go ahead. Where are you, James?"

Reception was a little weak and James hesitated a second before he went on, "Boyd, we've got a seven or eight car pileup on Interstate 90 east bound, with serious injuries. It looks like a tractor was hauling a load of people out on a trailer."

"HDX, did you say a tractor trailer? Over."

"Negative, a farm tractor, pulling a flatbed trailer loaded with people, over."

"Copy HDX. Oh and kid, you forgot your call signs. And one more thing, your Dad is looking for you. Over."

James puffed his cheeks and considered not answering. But he glanced at the injured people and quickly changed his mind. "This is KB7HDX. Tell Dad Heather and I are headed for the Red Cross Center in Renton. We're going to help, over."

"Commendable, HDX, just not very smart. I'll tell him. We already got a call on that accident. You should have help in a few minutes, over."

"Thanks Boyd, KB7HDX, out."

Boyd was right. In less than five minutes, two ambulances came from the direction of Yakima. For another twenty minutes, James and Heather assisted a registered nurse and four Medical Technician's with the injured. No one died and Heather was greatly relieved. Yet when she climbed back into the passenger side of the truck, she was clearly annoyed, "Idiot!"

"Who?" James asked, getting into the driver's side and closing the door.

"That guy in the green Camaro. He said he was so scared after the earthquake; he just got in his car and drove as fast as he could. The accident was his fault, he said so himself. He could have killed all those people. And they were coming out of the earthquake too, some of them were already injured. They left behind all they owned. Their cars were smashed, their houses were..."

James started the engine, eased back into inbound traffic and just let his little sister rant. More than a mile later, he pulled over again.

"Why are we stopping?"

"Didn't you hear? They're setting up roadblocks. We can't get in."

Dismayed, Heather stared at her brother, and then looked back out the window, "Quitter."

"You watch too much TV, Heather. What am I supposed to do, crash the barricade or sail over a drawbridge?"

"They need us in Seattle."

"For what? We're just a couple of kids."

"Well, the way I see it, nobody else is going to help Max and Collin. Somebody has to find their wives."

James considered it for a moment before he spoke, "We could go straight to the fire at South Center, but then what? We don't know what they look like. We don't even know what kind of car they're in."

"Yes, but we could find out. Once we get there, we'll radio Max and ask him."

James strummed his fingers on the steering wheel and stared at nothing at all. "Dad knows where we are."

"Really? Is he mad?"

"Don't know yet. I only talked to Boyd."

Heather shrugged and threw a hand out, palm up, "What's the worst he can do?"

"Ground us for life, take the truck away, or spank us. Or worse, he could send us to Uncle Harry's and make us work all summer in the packing sheds."

"Peach fuzz, yuk!"

"Still think we should go?"

This time it was Heather who thought it over carefully. "We're too big to spank. I'll miss this old truck, grounding us makes Mom crazy, and peach fuzz is manageable ... with enough baby powder. I say we go."

James started to laugh, "What do you mean, *you'll* miss this old truck? It's *my* truck!" Heather didn't answer and James didn't expect her to. Instead, he took up a new position amid the growing number of cars heading into Seattle.

"NP7WS."

"NP, go ahead," Sarah said.

"NP7WS wishes to pass along another message from the Navy. Be advised, rescue teams with search dogs are on their way from six states – Florida, Texas, Oklahoma, North Carolina, South Carolina and Kansas. They should be arriving as early as tonight. Also, Canada is sending teams of electricians to help restore power, and the Red Cross is asking citizens to place identification on the dead whenever possible. Over."

Copy NP. Does Navy know if the fire at South Center is out yet?"

"This is NP7WS, stand by." Just as before, silence filled the air while NP7WS talked to the navy. "South Center is still burning, but they've got the gas main turned off. They've been able to get two fire trucks in, and they've got a hand brigade dipping water out of the Green River and passing buckets. And one more thing, the US-

GS isn't sure, but we may have another big aftershock as strong as or stronger than the initial quake. Over."

"Copy that, NP. Can Navy still see our man on the cliff?"

"Stand by...Roger Net Control. They've got casualties coming on board. Afraid he'll have to wait a while longer. NP7WS, over."

"Copy NP, thanks. Come in, A7BB."

"This is A7BB, I heard, over."

"BB, how's the kitty?"

"Well, the dumb cat woke up and tried to swim for it. Most cats hate water, but this one got real wet before he figured that out. Nearly didn't get back on the board, but he looks okay now. I think when the tide comes in it will push him closer to shore. And Sarah, I can see more bodies. Two for sure and I think three more, over."

"Copy BB."

A7BB released the button on his hand-held and took a deep breath. His was the best seat in the house, although the view was of massive devastation and his tree was gradually slipping down a hillside. Even so, he marveled at the array of choppers increasingly filling the sky. Some he recognized as military. Others had markings he'd never seen before. He watched as they held their place in line, waiting to deliver the severely injured, and then quickly lifting off again. One helicopter, with a Canadian Maple Leaf emblem on the side, dropped a large black bundle near the edge of the deck. Almost immediately, seamen unbelted the bundle and began pulling out black body bags. The next Canadian chopper unloaded several men and women in white medical jackets.

The next sight was one he hadn't counted on. A tug boat, complete with a red stripe around it, and black smoke billowing out of its smoke stack, was pushing a long, wooden barge around to the back of the Aircraft Carrier. The tug expertly changed positions, turned, and then eased the barge up to the side of the huge ship. Soon, men still in Navy whites were lowered to secure the barge, and as soon as the tug pulled away, a small crane lowered the first occupied body bag.

A7BB shivered.

The time was 6:45 p.m.—a little more than two hours after the first earthquake and less than one hour remained until dark. The fires still burned, people were still buried, scant news was coming from downtown and in a place where rain fell in abundance, not a cloud appeared in the sky. A7BB would have to wait for that drink of water. Cautiously, he slid his hand around the tree branch and into his pocket. His spare batteries were safe and sound. Relieved, he turned the volume up on his hand-held. Finally, the first call came from downtown.

"NE7G."

"NE, this is net control, go ahead."

"Be advised the I-90, I-5 interchange south of downtown fell in the initial quake. We have traffic backed up for miles with no way to get people off. Is the Mercer Island Bridge out? NE7G, over."

"Affirmative NE. Where are you?"

"I was on the I-90 overpass. Now I'm standing on Airport Way South. Sorry it took so long to get in touch, but my car went off the freeway and I just now managed to crawl out. NE7G. Over."

"NE, are you hurt?"

"Sure I'm hurt. Isn't everybody? Sorry, Sarah, I didn't mean to snap at you, over."

"That's okay Ned. What can you tell us about downtown?"

"NE7G, well the retractable roof on Safeco Field flew off its rollers during the first quake. I watched it from the Freeway. But that's no big surprise; we all knew the fault ran right under the stadiums. I think the Kingdome fell too and I watched the new train station cave in. Chinatown's a mess. After the second quake, the freeway fell. People were so scared they just ran, the ones that could, I mean.

Was there a game today? Do we have thousands of people trapped in Safeco Field? Over."

"NE, I don't know." Sarah remained quiet, allowing the words to sink in and trying to think if there were events scheduled in either of the ballparks. She couldn't remember. She was getting tired and her ceiling looked an inch or two lower. Still the thirty-year-old turned back to her duties. "NE, this is net control. The Army and the National Guard are mobilizing and they'll need our help. Try to find the worst hit areas and keep me posted. You're the only Ham we've heard from downtown, over?"

"NE7G, roger. I'll head on over to Safeco Field. Pray it's empty, okay? Out."

In the attic radio station, Collin glanced around. "Max, what'd you do with that newspaper? We have any games today?"

"I don't think so. I think the Mariners are out of town. Of course, they're always holding boat shows or something on weekends in the Kingdome. Try that trash can, maybe I stuck it in there."

Collin got down off his stool and walked to the trashcan. He rummaged through, but found no newspaper. Nearer to the window than he'd been since the second building fell, he tried to resist looking out. But the temptation was too great. On the front yard of the second building lay a little boy, cold and unmoving. He walked back to his console and grabbed his cigarette pack, "Damn."

"Collin, we're on the air."

"Sorry, I forgot." He leaned closer to the mike and allowed his voice to override the Ham transmissions, "Sorry folks, but I'm down to my last cigarette. It's the little things, you know. I mean, the whole world is falling apart and I've only got one cigarette left."

"Collin!"

"Max, I got my rights. At a time like this, a man shouldn't have to do without the little things. I mean, how cruel is that anyway?"

"You're cracking up man."

"No I'm not. I'm just saying it's the little things. That's all. Hey, I just thought of something. You think the Prophet lived through this?" Suddenly, he drew in a sharp breath.

The earth was moving again.

THIS TIME JAMES AND Heather were close enough to Seattle to feel the strong aftershock, and James swerved just in time to keep from rear-ending a car. Yet for them, not far from the outskirts of Preston, the initial jolt of the 5.7 aftershock was more of an inconvenience. Just as other drivers did, he pulled to the side of the road and waited.

IN THE WINNINGHAM BLUE Building, Jenna screamed again and flew into Seely's arms. The earth rumbled and the enormous building once more screeched in agony, bouncing, twisting, turning, and wreathing.

Alone in the dark stairwell one floor up, Tim spent ten minutes climbing over large chunks of cement on the steps. The higher he went the more the devastation and he had only just made it to the door when it started. He quickly looked around for something secure to grab, but there was nothing, except the untrustworthy handrail and a doorknob. He grabbed the knob with one hand, sat down on a chunk of concrete, and scanned the frightening, shaking structure with the beam of his flashlight. Opposing walls appeared to be moving in different directions, shifting from side to side, while at the same time bouncing up and down. More concrete crumbled and fell, revealing larger areas of rebar. The air smelled of dust and the stairwell echoed deep, unnatural, guttural noises. Before it ended, the motion made him nauseous. He let go of the doorknob, laid the flashlight in his lap and held tight to his wrenching stomach.

AT KMPR, MAX AND COLLIN were back in the doorway. Neither man dared to look through the window. Instead, they tried to keep their heads bowed and their bodies steady. Just as it had before, the two story house shifted and hopped. Glass tinkled, books slid and the Amateur Radio moved closer to the edge of Collin's console.

NINETY-SEVEN BLOCKS north, Seely's daughter, Michelle, quickly pulled both children out of the back seat into the front. Wave after wave rolled the pavement under their parked car. Neighbors poured out of badly damaged houses, and before it stopped, Michelle's eyes filled with tears again, "Oh Momma, why did you go to work today? Please live, Momma...please."

SEELY'S HEART HAD BEGUN to hurt again. The wrenching pain contorted her face and she involuntarily clenched both fists.

Jenna struggled to open the purse and grab hold of the small bottle of pills. Urgently, she unscrewed the cap, reached in with two fingers, pulled out a tablet, and put into Seely's open mouth. When the aftershock stopped, Jenna found herself staring at Seely and still holding the open bottle.

SAM TAYLOR WAS MAD. The shock wave caught him by surprise and knocked him to the broken pavement. When the heaves diminished, he lifted his eyes to heaven and threw up his hands, "Enough, already! How much can these people take?" Instantly he was sorry for his outburst. He pulled his earphones off, bowed his head, and apologized.

Bone weary, Sam slowly got back up. Each block was beginning to look exactly like the last. His feet hurt, the empty canteen string cut into his neck, and now his butt hurt. Tenderly, he placed both hands on his rear end. Suddenly self-conscious, he quickly looked around. No one seemed to care. He walked another half a block, and then stopped. This time he made sure no one was watching before he hoisted himself onto the hood of an older model car. To his relief, no car alarm sounded.

In two hours, he'd covered only twenty blocks – twenty blocks of downed power lines, hurting people, backed up traffic, broken water mains, ruined homes, and unfriendly dogs. His white golf shoes were still new enough to cause blisters, so he took them off, examined the sore spots, and wiggled his toes. Thirsty, he set his shoes on the hood of the car and pulled the water bottle out of his pants pocket. He removed the lid and slowly drank, careful to conserve as much as possible.

Just then, his eyes focused on the green grass just beyond the bent chain link fence. It contained the usual broken and tilted slabs of earth with one exception. Beneath the dirt, and tilted on its side, was a silver object about six feet long and two feet wide – with handles. Sam's eyes grew huge. He quickly slipped his shoes back on, jumped down off the car, and shoved his bottle of water into his pocket. With renewed energy and great haste, he crossed the street, hurried down the sidewalk, and put as much distance as he could between himself and the Evergreen Cemetery.

"W7HEU."

"HEU, go ahead," Sarah said.

"The fissure closed, over."

"You get everybody out?"

"W7HEU, I think so, thanks to that chopper. Too late now if we didn't, over."

FROM HIS PERCH MID-way up the Magnolia Cliff, A7BB lightly bounced his body, testing the strength of the tree still holding him flush to the cliff. Next, he tried to gauge how far he'd slid in the last aftershock – two more feet, at least. Yet the massive root system and several top branches were covered with enough dirt to keep him from falling. Relieved, he tried to find the cat. It was nowhere in sight. He looked up just in time to see a good sized wave rock the Aircraft Carrier and race toward the shore. Seconds later it sent spraying water over recently accumulated wreckage. In Smith's Cove to his extreme left, a docked cargo ship filled with new cars from Japan was sideways, listing and rocking back and forth.

"Cat? Where are you cat?" With his free hand, he carefully moved a branch and looked straight down. To his relief, the cat was still on the board and closer to shore. But so were the bodies. Now, the body of a man lay in the water directly beneath him and the body of a woman was moving his way.

A7BB quickly turned his attention to other things. Lately, the loud clapping noise of multiple choppers filled the air, but just now, there were only two – one landing on the deck of the Aircraft Carrier and one waiting. So he concentrated on scanning the sky for the mysterious air crane. The closed fissure wasn't that far away and he hoped it would come for him next. When he spotted it, the basket was still attached to the undercarriage.

With growing anticipation, he lifted his free hand and waved, but the chopper quickly flew over him, crossed the Bay, and turned to hover high above the fire in West Seattle. When it started back, A7BB's eyes once more lit up. Again, he was disappointed. The air crane quickly disappeared behind the smoke of the downtown fire.

Suddenly, he noticed something wet dripping down the back of his neck. Cautiously, he twisted his body and turned his head. There, just barely visible out of the corner of his eye and sticking less than an inch out of the ground, was a small, broken sprinkler pipe. A7BB licked his lips. He turned back around and searched for some way to catch the water. Finally, he remembered the baseball cap still snugly on his head. Quickly, he flipped the cap off, held it behind his neck, and waited for the cool, luxurious drops of fresh water to collect.

# CHAPTER 16

STILL IN THE DARKENED stairwell, Tim stood up and tried the door to the forty-fourth floor. It was just as he expected—locked tight. When he heard the unmistakable sound of an approaching chopper, he grabbed the knob, put his shoulder to the door, and shoved hard. The door remained true to its lock, but its hinges were broken and it soon fell into a hallway identical to the one on the floor below.

He walked across the door, hurried down the debris filled hall, turned left, and made his way past the elevators. Instead of a conference room, this floor held two small offices, each void of furnishings. Tim rushed into the nearest one, and then stopped. The sound of the chopper was deafening, yet he couldn't see it. He eased forward, taking one cautious step at a time until he spotted the tips of the blades whirling below.

To no avail, he shouted into the noise, "Up here!"

For several minutes, the chopper kept its position opposite the forty-third floor where Jenna stood alone watching. Finally, it lifted until it hovered opposite Tim. It stayed for a time with its cameras clicking off a series of pictures, and then it turned sideways displaying the ID panel with tiny white lights. In bold black letters it read, "Go back down."

Reluctantly, Tim nodded. Inside the clear glass aft bubble, he spotted a man pointing down, so he nodded again, and only then did he notice a huge steel hook hanging from the undercarriage with a cable hanging down. He kept his eyes on the cable and waited while the chopper slowly lifted. At last, his expression turned to one of sheer joy. The cable was split into three lines, and inch by inch, a brown Balloon basket with a wide rubber rim appeared above the window's bottom ledge.

Tim quickly turned on his heels and went back into the dark, forbidding interior of the building.

WITH HER SHOES STILL off and a thick black cable extending through a hole in the floor behind her, Jackie softly spoke into her headset. "I was afraid they'd try to go up. Maybe we could drop a phone down the stairwell from the roof."

In the aft bubble, Michael's five o'clock shadow was beginning to show. "We just told him to go down. Let's go get that window washer off the Columbia Tower...if he's still alive."

Carl flew two blocks southwest, and then turned so the setting sun would not shine in Michael's eyes. From the belly of the air crane, the basket swung back and forth and in the street below, the tower's dark shattered glass glistened like black diamonds amid smashed furniture, broken cement and crushed cars. The man hanging from the ninetieth floor didn't seem to notice them. Still strapped in his safety harness, his legs were limp, his head was bowed, and right next to him, the scaffolding gently swayed in the breeze.

Jackie redirected camera three to get a better look, "Is he still alive?"

"I can't tell," Carl answered. "Wait, I think he moved his fingers."

She enlarged the picture and watched his hands until finally, his middle fingers moved again. "Poor guy, the straps have probably cut off his circulation. Let's bring the basket up under him."

Cautiously, Carl moved the chopper closer while Michael maneuvered levers in an attempt to minimize the basket's swing. Still, for the better part of five minutes, the balloon basket swayed back and forth, once striking its rubber rim against the building and bouncing away. At last, it dangled directly below the man, swaying only slightly in the wind.

Carefully, Michael eased the basket up. Abruptly, the earth once more rumbled. Both the scaffolding and the man began to jiggle and soon, each started an exaggerated sway. In horror, Michael watched the man use his last ounce of strength to grab hold of the basket cable. At the same time, the already frayed scaffolding safety lines scraped across the edge of the Columbia Tower roof. Suddenly, the first one snapped throwing the metal plank into a diamond shaped spin. Closer and closer it came to the window washer, its sharp upper corner aimed at his head. A fifth of a second later, the remaining line wore through and the scaffolding hurled downward. It shot through the bottom of the basket and for a moment, the falling cables wrapped around the basket's rim. When they uncurled, the scaffolding fell ninety floors to the street below.

Jackie held her breath. Now pointed straight down, camera two showed a terrified, trembling man at the end of a jagged rope. His grip on the basket cable was the only thing keeping him from falling. "Hurry you guys!"

Carl instantly moved the chopper up until the basket cleared the top of the building, and then maneuvered the swinging passenger toward the center of the roof. Inside the chopper, the cable spun over a pulley in the ceiling, turned toward the tail section, crossed a second pulley, and then shot downward and wrapped around a spinning four-foot spool. Finally, the cable stopped moving and Michael released his seat belt. He opened the aft door and hopped down on the roof. To his amazement, the earth was still moving.

Jackie grabbed a set of goggles, put them on, turned, and opened the chopper body door. Wind from the whirling blades whipped her hair while the steps unfolded from below. She too threw off her seat belt and hurried down. Working as fast as possible, she helped Michael unhook the safety rope, pry the man's hands off the cable and lift him into the chopper. While Jackie got back in her seat, retracted the steps and closed the door, Michael strapped the window washer into a passenger seat. Already, Carl was lifting away, dragging the damaged basket across the roof of the swaying building.

For several long moments, fractured nerves kept each of them silent. At last, Michael spoke, "Did you feel it? I bet that building was leaning twenty feet each way."

"Yes, I felt it." Jackie's hands trembled, but she managed to remove her goggles and put her headset back on.

Well away from the building and headed over the bay, Carl glanced through the aft bubble at their passenger. "Is he okay?"

"I don't know," Jackie answered.

"He's probably in shock. Saw a lot of guys in Nam like that. Michael, see if you can loosen his safety jacket and don't be surprised if he takes a swing at you. He's probably pretty fond of that jacket by now."

JUST BEFORE TIM GARTON stepped back into the cold clammy stairwell, he cupped his hands around his mouth and yelled, "Anybody here?" He waited, but no one answered. In the law offices of Hadley and White on the forty-fourth floor, no one ever worked on Saturday.

He made his way down the cement littered stairs, crossed the landing, and then darted into the hallway where Seely and Jenna were waiting, "That chopper's got a basket."

"We know, Jenna saw it." Seely turned the radio off and offered Tim the jug of water.

Sitting with her arms tightly folded, Jenna narrowed her eyes, "You're not getting me in a basket. No way! Besides, how come they're so interested in us? Don't they have anybody else to save?"

Seely reached for Tim's hand and let him help her up. "Jenna, you're acting like a child. Come on, they'll come back and we won't be there."

"I am a child, I'm only seventeen."

"I thought you were twenty," said Tim.

"I lied!"

"Okay then, you're seventeen going on twelve," Tim snapped. He took Seely's hand and led the way down the hall. But when he sensed her slowing, he stopped and turned around. "You alright?"

"I'll manage. It's just that I don't hear a chopper, at least not one that's very close and I'm terrified of leaving this hallway."

Tim walked on, pausing occasionally to scoot rubbish aside with his feet. "We don't have much choice if we want to get out of here. Are you getting tired?"

"Well, it takes a lot of strength to live through an earthquake and a heart attack all in one day. Let's just get this over with."

A couple of feet past the elevators, Tim stopped. "Stay here, I'll go see if I can spot the chopper. When she nodded, he went on, walked as far as he dared into the damaged conference room, and then slowly scanned the sky with his eyes. In the distance, he could see two black choppers hovering off the bow of the Aircraft Carrier. But no blue air crane. Finally he heard its distinctive thud and glanced back just as Seely walked up with her arm around Jenna.

It appeared from the north and already the air crane was turned sideways with its ID panel lit up. "Lost basket." The words disappeared and a new sentence scrolled in from the right, "Do you have water?"

Tim took another step forward and nodded.

In the air crane, Jackie got a close up of Seely's bruised face and tired eyes. She moved her mouth piece closer and asked, "What should I tell them?"

Back in his aft bubble seat, Michael answered, "Tell them to stay where they are."

She typed the words, and then turned to stare at him, "Now what, Michael?"

"We can't do anything more tonight. We have no equipment, we need more fuel, and our passenger needs a doctor. Besides, we've been up since the crack of dawn and tired people have accidents."

"Okay." Reluctantly, Jackie typed a final word, "Sleep."

Below, Tim stared at the chopper until it became little more than a speck in the sky, "Easy for them to say." He turned back and forced a grin, "Look on the bright side, a little sleep is just what we need."

Nearly in tears, Seely walked back toward the elevators.

"A7BB."

"BB, go ahead."

"Sarah, that blue chopper lost its basket. Darn, I was hoping they'd head my way, over."

"How did they lose the basket, BB?"

"I don't know, it just fell into the bay. The cable must have snapped. A7BB, out."

"NS7OPG."

"OPG, go ahead."

"NS7OPG we have a child with no parents. First name is Benny. He says he is three and doesn't know what his last name is or where he lives, over."

"Net Control, copy. One found child named Benny. Where are you OPG?"

"NS7OPG. I'm in Wallingford. We have severe damage to houses, traffic pile-ups, and water everywhere. Thirty-two reported dead so far and we're still digging. We have injured waiting for transport, but none critical. Man, we've got a lot of broken bones and people are in pain. We have one registered nurse and no supplies, over."

"OPG, copy. Give me a cross street."

"NS7OPG, I'm at 65th and Corliss Avenue right near Green Lake ... or what used to be Green Lake. Most folks around here got the lake in their yards, over."

"Roger OPG, don't forget to take names. Injured in need of transport at 65th and Corliss. Okay, I think A7FL is next. FL, you still at the I-5 landslide?"

"A7FL, affirmative. It's hopeless, just hopeless. Like I said, it's a forty-foot concrete drop. We can't get down and they can't get up. People are out of their cars and helping where they can, but that metro bus is a pancake. I've never seen anything so awful in my life. One guy tried to make it up the landslide and got himself buried. Is there any help coming—any help at all? Over."

"I hope so FL. They're trying to clear Highway 99 for emergency traffic."

"Ninety-nine? But that's clear across the city."

"I know FL, keep us posted. Who's next?"

"NV7HC."

"HC, go ahead."

"NV7HC, we have a live power line down on 34th NW, between Woodland Park Avenue and Stone Way, over."

"Net Control, copy. Jerry, do you know if they've taken care of that gas leak in your area? Over."

"NV7HC, not sure. Don't smell any gas here. Over."

"NB7J."

"NB, go ahead."

"NB7J, somebody must have gotten the gas turned off in Freemont. Don't smell it anymore. They're still working on the draw-bridge and hope to get it in the down position soon. Sarah, I checked on Tom Hansen. He's cut up pretty bad, over."

"NB, copy. Sorry to hear it, we sure could use his help. Anyone else? Injury and damage only please."

THE CLOSER TO THE CITY Sam got, the worse it was. Six miles from downtown, the homes were in shambles. Now choppers and small aircraft passed overhead more frequently. Dogs barked, cats meowed and birds chirped, but car alarms were silent. No televisions blared, no music played, and dazed, stunned parents kept children outside and close at hand. Some people wore tear-stained cheeks and blank looks. Others stayed near car radios listening to the news. No one drove far on the broken and battered streets. And in a city used to sirens, the lack of them upset their sense of security.

Sam Taylor stared at the broken water main sticking out of the ground. The street was flooded at yet another intersection. To avoid it, he found himself walking back an entire block, and then heading toward fifteenth – a more direct route to his bank and the Ballard Bridge. On he walked, the unthinkable damage dulling his senses and the steady blare of Ham Operators filling his earphones.

"WD7GK."

"GK, go ahead."

"WD7GK passing a message from AX7MNB. Be advised the Everett Mall Way overpass collapsed. Thorndike Memorial Hospital is in pretty good shape and can take more casualties. Everett Salvation Army is mobilizing in City Hall Park, over."

Sarah laid her pencil down, closed her eyes, and rested. Her bottle of water was empty and her ceiling was sinking lower, but soon she went right back to work, "Copy that NJ. Who's next?"

"KH7TDY"

"TDY, go ahead."

"KH7TDY, a freight train derailed in Carkeek Park. We have one injury and no deaths, over."

"Copy TDY."

TIM AND JENNA MOVED the door away and cleared enough space on the hall carpet for all three to lie down. For pillows, Jenna found forgotten coats and sweaters still hanging in a closet and for entertainment, they turned the radio back on.

Seely made herself as comfortable as possible and tried to close her eyes. But waiting for the next aftershock unnerved her, the floor was too hard and everything hurt no matter what position she was in. So she sat back up, laid the radio in her lap, and leaned against the insulation.

Exhausted, Jenna stacked broken tiles, sat down and stared into space while Tim made it his business to survey the supplies in the earthquake kit.

For the third time in less than ten minutes, Jenna looked at her watch and sighed. Too soon, the sunlight was beginning to fade. She changed her position again and began picking at her nail polish. "Seely, you really should try to sleep."

Seely turned the radio down and smiled, "I can't seem to relax enough."

Tim chuckled, "I know what you mean. I had the same problem in the men's room. You know you got to go, and then you realize every muscle in your body is as tight as a drum. It takes real concentration to relax after an earthquake."

"What we need is a bottle," Jenna snickered.

Tim's eyes instantly lit up. He grabbed a flashlight and started to rise, "Why didn't I think of that?"

"I'm as shocked as you are," Jenna teased. "Where are you going?"

"Guess."

"Paul's office?"

Seely's mouth suddenly dropped, "Paul? Our very own Paul McGill keeps booze at the office?"

Tim's voice was already fading down the hall, "You didn't hear that from me."

Jenna giggled and brushed blond hair out of her eyes, "You mean you never smelled it on his breath?"

"Only on Thursdays." Seely winked and struggled to bend one knee. "Ouch."

"Want some help?"

"No Darling, I'm just trying to work some of the soreness out. Want to hear something funny?"

"What?"

"Well, after that big fight Paul and I had over the earthquake kit, he bought a ten million dollar earthquake insurance policy."

"No kidding?"

Seely slowly bent the other leg and tried not to moan, "Guess who makes the payments?"

"His wife."

"Right, but she's not the beneficiary. His son by his first wife...the one he just made partner, gets the whole thing?"

"That slime ball."

Bottle in hand, Tim soon made his way back, "Who's a slime ball?"

It was Jenna who answered, "Paul. He bought a ten million dollar policy and made his son the beneficiary."

"In that case, I'm changing my name to McGill." He sat down, grinned and handed Seely a full bottle of vodka.

"Um, my favorite."

Jenna wrinkled her brow and glared at Seely, "Christians aren't supposed to drink."

"Sugar, we're Christians not saints. We have to die before we get perfect." With that, she handed the bottle back to Tim. "You're the guy, you open it."

Aimlessly, Jenna gazed at the ceiling, "I wonder what ten million dollars feels like. I'd never have to worry about my bills again and I could spend all I wanted next time I went shopping. Just once, I'd like to know what that feels like."

"I'm sure it's quite nice," Seely answered. "But sometimes wealth is a curse. It doesn't make Paul happy, his wife hates him, and his son is a spoiled brat."

Tim unscrewed the lid on the bottle and reached inside the earthquake kit for paper cups, "A spoiled brat with ten million dollars."

"True, but money can be more of a curse than a blessing, especially a lot of money."

Jenna's legs ached, the bruise on her face was a deep purple and her bones hurt. Even so, she picked up on Seely's comment, "You talk like you know."

"Well, I've been around a little. I'm old, remember."

"Come to think of it, I've never heard you talk about money. You don't even complain on payday. Are you rolling in it?"

Seely laughed, "Would I be working for Paul McGill if I was?"

Only half listening to their chatter, Tim set three paper cups on the floor, carefully poured, and then lifted each to gage the amount. "Hey, I just thought of something. Isn't a little booze good for bad hearts?"

"That's what I've always heard." Seely grinned, accepted the paper cup and took a slow soothing sip. Instantly, warmth spread throughout her body.

Tim handed a drink to Jenna and sat back down. "So, what should we do about the money?"

Confused, both women asked at the same time, "What money?"

"The cool thirty thousand Paul keeps in the vault. We can't just leave it here. I mean, who would be fool enough to come back for it? They'll condemn this building and all that cold, hard cash will come crashing down when they implode it."

Jenna set her cup down, folded her arms and stretched her legs out straight, "Oh no you don't. I'm not going back out there. Certainly not for Paul McGill's money."

"Who says it's his money?"

"You mean steal it?" Seely asked. "Timmy, we can't..."

"Maybe you can't, but I can. I've got a wife to take care of. Think of it as unemployment benefits. After all, our jobs are trashed and old Paul won't pay our wages while he rebuilds. Besides, if he recovered the money, he would have to claim it on his insurance. He would hate that."

"Yes, but it's dangerous out there," Jenna said.

"I'm not asking you to go with me. The problem is, I don't know the combination."

Seely looked into Tim's searching eyes a moment, and then turned her gaze downward. "Zip code."

"The combination is our zip code? Hot dog!"

# CHAPTER 17

COLLIN TOOK A LONG drag on his last cigarette, and then put it out. The early evening air was cooling and the sun no longer beat down through the damaged roof. Although the advent of night was foreboding, the lack of heat was a relief. Between calls, and right on time, he lifted the microphone and gave KMPR's frequency. He briefly reviewed his list of instructions, adding the number of dead across the street. It hadn't changed in an hour. Those most easily saved had already been pulled out, and without equipment the tired, overburdened workers moved slowly or not at all. Finally, he laid the mike back down next to the Amateur Radio speaker.

Something was wrong. Sarah's usually cheerful and calm voice sounded on edge, "SK, what is your location?"

"AV7SK. I'm on 16th Avenue east, over."

"SK, we need a cross street. Come on people, I've got eight calls backed up here."

Max instantly stuck his head through the adjoining window. "What's wrong with her?"

Collin shrugged and listened.

"SK, we've just had a major earthquake. I don't think anybody cares if traffic is backed up on Capitol Hill. Traffic is backed up everywhere, over."

"Sarah, I'm trying to tell you we've got a huge sink hole. Over."

Second after second ticked by before Sarah answered. This time her voice sounded as though she were near tears, "I'm sorry SK. I guess I'm getting a little tired. Can you give me the cross street again, I didn't get it written down, over."

At first, Max softly whispered, "This is not like Sarah at all. Something's seriously wrong. We need to go get her."

Collin eased off his stool and walked to the control room window, "Go get her? Where?"

"Next door."

"Right next door? I didn't know that. You want me to bring her up here?"

Max raised his voice a little and stood up, "No. I want you to mind the station. I'll get her this far, then you can carry her up the stairs. Deal?"

"I don't know how to work the controls."

Max hobbled around the corner into the studio and grinned, "Good. Don't touch anything. I'll yell when I get her this far." He headed for the door, and then abruptly stopped. This time his voice came across loud and clear, "On the other hand, I'll have to take Net Control. You go get her."

Collin rolled his eyes and headed out the door, "Isn't that what I just said?"

"And don't drop her. She can't walk, you know."

"I won't drop her." This time it was Collin who grinned, already starting his descent down the first flight of stairs. "We're still on the air, you know."

Max spun around and stared at the black microphone on Collin's console.

"WC7NJT."

Sarah didn't answer. Instead, tears streamed down her cheeks and her eyes were glued to her sagging ceiling. Tortured wood began to creak and groan as the duplex apartment attempted to settle on its mangled and broken foundation. And with it, her ceiling moved—slipping lower and lower.

"WC7NJT."

At last, she recognized the Mayor's office call sign, forgot her troubles, and instantly perked up, "NJT, how nice of you to call, Mister Mayor."

"It's me again Sarah, the underpaid public servant, better known as the hapless messenger. I have a word from the President, over."

"The president of what, the Mayor's yacht club? Over."

"WC7NJT. No, the President of the United States. Shall I go on? Over."

"Is this an election year? Over."

If he had listened, he would have heard the cracking and popping in the background when Sarah spoke. But he wasn't listening. "This is WC7NJT. Sarah, I know you're tired. We're all tired. The President sends his regards and wants us to know he's doing everything possible to help, over."

"Help? He can't help us, no one can. We're dying Mister President. We're trapped, we're all alone and we're dying. We..." She stopped talking when she heard someone yank open her dislodged front door. "Who's there?"

Collin carefully eased through the half opened doorway and looked around. Sarah sat near the end of the living room with the sagging ceiling not more than a foot above her head. Horrified, he bent down and shot across the cracked hardwood floor, nearly slipping in a puddle of wet, soggy fish tank water. "We've got to get you out of here. Max, if you can hear me, take the Net. Sarah's roof is collapsing." He grabbed hold of the back of her wheelchair and pulled. But the wedged doorstopper held it firmly in place. The building groaned louder and in a panic, Collin shoved his arms under her and lifted her out of the chair. Her 96 pounds were lighter than he expected, and he easily spun around and headed back across the room.

Next door, Max held his breath. With Sarah's radio still transmitting, he could hear the ripping and tearing of over-strained metal and wood. The ceiling gave way with a resounding crash and the apartment sounded as though it was ripping in two. After that, there was silence.

All across America, strangers sat glued to their radios or televisions. Worried commentators glanced at production managers, and then began whispering into microphones, "Ladies and Gentlemen, it seems all we can do now is wait. For the last few hours, Sarah, a lady whose last name we don't even know, has filled our lives and our imaginations with the graphic details of Seattle's growing tragedy. Bound to a wheelchair, Sarah's calm and steady voice kept others calm and steady, preventing the panic of dozens of Ham Operators in the Seattle area. Now, we wait.

At approximately 4:26 this afternoon, Seattle suffered a catastrophic earthquake measuring 9.2 on the Richter scale. It is believed that the 1964 Alaska quake measured 9.2. However, the Alaska quake occurred long before accurate measuring devices were in place and the exact magnitude is unknown. How well I remember the first pictures of damage coming out of Anchorage, and it is important to note that Anchorage is nearly eighty miles north of the underwater epicenter. A quake of equal strength may well have left Washington State's entire western slope in ruins."

MAX COULDN'T HEAR THE commentators nor imagine an entire country, maybe even the world, listening to the events unfolding in his small, upstart radio station. Instead, he nervously waited for each endless second to pass. Becoming impatient, he glanced around, but the only window in the attic faced the wrong direction. When AJ7OMR called in, Max ignored it. For the first time since the quake, he was alone, waiting and listening with countless others who held their collective breaths.

Just when Max could wait no more, got up and started across the room – the downstairs front door banged open and Collin yelled, "I got her!"

SEELY, TIM, AND JENNA missed all of Sarah's excitement. Instead, they sat on the forty-third floor with the radio off. When the building shuddered, Jenna's eyes darted all around, waiting to see if it was just the building or if the earth was moving. Just as abruptly it stopped. Several seconds passed before she began to breathe easier.

This time, Seely didn't panic. Her eyes were closed and she had a peaceful look on her face. A dull pain still ached in her chest, but it did not increase. "Let's talk about something else. Jenna, where do you think your Mom and sister are right now?"

"Mom didn't mention any special plans this morning. Oh Seely, was it just this morning? It seems like weeks ago."

"I know. Go on, what about your sister?"

"She planned to play tennis with a friend this afternoon. We live near a park with tennis courts and she's really quite good for only twelve. I'm not too worried about them; the houses in our neighborhood are fairly new. I wish we could call, though. Don't you have a cell phone?"

Tim was sitting on his tailbone with his knees up to his chin and his cup half empty. "Cell phones are out just like regular phones."

"Yes, but maybe they'll come back on. I know, maybe we can find one in one of the offices."

"Good idea." Seely said. "Turn the radio back on, will you? Maybe they'll say something about cell phones. In LA, I didn't have a radio when the earthquake struck, and I had no way of knowing what was happening in the rest of the world. I think that frightened me more than the quake. ...That's funny."

Jenna reached for the small radio and began stretching the antenna upward, "What?"

"Well, that earthquake scared me so bad. I've lived in fear of another one for years, but that one was a walk in the park compared to this."

The earth began to move again. Tiles shifted, glass clinked and exposed wiring swung back and forth, but it was a small aftershock and the Winningham Blue Building held. When it stopped, all three heaved a sigh of relief and Tim headed straight for the men's room.

"A7BB, HOW DO YOU READ?"

"Hey Max, is that you?"

"Yeah buddy, you alright? Over."

"A7BB, good as gold. If I keep slipping a little bit with each aftershock, I should be able to walk out of this tree in a mere three or four days. By the way, I found some drinkable water, over."

"BB, good for you. Can you give us a report? Over."

"A7BB, not much changed. The fire downtown is still burning and I count more dead bodies floating in the water. Must be from that ferry. The good news is we've got more choppers coming in. They're starting to get thick as thieves. By the way, did I tell you the Canadians have arrived? I just love Canada. Think I'll move there...if I ever get off this cliff, over."

"BB, what about the cat?"

"This is A7BB, let me get back to you on that. I'm having trouble spotting her, over."

"Copy BB. Okay, who's next?"

"KJ7DRF emergency."

"DRF, go ahead."

"KJ7DRF, we've got a near riot over here at Clifton Hardware. Are police available yet?"

"DRF, what kind of riot?"

"Owner's trying to sell flashlights for $50.00 each and $10.00 extra per battery. I think they're going to kill the man. KJ7DRF, over."

"Copy DRF. Anybody in touch with Seattle Police?" Max waited several seconds for an answer. Finally one came.

"A7SPD, Seattle Police here. We've got our hands full with injuries. Suggest you use fire extinguishers or stay clear of the area. What is that location again? Over."

"This is WJ7DRF, I'm at 15th NW and 100th place, over."

Max waited, but when no one spoke, he leaned closer to the mike, "Roger DRF. Did you get that Seattle Police? Over."

"Roger Net Control. Thanks. A7SPD, out."

Max took a long, deep breath, "Good to hear from you Seattle Police. Okay, who's next?"

"WJ7V."

"WJ, go ahead."

"We just got help at the Department Store. I don't know how he got through, but that guy at the Construction Company made it, and he brought two crews. The little girl is still buried, but she's alive. Her name is Charlie and now she says her stomach hurts. We sure could use a Doctor. Is Sarah hurt? WJ7V, over."

"Negative, WJ. She's sitting here on the floor telling me what to do just like always. Soon as we get her a chair, I'll gladly give this job back. Who's up next?"

SAM TAYLOR SUDDENLY stopped in the middle of the road. Fifteenth NW and 100th place couldn't be that far away. Cautiously, he approached a bent street sign and tipped his head to read the numbers.105th—only five more blocks. Squinting his eyes, he tried to look down 15<sup>th</sup>, but another of Seattle's rolling hills kept him from a full view of the hardware store and the flashlight crisis. 100th place had to be just over the next ridge. He grinned and walked on.

A7BB MOVED THE BRANCHES of the tree one way, and then the other, trying to spot the cat. He couldn't see it, even amid the bodies and the mounting slabs of broken wood gathering along the shore. At length, he gave up and searched for the blue air crane instead. The sky seemed filled with choppers now, flying over the city or bringing precious cargo to the Aircraft Carrier, but none of them were blue. The noise of one coming in soon became overwhelming, so A7BB held his radio closer to one ear, and then covered the other ear with his free hand. It didn't help.

A chopper flying low over downtown quickly peeled away and headed across Elliott Bay. Behind it, another banked and turned the same direction. A7BB followed both with his eyes. The Bremerton fire, where the Navy housed its weapons at a massive shipyard, looked larger. He watched for a long time, but Bremerton was too far away to see details, so he turned his attention back to his Ham Radio.

"N7UES."

"UES, go ahead," Max answered.

"Roosevelt Hospital here. Any ETA on that blood? Over."

"On its way Doc. Red Cross reports 300 units of "O" positive coming from Portland with another 200 units out of LA. Will advise as soon as it arrives. Over."

"N7UES, copy. We're nearly out of sutures and bandages. Over."

"Roger UES, sutures and bandages needed at Roosevelt Hospital."

TIM WAS IN THE KITCHENETTE trying to determine the best way to get to the vault when he heard a chopper. In fact, he heard several. Downtown was becoming a sea of them and as he ventured as close as he dared to an outside window, he tried to read the markings. "A Portland News chopper. How about that, the press finally heard about our little disaster. I bet they're getting some great pictures. Wish I were home, in front of my TV watching."

As soon as the chopper disappeared, he went back to finding the easiest way to the vault. It stood with its door closed against the far wall and to his relief, not that much debris blocked the path. He stepped out of the kitchenette and started toward it.

Behind him, Jenna stood with her hands on her hips, "I'm not going to rescue you again, Timmy."

"Not even for half? That's fifteen thousand. Think about it Jenna, you and Kevin could have a great honey moon with fifteen thousand."

NE7G WAS A TALL, THIN man with dark hair, and the only Ham reporting in from downtown Seattle. Injuries received when his car plunged off the I-5 freeway included a broken rib, multiple contusions, abrasions, and a long, superficial cut on the front of his upper right leg. Cautiously, he leaned down, moved his torn pant leg and checked the butterfly bandages. They were still in place.

Well away from shopping districts and buildings higher than one floor, South Royal Street was deserted. Huge chunks of pavement and sidewalk jutted in odd directions, yet little debris lay on top. Across the street, one end of Safeco Field's black, iron, and steel retractable roof lay buried in the roof of a warehouse. The other end lay flat on the ground, crushing two adjoining warehouses beneath it. Cautiously, NE7G made his way another two blocks down the street, toward the thick outside walls of the black baseball stadium. Then he paused to listen. He heard no screams, no yells for help and no moans coming from inside.

Relieved, he walked another torturous block to the Kingdome's massive parking lot. It was empty. Again he heaved a sigh of relief. The Kingdome's white circular dome sat only one forth as high as it had before the quake, its ribbed roof was cracked in odd directions with some sections missing and some higher than others. NE7G turned and headed down the street, toward both the old and new railroad stations.

"A7FL."

"FL, go ahead." Max was completely engrossed in the Ham Radio, forgetting about the control room and enjoying himself immensely.

On the floor beside him, Sarah sat with her arms folded watching. Her disheveled dark hair hung in her face, her crystal green eyes flashed with mischief and deep dimples appeared in her cheeks. Too soft for the public to hear, she whispered, "Hey Handsome, who's going to take me to the bathroom?"

Max winced and rolled his eyes, "A7FL, could you repeat that?"

"We got a visit from that blue Angel. They dropped a harness and some ropes. At least now we can get the injured kids to a hospital. Does anybody know who those guys are? A7FL. Over."

"We don't have a clue, over."

"Well, whoever they are, they deserve a medal. A7FL, out."

"AE7VW."

"AE, go ahead."

"AE7VW relaying a message from Spokane. Seven fully loaded trucks in a convoy are headed your way. They're bringing blankets, food, diapers, and medical supplies. Estimated time of arrival, midnight, over."

"Copy AE. Tell them not to take Interstate 90, its out."

"Roger Net Control. They'll take it to Preston, and then swing south on Highway 18 and try to come in through Renton. Meanwhile, we've got Army transports with supplies due to land at Paine Field in Everett. The runway has damage and they're assessing it now. If we can't land, we'll try for one of the military bases, AE7VW, over."

"Copy AE. We can use all the good news we can get." Max rested both arms on Collin's console, smiled and turned to Sarah, "I've forgotten how much I enjoyed the net. I should do this more often."

Sarah brushed her hair aside and smiled, "Yes you should. We've missed you." She turned to watch as Collin carried an armchair through the door, "Oh there you are handsome. Put that chair right in Max's way, will you? I'm anxious to get back to work. They can't live without me, you know."

"I know." Collin waited for Max to get up, moved his stool, and then set the sturdy wooden armchair in front of the radio.

When he bent down, Sarah wrapped her arms around his neck, "Careful handsome, don't drop me."

"Why is everyone always saying that?" He lifted her up, set her down in the chair, and scooted it forward, "I've never dropped a woman in my life."

Sarah giggled and grabbed the pencil, "Okay, this is Sarah. I'm back, and if you think you've got it bad, you should be up in this attic with these two guys. Who's next? Over."

Collin heard pounding footsteps on the stairs below, and turned just in time to watch a man rush up the last flight.

Drawing in huge gulps of air, the horrified man grabbed hold of Collin's shirt, "You gotta help. We...lifted a slab of concrete off a woman's arm...and it's nearly tore off. Now we can't stop the bleeding. And, she's got blood coming out her ears. She's gonna...bleed to death."

Collin spun around and stared at Sarah, but Sarah was already on it.

"This is net control emergency. We've got a woman with a severed arm, and possible head injuries at the collapsed building across the street from KMPR, over."

"KG7SD."

"SD, go ahead."

"KG7SD, University Hospital. Sarah, have they got a tourniquet on the arm? Over."

Sarah glanced at the man just as he began to nod, "Roger SD."

"Tell him to keep it tight. We'll send the next available chopper. KG7SD, out."

"Copy SD, thanks. Okay, who's next?" When Sarah turned, the man was gone.

FROM HIS CLIFF, A7BB watched a man and woman in white jackets on the Aircraft Carrier quickly climb into a chopper, but just as the deck crew started to close the sliding side door, a man in dress whites rushed forward. He handed a box to the woman, and then stood back. Almost immediately, the chopper lifted off. With its door still open, the chopper glided across the Bay, climbing as it went up the southern slope of Queen Anne Hill.

"A7BB."

Sarah grinned, "BB, go ahead."

"I think you're about to get your medics. Don't be surprised if it gets a little noisy, over."

"Thanks, BB. We can hear it now."

# CHAPTER 18

STANDING IN THE MIDDLE of McGill Accounting's main room, Tim judged the distance to the safe—a good thirty feet. Most of the room's belongings were piled on the east side where the last sway left them, but the built-in vault remained along the outside southern wall. Only two medium-sized heaps of rubble blocked a direct path. He estimated the best way around, considered the sturdiness of the floor and quickly glanced back at Jenna. Then he shrugged, "I'm probably going to die anyway."

With thin red lines marking the multitude of glass cuts on his face and the wind ruffling his short, red hair, he quickly dashed across the room, side-stepped the first, and then the second heap. He reached the vault, pounded in the five-digit zip code and pulled on the handle. But his hand met cold, hard resistance. "Crap, no electricity."

Tim turned around, marched back to the kitchenette, and started down the hall, "Come on Jenna, this is definitely not my lucky day."

JACKIE WAS EXHAUSTED. The window washer, securely strapped into the first passenger seat, still hadn't said a word. Seely's heart rate held steady on the monitor, but the images of her bruised and swollen face were hard to look at. And just now, camera three was trained on a news chopper giving chase.

In the aft bubble, Michael released his seat belt and climbed into the copilot's seat to hide his face behind tinted windows, "Looks like we've been discovered, Jackie. You got our ID up?"

"Yes, in Russian. Slow down and let them have a peek, Carl."

Carl grinned, "Give 'em my ex-wife's phone number too. She can tell them all about the drug company."

Jackie laughed. She watched the news chopper make one complete circle around them, and then held on while Carl sharply banked and darted northeast. She glanced back at her passenger, noticed the red light flashing on the corner of the lower right hand screen and quickly answered, "Mister Cole, I nearly forgot about you."

"How is she? I'm out of my mind with worry."

"She's doing pretty well, all things considered. She walked around a little more and her heart rate is steady. She's with two other people and they've got water. Did you make the arrangements?"

Evan Cole stood in front of sliding glass windows in the top floor honeymoon suite of a Vancouver, British Columbia hotel, "Everything is all set. I've reserved several rooms, the hotel has a landing pad on the roof, and the Canadians are more than willing to help with all the equipment and fuel you need."

"Good. We've got a passenger to drop..."

"I know. I've been watching pictures of the rescue on TV. They're calling you the Blue Angel."

Jackie puffed her cheeks and let out a slow breath, "Oh great. Evan, can you make sure the press doesn't get in the hotel? What we need most is rest."

"Consider it done," he replied.

"Have you found Loraine?"

"No. No one seems to know where she is. However, my bank called. They said she claimed the foundation's checkbook had been lost and asked to have all twenty-two million transferred to a new account."

"Do you think she's taken off with the money?"

"That was my first thought. She could easily have done that, but she didn't touch a dime. Instead, she put the new account in my name only."

AS SOON AS THE NOISE of the Navy chopper increased, Max turned the station's broadcast volume way down. Sarah covered her ears while Max and Collin went to the window to watch. The cluttered street offered no place to land, so the chopper hovered and lowered a stretcher.

Two short minutes later, the injured woman was put in a boat shaped stretcher and hoisted into the chopper. However, just before it flew away, the woman medic tossed a box out the open door. On the ground, the same man who'd come to tell KMPR about the injury picked it up and turned it over. He looked toward Max and Collin, and then waved.

"I'll go," Collin said, heading for the door. "Hey Max, from here on out you're paying me double time, right?"

Max winked at Sarah and hobbled back to the control room. He turned the appropriate dials, renewed the station to its normal broadcasting volume, and eased his broken foot back up on the stacked books under his console.

Sarah went right to work. She took two more calls, wrote down the pertinent information, and then asked for the next. When she glanced up, Collin was back on his stool, preparing to take the mike for his next station break. Just before he did, he handed her the white cardboard box tied with a pink ribbon.

First she stared at her name written across the top, and then she went back to her caller, "OT, copy. Minor injuries at west Emerson and 15th avenue. W7KS, you're up next, over." Sarah slipped the ribbon off the end of the box and opened the lid. Inside were three sandwiches, three bottles of water, and one long stemmed, red rose. Sarah curled her lips into a wide grin; her eyes twinkled like diamonds and the dimples in her cheeks had never been deeper. "Roger, KS. Keep me advised. And by the way, thanks Navy, over."

Collin grinned, took the station microphone, and began his station break. "This is KMPR, 760 AM in Seattle. The noise you just heard was a Navy chopper air lifting our seriously injured woman from the collapsed buildings across the street. Hundreds, maybe thousands are still buried alive. Some help has arrived, but we're way short of equipment and manpower. Night is closing in and frankly, I've never felt so useless. I'd rather be out there digging, but Max says our job is to stay on the air and help the living by directing them to food and water. So the following is a list of places the Salvation Army and The Red Cross are setting up. "Abraham Cook High School, Broadmoor Golf Course, City Hall in Everett..."

He ran down the short list, renewed his survival instructions for the night, and then paused to glance at Sarah's rose. "There is one bright spot in all this gloom. Our friends aboard the USS Carl Vincent sent us something to eat and Sarah got a rose. We're glad she made it out alive too. Only next time guys, could you send a pizza and a pack of cigarettes?" Collin quickly glanced at Max's disapproving glower, smiled, and laid the mike next to the Ham Radio.

TIM CHUCKLED AT COLLIN's remarks, and then turned the transistor radio down, "I used to smoke, I know just what he's going through."

"Well I for one am glad you don't smoke now," Seely said.

"I'm not. I could use something right about now to steady my nerves and I know a lot of cranky people who ought to take it up."

Seely smiled, but Jenna looked disturbed, "What if they don't come back for us?"

"Why wouldn't they?" Tim asked.

"What if they crash, everything else has."

"You worry too much, Jenna. If it doesn't come back, we'll just climb down the side of the Mainland Tower."

Seely frowned, "The one that fell into us? Climb down it how?"

"Well, last time I looked it was at an angle, you know like this." Tim held a flattened hand straight up, and then tipped it a little.

Jenna's jaw dropped, "But that's almost straight up and down. Climb it with what? We don't have any ropes."

"See, that's why it's important to watch movies. We've got fire hoses, Jenna."

"Long enough to climb down a whole building?"

"Well, movies don't tell you everything." Tim scratched his head and glanced at Seely. "You got a better idea?"

Seely softly shook her head.

"Okay, that settles it. Let's eat, then I'll go take another look outside."

But Jenna quickly grabbed hold of Tim's arm. "Oh no, I'm not climbing down the side of a building in the dark. And we sure can't do it before night."

Tim thought for a minute, and then shrugged. "In that case, we can eat slower."

"BB, YOU FIND THAT CAT? Over."

"Not exactly, the cat found me. Can you believe it? It climbed the cliff and is sitting on my shoulder. Guess it didn't have much choice since there's no place else to go from the water. I thought you might like a little update on the fire downtown. The wind is starting to shift, so don't be surprised if you get a little smoke your way. Wait, I got another chopper headed straight for me." With that, A7BB released his speak button. Overhead, a red and white news chopper slowed. Its nose was pointed directly at him and a passenger was half hanging out the side door with a large camera on his shoulder.

At first A7BB considered his potential fame and the possibility of being rescued. A lot of people were listening to Magnolia's Network of Hams, via KMPR. But as the chopper moved closer with no hint of rescue equipment, he reconsidered. He reached up, pulled a branch closer and hid his dark eyes behind the leaves. The news chopper hovered for a time more, turned its attention toward the body bags carefully laid out on the barge next to the Aircraft Carrier, and then flew back toward downtown.

"A7BB, you still there?"

"Yep, Sarah. As I was saying the fire looks nearly under control. I've been watching those huge fire helicopters drink water out of the Bay, and then dump it on the fire. I read once where they can draw up a full load of water in forty-five seconds. They mix it with foam, you know while they're in flight to the fire. It's truly a sight to behold. I gotta tell you Sarah, I'm thinking about changing careers. A7BB, over."

"NJ7F."

"NJ, go ahead."

NJ7F's transmission was weak and filled with static, "We ... use a couple of those fire...in south...Over."

"NJ, having trouble hearing you. Did you say South Center? Over."

"Roger. Fire...of control...brigade useless...help. Over."

Max rushed out of the control room and leaned into the mike, "NJ7E, can you look for a green van, license plate Walker, Charley, Charley 573? Over."

"...wife?"

Sarah glared at Max until he reluctantly gave the mike back, "Roger NJ7E. A green van, Washington license plate WCC573, over."

"...J7F. ...cars burned. Will..."

"NJ, you're breaking up, over." Sarah waited, but the transmission from South Center was just too weak.

Collin slumped on his stool, put his elbows on his console, and buried his face in his hands. Max stared at the radio for a moment more, and then went back to the control room. He sat down, peeled off his shoe, and began pulling the ace bandage off his hurting foot. "Too tight!" By the time he got it re-wrapped, some good news came over the Ham Radio.

"NP7WS."

"WS, go ahead."

"NP7WS. I have a message from Navy. Fire Units out of Idaho and Northern California enroute to fires at South Center and Bremerton, over."

Sarah smiled, "Thanks, Navy. When this is over, I plan to buy you guys a drink, over."

"This is NP7WS, on behalf of the United States Navy, I accept. Out."

Sarah's eyes widened and she turned to stare at Max, "Did he say the whole Navy?"

Max chuckled and enthusiastically nodded.

But Collin was at the window again, staring more into space than at the grizzly ruins across the street. He didn't notice when Max walked up beside him, nor was he aware of Sarah's calls. Finally, Max's voice interrupted his thoughts.

"How long?"

Collin quickly turned his head, "What?"

"How long do you think we have, until we have to worry about disease?" When Collin still didn't understand, Max leaned closer. "The dead bodies. How long..."

"Oh. I have no idea."

"Neither do I. They keep telling us help is on the way, but it could take days before they get around to burying bodies. It's hot and we've got kids to think about."

"Yes, but Max, we don't have the man power to dig out the living. Who's going to bury the dead?"

"I don't know. That's why we need to find out how long before it becomes critical." Max turned to glance at Sarah, and then leaned still closer to Collin's ear. "The next time you do a spot, talk loud enough to cover her voice. I'll have Sarah find out."

"Okay."

INBOUND SEATTLE TRAFFIC crept at a snail's pace, inching forward, and then stopping again. Finally, James reached the Preston off ramp and drove down the curved grade to the bottom. At the stop sign, he turned left toward the heart of town. A short twenty-five miles from the epicenter, the earthquake had wreaked havoc on Preston's citizens. Chimneys were broken, houses had slipped off foundations, and an apartment building was still burning. Power and water had not been restored and people were jammed into parking lots and parks to spend the night.

Heather stared at the destruction, while James slowed before driving over a wide crack in the road, "What'll we do now?"

He turned down a side street and found a place to park, "I say we eat. I'm starved."

Heather climbed out of the passenger side, went around back, and pulled the pickup gate down. She hopped on, spun on her bottom, and got to her feet. Next, she pulled the cooler and the bag of groceries toward the tailgate and sat back down.

"At least now we know what kind of van to look for."

"Yes, and I've been thinking about that convoy from Spokane. It's supposed to come through here in an hour or two. We've got Mom's Red Cross arm band in the glove box, and if we could get a few donations to put here in the back, we could maybe follow them through the barricade."

"And if we get caught?"

"We're both under age. The worst they can do is send us home."

"Yes, to Dad."

"NE7G."

"NE, go ahead Ned."

"Sarah, it's really awful downtown. I don't know where to begin. NE7G, over."

"NE, what's your location?"

"NE7G. Well, as best I can tell I'm in Pioneer Square, or what's left of it. The Smith Tower held, but that's about all. This is the oldest part of the city and it just crumbled. We've got injured walking toward the courthouse and more just sitting in the streets. People are covered with blood. There's a guy with a megaphone somewhere, but I can't get what he's saying. Army just dropped a dozen or so guys from a chopper and they've got more coming in. Over."

"Glad to hear you're getting help. NE, we got a report that the bus tunnel collapsed. Can you confirm that? Over."

"Negative. I can see what's left of the Mainland Tower leaning against the Winningham Blue Building though. The tower has a huge crack in the middle and could fall at any time. But the Mainland Tower is on the other side of the bus tunnel which runs under third and I'm on Second...maybe I'm on third, I can't tell, everything shifted. Let me get back to you on that, NE7G, out."

Collin turned from the window to look at Max. Max had his head down, concentrating on something, so Collin walked to the control room. "There must be a dozen news choppers up there by now. We got enough power to turn on a TV?"

"Power yes, cable no...unless you've got an antenna."

Collin folded his arms and stared at the floor. "They still make TV antennas?"

"I don't have one either. On the other hand, we could use speaker wire. Of course that would only work for local stations, but it's worth a try."

"Great. I'll go see what I can find." With that, Collin headed down the stairs to his apartment.

"NV7SK"

"SK, go ahead," Sarah said.

"I finally made it to Broadmoor Golf Course. University Hospital set up another Triage area there. Sure could use the Mountlake Bridge cleared. I count 27 critical awaiting transport, 173 serious and more than 400 with minor injuries like broken bones. It looks like that war scene out of a movie. NV7SK, over."

"Copy SK. What about the sink hole?"

"NV7SK. They got everybody out, but it looks like it's growing wider. Sarah, I can see the Evergreen Point Floating Bridge from here, at least part of it. I think it held, but traffic is stopped so there must be a problem somewhere, over."

"Roger, SK. Okay, anybody in contact with the Red Cross in that area yet?"

"A7MMA."

"MMA, go ahead."

"A7MMA, First Hill Red Cross. We have serious staffing problems, only three reporting in so far. First Hill has major damage, mostly to older buildings and people have lost their minds. They don't know what to do or where to go. Most are too scared to do anything. And Sarah, looters raided our warehouse. We have very few supplies left and we've had a shooting. Ray Croft is dead. Over."

Max hung his head, "Maybe we do need a curfew."

"Copy, MAA." When Sarah glanced up, Max was waving to her. "This is Net Control, stand by."

"It's after seven. We need food, we need rest and most of all, we need to tell people where to go."

Sarah nodded, and then went back to her duties, "All stations, this is Net Control. We have less than an hour before our dear Mayor's curfew. Max wants a list of shelters. Unless you have an emergency, please stand by. Give me shelter locations only, over."

SAM WAS AMAZED AT THE size of the angry mob gathered outside Clifton's Hardware store, and he was careful to stay well away. So was KD7BN, a rotund man with light hair and a matching beard. Both men stood atop a hill, not ten feet apart, gazing into the threatening mob.

It was Sam who spoke first, "Think they'll kill him?"

"If they haven't already? I know I'd be tempted. Aren't there laws against price gouging in a disaster?"

"I think so. If not, there should be. $50.00 for a flashlight? It's obscene."

Just then, two shots rang out. The crowd froze for a moment, and then the double doors to the hardware store came open and the crowd moved forward, nearly trampling each other.

"Well, that answers that," Sam muttered. "By the way, could you let Max know his Dad is alive?"

"You're Max Taylor's Dad?"

Sam smiled and nodded, "Sure am. The boy's probably beside himself with worry about me."

"I'll do it as soon as I can, Mister Taylor."

"No hurry." Sam brought a finger up and tapped his earphones. "It can wait till they've finished with the shelters."

AT LENGTH, COLLIN RETURNED from downstairs empty handed. He looked at Max, slowly shook his head, and then mouthed the word, "Smashed."

Max motioned for him to help Sarah and Collin agreed. He walked up behind her, and then watched as she tried to write down the locations. Collin quietly moved his stool closer, pulled out his drawer, removed pencil, and paper, and then whispered in Sarah's ear. "I'll take every other one."

Relieved, Sarah nodded.

"NP7WS."

"WS, go ahead, over."

"Passing along a list from the Navy, Sarah. Ready? Over."

"Roger, WS, go."

The loud clapping sound of an incoming chopper interrupted them. The red and white news chopper hovered briefly over the collapsed buildings across the street, and then turned toward the attic station. Slowly, it moved closer and closer, until the noise became deafening. Collin raised an arm and motioned for the chopper to move back, but the cameraman hanging half out of the side door was not satisfied. Instead, he pointed the camera at Sarah.

Furious, Collin stood up and blocked the view. Livid, he glowered and narrowed his eyes – until at last, the chopper flew away. As soon as the noise dissipated, Collin grabbed the station mike. Mister President, if you're listening we need a no-fly zone around the station. We're trying to save lives here, not make the evening news!" He shoved the mike back where he got it and sat down hard on his stool.

Sarah watched the muscles in his jaw twitch, and then got back to work. "Okay, WS give me your list again."

# CHAPTER 19

PATIENTLY, KD7BN WAITED outside Clifton's Hardware until finally, Sarah finished listing shelters and asked for regular calls again. Anxiously, he pushed his speak button, "KD7BN reporting a probable murder at Clifton's Hardware, over."

When two Hams tried to call in at the same time, Sarah reeled back, "That was another double, and I didn't get either of you. Let me have the one about the murder first, please, over."

"This is KD7BN. I'm at Clifton's Hardware and I think they killed that guy over the flashlights. I haven't been inside yet because people are still going in and out. Oh, and tell Max I just talked to his Dad. He's fine, over."

"Copy KD. Is he there with you now? Over."

"Negative, Sarah. He left here about half an hour ago, headed up 15th on foot. He said a fissure opened up on the golf course and swallowed two guys right before his eyes. He also told me about some unearthed caskets over at Evergreen Cemetery. KD7BN, over."

The next Ham was WJ7V.

"WJ, go ahead."

"Sarah, we're still trying to get that little girl out of the department store. She's alive and a chopper dropped off a doctor. We've got nearly a hundred people pulled out of the top floors, but we're gonna need lights so we can keep digging after dark, over."

"Roger Mattie. WJ7V needs lights at the Cleveland Department Store. Anybody else? Over."

"SC7NJT."

"Well, if it isn't the Mayor's office. Is that you Mister Mayor or just the hapless messenger? Over."

The Mayor's attitude and tone came across much more mellow than when he first called, "Sarah, I want you to know I...that is we, think you're doing a great job. You, and the boys at KMPR, over."

Sarah snickered, glanced at Max, and whispered, "Boys." She giggled, deepened her southern drawl, and then leaned into her mike, "Why thank you Mister Mayor. Why ever did you call...Hun? Over."

"Now you listen here, Sarah. You tell your people I've ordered all looters shot on sight. We'll have none of that in Seattle, not on my watch! Over."

"Oh really? And how are you going to get the cops up the streets? We need the cops, Mister Mayor, to help us save people, not shoot 'em. Net Control out!"

Sarah slammed her pencil down and folded her arms in a huff.

Several seconds later, A7BB broke the silence, "Net Control can't say 'out.' Everybody knows that, Sarah."

Sarah started to laugh, "Good heavens, BB, you off that cliff yet?"

"Don't I wish. The good news is; I think the aftershocks have stopped. The bad news is, the Mayor forgot to give his non-existent call sign. A guy can get in a lot of trouble with the FCC over that. A7BB, over."

Both Max and Sarah started to roar with laughter.

"NE7G, emergency."

Sarah quickly grabbed her pencil again, "Go ahead, NE."

"NE7G, the whole city fell in. It's a blood bath down there. We've got people on the sidewalks covered with glass and bricks ... and cement. All I can see are hands and legs sticking out. They're dead Sarah, they're all dead."

"NE, give us a location, over."

"I'm on a bluff on Third Avenue, NE7G, over."

"NE, take a deep breath and tell us – what bluff?"

"The city sank, Sarah. It must have. God in heaven, what are we going to do?"

Sarah waited for him to say, "Over." When he didn't, she went on, "NE, what's wrong with you? You sound like you're having trouble breathing, over."

"Just a broken rib, I think. I can't do this, Sarah. I just can't. NE7G, out."

IN THE LAST RAYS OF sunlight, Seely's daughter, Michelle, helped her husband bring the barbecue out of the back yard to the front. Theo started a charcoal fire while the girls sat in lawn chairs and played with dolls.

When he finished, Theo Wesley wrapped his arms around his wife, "I really owe your Mom an apology. I've never been so scared and the next time she tells me to check the earthquake kit, I'll actually do it."

"Me too. How long till the phones work again?"

"Who knows? Meanwhile, my business is looking up. Lots of rich people will want their yards groomed after this. Maybe they'll even want me to replant. I don't think two crews will be able to handle it all."

Michelle snuggled deeper into her husband's arms and watched the sunset. "Have you decided what we should do?"

"Decided, no, thought about it yes. I think we should make all future decisions together. Isn't that what you're always telling me?"

Michelle smiled and moved away just a little to watch his eyes, "I guess earthquakes have a purpose after all."

"The truth is, I didn't know how much my family meant to me until today. Honey, I think we should stay here. If your Mom makes it out, she'll look for us here."

"What about our supplies?"

Theo grinned and pulled her close again, "No one knows how much we've got. When they ask, we'll share, but pretend to share our last crumb. What else can we do?"

"I think you're wonderful."

"I think you're wonderful too." He kissed her forehead, and then glanced up the street. A white-haired man with earphones, white shoes and a checkered red vest was headed their direction. "Would you look at that? He looks like something out of a golf magazine."

Michelle turned and studied the face, "Hey, that's Mister Taylor from the bank. You know, the guy who loaned us the money for the house."

"By golly, you're right." Theo released his wife and started to wave, "Mister Taylor, over here."

At first, Sam couldn't tell who was yelling at him. It didn't matter, he was tired enough to call just about anybody friend. Finally, he saw who it was, hurried on, grabbed Theo's outstretched hand and vigorously shook it. "Am I ever glad to see a friendly face! You all okay? Anybody hurt?"

"We're fine," Theo answered. "Have a seat."

Gladly, Sam lowered his aching body into a soft lawn chair and removed his earphones, "I've never felt anything so wonderful in my life."

Michelle giggled. "Are you thirsty? We've got water."

"No thanks. I managed to buy some up the way. Tell me, have either of you been to Ballard? I've been worried sick about the bank, what with looters and all."

"No, we've been here all day." Theo leaned against the car and once more put his arm around his wife. "Where did you come from?"

"Evergreen Golf Course. Saw two men fall head first into a fissure. Don't think I'll ever forget that. The city's a mess, but I guess you already know."

Michelle lowered her head and stared at her feet, "We haven't heard much. The radio stations don't seem to know anything and we're worried about running the car battery down."

"My dear, you've been listening to the wrong station. My son Max owns KMPR and he's had the wherewithal to let us listen in on the Ham operators. I suspect I know just about everything that's happening. You just ask me, go ahead, ask me."

Michelle bit her lip and looked into her husband's eyes. "My mother is in the Winningham Blue Building."

"Still standing."

Instantly Michelle's eyes brightened, "Thank God."

"Thank God indeed. Several others fell but NE7G mentioned that one by name. It's still there, all right. Say, you folks don't know of a place I can spend the night?"

"We'd be pleased if you stayed with us," Michelle answered. "I was just thinking about cooking some of the meat in the freezer before it spoils."

Sam's grin was as wide as his vest was bright, "My dear, I was hoping you would offer."

TIM EYED THE FREEZE dried food Seely pulled out of her earthquake kit with a suspicious glare, "Are you sure that's edible?"

"Well, I've never tried it, but the guy at the store assured me it was."

"Aren't you the one who wanted to break into the candy machine?" he asked.

Seely's eyes lit up, "Indeed I am. Help me up, I wouldn't miss this for the world.

Worried, Jenna kept her hold on Seely's arm, "How's your heart? Are you okay?"

"I feel pretty good, but maybe you should bring the pills just in case."

Jenna reached down, grabbed the bottle, and then followed Seely and Tim through the rubble. Soon, they entered a short passageway leading to another hallway on the east side of the building.

Tim moved cautiously, repeatedly glancing up at the ceiling. It appeared stable. He walked into the lunchroom, turned left and grinned at the toppled and smashed snack machine with candy bars, chips, and gum packages strewn across the room. "What's your pleasure, ladies?"

"All of it," Jenna giggled.

"Good idea." Tim swooped down, gathered snacks off the floor, and then handed them off. "Let's eat, then have another look around. You never know what people hide in their offices."

"KR7BM."

"BM, go ahead."

"Sarah, the Freemont drawbridge is still stuck in the up position. However, people are gathering at Waterworks Park. They're bringing canned goods and have camp fires started. At least we don't have to worry about water. Lake Washington is fresh, not salt water, over."

"Copy, BM. You're right. Water shouldn't be a problem for people near Lake Washington or Lake Union. Thanks. WD7DHZ, you're next, I think."

"WD7DHZ, passing a message from the governor. All hospitals able to provide services in Tacoma, Olympia and surrounding areas are full. The Governor is shutting down Lincoln Hospital in Tacoma and transferring patients. Engineers say it isn't safe, over."

"DHZ, copy. Anybody else?"

"A7GLG."

"GLG, go ahead."

"A7GLG, we've got a sewage spill off West Point, over."

"GLG, where is that exactly? Is it salt water or fresh?"

"I'm just south of Shilshole Bay on the tip of Fort Lawton Military Reservation. It's dumping into salt water, Sarah. Hope you don't mind if I don't stick around. It stinks out here. A7GLG, over."

"GLG, I don't blame you a bit. Can you go to the east side of Discovery Park? We should have a shelter setting up there, but we haven't heard?"

"Roger Sarah, I'm on my way. A7GLG, out."

"This is net control, anybody else?"

"WC7NJT."

"You sure are a busy man today, Mister Mayor. What now? Over."

"It's me again, Sarah. The mayor wants to remind people we have industrial businesses on Lake Washington. As a precaution, we should boil the water. WC7NJT, over."

"I forgot about that. Tell the Mayor we appreciate the reminder."

FOR MORE THAN AN HOUR, Tim and Jenna rummaged through the forty-third floor offices—the ones that looked safe to enter. When they came back, they handed Seely an apple, a banana and one cell phone.

Tim anxiously sat down and licked his lips, "Hand me the booze, will you. I feel like celebrating."

Jenna huffed and sneered, "Celebrate what?"

"Seely feels better, my face doesn't hurt so much, you look a mess, and we stopped having aftershocks."

"What do you mean, I look a mess?"

"Jenna, you're always so, you know, well dressed, and immaculately kept. Finally, you look like a regular girl."

Jenna giggled, "You like regular girls better?"

"Yes I do. My Sue is as regular as they come. She helps fix the car, works in the yard ..." Suddenly, his eyes turned sad.

"Don't go belly up on us, Tim." Seely finished pouring a drink into his paper cup and handing it to him. "We need you to stay level headed."

"I know. I was just wondering if she's okay. Turn the radio up will you. Maybe they'll say something about Northgate."

"She wasn't at that new department store, was she?"

"I don't think so. She said something about getting more plants for the back yard at Northgate Mall. She loves pansies." He took a deep breath, drank several gulps, and then reached for the radio. "Okay, I'll do it myself." With that, he turned the volume up.

THE MAYOR'S CURFEW came and went with little change at KMPR. Hams still reported damage and injuries, Collin still took his station breaks and Max downed more ibuprofen. When the sun faded, Collin went downstairs, found a lamp with an unbroken bulb, and brought it back up. They had the only electric light for blocks.

"NP7WS."

"WS, go ahead," Sarah answered.

"Navy wishes to know if you have enough food and water. Over."

"WS, tell Navy we're fine. We've got a well-stocked refrigerator full of drinks and generator power. Can you tell us about the fire at South Center? Over."

"NP7WS. The fires in West Seattle, Bremerton, and South Center are still burning, but more help is on the way. Hospitals report 963 dead, but we could have duplicate reports. We have over five hundred collapsed buildings, not counting the ones downtown. Several search teams will arrive in the night and we are assessing which buildings show the greatest potential for saving lives. We..."

Collin walked to the window and looked at the buildings across the street. Even in the fading light, he could tell the chances of people still being alive in the ruins were slim. Even so, loved ones and neighbors still struggled to remove debris piece by piece with their hands.

"...more troops should arrive by dawn to help downtown, over."

"Copy WS. A couple of hours ago, A7BB reported an explosion in the south. Can you tell us what that was? Over."

"NP7WS stand by. ...Sarah, some guy in a small plane either didn't know about the quake or didn't care. He tried to land at Boeing Field, hit a lifted section of the runway, and flipped. His plane caught on fire, skidded under the belly of a Boeing 777 and blew it up. And Sarah, we've got potential refueling problems for the choppers. Hope to have that resolved by morning, over."

GUSTS OF WARM WIND were whistling down the darkened hallways of the Winningham Blue Building, by the time Tim and Jenna lay down beside Seely on the floor. Each held a flashlight and none had a blanket. A few seconds later, Tim turned on his side and propped his head up on his hand. "I've begun to hate that sound."

Lying on the other side of Seely, Jenna did the same, "The wind or that train."

"The train. Of course it's not really a train. The tracks are out, remember?"

"What is it then?"

Seely glanced at one, and then at the other. "Don't freak, but I've heard that before. It's the earth."

"You mean it's still moving?"

"Sugar, I haven't got a clue. I've read a lot of books on earthquakes and few ever mention the horrid screech right after, or the train noise it makes for weeks. I guess no one knows what causes it."

Tim thoughtfully listened. "Maybe gas escapes through the new cracks or something."

"That's the best guess I've heard yet. Or maybe that sound is always there but we can't hear it until the dirt is dislodged. At any rate, it goes away."

Jenna sighed, "Good. I'll be glad when that happens. What time is it?"

Seely raised her flashlight and looked at her watch, "a little after nine-thirty."

"Nine-thirty? I haven't gone to bed this early since I was twelve."

"Yes, well going to bed after an earthquake is one thing. Going to sleep is quite another."

Tim lay back down and closed his eyes, "The booze will help with that, I hope."

A7BB WAS TIRED. THE air was still warm and the cat was curled up on his shoulder. Fewer choppers broke the stillness with their thudding noises and the bright Aircraft Carrier lights seemed to be dimming. On far off shores, tiny flickers signaled make-do campfires and small spot lights cast ghostly, elongated shadows on downtown buildings. In a dark sky normally brightened by city lights, stars twinkled in the heavens. The rhythm of the sloshing water below seemed mellow and comforting, and for a little while, A7BB slept.

"Net Control, this is NP7H, care for a little good news? Over."

"NP, go ahead."

"NP7H, Sister Elizabeth's weekend daycare in Northgate is in good shape. Moderate damage, but all nineteen kids are safe and they've got a working generator. They could use diapers, formula, and some extra hands if anybody can help, over."

"NP, that's the best news we've had all day. You got an address? Over."

"NP7H, 92nd and Linden. There's a big sign, tilted a bit sideways, with a duck on it. Bet we've got some relieved Moms out there somewhere, over."

"Bet we do too. Thanks NP7H. Anybody else?"

"KB7MN."

"MN, go ahead."

"Sarah, I forgot to tell you. The statue of Lenin fell. It smashed into a thousand pieces. KB7MN, over."

"The one that guy brought from Russia? Over."

"That's the one. A lot of folks in Freemont will be pleased about that. Night Sarah, I'm going to turn in now. KB7MN, out."

"Good night, KB. Who's next?"

"NP7WS."

"WS, go ahead."

"NP7WS. Navy wants to take your net for the night so you can rest, over."

Sarah stared at the radio, and then lightly rubbed her brow.

Before she could answer, Collin leaned into the mike, "WS, tell Navy thanks. We've got a real tired lady here."

"NP7WS, will do. By the way Sarah, you've become pretty famous these last few hours. The press got hold of your picture and half the guys on the ship have flipped over you. They interviewed your Mom in Atlanta. She's worried, but holding up. She said she felt bad for all the mothers who couldn't hear their daughters on the radio. NP7WS, over."

Sarah's eyes brightened a little, "That sounds like my mom. WS, thanks, she's been on my mind too. Did you say you were on the ship? Over."

For a moment, NP7WS didn't answer. "Well, yes. It's not exactly protocol, but I've got my own Ham License out of LA. Captain okayed it as long as it doesn't interfere with my duties. Good night, Sarah. This is NP7WS. Over."

"Good night, over."

"John, over."

"Good night, John."

Sarah flipped the Amateur radio microphone off and briefly listened to Navy take her next call. Then she hung her head and cried. For a long time, she let Collin hold her in his arms while she sobbed like a child. When she finished, she pulled away and glanced up at him, "This is the worst chair I've ever sat in."

Collin got up, lifted her out of the chair and carried her to a pile of pillows on the floor, "What? You miraculously got feeling in your butt now?"

"No, but I still have a back bone."

"Fine. Tomorrow, I'll put you on pillows."

"Good."

Max's grin was wider than it had been all day, "Guess what, we're still on the air.

Collin rolled his eyes, walked back to the microphone and lifted it to his lips, "This is KMPR, 760 AM in Seattle signing off for the night." He nearly signaled Max to shut down, and then thought better of it. "Seattle, this has been the worst day of our lives and those of us who came through in one piece send our love to all those injured, suffering and still waiting for help. Sleep if you can." He closed his eyes and bowed his head, "Beth, I love you. Wherever you are, try to rest. Max wants you to give Candy and the boys a hug for him. Be safe Beth...and please, please be alive." He nodded, and Max shut down the controls.

Collin hung his head for a long, long moment. Then he walked to Sarah, unfolded a thin blanket, and spread it over her. When Max sat down beside her, Collin began unwrapping the ace bandage on his foot. "So Sarah, how come you hate the Mayor?"

"He's a twit."

Max chuckled. "A bunch of us Hams went to see the Mayor a short time after he was elected. He took one look at Sarah's wheelchair and left the room, mumbling something about not having time to look at Seattle's disaster plan."

When Collin looked at her, Sarah only shrugged, "I'm used to that. A lot of people don't look me in the eye. They don't know what to say or how to treat people in wheelchairs."

Collin frowned at the black bruise on Max's foot, and then carefully began to re-wrap it. "I hate to admit it, but I never know what to say or do either. Besides, some people with disabilities are so cranky, all I wanna do is stay out of their way."

"They get angry and with just cause. They get to a door they can't open and they get frustrated. I was lucky, I was in a car accident when I was little, and my mom never let me get angry. She said I was beautiful, intelligent, alive, and I'd better be grateful for what I had. Once, when I was having a particularly rebellious day, she tied a scarf over my eyes so I could see what it was like to be blind as well. Boy did that teach me a lesson. I don't think I've wallowed in self-pity since. Still..."

"Still what?"

"Well, I have days when I am angry. I would like to find a good husband and have kids, but it's a lot to ask of a guy. So I keep telling myself I just have to be content with my little home Internet business and my Ham Operator hobby. With a radio, a girl can have dozens of guy friends and none of them care if she's in a wheelchair."

THE EVENING AIR WAS still warm when John Carson walked across the flat top of the USS Carl Vincent and stood by the rail facing the city. Still in his dress whites, he removed his cap and ran his fingers through his dark, curly hair. His soft eyes looked tired and his tall frame slumped a little. Calm waters sloshed against the side of the ship, but the noise on deck where dozens of his shipmates still loaded and unloaded choppers obliterated the peaceful sounds.

He gazed at KMPR's light on top of the hill for nearly ten minutes before Ted Walker casually walked up beside him. "I've never seen you like this old friend. Sarah's got some sort of magical hold on you."

John chuckled and rubbed the back of his tired and aching neck, "You've got to admit, she's some kind of woman. Most of the men I know couldn't hold up under that kind of pressure. After she gave the net to us, you know when she cried, I nearly lost it. Didn't you?"

"Yes, but..."

"But she's crippled?"

"Well..."

"So was my mom." Lieutenant John Carson smiled, put his cap back on and walked away.

# CHAPTER 20

AT SHORTLY AFTER TEN o'clock p.m., James flashed his Mother's Red Cross arm banner at a man directing traffic, smiled, and then fell in behind the fifteen-truck Spokane convoy. The back of the pickup was fully loaded with jugs of water, day old bread, canned goods, and blankets donated by people in Preston. Darkness hid the devastation and the previous trucks bounced back and forth on the broken pavement. Nevertheless, the convoy followed the Auburn Echo cut off to Highway 169, and then turned north toward Renton.

At the first of two bridges over the Cedar River, the trucks stopped. Men in Army uniforms cautiously waved the trucks forward, allowing only one at a time to drive across the bridge. But none paid attention to James and Heather in the small pickup. As soon as they were past, James took a deep breath. "That's finished. Good." Then the convoy slowed again.

Inch by inch, the truck eased through free standing water, which made Heather nervous, "Why is there water everywhere?"

"Maybe the river changed course."

"Oh. Are we gonna sink?"

James turned an incredulous glare on his sister, and then he suddenly smiled. "That's right, you can't swim."

Soon, they were back on dry land, but in less than half an hour, the convoy stopped. All along the side of the road, tents with blaring lights housed duty minded men in uniform. James waited, moved up each time the line moved, and waited some more. Finally, the last truck in the convoy pulled away.

He was a short man with a fully loaded rifle and a silly grin on his face. He paused in front of the pickup's headlights, looked at the license plate, and then glanced at James and Heather. Finally, he made a smart, military turn, marched forward four steps and stopped. He turned again, marched down the driver's side of the pickup, and turned once more. His face was less than six inches from James when he grinned, "Mister McClurg, I assume."

James swallowed hard and slowly nodded.

"We've been expecting you. Your Dad said your Uncle Harry needs help in his packing shed."

Heather closed her eyes and let her head drop, "Peach fuzz, yuk!"

LONG AFTER THE STATION shut down, Max, Collin, and Sarah were still wide-awake. Their tangled nerves felt every vibration in the earth and their ears caught even the softest noise. The volume was turned way down low, but they could still hear the Ham's.

Max soon began to talk about Candy, "My wife tells me we met in a sand box at age three, but I don't remember it. She decided I loved her and that was that. We grew up next-door neighbors and when I went off to college, I realized I did love her. I missed her so much, I got off the plane, grabbed a phone and proposed. She said yes, and we are still best friends." He thoughtfully paused for a moment, and then went on, "When she comes home, I'm taking all of them on the best vacation ever."

Sarah giggled, "You want to take her on a vacation with three little boys? Some favor."

"What do you suggest?"

"Well, if I were her, I'd like a nice long bubble bath with soft music and candle light. Then, dinner out at the most romantic place he can think of, and maybe a movie with no kids, no worries and no aftershocks."

"Amen to that," Collin said. "Maybe Beth would like a cruise."

"I think she would." Sarah adjusted her pillow and laid her head back down, "I like Beth very much."

"I didn't know you knew her."

"I know." Sarah giggled and turned to look at Collin, "Don't you recognize my voice?"

Collin thought for a moment, and then shook his head.

"Amazing. I'm better at disguising my accent than I thought. Beth comes over in the afternoons. We share a pot of tea, and then make as many calls to the station as we can dream up."

"I had no idea."

"See if you recognize this—Carl, he's your Aunt Jo's boy, never did a lick of work in his life."

"Mom?"

Sarah shrieked with laughter, reached out and playfully smacked his shoulder. "Beth and I have more fun with that one. In fact, we've been talking about maybe asking if I could do a spot on your show. You know, like a half hour or so. I could talk about all sorts of things, like Internet businesses, Ham Radios, girl stuff and..."

Collin quickly turned on his side, "I love the idea. If you did it around noon or one o'clock, Beth and I could have lunch together."

But Max was not so enthusiastic, "Sure, if we rebuild. This place is totaled, and it took every dime I had to build it."

"Well the equipment still works and that's the expensive stuff, right?"

Max stared at him in disbelief, "You're going to stay, even after all this?"

Suddenly, the earth jolted. Collin shot up off the floor, shoved his arms under Sarah, blanket and all, and headed for the door. Max sat straight up, quickly flipped over, and then cried out in pain as he put weight on his sore foot. Even so, he wedged into the doorway beside Collin and Sarah. The earth began its shaking again, sending forth its horrendous thunder, it's frightening twists and its murderous heaves.

In the bay, the water once more swirled and churned, alarm bells sounded on the Aircraft Carrier and all hands dashed to the safety of the lower decks.

IN THE WINNINGHAM BLUE, Tim sat up with a start and grabbed his flashlight, trying to hold its beam on the rolling ceiling. Seely wrapped her arms around Jenna. Her eyes darted, her heart raced and Jenna began screaming in her ear. In the frightening dark of night, the battered and weakened building rode the 8.3 shock wave – dipping, rising, screeching, twisting, shaking, and falling.

ASLEEP ON THE GRASS, Sam jerked awake, stood up and tried desperately to keep his balance, but the earth rolled too quickly and he fell on his face. Theo wrapped his arms around his terrified family and kept them seated on the ground. The wood and brick house behind them cried out in torture and car alarms once more went off.

FOR JAMES AND HEATHER, the thunder was not as loud, but their first real experience with a moving earth terrified them both. Water began seeping onto the wooden floor of their bouncing, twisting tent as the Cedar River sloshed over its banks. In a panic,

Heather got to her feet and darted outside. Almost instantly, a young Private grabbed her around the waist, held on tight and whispered in her ear. "You're okay. Nothing can fall on you here." Even so, the tall pines danced in the distance and the water kept rising. Seconds later, James emerged from the tent just before the rolling earth began to quiet. His eyes were wide and his face was nearly colorless.

TWICE DURING THE AFTERSHOCK, the lamp at KMPR flickered and dimmed. Twice it returned to its full capacity and now that the shaking stopped, Max stared at its base sitting nearly half way off of Collin's console. Again worried about the stability of the floor, he took cautious steps toward it until he could reach out and shove the lamp to safety. He grabbed his forgotten flashlight, turned it on and shined the beam at the satellite dish. It was still there. Next, he pushed the Ham Radio farther back on the table and turned the volume back up.

Sarah was trembling even though Collin still held her in his arms. She relaxed just a little and buried her head in his neck, "At least you didn't drop me."

At last, Collin allowed himself to breathe, "How could I? You've got your fingernails in my neck."

Sarah quickly let go, "Oh, sorry."

Gently, Collin laid her back down on the pillows, and then sat down beside her and turned his attention to the radio.

"A7BB, this is Navy. How do you read?"

A7BB didn't answer. Max held his breath, made a slight adjustment to the frequency tuning dial, set Collin's stool upright again and sat down.

"Navy to A7BB, over." Aboard the Aircraft Carrier, John Carson watched the last of the waves hit shore on his radar screen, and then ordered a spot light turned on the cliff. "A7BB, come in, over."

"Hey, what's with the light? Can't a guy get any sleep around here?"

Sarah giggled, and Max slapped a hand on the console, "Awesome."

"A7BB, you slid a bit more, over."

"Are you asking or telling? If you ask me, I slid a lot more and I got all wet. You know that stupid cat, the one I was growing fond of? Well it scratched up the whole side of my face, and then took off up the cliff. So much for loyalty. A7BB, over."

"Navy to W7LGG. Over."

Max quickly flipped on the mike, "W7LGG."

"Max, we got a guy named John who'd like to know if Sarah's alright, over."

"W7LGG. She's okay. A little shook up, but okay. We lost the other half of our roof, over."

TIM WAS TOO SCARED to breathe. The ceiling looked okay, but he wasn't sure. The floor beneath them felt strong, but the building still echoed its settling noises. "Maybe we should go lower."

Jenna sniffed her nose and wiped the tears off her cheeks, "But Seely said higher was better."

"Maybe, but my gut tells me to go lower."

Seely didn't quickly comment. Instead, she again concentrated on breathing normally. She waited for the pain to shoot across her chest, but it didn't and in a little while, she relaxed. "Tim might be right. Maybe we should try to go down a flight or..."

It began with a sharp cracking noise somewhere below and all three instantly resumed their huddled positions. The odd sounds of splitting wood and metal reverberated through the devastated building and objects started crashing to the street below. Even so, the ground didn't seem to be moving, but then suddenly, the forty-third floor shuddered, its walls popped and its floors convulsed. Long, endless seconds passed, and then the Mainland Tower broke apart and fell, sending a horrendous crashing noise up the walls of the Winningham Blue.

Tim laid his flashlight in his lap, covered his face with his hands, and took several long, heavy breaths. In the eerie glow of the flashlight, Jenna's eyes looked distorted and huge. Tears once more ran down her cheeks and Seely bowed her head in prayer.

Stiff and sore, Tim slowly got to his feet. "I guess going down isn't such a good idea after all...now." He moved down the hallway and shined his light on the walls. Tiny molecules of dust still filtered down and wires yet swayed, but the walls and ceiling seemed to be holding.

The cracking erupted again – this time within the building. Tim dove back down the hall, sat down next to Seely and threw his arms around her. Jenna shivered, Seely cringed, and for more than a minute, no one moved while the building rested. Finally, newly stirred dust began to settle.

THE NOISE OF THE CRASHING Mainland tower took a good ten seconds to reach KMPR. When it did, Collin jumped up and went to the window. Car headlights cast a faint glow on the collapsed buildings across the street and a lone man continued to dig in the rubble. In the dark, Collin couldn't tell if the other buildings were still there.

THE "BLUE ANGEL" FLEW north to Everett, dropped off its passenger at Thorndike Memorial Hospital and turned south again. They were flying over Lynnwood when Seely's heart rate abruptly increased. Instantly, Jackie knew what was happening and instructed

Carl to stop. She waited and watched as the heart rate slowed, and speeded up twice more before it held steady. Below the chopper, people poured into streets and she slowly scanned the area with her cameras looking for new fires. There were none.

In the right hand top screen, an enlarged Seattle map indicated Michelle's house and the playground across the street. The monitor next to it showed a view through the sprinkler head camera of a dim charcoal fire in the barbecue, and shadowy figures standing around it. "At least we won't have to wake them up. Go ahead, Carl."

The air crane picked up speed and quickly flew over the more than fifty city blocks to Crown Hill.

On the ground, Sam, Theo, Michelle, and the girls quickly spotted the chopper lights. Mesmerized, they watched it land in the middle of the play field. A side door slid open, steps unfolded and the bright interior lights silhouetted the figure of a nicely dressed woman. Flashlight in hand, the figure descended the stairs.

In high heels, Jackie struggled to walk through the broken patches of grass. The sidewalk and the street with slanted slabs were equally difficult, but at length she arrived. She extended a hand first to Theo, and then to Michelle. "My name is Jackie Harlan. Your mother is alive."

Michelle instantly slumped against her husband. "Where is she?"

"She's still in the building, but we're going to do everything we can to get her out. Look, I've got a tired crew on my hands and rooms for all of us in Vancouver, BC. Will you come?"

Theo wrinkled his brow and frowned, "To Canada?"

"Yes."

"Why us? There are millions of people trapped in this mess."

Jackie hesitated, looking first into Theo's eyes and then Michelle's, "I'm a Private Detective. I'm being paid to find you and bring you out."

"Paid by whom?" Michelle waited for an answer while Jackie glanced back at the chopper.

"Your father."

"My father is dead."

Jackie took a deep breath and once more glanced at the chopper. "It's a long story and one I'd love to tell you on the way. The important thing is, your father wants you safe. He wants your mother out of that building and my crew needs a rest. Please come, your children will be safer in Canada."

Michelle searched her husband's eyes, and then nodded. "What about Mister Taylor? We can't just leave him here."

"Of course you can, my dear," Sam said. "I'll be perfectly fine, with a little sleep. You go on."

Jackie smiled, "Good."

THREE TIMES, EVAN COLE went up on the roof to look for the chopper, and then hurried back to his room to watch the news on TV. Dozens of planes and choppers flew in and out of Vancouver, but none landed on the Hotel's landing pad. The 8.3 aftershock toppled a few more chimneys, rattled windows and sent Canadian citizens to the streets again. Now, local news was filled with new local damage reports. The lack of information from Seattle sent chills down his spine and now he sat next to a radio waiting to see if KM-PR would come back on the air. It didn't.

When Jackie called, he nearly jumped out of his skin. "Jackie, what's happening?"

"She's okay, Mister Cole. She's still in the building, but her heart rate looks good. We just picked up your daughter and her family. Our ETA is half an hour. Is everything set?"

"Yes. Ask them if they're hungry. I can order..."

"They can hear you, Mister Cole, and they're shaking their heads no. but I'll have prime rib. Carl likes anything Mexican and Michael says he could eat a horse. Do they have horse on the menu?"

Evan Cole laughed, "I'll see what I can do. A half hour then?"

"See you there." With that, Jackie disconnected the call. When she turned in her swivel seat, Michelle was staring at the picture of her father.

In the time left before the chopper arrived, Evan turned his attention to finding just the right words to say to a daughter he had never seen – a daughter who probably thought he was dead. As hard as he tried, nothing came to mind. He watched the chopper land and there she was, looking very much like her mother had at that age, and he wanted nothing more than to take her in his arms. Instead, he just nodded and watched her follow the hotel attendant assigned to show them to their rooms. Without a word, his daughter walked with her family through the roof's hotel entrance.

Again, there was nothing left to do but wait. He made sure Jackie and the others had everything they needed, watched continuous repeats of the day's news on TV and nearly two hours passed before Michelle finally knocked on his door.

He calmly let her in, asked if he could get her anything, and when she refused, took a seat opposite her at a small table. "It's a lot to take in, isn't it?"

"Yes, it is." Michelle let her eyes drop and struggled to find something to say. She was wearing the expensive sleeping gown and robe he'd ordered for her from the downstairs gift shop.

"Do all the clothes fit? You can exchange them, if you'd like."

"They're perfect. The girls love the pajamas and you must have wiped out a toy store. I had a devil of a time getting them to go to bed." Without even taking a breath, she changed the subject, "Mr. Cole, Jackie told me about Christina and about the ring you found, and about you being married to somebody else, but I still don't understand. What happened?"

"I wish I knew. One minute I was the happiest man on earth with a beautiful bride and the next, I was cast into a pit of the deepest, darkness sadness in the world. To tell the truth, it never occurred to me to question Christina's death. I saw nothing amiss at the time, nothing that would make me doubt what the authorities said."

Michelle was beginning to relax a little, so she got up and helped herself to a drink. "She's always had those scars around her wrists, you know. I asked about them when I was very young, but she passed it off as though it were nothing. Still, I guess I always knew something was wrong because she was so over-protective of me. When I got older, it was a real struggle to get her to let me go out. Maybe now I know why, someone tried to kill her."

"Yes, but I have no idea who?"

"Neither do I." Michelle brought her glass back to the table and sat down.

"Didn't she ever remarry?"

"Remarry? She wouldn't even date, although men always flocked around her like flies. She said she loved you, you were dead and that was the end of that. Just a couple of weeks ago she told me she was happy to be getting older – there aren't as many flies these days."

"Legally, she couldn't remarry. Come to think of it, I have been a bigamist all these years. What a mess."

Michelle finally grinned, "I can't wait to find out what happened. Do you really think they can get her out of that building?"

"I hope so, I couldn't bear to lose her again."

SUNDAY MORNING AT EIGHT-thirty a.m. Eastern Daylight time, TV news was still showing yesterday's devastating pictures over and over, and reporting the number of hours before Seattle would see daylight. They replayed Sarah's calm voice, Ned's refusal to accept the devastation downtown and Mattie's heartfelt concern for the child buried in the department store. For a full hour, an expert talked about the intricate network of Hams and explained more about Amateur Radio. Finally, they identified Sarah and interviewed people she'd known in high school and college.

Seated in her living room in Atlanta, Georgia, Sarah's mother turned her television off. In another two and a half hours, more pictures would come and God willing, she would hear Sarah's voice again. That was a long time to wait – especially with another 8.3 aftershock reported during the night. Slowly, she got up and picked up her purse. She closed the door softly behind her and walked down the street to the nearest church.

When she got there, the double doors were open and a man greeted her with a smile, "You're Sarah's Mother, aren't you?"

She nodded, tears welling up in her eyes, "I haven't thanked God for anything in twenty years. It's about time I did." She walked down the aisle and took a seat in the front row.

IT WAS THE LONGEST night anyone could remember in Seattle. For most, sleep didn't come until the early hours before dawn. Ham calls were few, the earth remained relatively calm and dogs didn't bark. Exhausted minds finally shut down and rested until the sky began to brighten.

His chest filled with pain each time he took a breath, and the cleared off park bench was as hard as a rock. Even so, NE7G was out like a light for most of the night. When at last he opened his eyes, a woman was smiling down on him. She held a cup in one hand and pot of coffee in the other.

"Lady, I've never been so glad to see anyone in my life. Could you set that down and help me up?"

"You hurt?"

"Broken rib."

She set the pot down, wrapped his arm around her shoulder, and helped him rise to a sitting position. "I've had one of those. You're in for about six weeks of pain. They're not taking broken bones yet." She lifted the pot, and then poured him a cup of coffee. "It doesn't matter. There's not much they can do about a broken rib except wrap it. Mind if I sit down?"

"Not at all. Tell me, where did you come from?"

She handed him the coffee, and set the pot down on the ground, "The courthouse. The Salvation Army set up on the grass. Sure is a fine time for the street people, the ones that lived through this. They'll likely get three good meals a day till this is over. And how hard will it be for them to steal booze with all the windows smashed. On the other hand, maybe all the booze got smashed too."

NE7G smiled. "Tell me what's happening?"

"Well, that aftershock scared hell, sorry, heck out of me. We heard a big crash after it stopped, but I don't know what fell. Probably another building."

"Yes, I heard it too. You got any food at the courthouse?"

"Sure do. The Army dropped some from the air last night. It's not bacon and eggs, but on a day like this, who cares."

He herd the engine of a snowplow start less than a block away. "Where did that come from?"

"Army dropped that too, early this morning. Didn't you hear the chopper?"

"Guess I passed out."

COLLIN OPENED ANOTHER box of crackers and then popped the lid on a new jar of cheese. "I've always wanted to eat cheese and crackers for breakfast. Wonder why I didn't think of this before."

Seated on the floor with her back against the wall, Sarah swallowed her last bite and smiled, "Guess you've been a little too proper. Beth told me about you. You like things in order, just like the day before and the day before that. You need to branch out. I had a friend like that once. He..."

Max poked his head through the window and frowned. "Hey you two, time to go to work."

Collin walked to Sarah, leaned down, and instead of lifting her, grabbed two pillows. "See, I remembered." He put the pillows in her armchair and switched off the lamp. He came back, leaned down, picked her up, and set her on the pillows. He watched her turn to a new page in her notebook. "Do you want to go first, or shall I?"

"You go first."

"Okay." He sat down, put his lips close to the station microphone, and waited for Max to nod. "This is KMPR, 760 AM in Seattle. Folks, we need another check. If you're on Queen Anne Hill and you can hear us, honk your horn." He waited, heard three different car horns, and smiled. "Thanks. When this is over, I'd like to shake your hands. As those living in Seattle already know, we had another strong aftershock during the night. Reports are not expected to be very good this morning.

And now, you need to brace yourselves. What I am about to say will hurt. We have to keep our eyes on the living, especially the children, and dead bodies carry disease. Experts tell us the sooner we get them buried, the safer the children will be. Today, we must focus not only on search and rescue, but on the grim task of saying good-bye to the dead. The Red Cross asks that you try to identify as many people as you can.

Just like the rest of you, we at KMPR hardly slept a wink. Nevertheless, we do have a little good news. A7BB didn't fall off the cliff and Charlie, the little girl trapped in the department store is still alive...and still trapped. The truck convoy reached Renton and is unloading badly needed supplies at a Red Cross center. Help is on the way.

At the collapsed buildings across the street, I see fresh faces, and sadly, another two bodies. If I remember correctly, we should see rain tonight or tomorrow, and before you curse the rain, remember those still trapped in buildings need the water."

Collin paused to take a deep breath. "Max and I have yet to hear from our wives in South Center, but Sarah manages to keep our spirits up. She's well, sitting right next to me and anxious to go back to work. One last thing before she takes her net back—I sure could use a cigarette."

This time it was Sarah who rolled her eyes and shook her head. Her voice sounded crisp and clear as though she'd slept for a week, but her eyes were heavy and drooping, "Navy, this is Magnolia Net Control extending great appreciation for your help. Okay guys, please check in."

"NE7G."

"NE, good to hear your voice this morning, over."

"Sarah, I'm at the park next to the courthouse downtown. I walked over to the bluff a while ago and looked down Third Avenue. If you haven't already heard, the bus tunnel did collapse. The Mainland Tower, the one that was leaning against the Winningham Blue Building, fell in the aftershock. We've got all kinds of help down here now. I can't imagine where they all came from. The Salvation Army has coffee and food and snowplows are trying to clear the streets. NE7G, over."

# CHAPTER 21

ON THE FORTY-THIRD floor, Tim sat with his legs crossed listening to the transistor and munching on a small bag of chips. "Coffee ... hot coffee. I can smell it clear up here."

Jenna giggled and took another sip of water. "I sure hope that chopper comes back. Are you sure we can't go down the stairs?"

"No, I'm not sure. But suppose we go down and the chopper comes?"

Seely lightly touched her swollen jaw and slowly exercised it. When she talked, her words were slightly slurred, "You know, I hardly remember getting hit. I'm not even sure what hit me."

"Well I know what hit me," Jenna said. "That putrid modern art painting by the elevators just flew off the wall. Oh Seely, I was hoping we would wake up and this would be just a bad dream. It's real, isn't it? I wanna go home."

Seely tenderly touched Jenna's hand, "Me too."

"I think we should try to go down the stairs. We don't know for sure the stairs are blocked and the chopper might not ever come back," said Jenna.

Tim lowered his head and looked at Jenna through the tops of his eyes, "I've got ten bucks says we can't get down. A floor collapsed, remember?"

"Well, maybe we can find a way to climb around that floor, you know, down the side of the building. The windows are broken and we could get back in."

Instantly Timmy perked up. "Hey, you might be right. We might get to use the fire hoses after all."

A7BB WAS AWAKE. THE early morning glow began behind the city where scattered clouds dotted the sky. The fire was out downtown, but South Center still burned, as did Bremerton. On the Aircraft Carrier, a dozen choppers sat ready to lift off and teams of men with search dogs climbed into three. Boxes of blood and supplies bound for hospitals were loaded onto others and just as the day before, Canadian choppers waited to land.

He moved a tree branch and looked down. Beneath him, several more bodies sloshed in the water. Quickly, A7BB released the branch. The cat was nowhere to be found and none of the choppers coming or going seemed at all interested in him. Jim Sarasosa sighed, wiggled his hand between the tree and the dirt, and then dug a fresh radio battery out of his pants pocket. He loaded it, closed the cover, and listened to his friends report in.

Mattie called in to say a team with a search dog arrived at the department store in the night. They pulled six more people out of the rubble, but not the little girl. Now, the little girl named Charlie was quiet. Hopefully, she was just sleeping. Nevertheless, the searchers were trying to get a microphone down to her. Reports of more collapsed buildings poured in, each sounding grimmer than the last. Emergency calls took priority and occasionally, A7BB saw a chopper head in the direction of the call.

On the I-5 freeway, where a landslide buried cars and an overpass crushed a metro bus, Marines dropped from choppers with a cherry picker and equipment. All who could be saved would soon be on higher ground. Attention then turned to the collapsed Convention Center tunnel where the drunk driver started a chain reaction pile-up. Yellow tiles were scattered in front of the collapsed tunnel entryway.

A7BB watched a chopper hover over the people trapped in cars on what remained of the Alaskan Way Viaduct, now several yards out in the bay. Chopper after chopper flew to downtown, returning to the Aircraft Carrier with still alive, but horribly injured Saturday shoppers.

Water still dripped from the pipe behind his head, although he'd slid nearly out of reach. Occasionally, Sarah checked on his welfare. Occasionally the ground trembled a little and a chopper seemed to be heading his way, but none came and the sun rose higher and higher in the sky. He spotted the big blue chopper right away. It had a distinctive sound amid the other choppers, but there was no new balloon basket hanging from its belly. When it flew right over him without stopping, he put his free hand on his hip, "You saved everyone else, why not me?"

AT KMPR, SARAH TOOK call after call, seldom pausing to drink or rest. "Okay, who's up next?"

"WC7NJT."

"Well good morning, Mister Mayor."

"Sarah, it's me again. Please tell everyone the water in Lake Washington has been tested and is contaminated. Continue boiling the water before you drink, over."

"Thanks, we'll do that. Next?"

"NG7L"

"NG, go ahead."

"NG7L. We've still got people stranded on Interstate five between NE 75th and 85th. We sure could use some help. The off ramps have fallen on both ends, over."

"Copy NG, do you have injured?"

"Negative. We've got about fifty people here and some are kids with nothing to drink. NG7L, over."

"NG, you might have to wait awhile, but we'll put you on the list."

SEELY WAS EXHAUSTED. So much so that the sound of an approaching chopper hardly interested her. Several times Tim went to the conference room and watched, but the blue Angel didn't come back. Finally, he gave in to Jenna and was about to head down nearly thirty flights of stairs when at last, he heard it. Instantly, he grabbed Jenna's arm and nearly pulled her back down the hall. Well-traveled by now, the carnage in the hallway seemed easier to navigate and soon they turned, passed the elevators and walked into the conference room.

Again, the noise was deafening and again they couldn't see it. The chopper hovered somewhere above and the waiting seemed endless. Jenna was about to turn back when two feet appeared at the top of the blown out window. Inch by inch, legs, knees, thighs, and a woman's waist descended from above.

Tim quickly glanced around, scouring the carnage on the floor for something to pull her in. But there was nothing. Helpless, he turned back to watch.

Jackie sat in a full sitting harness with a thin steel rod across her lap. On the end of the rod was a small hook. She wore a headset complete with earphones and a microphone wired to a cell phone in her pocket. When she was low enough, she reached inside her vest and withdrew a rope. Already tied to the seat, she looped it around her hand several times, aimed and tossed the other end of the rope toward Tim. The first time, he missed. So Jackie coiled the rope again and hurled it harder.

As soon as he caught hold, Jackie put a hand up palm out to keep him from pulling. Assured of his compliance, she took hold of the long steel rod. Cautiously, she brought it out of the safety belt, turned it and shot it toward an inside wall. The rod bounced off the wall, fell to the floor and began to roll toward the window.

Jenna grabbed Tim's arm, reached out and grabbed the rod.

Jackie heaved a sigh of relief, nodded to Tim, and then spoke into her mike.

As Tim pulled her in, the cable holding her up lengthened, allowing Jackie to step inside the badly damaged, monster of a building.

"Boy are we glad to see you!" Tim said.

Jackie wasted no time unbuckling the safety seat and letting it fall to the floor, "The girl goes first."

"Jenna's eyes grew large, "Me? But I..."

Tim glared and yanked the rod out of Jenna's hand, "You want to go home or not?"

Jenna slumped and stood still while Jackie and Tim helped her into the harness.

"Here's the deal," Jackie said, tightening the strap over Jenna's legs, "don't jump. Just walk to the window. When you step off..."

"Step off? But I ..."

"Look, rollercoasters are more dangerous than this. The trick is to let the chopper pull you away from the building. Don't hang on to anything except the seat. Just relax and let us do the worrying, okay?"

Jenna didn't have time to protest. Instead Tim and Jackie were walking her closer and closer to the edge. Suddenly, she was two steps away from the window, and then one, as the cable above her head got shorter. She closed her eyes, gripped the side of the chair and stepped off. Instantly, her body sailed through the air, swinging away from the building as the chopper quickly banked and veered away.

Jenna was barely away when Jackie grabbed Tim's arm. "We don't have much time, this building is in trouble. Where's Seely?"

"This way." One last time, Tim traveled the beaten path into the dark bowels of the forty-third floor.

Behind him, Jackie's eyes darted, her ankles twisted in the rubble and hanging electrical wiring repeatedly got in her face. Finally, she spotted Seely Ross sitting on the floor near the ladies' room. In one sweeping motion, she dug a hypo out of her pocket and knelt down. She quickly ripped the small slender cap off, pushed the liquid through the tip of the needle and jabbed it into Seely's arm.

"Ouch!"

"Sorry, I didn't have much time to practice."

"What's that? And who are you?"

"That was something to keep you calm and I'm Jackie." She tossed the hypo away, and then looped Seely's right arm around her neck. "Come on, we've gotta get moving."

"Jackie from the Internet?"

"That's right, I've come to take you home." Just as they got Seely up, the building began a sorrowful groan. "Don't stop, keep going." Yet, it was Jackie who was terrified, stumbling through the rubble, gasping for air and fearing each new sound of the screeching, wailing building. Endless seconds passed and Seely grew more and more dependent on their strength, and when they at last reached the conference room, the chopper wasn't there.

Jackie nearly yelled into her mike, "Michael, where are you?"

In the aft bubble, Michael began lowering the chair again, "The girl panicked. We just now got her inside."

"Hurry Michael, hurry!"

Suddenly, there was a different sound deep within the building—a whining. It was loud at first, and then seemed to drift away, growing softer and softer, "What is that?"

Tim shrugged, "We think it's the elevators. That's the third one this morning." Finally, it hit the bottom; its sickening crash muffled somewhere below.

Jackie's eyes grew still wider, "Do you think..."

"I hope not."

"Man, I can't wait to get out of here."

"I know what you mean."

Finally, the dangling seat appeared. Jackie quickly picked up the hook, looped it through the harness, and pulled it in. Working as quickly as they could, Jackie and Tim strapped Seely in and walked her toward the edge.

But Seely balked. She stiffened her legs and refused to budge, "No!"

"You have to, it's the only way out," Jackie said.

"No, you're trying to kill me."

Jackie grabbed hold of Seely's arm. "Listen to me. No one is trying to kill you and if I wanted you dead, I'd just leave you here. Now Go!"

Seely's mind was a fog and just before she stepped out the window, she thought she heard Jackie say that Evan was waiting for her. That was impossible. Still, she smiled. She became oddly relaxed and calm, moving through the air with music in her head, and a long forgotten memory of a silk pink dress and Evan Cole. The sky was a bright blue, the sun felt warm on her skin and she could see forever. White fluffy clouds drifted across the western horizon, the waterways of Puget Sound shimmered, and she was swinging back and forth, back and forth – just like a child in a backyard swing.

Below, the Winningham Blue still voiced its distress with odd screeches, deep-throated moans and frightening shivers. Tim took a slow look at the broken and cracked ceiling. "It's starting to lean, isn't it? That pole wouldn't have rolled last night."

"Yes. The eighth floor can't hold up much longer and one side looks weaker than the other. You mind if I ride piggy back?"

Tim grinned. He removed his imaginary hat, and then slowly and elaborately bowed. "My pleasure." Then he paused, "How much do you weigh?"

Jackie nearly laughed, "A lot less than this building."

"Good point."

At last the chopper came back and once more the harness appeared. Jackie quickly hooked it, pulled it in and helped Tim with the straps. As soon as he was secure, she climbed into his lap, wrapped the rope around both of them, and tied a quick knot. "Ready?"

"You bet." He walked closer and closer to the edge with Jackie's weight full on him and her arms gripping his. Finally, he heard her say, "Go Michael, go!" And they were away, swinging through the air a thousand feet above the ground below the Blue Angel.

The top floors of the Winningham Blue began a slightly more exaggerated and torturous sway. As it seesawed, it added and subtracted weight on the weakened and crumbling eighth floor. Abruptly, it stopped and for a moment the building rested. Suddenly, the entire eighth floor collapsed. The upper floors landed with a reverberating bang, sending a new round of broken metal, concrete, dirt, and glass cascading out of the windows to the streets below.

Tim cast his eyes upward, gazing at the hole in the belly of the air crane. The cable became shorter and shorter with the giant hook growing bigger and bigger until, at last, the huge pulley drew both he and Jackie into the helicopter. With the flip of a switch, Michael retracted the steel doors in the floor, unbuckled his safety belt, and scrunched through the small door into the chopper body. In the first passenger seat, Jenna gazed aimlessly out the window. Behind her, Seely sat slumped with her head bowed and her eyes closed.

Michael un-strapped Tim and smiled. "Welcome to HDA1. She's big and she's beautiful. Now, where can we drop you?"

Tim wrinkled his brow. "Don't say drop, okay?"

FOR SEVERAL MINUTES, Collin paced nervously across the studio floor. His latest station break was complete and with no word from Beth or Candy, he could think of nothing else to do. Max kept busy in the control room and Sarah hardly ever looked up. He walked away from the window, stopped, and turned back just in time to see a pebble fly in and roll across the floor. Cautiously, he eased closer until he was able look straight down.

A woman dressed in a dirty shirt and blue jeans smiled up at him, and in her hand, she held a fresh, unopened pack of cigarettes. Using her best aim, she threw the pack as high as she could and then watched as Collin reached out just in time to grab it. She smiled and yelled up, "Don't worry, the guy I took those off of won't be needing them anymore." With that, she turned and headed on down the street.

Collin eyed the pack in his hand, and then muttered under his breath, "I sure wish she hadn't told me that." He shrugged, ripped the plastic seal off, opened the pack and lit his first cigarette in nearly 24 hours.

BY TEN O'CLOCK IN THE morning, Sam Taylor had had enough. He paid fifty dollars for a ride on the back of a motorcycle – a dangerous one at that – over broken and traffic-snarled side streets. When he reached the Lake Union Ship Canal, he paid another hundred and fifty dollars for a small rowboat and two oars. In less than two hours, he rowed out of Shilshoe Bay, passed the bustling Aircraft Carrier, and landed on the littered beaches of West Seattle. His favorite pier was gone.

He got out, pulled his boat alongside huge chunks of a broken ship, tossed the oars inside and started toward home. He was still mad when he finally stopped to take a good look around. The air smelled of dead fish. Remnants of small boats and back-washed houses were everywhere. A compact car was near the water's edge and lying on its top. When he noticed a body, he immediately turned and walked away. Half way up the hillside, he put both hands in the small of his aching back, stretched from side to side a time or two, and then headed on. He hardly recognized the broken and splintered remains of the missing ferry.

There it was at last – home. It stood where it always had, with its front porch still oddly intact and only part of the front siding gone. Located high enough up the hill, the water damage was minimal and he wondered if it could be repaired. Suddenly hopeful, he hurried up the steps and opened the door. The living room was gutted and the back half of the house was gone. Sam slowly closed the door, walked across the porch and sat down on the steps. "Well Lord, at least I've got my Max. That's more than most folks. On the other hand, couldn't you have left me a pair of softer, kinder shoes?"

He fretted for a time more and then the Ham Radio call he'd prayed for came over his transistor.

"K7PNO."

"PNO, go ahead," Sarah said.

"K7PNO relaying a message from Candy Taylor. Boys safe, injuries are slight and car burned. Beth Slater unaccounted for."

At KMPR, Collin Slater bolted. He ran down both flights of stairs, yanked open the front door and raced into the street. With tears in his eyes, he abruptly stopped. He put his head in his hands, slumped to his knees and cried out, "No, Beth, no!"

THE BLUE CHOPPER, COMPLETE with "HDA1" lit up on the side panels, glided through the air above Vancouver, British Columbia. Standing in wait atop the ten-story hotel, Evan Cole kept his eyes glued to the approaching dot. Steadily it drew closer, its long blue blades whipping the air and its engines filling the afternoon breeze with sound. A few feet away, a doctor and a nurse waited beside a gurney, and Michelle stood beside her husband and daughters. Slowly, the helicopter descended until its hydraulic legs touched down on the chopper pad.

Instantly, the doctor and nurse shoved the gurney forward. At the same time, Jackie opened a side door, let down the folding steps, and then disappeared back inside the body of the air crane. Apprehensive, Michelle and Theo took a step forward and paused, while both the Doctor and Nurse climbed into the chopper.

Evan Cole did not move. The slow turning blades generated wind, mussing his hair and fluttering the collars of both his shirt and jacket. His pant legs waved and his jaw tightened, relaxed, and then tightened again.

Finally, the doctor rushed back down the stairs. Theo bolted forward and reached out two strong arms just as Jackie and the nurse brought Seely to the door. Her hair was streaked with dried blood and below the cut on her head; a dark bruise discolored her right eye. Her left lower jaw was swollen, her white blouse was blood stained and both legs of her blue jeans flapped with rips and tears. One shoe was missing.

She didn't look his way, her pain-ridden eyes fixed instead on the steps and the long awaited soft bed of the gurney. She hardly recognized Theo and when the gurney rolled past Michelle, she only half-heartedly smiled, and then her eyes drooped and closed.

Less than six feet away, Evan Cole looked on. He watched them take her to the waiting elevator, nodded as Michelle glanced his direction, and then bowed his head when the door closed.

Suddenly, Jackie was standing beside him, "I drugged her."

Evan turned to stare, "What?"

"Don't worry, I've got a doctor friend who supervised the whole thing. She's going to make it. I monitored her heart all the way back and sent the tape to my doctor friend. Her heart looks great for what's she's been through. Just give her time to rest. Meanwhile, fill her room with flowers."

"Did you tell her about me?"

"I tried, but who knows how much she heard. The poor thing is exhausted, and drugged. I was hoping it would wear off a little sooner, but it hasn't."

Evan smiled and wrapped his arms around Jackie, "How do I thank you?"

Jackie giggled and cocked her head to one side, "Well, you can start by giving me a bonus. I've suddenly become homeless."

"Done."

"And you can hand me that basket. We ordered take out on the way in."

"You'll go back then?"

"There are a lot of people still in trouble in Seattle."

With his arm still around her, he scooped up the basket and walked her back to the chopper. He waited until she climbed the stairs, handed her the basket, moved back, waved and watched her close the door. The chopper's blades took on speed and in a matter of moments; it became nothing more than a dark speck in the distant sky.

THIS TIME THE HUGE bubble-faced air crane came from behind, high in the air above Magnolia Hill. Already, a man wearing a safety vest and full headgear hung from the strong cables beneath the chopper. Attached to another cable was a second safety vest and both were slowly descending toward A7BB and his tree.

Overjoyed and hidden by branches and leaves, Jim Sarasosa reached up his free arm and began to furiously wave, "Over here!"

Jackie sat in the aft bubble working the controls—with Carl's constant supervision. She lowered the line until Michael dangled in the air just opposite the trapped man. "See, this is not so hard."

In the Pilot's seat, Carl rolled his eyes.

Dangling below, Michael examined the situation, glancing first at the roots of the tree, and then the branches. With a hand, he motioned for Jackie to lower him until he could see beneath the tree where A7BB's legs hung free. Again, he motioned and Jackie lifted him higher and up over the trapped man. Once more, she returned Michael to his original position.

Michael looked A7BB in the eye, and then scratched the side of his face. A second later, he began speaking into a thin, vest mounted microphone. At length, another—stronger cable with a giant hook and two long chains began a slow descent from above.

A7BB never said a word. Instead, he watched Michael maneuver one chain around the trunk of the tree and the other around the branches on the opposite side of him. Next, Michael grabbed hold of a branch. Hand-over-hand, he walked his way toward A7BB until he was close enough. He opened the spare safety vest and tried to slip it over the man's head, but not enough of A7BB's chest was exposed. Michael thought for a long moment more. Suddenly, his eyes lit up.

He spoke quickly into the mike and Jackie lifted him away. He turned in midair, and then Jackie lowered him behind A7BB. With his feet spread apart as wide as possible, Michael put his feet on the tree. He quickly crouched down, slipped his arms under A7BB's armpits and then locked his hands around Jim's chest.

Suddenly they were in motion. The tree pulled away from the cliff, causing loose dirt to slide down on the bodies below. Leaves fluttered and Michael strained to hoist A7BB up over the trunk.

Jim Sarasosa threw his arms up and dug his fingers into the bark. but he was sliding. He kicked his dangling feet, arched his back and tried to hoist himself higher and couldn't. Michael's chest grip was all that kept him from falling to the shallow water below. The tree started to turn and his hand-held radio fell, sailing downward and splashing into the bay. And still they moved upward, faster now with the tree swinging, tilting and starting to spin. The tree stopped moving and Michael abruptly let go.

A7BB panicked. His eyes widened in terror, his heart pounded, his breathing stopped and his hands began to slip. Horrified, he quickly looked behind him. To his amazement, Magnolia Park's lush green grass lay right below his feet. After nearly twenty hours, A7BB gingerly stepped down to safety.

"NP7WS."

"NP, go ahead Navy."

"Your man on the cliff has been rescued, over."

Sarah heaved a sigh of relief, "Thanks Navy."

ALL THROUGH THE DAY, Ham calls came. The little girl named Charlie died before she could be rescued, but help began pouring in – by land, by air and by water. Sarah got a personal apology from the Mayor and John asked her to dinner. Max wrapped and re-wrapped his aching foot a dozen times and listened to each exchange on the Ham Radio intently, but no word came of Beth. The aftershocks still struck, but none so great as the initial quake and by nightfall, Max and Sarah quickly fell asleep.

Many hours later, Collin still stood at the window, staring into the night.

# CHAPTER 22

"MOMMA?"

Seely's mind was still a fog and the familiar voice sounded so far away. Slowly, she forced her eyes open a bit and drank in the golden sunlight streaming through fluttering white sheers. The air held a hint of freshly brewed tea, soft music played and the voice was growing louder.

"Momma?"

When she at last fully lifted her heavy eyelids, Michelle's glowing face greeted her with a loving smile. "Oh there you are. Are you okay? Where are the girls?"

"We're fine, Momma. We're all just fine."

Tears rimmed the bottom of her mother's eyes so Michelle leaned over and kissed her cheek. She sat back down in a chair next to the bed and took Seely's hand. "How are you feeling?"

"Truthfully?"

"Truthfully."

"I hurt everywhere. Did Jenna and Tim make it? Where am I?"

"Tim and Jenna are home with their families and you've in a hotel in Vancouver, BC. The doctor said you needed rest more than anything else and the hospitals are full. Besides, we wanted you here with us."

"How long have I been here?"

Michelle glanced at her watch, "About a day and a half. Momma, do you remember how you got here?"

Seely though for a moment, "I remember a woman with a hypo. She frightened me. Baby, help me sit up will you? And I sure could use something to drink."

Michelle did as her mother asked, and then walked to the small table and poured a cup of hot tea.

"Where are Theo and the girls?"

"Downstairs shopping. We left everything behind. Momma, do you remember the blue chopper?" She sat back down, and then blew on the hot tea.

"I remember hearing about it over the radio and I think I did see it once. Oh Michelle, Seattle is ruined. How many are dead?"

She handed her mother the cup of tea and scooted back in the chair. "The last count was fourteen hundred and thousands are still unaccounted for. But Momma, do you remember..."

"Baby, what is it? That's the third 'do you remember' in a row."

"Okay, but promise me you won't get upset."

"Why would I get upset? Are the girls hurt?"

"No, I swear we're all fine. It's just that, well, I know the truth now."

For a long moment, Seely searched her daughter's eyes. "The truth?"

"Uh huh, and Momma, there's no reason to be scared or upset. In fact, everything is wonderful. I've met him and he's just the way I always imagined. Momma, he still loves you."

Seely quickly grew suspicious. She narrowed her eyes and hesitantly asked the next question, "Who still loves me?"

"My father. Don't be scared, Loraine is in jail. She turned herself in. Oh Momma, he's so wonderful and so easy to talk to. I have two half-brothers and my father was the one who saved us. He found out you were still alive, he hired the blue chopper to find us and he..."

Seely's mind was suddenly alert. Her hands began to tremble and her voice sounded like thunder, "Michelle, where is he?"

Taken aback by her mother's harsh tone, Michelle quickly got to her feet, "He's in the next room."

"Get him! Get him now, Michelle!" Seeley watched her daughter rush out of the room, threw her blankets off and painfully climbed out of bed. She reached for the robe on the back of the chair and almost had it on by the time they returned. She ignored both Evan and her daughter. Instead, she walked to the phone and picked it up. "Would you please page Theo Wesley?"

Her eyes filled with anger, Seely held the phone next to her injured face, mindless of the pain, "Theo, bring the girls upstairs and do it quickly. You'll understand when you get here, and be careful, you're in grave danger." As soon as she hung up, she turned her furious expression on Evan. "Where is the other sister?"

He was hesitant, trying to understand, "Whose sister?"

"Jennifer's! There were four sisters, one died years ago, Loraine is in jail and Jennifer died of cancer, but Susan was always the dangerous one."

Shocked, Even Cole could only stammer, "I only know about Jennifer and Loraine. I've never heard of anyone named Susan."

"You're kidding. Evan, you supported all these people for thirty years. Think! Even if you didn't know her by that name, wasn't there anyone suspicious, anyone both Jennifer and Loraine knew?"

Evan brought both hands up to his face and tried to concentrate, "No, Jennifer only had one sister and neither of them had close friends."

Confused, Michelle just stood there and watched Seely walk to the window and lowered the blinds.

"Christina, please calm down. You've nothing to be afraid of now, Loraine confessed," Evan went on.

"Confessed to what, stealing your money?" Seely turned around and glared at the man she was once married to. "Do you really think I would have stayed out of your life all these years if I didn't believe Susan was capable of killing us all? Believe me, Loraine is not the problem. In fact, Loraine saved my life. Susan killed Julie Wilcox, her own sister, and arranged for that little boat accident. She killed seven good men that night, just so she could get me out of the way. Only I didn't die. God knows how many others she's killed. She's a monster who would do anything to keep her hands on your money, with or without Loraine's help."

Just then, someone knocked on the door. Seely rushed to it, peeked through the hole and yanked it open. Forgetting her injuries, she happily threw her arms around her granddaughters. "There's my babies, let me look at you. Did you get scared in the earthquake?"

While Seely chatted with her granddaughters, Michelle whispered in her husband's ear, "Get her to go back to bed. She listens to you."

Theo nodded and soon took a turn at hugging Seely, "Mom, I owe you an apology." He slipped an arm around her waist and guided her back toward the bed. "From now on, whatever you're worried about I'm worried about too. I nearly had a heart attack of my own."

Seely finally relaxed a little and let him help her back into bed. She waited until he covered her, and then looked long into his eyes. "I should have warned you about a whole lot more. You married into a real mess son, and I should have told you about it years ago."

"What sort of mess?" Theo asked, allowing the girls to climb up on the double bed with their grandmother.

Timid no longer, Evan sat down next to Seely and took her hand, "Christina, tell us what happened."

Seeley thought for moment before she began, "We'd only been out to sea a few hours when the storm blew in, so we quickly turned back. It was such a fierce and sudden storm that everyone was concentrating on that instead of watching for other boats. Suddenly, there it was, just off our bow and we couldn't get out of the way in time. Captain Marrow grabbed me and threw me overboard, and then jumped in himself. We both had lifejackets, but the water was bitter cold and I was afraid for my baby. So when a cabin cruiser appeared to pick us up, it never occurred to me to refuse. Two women pulled me in, but when I was safe and expecting them to pull the Captain aboard, they turned the boat and left – they left him there to die.

I couldn't believe it! I remember screaming until I passed out. The next thing I knew, I was tied up and lying in a bed below deck. Jennifer was sitting opposite me with a gun in her hands. The sea was calm and I could hear Susan and Loraine having a horrible fight in the next room. Susan wanted to kill me and be done with it, but Loraine said no. There had been enough killing. "Why not?" I wondered. They'd already killed the others. Why didn't they just let me die with the Captain?

Anyway, Loraine was smarter, that's all. She'd kept the evidence and could prove Susan killed Julie Wilcox. Did you know Julie Wilcox was their sister? She was the only sane one of the bunch." Seeley paused, reached for her teacup, and took a long sip.

"But why didn't Susan just kill Loraine?" Evan asked.

"Because Loraine left a letter with someone to be mailed to the police, in the event of her death or disappearance. I don't know if that was really true, but Susan believed her. So they drove me to California and made me assume another identity. In those days, it wasn't hard to do. Loraine made me promise to stay away and Susan vowed to watch every move I made. She said if I went to the Police, she would kill you."

"But surely there was some way to let me know. I would have come to you, I would have protected you with my life," Evan said.

"I know, and I tried to once. After Michelle was born, I made sure I wasn't being followed and called you from a pay phone. You had a new secretary and I didn't recognize Loraine's voice in time. She refused to put me through. The next morning, I found a note from Susan in Michelle's crib. The doors and the windows were locked tight and she couldn't have gotten in – but she did. The cat was lying on the kitchen floor with its throat cut. I never tried again."

Michelle, wrinkled her brow, "So if Susan was the dangerous one, why did Loraine turn herself in?"

"Because she's smart. Jail is the one place Susan can't kill her."

Evan got up and went straight to the phone. First he called hotel security, and then he placed a call to his eldest son and insisted on security for the rest of his family in New York. When he was finished, he found himself alone in the room with Seely. He walked back to her bed and sat down in the chair. "How can you ever forgive me, Christina? I never guessed you were still alive."

Seely dropped her eyes and fiddled with the edge of the blanket. "I haven't been called Christina in years. It's good to hear it again. For years, Susan called to report how happy you were with Jennifer." With a hint of mischief, she looked into his eyes, "I didn't believe her. Jennifer didn't even like you."

Evan chuckled and took her hand again, "I found that much out for myself. I did a lot of drinking after you...died, and one day I woke up in her bed. When she said she was pregnant, I married her. Why not, I knew I would never love anyone but you." He brought her hand to his lips and lightly kissed it. "We'll find Susan. I have a friend on the Police force and he'll see to it. In the meantime, are you hungry?"

"Starved."

A LITTLE MORE THAN a week after the earthquake, they stood among several others on opposite sides of a long conveyor belt in the sweltering Yakima heat. Each wore a sweatband, shorts, cotton shirts, and slip on shoes. Finally, round ripe peaches began streaming down the belt, rolling and turning as they went.

Heather McClurg sighed, grabbed hold of a can of baby powder and quickly dumped the contents on the inside bend of both arms. She set it down and with two dainty fingers lifted the first over-ripe peach off the belt and tossed it in a nearby basket. She cringed, and then turned to glare at her brother.

"What Heather?"

"We could have escaped."

"How? The Army had us surrounded. Face it Heather, we gambled and lost. At least Dad let us keep the truck."

"Us? The truck is yours, remember? And the only reason they let you keep it was because Mom doesn't want to drive us. They didn't even take your Amateur Radio away."

"Yes, but the only one I'm allowed to talk to, is Aunt Blanch in Iowa. How old is she anyway, sixty, seventy? She doesn't even know what a CD is. You still get to go to summer camp, don't forget."

Heather soured her face and grudgingly took another rotten peach off the belt, "Some favor. For two whole weeks I get to set tables, peel potatoes and wash dishes. I think I'll probably die there."

JUST AFTER SUNDOWN on the eighth day, Collin Slater stood amid the rubbish on Alki Point. Aimlessly, he stared across the still water at the gold and amber reflection of a fading sunset. Behind him the darkened city of Seattle lay in ruins. The space needle was still there but the people had gotten out of the glass elevators. The Winningham Blue still stood, but it dangerously leaned toward the water and men wearing cloth masks still tended the burial of unclaimed bodies. Huge cables stretched from the Aircraft Carrier supplying badly needed electricity to hospitals. Heavy equipment steadily moved from telephone pole to telephone pole while workers restored service. Ships of varying sizes sailed into the bay bringing water and supplies to displaced families. And Hams, including Sarah and Max, still passed messages.

The sparkling water gave no hint of its destructive force. No lingering memories marred its surface and no healing did it offer to the wrenching pain in Collin's heart. It simply rippled with the coming tide.

One block back amid the other damaged homes on the hillside, Max, Candy, and Sam Taylor stood on Sam's front porch watching. Three little boys played with toy cars at their feet and Sarah sat in a new wheelchair donated by the US Navy.

Suddenly, the familiar, repetitive thud of a helicopter broke the silence. It was a royal blue chopper with a bubble face resembling a mutant dragonfly. Beneath it, heavy cables with giant hooks led to a forest green, forty-foot mobile home. At first, the air crane seemed to struggle, its heavy load swaying forward and back. As it glided toward Collin with its cargo just above the water, it slowed. He watched in awe as the chopper began to turn in midair, gradually coaxing the mobile home to turn with it.

With his eyes, he followed the cables upward; examining the huge blue crane he'd heard so much about. He lifted his eyes higher to the side panel where hundreds of small bulbs were coming alive. Suddenly, large black letters began to drift across the panel. Standing too close, Collin wrinkled his brow and strained to make the letters into words.

Behind him, Max shouted something and started down the porch steps. Then Candy caught her breath and started to cry, throwing her arms around Sam.

Yet, Collin was at a loss. The dark letters steadily moved across the panel again. Behind him, Max was shouting louder, waving his arms, and trying to run down the beach with his right foot in a walking cast. Collin didn't hear him. The chopper turned just a little to its right, and soon the letters repeated –

BETH ALIVE
ST. LUKE HOSPITAL
PORTLAND OREGON.

Finally, Collin understood. At first, his jaw dropped, and then his eyes brightened. He threw his arms up, clenched his fists, and shouted, "Yes!" He spun around and started toward Max, running between broken boat hulls, jumping over debris, and sprinting past mounds of rubbish. He landed in Max's arms, knocking him to the sand, and then rolled onto his back in shrieks of laughter.

AIR CRANE PILOT CARL Kingsley watched through the tinted front windows, Michael grinned through the clear aft bubble and Jackie watched in the full color monitor fed by camera one. Gradually, the air crane lifted higher and higher, moving westward and picking up speed—and the mobile home moved with it.

Michael pushed his glasses up, interlocked his hands behind his head and leaned back, "Where to now?"

"Hilo."

"Hawaii? Great!"

Jackie's eyes danced with mischief and her mouth curled into a sly grin, "Think you need a vacation, do you?"

"Well yes, don't you? I mean a month or two with wine, women, and song can perk a man right up."

Jackie typed a command, transferred an image to the small screen in the aft bubble, and then enjoyed the fading grin on Michael's face. "Her name is Melissa Green. She was born in South Africa and disappeared on the twelfth day of April 1966. She was ten years old, loved horses, hated fish and..."

IN THE DAYS IMMEDIATELY following the earthquake, Seattle took up the task of providing food, water, and medical attention to its homeless residents. The grim chore of burying the dead, condemning buildings, and comforting families seemed endless. Next came a time of public mourning, with weary survivors huddling near Red Cross centers or attending services at mass graves. Some would never know which impromptu cemetery their loved ones were buried in. Twenty-six thousand, two hundred and eighty-nine people lost their lives and the still missing numbered in the thousands as well. Thousands more became homeless and double that number lost their jobs.

Insurance adjusters, architects, lawyers, and government advisors flooded in and began to build a future out of the senseless carnage.

Then the day came when Amateur Radio Operators could ease back into obscurity, happy to concentrate on their own lives and do what they do best - pass information and prepare for the next major disaster.

With the help of Loraine Whitcomb, AKA Eilene Black, Susan was arrested getting off a plane in Mexico. Their mother, the elderly woman who visited Evan's fake grave, died in the earthquake. It is unknown who is actually buried there. Loraine was convicted of concealing evidence, and then given a suspended sentence after Christina testified on her behalf.

To the delight of all their children, Evan and Christina were remarried in the largest church service New York has ever seen. Evan retired and together they travel the world.

Max rebuilt KMPR, Collin stayed on and Beth gave him a son.

Sarah married John Carson in December of that year and keeps the home fires burning in a new house next door to the radio station.

And in the earth...two massive sheets of solid rock strain to move in opposite directions.

The end

(Read a sample chapter of *Love and Suspicion* below.)

# Acknowledgements

A special thanks to Ed Mitchell of Ham Radio Online in Spokane, Washington and Mark Tharp of Yakima, Washington who were instrumental in helping me learn about Hams. Also, my thanks to Kevin Talbott for information concerning Aircraft Carriers and the US Navy.

Author's note: All references to call signs and locations in this work of fiction are coincidental and solely from the Author's imagination.

# A Survivor's Earthquake Kit

While most earthquakes are so small they are rarely felt, modern technology records between 12,000 to 14,000 earthquakes each year, the larger ones claiming thousands of lives in a matter of seconds. Amazingly, earthquakes are also occurring in such unlikely places as the Texas Panhandle, Idaho, Colorado, New York, and the Mississippi Valley. We can't prevent them, but with a little forward thinking, we can do everything possible to survive them.

**The first sign:** Earthquakes often begin with a short, quick pre-shock that rattles windows and feels like someone just bumped into your chair. Normal reaction is to stop, look around, and see what's happening. But what you do or don't do in those few seconds could save your life.

**Do**—train yourself to be sensitive to movement under your feet. If the floor moves, it's a pre-shock. Plan the safest place to be during the quake, (preferably an area with close walls like the bathroom or a stairwell) and your escape route out of the building. Always keep hallways and doorways clear of boxes, suitcases, toys, etc. As soon as you are outside, immediately turn the gas off to prevent fires.

**Don't**—get in an elevator! Earthquakes cut power as well as change the door alignment and you may not be able to get out.

**Don't**—go back inside damaged buildings after the quake. It's not over! Aftershocks begin in as little as thirty seconds and can be as strong or stronger than the initial quake.

**The size of the quake** –

A **5.0** earthquake will frighten you, knock a few things off shelves, and perhaps topple a bell in the church tower, but for the most part injuries will be slight.

A **6.0** (100 times stronger than a 5.0) will cause some buildings to fall, interrupt power, water, phones and gas, crack foundations, break windows, and topple weaker chimneys and some freeway on and off ramps. A few people will die and several will be injured.

A **7.0** and above are the real killers. Many buildings will fall trapping hundreds. If you live near the water, you need to think about tsunamis. A tsunami depends on the amount and location of land sliding into the water. Don't wait to see what will happen, head for higher ground immediately.

**Supplies**—Prepare for AT LEAST a three-day disruption in basic services and store your supplies just inside a front or back door, or in the trunk of your car (unless you park in a garage). Keep extra bedding in your car.

**Water**—Enough for drinking, cooking, washing wounds, dishes and hands.

**Food**—Anything you can eat cold, crackers, cereal, canned beans, etc. Don't forget a can opener.

**Clothing**—A change of clothing for each member of the family, blankets, diapers, washcloths. Don't forget toilet paper.

**Medical** – Sun tan lotion in summer, burn medicine, butterfly bandages (to temporarily close cuts), miscellaneous bandages, scissors, tweezers (for removing glass), cotton balls, antiseptic (peroxide is cheap and excellent for cleaning wounds and purifying water—2 drops per liter).

**Misc.**—Candles, matches, flashlights with extra batteries, charcoal for cooking/keeping warm, lighter fluid, a transistor radio with plenty of spare batteries (a 9 volt lasts about 20 hours) and extra prescription drugs.

# Missing Heiress

Book 2
A Jackie Harlan Mystery
(sample chapter)

The Harlan Detective Agency was the best there was when it came to finding missing people. They were also the most expensive, so it was no coincidence that they were hired to find the heir to a fortune totaling over 1.6 billion dollars.

Nicholas Gladstone left everything to a granddaughter he didn't know he had until a week before he died, but which one was it - the maid secretly working in the parent's home, an office worker, or the young woman tragically killed in a car accident?

# CHAPTER 1

IT WAS NO ACCIDENT that Teresa Gregory secured a position as maid to Mathew and Laura Connelly – she planned it that way. She asked around, found out which temp agency the Connellys used, signed with that agency, and then waited her turn. Word was that Laura Connelly went through maids like water, and Teresa didn't expect it to be very long before the agency sent her there. The American wealthy favored pretty girls with British accents, and she was certainly all that. As it turned out, she was not offered the position until two weeks before she was due to return to England.

The agency carefully explained the Connelly situation to her, and it soon became clear – the reason the Connellys couldn't keep a maid was because Laura was a drunk and Mathew was a letch. The position required fulfilling Mrs. Connelly's needs, doing laundry, cleaning, serving meals, answering the phone, and keeping the Connelly's social calendar up-to-date.

The agency didn't say anything about fulfilling Mr. Connelly's needs.

It was early morning when Teresa arrived at the wealthy gated community on Chester Street in Denver. She got out of the taxi at the gate, was let in by the security guards, and walked up the street. There were several houses facing the circular drive, but according to the internet map, the sprawling, two-story, Federation style mansion in the middle belonged to the Connellys. It had a four-car garage and a limousine, complete with a driver, waiting in the wide driveway. The expansive lawn was well cared for, and was bordered with rose bushes that gave off their sweet aroma.

Carrying a small bag, she walked up the drive to the front door, nodded to the waiting driver, rang the bell, and was let in by a middle-aged woman who introduced herself as Eleanor.

"I am the cook, and my husband, Mark, does odds and ends, and drives the Connellys' limo," Eleanor explained, as she led Teresa to a bedroom located on the bottom floor just beyond the indoor swimming pool. "Mark and I have the room next to yours. You can knock on the wall if you need help."

"Will I need help?" Teresa asked.

"I hope not. Mr. Connelly ain't here much, and when he is, you best just stay out of his way."

"I see." Teresa set her bag on the bed and looked around. It was a comfortable enough room, especially for her purposes. It had a bed, an easy chair, a table, and a television on a stand. The door, she noticed, had a deadbolt on the inside.

"There's an elevator for when Mrs. Connelly can't make it up the stairs." Eleanor took hold of the doorknob. "You hungry? The Connellys don't eat breakfast, but I'd be pleased to make you up something."

"No, thank you, I've already eaten." She smiled as Eleanor closed the door and then she took a deep breath.

She was in...at long last.

A TALL WOMAN, WITH long dark hair and blue eyes, twenty-two-year old Teresa was dressed in the required gingham, short sleeved, French style uniform. It was blue with trim on the sleeves that matched her white half apron. Her first glimpse of the Connellys was a brief one. Mathew hurried his wife out the door and climbed into the back of the limo beside her. They didn't say where they were going and Teresa didn't ask.

Once they were gone, she took her time becoming familiar with the place. Oddly, the furnishings and the decor in the eight-bedroom, ten-bathroom house clearly had not been updated for at least twenty years. Most of the rooms hadn't seen much use either. Yet, there was plenty of work to keep a small staff busy and then some.

Teresa decided to ignore the other rooms for now, made the beds in the separate bedrooms the Connellys apparently occupied, and located several places to hide...should the need arise.

When the Connellys came home later that afternoon, Teresa was in the dining room dusting the tall china cupboard. Laura immediately headed for the liquor cabinet in the living room to make herself a drink, while Mathew watched. Neither of them seemed to care who might be listening, so Teresa moved a little closer to the arched doorway between the two rooms.

Mathew glared at his wife. "She told me she called you. What did you tell her, Laura?" A little too thin for his height, Mathew's tailored, dark blue suit fit him well enough. He was an unusually handsome man with slightly graying sideburns. His dark hair was fashionably short, and he had intense blue eyes.

"I told her the same thing I told all the others," Laura answered.

It was obvious Laura had once been quite a beauty, but the alcohol she consumed over the years made her face puffy and her cheeks red. Even so, she still had a girlish figure, dark hair, pretty blue eyes, and a nice smile – although her smile was disingenuous just now.

"Laura, I need to know exactly what you said."

"Why? Is she the one you *truly* love these days?" She finished pouring her drink, took a long swallow, and then headed up the mahogany staircase.

Mathew soon followed. "I don't love her, but I *do* need her."

Drink in hand, Laura stopped halfway up and turned around to face him. "I can't imagine what for. Darling, don't you have some-place to go? Why don't you just run along? You know you want to."

"There was a time when you wanted me to stay home."

"There was a time when..." Laura stopped in midsentence and continued up the stairs.

He watched her disappear around the corner, closed his eyes and rubbed his forehead. When he turned to go back down, he spotted Teresa standing in the archway. "See that she doesn't hurt herself, and remember to make sure she takes her medicine every morning."

"Yes, Mr. Connelly, I'll remember."

As soon as he reached the bottom step, he stopped, looked at her for a long moment, and started to say something. He changed his mind, and instead, walked out the front door, letting it slam behind him.

Teresa went to the window, moved the curtain aside and watched. One of the garage doors opened, Mathew backed out, and then drove his red Ferrari around the curved driveway toward the gate. After he was gone, she let the curtain close and went upstairs to see about Laura.

THE NEXT MORNING, TERESA stood beside the bed, opened her palm and offered a pill to Mrs. Connelly.

Laura Connelly's enormous bedroom on the second floor was decorated in outdated pastel mauve and blue. The room held a dress-ing table, a sofa and loveseat with a matching reading chair, a reading lamp, a magazine rack and a coffee table. Her walk-in closet was big-ger than most bedrooms, held three dressers and more clothes than any one woman had a right to own. Teresa expected to spend an en-tire week just organizing it.

"I don't want that, take it away," Laura moaned. In her king-size bed, complete with a lace trimmed mauve canopy, she turned her back to the maid and buried the side of her face in a pillow.

"Mr. Connelly gave me specific instructions to see that you take your blood pressure medicine."

"Of course he did, he wants me alive, not dead...at least not yet."

"You wish to die?"

Laura turned back over. "No I don't. I can't die now; I would miss all the fun."

"What fun is that?"

Laura sat up and then held her head as her hangover pain began. She waited for it to subside, took the pill, put it in her mouth, and then washed it down with the glass of water Teresa handed her. "The inheritance, my dear, we have to go to court to settle the matter of my inheritance."

"Is that why you were gone yesterday?"

Laura wrinkled her brow. "Didn't I tell you?"

"I'm new, remember?"

Laura thought about that for a moment. "Of course you are. We are contesting the will, you see, and I...what day is this?"

"Tuesday, the ninth."

"Tuesday? I guess I must be in court again today. What shall I wear? Black would be proper in honor of my father, I suppose."

Teresa set the glass of water on the nightstand, walked into the bathroom, and turned on the shower. "I think your red suit will do nicely."

Laura moaned a second time. "I hate red."

"Yes, Mum, but it brings out the color of your hair. Do you not want to please your husband?"

"Please him, no; taunt him, yes. Come to think of it, I might enjoy reminding him of what he is missing. Red it is." Laura struggled to throw the covers back. "Who am I fooling? He hasn't been tempted in years. We don't even sleep in the same bed, and not even the same house most of the time. Crumbs, that's all he ever gave me. I truly hate the man, but Connie, I still long for his crumbs sometimes."

"Teresa."

"Oh yes, Teresa."

The maid held out a silk robe while Laura stood up and slipped her arms in the sleeves. "Come along, it is time for your shower."

Laura followed her to the bathroom, and then leaned against the doorjamb while Teresa tested the temperature of the water. "You know, it is almost spooky."

"What is?"

"How much you remind me of me when I was your age."

"NICOLE JUST FIRED COLLEEN," Jim whispered as he walked past Maggie's small office cubical. She stood up, made certain Nicole was not around, and followed him to the break room. She liked her dark hair long, but not long enough to reach the middle of her back as it did now. Sadly, a hairdresser was something she could not afford. Her wages were scandalously low, but considering her circumstances, she was happy to find any position with a Human Resources Department that didn't require American references.

The Gallaher Superior Telephone Service office building in downtown Denver once housed over 500 people. With the failing economy and so many improvements that GSTS couldn't match, the number of employees had dwindled to one-hundred-twenty-six. In Maggie's department, that left only five.

Maggie Jackson was an Account Cancellation Specialist for a phone company. Simply put, it meant she cancelled accounts, generated a final invoice and refunded deposits. The more their customers moved on to other providers and cancelled their GSTS accounts, the more secure Maggie's job was.

For three years, she watched fellow employees come and go, most of who were good workers and didn't deserve to be fired. Unfortunately, there was more going on than met the eye, and some didn't figure that out until it was too late.

As she hoped, Jim was the only one in the break room and he was at the vending machine getting a candy bar when she walked in. Dressed in jeans and a summer blouse, she sat down at one of the tables and waited for him to join her.

"Did you hear what I said?" Jim whispered, as he chose a chair across the table from her. Wearing casual clothes as well, he had a stout build, curly red hair, and pleasant green eyes.

"She got fired on a Wednesday morning? I thought Americans liked to do their firing on Friday afternoon."

"Normally, they do. Issuing a last check for a full week is easier than trying to figure out the hours in the middle of the week."

Maggie adored Jim McMorrow. Her first day there, he took her under his wing and taught her how to use the complicated, nightmarish software. When she spoke, she lowered her blue eyes, as well as her voice. "Did you have to issue her final paycheck?"

Jim peeled the wrapper back on his candy bar and took a bite. "That's the part I hate most about this job. Nicole should do it herself, but she always has me do it. I am the first to know when someone is getting fired and I truly, truly hate it. I can't even look some people in the eye."

"Why did Colleen get fired?"

Jim puffed his cheeks. "Since when does Nicole need a good reason?"

"Never. Whose toes do you suppose Colleen stepped on?"

"Nicole's probably. I don't know the details yet."

Maggie pushed a wayward strand of hair away from her face, and remembered to keep her voice down. "Another one bites the dust, as you Americans say. I thought Colleen was doing her job well."

"Yeah, but when has a department manager ever lasted more than six months?"

"Not since I've been here."

Jim broke off a piece of his candy bar and offered it to her. When she shook her head, he put it in his mouth. "I've got a feeling she'll offer the job to me and I don't want it."

"Neither do I."

He took another bite and glanced at the empty doorway just to make sure no one was coming. "Last time she fired a manager, she combined both our departments and put Colleen over all of us. That's a lot of work for one person and I don't know who else is qualified."

Maggie dropped her gaze and thought about that. "You and I have been here the longest and we know the computer system the best."

"That's why I'm worried. If we had half a brain, we'd go job hunting tomorrow."

"It is not that easy to find something else. I was one step away from being homeless when I found this job."

"You started here as a temp, right?" he asked.

"Right, and for two years, they wouldn't give me a raise because they had to pay the temp agency fee to get me."

Jim shook his head in disgust. "They punished you for that? Now I've heard everything."

"I wasn't supposed to tell anyone."

"I can see why. Did you protest?"

"I was afraid they would fire me if I complained, and this is my only American reference," Maggie admitted.

"All the more reason to get out before we get fired. You could always go back to that temp agency, right?"

"Right." Maggie went to the soda machine, dug some change out of her pocket, and made her choice. By the time she returned to the table, Jim was finished with his candy bar. He wadded up the wrapper and pretended to shoot it like a ball into the basket. When it went in, he smiled.

"Are all American companies like this one?" she asked, taking a drink of her soda.

"This is the worst one I've ever seen, but then, other companies don't let people like Nicole run them. They are scared of getting sued."

"No one sues this company?"

"Maybe they do, but we'll never hear about it. The owner's lawyer is his daughter and she doesn't talk to anyone but Nicole."

Maggie leaned forward. "Nicole actually brags about not celebrating American holidays. If she hates it here so much, why doesn't she go back to Germany?"

Jim reeled back. "You've been here for three years and you don't know? I'm shocked."

"Know what?"

"She lost custody of her daughter to her American husband."

Maggie's mouth dropped. "She lost custody? What did she do wrong?"

"Well, if you dress like a hooker, and walk like a hooker, I guess you're a hooker."

"That can't be true...is it? She talks about her boyfriend constantly."

When Susan walked into the room and went to the candy machine, both of them stopped talking. Jim finally said, "Nice weather we're having."

"A bit too hot to suit me," Maggie returned. "When do you think the air-conditioning will be fixed?"

"I have no..." Jim noticed Susan's glare as she walked out, and as soon as she was gone, he chuckled. "She probably thinks we were talking about her," he said, loud enough for Susan to hear, just in case she paused in the hall to listen.

Maggie got up, went to the door, peeked out, and then came back. "She's gone. What about Nicole's boyfriend?"

"Which one? Boyfriends don't last long either; they can't keep up with her. Some guys like sex to be their idea."

Maggie tipped her head to the side. "You're making that up, right?"

"Nope." This time Jim talked just above a whisper. "If you only knew how many times Nicole has propositioned me...and every other man in the company, you would be mortified."

"Really? Isn't that sexual harassment?"

"It is in my book."

"Why doesn't someone say something?"

"You mean file charges?"

"Yes," said Maggie.

"Well, she is an attractive woman and some guys fall for it. Others don't want the hassle of having to stand up in court and testify. I know I don't. Besides, the owner of the company likes her, and who knows what he would do to the guy who complains. We all need our jobs."

Maggie frowned. "I don't like Mr. Gallaher either. There is something about him that makes me..."

"Yeah, well, if he ever offers you a way to make extra money, turn him down."

"Why?"

"Harold Gallaher runs a phone sex business on the side."

She slumped in her chair. "So that part *is* true. At least he doesn't bring that business into the phone company."

"Who says he doesn't? If you own a small phone company, then it is easy to set up as many phone-sex lines as you want without having to answer too many questions."

"I suppose it would be."

Jim reached across the table and playfully patted the top of her head. "How I would love to be as innocent and as unsuspecting as you are."

"I'm not all *that* innocent."

"Just be careful, my favorite little Brit. Nicole likes the power she has over people, and you and I are probably moving up on her hit list."

"I'll do my best to stay out of her way."

"I wish I could." His eyes suddenly widened. "Know what would be worse than getting fired?"

"What?"

"If Nicole makes Susan our manager."

"Oh gosh, that would be awful. Susan has only been here a few months and she still doesn't know what she's doing."

"That's what I mean...things could get worse."

Maggie rolled her eyes. "Especially for me. Susan is mad at me again."

"What did you do this time?"

"I insulted her. You know how she stands too close when she asks a question?"

"I hate when she does that."

"Me too. Her eyelashes are very long and hang down over her eyes. I can't imagine why it doesn't bother her. Anyway, a couple of days ago, I told her it made her look like she's in prison."

Jim started to laugh and covered his mouth. "You didn't."

"I did. Today she came to work with her eyelashes curled. I should say something about how much better she looks, but truly, it would take a lot more than an eyelash curler to make her as lovely as she could be, if she tried."

"I think she's a little off in the head anyway."

"Do you? In what way?"

"Susan worked for a collection agency, so she's used to making up lies. Ursula needed to find a vendor zip code, and Susan started to make up this long, involved reason Ursula could use as an excuse to get it. Rubbish, I said. I called, asked for the zip code, wrote it down, hung up, and handed the paper to Ursula. It took about two seconds."

She giggled. "You humiliated Susan in front of a co-worker? You're worse than me."

"Maggie, I can't handle stupid sometimes."

"She might try to get even with you later."

"She'll have to get in line behind Nicole." He looked at the clock and stood up. "Time to go back. You coming?"

"In a minute." With two minutes of break time left, Maggie stayed and took another sip of her soda. Being a foreigner in America was harder than she expected it to be. She wanted to blend in, and to do that, she spent a great deal of time learning the American vocabulary instead of the one she grew up with. Even after three years, she sometimes used a word that brought about strange looks.

She only had one American friend, other than the people she worked with. Her friend was a man she talked to in a private chat room every night – at least he *said* he was a man. Bronco8881 seemed nice enough and she liked him. He could carry on an intelligent conversation, often made her laugh, and talking to him was the highlight of her day.

She couldn't wait to tell him what Jim said, but she had to be careful not to give Bronco8881 too much information. The internet made it easy for people to find someone if they tried hard enough, and the last thing she needed was for him to show up at her apartment.

As soon as her break time was up, Maggie begrudgingly went back to work. The basement was filled with equipment that softly hummed, but she had grown used to that. The top floor held meeting rooms and offices for the owner and his corporate lawyer daughter, neither of whom Maggie saw very often. Her cubical was on the middle floor, and when she looked in the one across the hall, the department manager's desk was indeed cleaned off, and Colleen's chair was empty.

WITH BILLIONS OF DOLLARS, thousands of employees, and the fate of several lucrative companies at stake, Mathew and Laura Connelly vs. The Estate of Nicholas W. Gladstone was the best kept secret in Denver. The small courtroom offered enough seats for a six-member jury, but a jury, even one that was sworn to absolute secrecy, could not be trusted.

Instead, Marcus Stonewall Hawthorn, a direct descendant of the famous Colorado Hawthorns on one side, and Stonewall Jackson on the other, served as both judge and jury.

The judge wore the usual black robe and sat behind the usual podium with an American flag on one side and a Colorado State flag on the other. The walls were polished wood paneling and a short fence, complete with a center gate separating the proceedings from two rows of spectator pews, all of which were empty. Facing the judge, Attorney Bradley Hyde sat at a table with his clients, Mathew and Laura Connelly, while the estate Attorney, Austin Steel, sat alone at the other table.

The argument between the two attorneys had already lasted well over two hours. Laura looked bored and Mathew looked irritated.

Once more, Austin Steel respectfully stood up. "Your Honor, the will specifically states that proof of Miss Connelly's death must be conclusive. The Connellys have admitted they registered their daughter in a boarding school in the United Kingdom, under the name Georgia Marie James. I submit to you, that the photograph of the dead woman they claim is their daughter is anything *but* conclusive."

Bradley Hyde slowly stood up too. "Your Honor, Miss James' identification was found on the body after the accident. Who else could it have been?"

"It was found several feet away, Your Honor," Austin countered.

"Yet, no other identification was found anywhere near the site of the accident," Bradley Hyde argued. "The body was cremated; therefore, there are no fingerprints and there is no DNA. How else are my clients to prove their daughter is dead?"

"Your clients wouldn't know their own daughter if..."

Judge Hawthorn banged his gavel twice. "Mr. Steel, I have already heard what you think of the parents. Please refrain from mentioning it again."

Austin lowered his gaze. "Yes, Your Honor."

"Counselors, both sides agreed not to call any witnesses and to have me judge this case based on the facts presented. Am I mistaken about that?"

"No, Your Honor," said Bradley Hyde.

"No, Your Honor," Austin sadly agreed. Just then, a bailiff walked in through the side door, whispered in the Judge's ear, and when the judge nodded, walked down the steps and handed a note to the estate attorney.

*Highline hotel, 24ᵗʰ floor, Suite A*
*Jackie Harland.*

Austin Steel couldn't help but take a relieved breath. "Your Honor, some new evidence has just been handed to me. I will need time to verify it."

"What new evidence?" the opposing attorney asked louder than he should have.

"I believe I can prove Miss James is quite alive. I ask...no, I beg the court for a continuance. Miss James' grandfather wanted her to have it all, and we owe it to her to at least..."

"How much time?" Judge Hawthorn asked.

"A month, Your Honor."

"A month!" Bradley shouted. "Your Honor, my clients have waited six months already."

"Two weeks and not a day more," said the Judge. "I want this trial over and done with before I am old enough to retire." He banged his gavel once, stood up, and left the room.

Frustrated, Mathew slammed his fist on the table.

"Ah, poor baby. Another two weeks," Laura mocked. She stood up and smoothed the wrinkles out of her red skirt.

"Whose side are you on, Laura?"

She cunningly smiled. "My side, Darling."

(end of sample chapter)

Pick up your copy of *Missing Heiress* today!

# More Books

www.martitalbott.com

To discover free Marti Talbott books and more historical novels filled with castles and kings, love and war, triumph and tribulation - click here[1].

Follow Clan MacGreagor through multiple generations beginning with *The Viking*[2] where it all began, *The Highlanders*[3] and their struggle to survive, *Marblestone Mansion*[4] and the duke who simply could not get rid of his scandalous duchess, and still more historical stories in *The Lost MacGreagor Books*[5]. Then check out **Marti's contemporary romance/mysteries**[6] in *Missing Heiress, Greed and a Mistress, The Dead Letters*, and *The Locked Room*. Other books include the **Carson Series**[7], **Leanna, (a short story)**, and **Seattle Quake 9.2**[8].

Find direct links to your next Marti Talbott novel at your favorite bookseller here.[9]

---

1. http://www.martitalbott.com

2. http://www.martitalbott.com/viking-series

3. http://www.martitalbott.com/highlander-series

4. http://www.martitalbott.com/marblestone-mansion

5. http://www.martitalbott.com/The-Lost-MacGreagor-Books

6. http://www.martitalbott.com/m-t-romance

7. http://www.martitalbott.com/the-carson-series

8. http://www.martitalbott.com/more-marti-talbott-books

9. http://www.martitalbott.com/direct-links

See what's Marti's working on next and sign up to be notified when it is released.[10]
Marti's Website[11] Talk to Marti on Facebook[12]

10. http://www.martitalbott.com/Home/notify-me

11. http://www.martitalbott.com

12. https://www.facebook.com/marti.talbot

# Also by Marti Talbott

**A Love Story**
The Dead Letters
The Locked Room
Love and Suspicion


**Carson Series**
Broken Pledge
The Promise


**Marti Talbott's Highlander Series**
Marti Talbott's Highlander Series 1
Marti Talbott's Highlander Series 2
Marti Talbott's Highlander Series 3
Marti Talbott's Highlander Series 4
Marti Talbott's Highlander Series 5
Betrothed
The Golden Sword, Book 7
Abducted, Book 8
A Time of Madness
Triplets

Secrets
Choices
Ill-Fated Love
The Other Side of the River
Marti Talbott's Highlander Omnibus, Books 1 - 3
Leanna: A Clean Highlander Short Story

**Scandalous Duchess Series**
Marblestone Mansion, Book 1
Marblestone Mansion, Book 2
Marblestone Mansion, Book 3
Marblestone Mansion, Book 4
Marblestone Mansion, Book 5
Marblestone Mansion, Book 6
Marblestone Mansion, Book 7
Marblestone Mansion, Book 8
Marblestone Mansion, Book 9
Marblestone Mansion, Book 10
Marblestone Mansion, (Omnibus, Books 1 - 3)

**The Lost MacGreagor Books**
Beloved Ruins, Book 1
Beloved Lies, Book 2
Beloved Secrets. Book 3
Beloved Vows, Book 4

**The Viking Series**
The Viking

The Viking's Daughter
The Viking's Son
The Viking's Bride
The Viking's Honor
Viking Blood
The Unwanted Bride

**The Wheeler Triplets**
Ondrea
Yvette
Adison
The Wheeler Triplets Box Set

**Standalone**
Seattle Quake 9.2
Missing Heiress
Greed and a Mistress

Watch for more at www.martitalbott.com.

# About the Author

Marti Talbott (www.martitalbott.com) is the author of over 40 books, all of which are written without profanity and sex scenes. She lives in Seattle, is retired and has two children, five grandchildren and three great-grandchildren. The MacGreagor family saga begins with The Viking Series and continues in Marti Talbott's Highlander's Series, Marblestone Mansion, the Scandalous Duchess series, and ends with The Lost MacGreagor books. Her mystery books include Seattle Quake 9.2, Missing Heiress, Greed and a Mistress, The Locked Room, and The Dead Letters. Other books include The Promise and Broken Pledge.

Read more at www.martitalbott.com.

Made in the USA
Middletown, DE
21 November 2018